Do you mind?

"No common ground with the Traders exists," Tikal said.

"We have to try," Kelric said, frustrated.

Tikal slapped the table. "The rest of humanity may view you as an Imperialate sovereign, but you don't rule here. You answer to me. And I say no."

"He answers to us both," Dehya said sharply. "I say yes."

"I won't give on this one," Tikal told her.

Dehya met Tikal's gaze. "I won't give on this one, either."

"Then we're deadlocked," Tikal said. "We'll have to turn it over to the Assembly for a vote."

Kelric made an incredulous noise. "What the hell kind of secrecy is that? The whole point is that Qox and I would meet in private, unaffected by outside influences."

Tikal crossed his arms. "It's the only way to resolve a deadlock between Pharaoh Dyhianna and myself."

Even if Kelric had been willing to send it to the Assembly, he knew it would never pass. He spoke with difficulty. "Very well. I withdraw the proposal."

Kelric felt defeated on a much larger scale than with this one question.

Then he looked at Dehya.

Her face showed only disappointment. Nor did her mood hint at any other response. But she was the most nuanced empath alive; if anyone could hide from even the psions at this table, it was Dehya. Kelric understood her as no one else, and the moment he looked at her, he knew. She wanted him to do this *without* Tikal's consent.

She wanted him to commit treason.

Baen Books by Catherine Asaro

Sunrise Alley
Alpha

The Ruby Dice
Diamond Star (forthcoming)

THE RUBY DICE

CATHERINE ASARO

BAEN

THE RUBY DICE

A Baen Books Original

Baen Publishing Enterprises
P.O. Box 1403
Riverdale, NY 10471
www.baen.com

ISBN 10: 1-4165-9158-3
ISBN 13: 978-1-4165-9158-0

Cover art by Alan Pollack

First Baen paperback printing, April 2009

Distributed by Simon & Schuster
1230 Avenue of the Americas
New York, NY 10020

Library of Congress Cataloging-in-Publication Data:
2007037314

Printed in the United States of America

10 9 8 7 6 5 4 3 2 1

To Jim Baen
1943-2006

❖

In memory of one of
the great publishers

Acknowledgements

I would like to thank the following readers for their much appreciated input. Their comments have made this a better book. Any mistakes that remain are mine alone.

To Aly Parsons, Kate Dolan, Sarah White, and Maria Markham Thompson for their excellent reading and comments on the full manuscript; to Aly's Writing Group for insightful critiques of scenes: Aly Parsons, Simcha Kuritzky, Connie Warner, Al Carroll, J. G. Huckenpöhler, John Hemry, Bud Sparhawk, and Bob Chase. To my editor and publisher, Toni Weisskopf; to Hank Davis, Marla Anspan, Danielle Turner (Managing Editor), Mary Ann Johanson (copy editor), and all the other people at Baen who did such a fine job making this book possible; to my excellent agent, Eleanor Wood, of Spectrum Literary Agency; and to Binnie Braunstein for her enthusiasm and hard work on my behalf.

A heartfelt thanks to the shining lights in my life, my husband, John Cannizzo, and my daughter, Cathy, for their love and support.

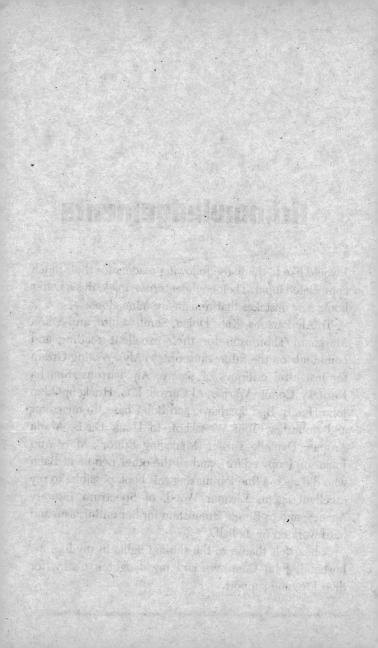

Prologue

The Emperor of the Eubian Concord ruled the largest empire ever known to the human race, over two trillion people across more than a thousand worlds and habitats. It was a thriving, teeming civilization of beautiful complexity, and if it was also the greatest work of despotism ever created, its ruling caste had managed to raise their denial of that truth to heights greater than ever before known, as well.

Lost in such thoughts, the emperor stood in a high room of his palace and stared out a floor-to-ceiling window at the nighttime city below. The sparkle of its lights created a visual sonata that soothed his vision, if not his heart. At the age of twenty-six, Jaibriol the Third had weathered nine years of his own rule. Somehow, despite the assassination attempts, betrayals, and gilt-edged cruelty of his life, he survived.

Tonight the emperor grieved.

He mourned the loss of his innocence and his joy in

life. His title was a prison as confining as the invisible bonds that held the billions of slaves he owned and wished he could free.

Most of all, he mourned his family. Ten years ago tonight, his parents had died in a spectacular explosion recorded and broadcast a million times across settled space. In the final battle of the Radiance War between his people and the Skolian Imperialate, the ship carrying his parents had detonated. He had seen that recording again and again, until it was seared into his mind.

Jaibriol's father had descended from a long line of emperors, every one of them dedicated to the destruction of the Imperialate. On that day, the Skolian Imperator had captured his father. Rather than see him imprisoned, his own people had destroyed the Imperator's ship. So had come the death of Jaibriol's father, the Emperor of Eube.

And so had come the death of Jaibriol's mother—the Imperator of Skolia.

How two interstellar potentates ended up in the midst of a battle, Jaibriol would never know. Perhaps they had been fleeing into exile, seeking a place where the hatred between their peoples couldn't destroy them. Whatever the truth, they had taken it to their graves. Now both were ten years dead, and Jaibriol sat on the Carnelian Throne. His mother had ruled the empire of his enemies. He carried the secret of his heritage like a bomb ready to detonate within him.

He kept his bedroom darkened as he gazed at the city below, Qoxire, the capital of his empire. He could no longer see the lights that glistened on the lofty towers, nor could he see beyond the city to the thundering waves that crashed on a shoreline of dazzling black sand. The scene's luster blurred into luminous washes of color, for tonight the emperor wept.

A door hissed across the room. He tensed, knowing it could be only one person. His bodyguards would stop anyone else. Unless they were dead and this was an assassination attempt. He felt more sorrow at the thought of their possible deaths than the thought of his own. He continued to gaze out the window. If an assassin had come upon him tonight, perhaps he should let the killer free him from the agony of his so-called glorious reign.

Footsteps whispered on the deep-piled rug. Someone stopped behind him, and he heard breathing.

"If you have a knife," Jaibriol said, "I would suggest placing it between my third and fourth ribs."

A woman spoke in a dusky voice. "I never carry knives. They're too obvious."

Jaibriol turned around. The woman stood at nearly his height, her leanly muscled body taut with coiled energy. Glittering black hair brushed her shoulders, and her upward-tilted eyes were as red as gems. Her high cheekbones underscored her aquiline beauty, giving her the profile that graced several Eubian coins. Her black jumpsuit resembled a uniform, except that it fit snugly, accenting her sultry, pantherlike sensuality. She could have passed for thirty-five, but Jaibriol knew the truth. His wife was more than a century in age.

"You don't need a knife," he said. "You cut to the bone without it."

Her lips curved upward. "I thank you for the compliment."

"What would you consider an insult?" he asked dryly. "If I called you sweet and accommodating?"

She raised her sculpted eyebrow at him. "For what possible reason would you say such a thing?"

Perhaps because just once, he thought, *I would like a wife who showed even one of those traits.* She didn't catch his thought; she had no telepathic ability. Although she wasn't an empath, either, she was far more attuned to his moods than he would have thought possible for a member of the Highton Aristo caste. Of course, he was supposedly Highton as well. He had the shimmering black hair, red eyes, and alabaster skin. No one had any idea he possessed the forbidden abilities of a psion.

"I was curious to see your reaction," he said. It was even true.

"No games, Jai. Not tonight." She sounded tired. Or more accurately, she let her fatigue show. Although she presented a perfect, cool exterior to the world, he knew her too well to be fooled.

"Why not tonight?" he asked. It was refreshing to ask a straight question. In normal discourse, Hightons never did. Direct speech was an insult, for Aristos used it only with their slaves. Except, of course, between lovers. He had long ago decided not to dwell on the implications, that they used the same form of speech with lovers and slaves.

His wife, Tarquine, walked away, across the dimly lit room. "It's the mercantile Lines," she said, sounding distracted.

Well, hell. If Tarquine decided some group posed a threat, she could do a great deal of damage. As Finance Minister, she wielded far too much influence over the economics of the Eubian empire; her reach could affect even the other two civilizations that shared the stars with them, the Skolian Imperialate and the Allied Worlds of Earth.

"Merchants in general?" he asked. "Or one in particular?"

She turned to him. "The Line of Janq."

"They're the ones who own so many export corporations in Ivory Sector, aren't they?" As Diamond Aristos, they dealt with Jaibriol less than his Highton Aristo advisors.

"If this consortium they are putting together succeeds," Tarquine said, "they will own all of them."

Jaibriol frowned. That would give one Aristo Line a lock on nearly one quarter of the empire's most lucrative export institutions. "Can you get me a report on what you know?"

"A report." She watched him, her eyes dark in the dim light. "So you can prepare for a meeting with them that will allow us to negotiate this situation in a reasonable manner."

His jaw ached, and he realized he was clenching his teeth. He forced himself to relax. "That's right."

She came back over to him. "Of course, Jai. I will provide you with a report."

He hated it when she agreed that easily; it almost always meant trouble. She unsettled him as much today as when he had met her, perhaps even more now that he knew her better. Nine years ago, his joint commanders of Eubian Space Command, or ESComm, had conspired to kill him and nearly succeeded twice, including on his wedding day, though no proof existed. In the end, they had both died by assassination. Three civilizations believed they had arranged each other's deaths. How could it be otherwise? No one could touch those two warlords who led the massive, relentless military machine of the Eubian empire.

Except Tarquine.

She would never acknowledge it, but Jaibriol knew. She had arranged the death of the admiral through the explosion of his ship, making it look as if the other commander killed him. The retaliation of the admiral's kin had been fast; before Jaibriol knew even one of his commanders had died, both were gone.

"Tarquine," he warned. "Keep out of it."

"I am the Finance Minister," she said mildly. "I cannot 'keep out of it.'"

"You know what I mean."

"You worry too much," she murmured.

"When you say 'don't worry,' I get hives."

She laid her finger on his cheek. "It will be fine."

He folded his hand around her fingers and moved them away. He was no longer the naïve youth who had married her out of desperation, because he was safer with her as his empress than as his enemy. He was still young compared to his advisors, hardly more than a boy by Highton standards, but he had learned a great deal over the past ten years. And if it meant he had lost his innocence, it also meant he kept his life.

Jaibriol had never lost his dream—to make peace between his people and the Skolians. He would never have the chance to know his family, the Ruby Dynasty who ruled Skolia. Their Imperator, Kelric Valdoria, would never know he was the uncle of Eube's emperor. That secret would remain locked within Jaibriol. But perhaps they could meet at the peace table. It was the only way he knew to honor his mother and father, who had dreamed of ending the hostilities between their two peoples.

He didn't want his parents to have died in vain.

The night mourned with silence, as if it were a sonata with no music left to play. More than ever, tonight Kelric Skolia—Imperator of the Skolian Imperialate—felt his age. The years weighed on him.

He sat on the bed, in the dim light, and watched his wife sleep. White hair curled around her face. Her skin was smooth, with only a few wrinkles, but it had a translucent quality. Her torso barely rose and fell with her shallow breaths. The crook of her nose, broken decades ago, shadowed her cheek. She had never wanted it fixed, though he could have given her anything, anything at all, any riches or wealth or lands or gifts.

Anything except her life.

"Jeejon," he said. A tear formed in his eye, and he wiped it away with the heel of his hand.

She seemed small under the blankets, wasted away. He had searched out every remedy medical science could provide, but it was too late. By the time he had met Jeejon, nine years ago, her body had nearly finished its span of life. She had been born a Eubian slave. They designed her to last sixty years, and she had been fifty-seven when his path crossed hers. His age. But he had benefited his entire life from treatments to delay his aging, even nanomed species passed to him by his mother in the womb. Jeejon had received nothing; her owners considered her a machine with no more rights than a robot. Kelric had managed to extend her three years to nine, but now, at sixty-six, her body had given out.

A rustle came from the doorway. He looked around to see Najo, one of his bodyguards, a man in the stark black uniform of a Jagernaut, with a heavy Jumbler in a holster on his hip.

"I'm sorry to disturb you, sir," Najo said. "But you have a page on your console."

Kelric nodded. Nothing could stop the Imperialate in its vibrant life, nine hundred worlds and habitats, a trillion people spread across the stars. It slowed for nothing, not even him, its Imperator.

He rose to his feet, watching Jeejon, hoping for a sign she would awaken. Nothing happened except the whisper of her breath.

Kelric went with Najo. His other bodyguards were in the hall outside: Axer, a burly Jagernaut Tertiary whose shaved head was tattooed with linked circles; and Strava, tall and stoic, a Jagernaut Secondary, her hair cut short. They had accompanied him here to his stone mansion above a valley of green slopes and whispering trees. He lived in the Orbiter space station, which had perfect weather every day. The big, airy spaces of his home accommodated his large size, as did the lower gravity, two-thirds the human standard. He didn't need bodyguards in this house; the entire habitat protected him. Najo and the others had come with him today as a buffer, to shield his privacy in these last days with Jeejon. His moments with her seemed faded by antiqued sunlight, as if they were aged gold.

His officers had to be able to reach him, however. As Imperator, he commanded all four branches of Imperial Space Command, or ISC: the Pharaoh's Army, the Imperial Fleet, the Jagernaut Forces, and the Advance Services Corps. He didn't rule the Skolian Imperialate; that job went to a contentious, vociferous Assembly of elected representatives and to his aunt, the Ruby Pharaoh. But Kelric had the loyalty of ISC.

He crossed his living room, limping slightly from an old injury that even biomech technology had never fully healed. The large space of polished grey stone soothed him. This mansion had belonged to his half-brother, Kurj, a previous Imperator. Kurj had been a huge man, tall and massively built, and Kelric looked a great deal like him. The house was all open spaces and stone, with no adornment except gold desert silhouettes that glowed on the walls at waist height. Kelric had thought of adding color to the grey stone, but with Jeejon here, the place had always seemed warm.

When he reached the console by the far wall, he found glyphs floating above its horizontal screen. The message was from his aunt, Dehya Selei. The Ruby Pharaoh. She descended from the dynasty that had ruled the Ruby Empire thousands of years ago. As a scholarly mathematician, she was far different from those ancient warrior queens; Dehya wielded a vast and uncharted power in the shadowy mesh of communications that wove the Imperialate together.

Her message glowed in gold:

Kelric, we've a diplomatic glitch with the Allied

Worlds of Earth. It isn't urgent, but as soon as you have a chance, I'd like to brief you.—Dehya.

He rested his palm on the screen, and the holos faded above his skin. She could have paged his gauntlet, but it would have been an intrusion. *Thank you,* he thought to her, for understanding he needed this time with Jeejon before his voracious duties devoured his attention.

As a member of the Ruby Dynasty, Kelric had inherited his title as Imperator after the death of his sister, the previous Imperator. He commanded one of the largest militaries in human history—yet all his power, all his titles and lineage and wealth meant nothing, for they couldn't stop his wife from dying.

Kelric's bedroom was huge and spare, all polished stone and high ceilings. Breezes wafted in through windows with no panes. The bed stood in the middle of the stone floor; walking to it, he felt as if he were crossing a desert. The room echoed, and Jeejon hadn't stirred.

With a sigh, Kelric lay beside his wife.

"Kelric?" Her voice was wispy.

He pushed up on his elbow to look at her. She watched him with pale blue eyes, worn and tired, wrinkles at their corners.

His voice caught. "My greetings of the morning."

"Is it . . . morning?"

"I think so." He hadn't been paying attention.

Her mouth curved in the ghost of a smile. "Come here . . ."

He hesitated, wanting to hold her but afraid. He was so

large, with more strength than he knew what to do with, and she had become so fragile.

"I don't break that easily," she said.

Kelric drew down the covers. She was wearing that white sleep gown he loved. He pushed off his boots, then lay on his back and pulled her into his arms. She settled against his side, resting her head on his shoulder. They stayed that way, and he listened to her breathing. Each inhale was a gift, for it meant she lived that much longer.

"I remember the first time I saw you," she said.

"At that mining outpost."

"Yes." She sighed. "You were so incredibly beautiful."

He snorted. "I was so incredibly sick."

"That too."

The memories were scars in his mind. He had been one among millions of refugees caught in the aftermath of the Radiance War that had devastated both the Imperialate and Eubian empire. Alone and unprotected, he had feared to reveal his identity lest he risk assassination. Not that anyone would have believed him. He had been dying, stranded on a mining asteroid, his body in the last stages of collapse. Jeejon was processing people through the port. A former Trader slave, she had escaped to freedom during the war. If she hadn't taken him in, he would have died, alone and in misery.

He laid his head against hers. "You saved my life." If only he could do the same for her.

She was silent for a while. Then she said, "You were kind."

Although he laughed, his voice shook. "I made you a Ruby consort. That's more cruel than kind." One reason he lived here, instead of on the capital world of the Imperialate, was so she wouldn't have to deal with the elegantly cutthroat world of the Imperial court.

"It has been a treasure." Her voice was barely audible. "I was born a slave. I die a queen."

His pulse stuttered. "You won't die."

"It was a great act of gratitude, to marry me because I saved your life."

"That's not why I married you." He wasn't telling the full truth, but he had grown to love her.

She breathed out, her body slight against his. "When we met, you were wearing gold guards on your wrists."

Kelric tensed. "I took them off."

"They were marriage guards."

Had she known all these years? "Jeejon—"

"Shhhh," she whispered. "I never knew why you left her."

"Don't."

"You never went back to her. Even though you love her."

"You're my wife. I don't want to talk about someone else. Not now." Not when they had so little time left.

She pressed her lips against his chest. "No one knows what happened to you during the war, do they? It isn't just me . . . you never told anyone about those eighteen years you vanished."

"It doesn't matter." Moisture gathered in his eyes.

Her voice was low. "Such a tremendous gift you have given me, waiting while it took me nine years to die."

"Jeejon, stop."

"Someday . . . you must finish that chapter of your life you left behind for me."

He cradled her in his arms. "You can't die."

"I love you, Kelric."

"And I, you." His voice broke. "Always."

"Good-bye," she whispered.

"Don't—" Kelric froze. Her breathing had stopped. Somewhere an alarm went off, distant, discreet, horrifying.

"*No.*" He pulled her close, his arms shaking, and laid his cheek against her head. "*Jeejon, no.*"

She didn't answer.

Kelric held his wife, and his tears soaked into her hair.

I
Hall Of Circles

The Highton language was rife with allusions to the Carnelian Throne that symbolized the reign of the Eubian Emperor, phrases such as "He commanded with magnificence from the throne" or "His glorious Highness sat on the esteemed Throne of Carnelians" or "Only a fool would put a half-grown boy on the damn throne." None of those phrases referred to the emperor actually sitting on a chair, of course. Unfortunately, however, the Carnelian Throne did exist. And it was about as comfortable as a rock.

Jaibriol sat in the throne, leaning to one side, his elbow resting on its stone arm. He was alone in the Hall of Circles except for his guards. The room was like ice. Its white walls sparkled, designed from a composite of diamond and snow-marble. Rows of high-backed benches ringed the chamber, all snow-diamond and set with red cushions like drops of blood on frost. A white dais supported his throne, and red gems glinted in the chair, as hard and cold as the Hightons who sat atop the empire's power hierarchy.

His bodyguards were posted around the walls, three of the mammoths where he could see them and four others behind him. They wore the midnight uniforms of Razers, the secret police who served the emperor, their dark clothes jarring against the brilliant white walls. These Razers had so much biomech augmentation, they were considered constructs rather than human beings. Their thoughts lurked at the edges of his mind, mechanical, not quite human.

The captain of his guards waited by the dais, alert and still, his feet apart, his arms by his sides. Although his face remained as impassive as always, Jaibriol never felt ill-at-ease with him. He had selected these men over time, choosing those with no Aristo heritage.

It disturbed Jaibriol that the Aristos identified their Razers only by serial numbers. His guards seemed more human to him than the supposedly exalted Aristos. He had named the captain Vitar, because the guard resembled Jaibriol's younger brother. But he had come to think that wasn't right, either; he should have asked the Razer what he wanted to call himself.

A chime came from his wrist comm. Jaibriol lifted his arm and spoke into the mesh. "Yes?"

The voice of his personal aide, Robert Muzeson, came out of the comm. "Your joint commanders are here, Your Highness."

"Send them in," Jaibriol said. His pulse ratcheted up, and he took a breath, schooling himself to calm. He had summoned them to this frozen place rather than to his office because the presence of the throne accented his authority.

The towering doors across the hall swung open like cracks widening in ice. Vitar's biomech arm flashed as he communicated with the other Razers, and they moved into position, flanking the entrance. A retinue of military types swept into the hall, a general and an admiral, with six other officers in a crisp formation. The Razers fell in around the retinue and accompanied them down the central aisle.

General Barthol Iquar strode at the front of the group. He was Tarquine's nephew, a powerfully built man in a dark uniform. Admiral Erix Muze, a leaner man in cobalt blue, walked with him. Both commanders were Hightons, members of the highest Aristo caste, which ran the military and government. They topped the hierarchy of ESComm; together, they commanded the Eubian military.

Jaibriol remained relaxed on his throne while they came to him. He allowed neither his posture nor expression to reveal his discomfort. Their minds were great weights pressing on his, smothering him; as they came nearer, his perception shifted and they seemed like chasms that could pull him into darkness and pain and swallow his sanity. He shored up his mental shields, both protecting himself and hiding his mind, for he could never let them suspect he was a psion. He carried out this farce that defined his life, every day of every year, until he felt as if he were walking down an infinite corridor of frost.

Seeing their hard faces, it was hard for Jaibriol to remember they existed because of an attempt to *protect* empaths. That well-meant research had produced a monstrous result. The geneticists tried to mute the painful emotions empaths sensed, but instead they created a race of antiempaths. Aristos. When an Aristo's brain detected the pain of a psion, it shunted the signals to its pleasure centers. The stronger the psion's agony, the greater the effect. Aristos considered the resulting explosion of ecstasy they experienced the greatest elevation a human being could experience. They named it "transcendence" and called the psions they tortured to make it possible "providers."

In their brutally warped logic, the Aristos believed their ability to transcend raised them into a superior form of life, and that the agony of their providers elevated them. If the Aristos ever suspected their emperor was a Ruby psion—the ultimate provider—his life would become a hell almost beyond his ability to imagine.

Almost.

Watching the approach of his commanders, Jaibriol fought to maintain his mask of indifference. Robert, his personal aide, came in after the retinue. His presence both calmed Jaibriol and stirred his guilt. Robert's unusual name came from Earth. Eubian merchants had "liberated" Robert's father from his ship. Of course they weren't merchants and they hadn't liberated anyone, but that sounded so much more palatable than saying pirates had kidnapped him and sold him into slavery. Jaibriol couldn't undo the sins of every Aristo, but he had managed to bring Robert's father to the palace and reunite him with his son after decades of unwanted separation.

The retinue stopped at the dais, and Barthol and Erix bowed to Jaibriol. None of the aides were full Aristos, so they all went down on one knee. Jaibriol had to stop himself from shifting his weight. He had never liked having people kneel to him. His parents had raised their children in secret on a world with no other people, so they never bothered with court protocols. He wasn't certain which disturbed him more, that Eubians believed all human beings except Aristos should kneel to their emperor or that he was becoming accustomed to that treatment.

He didn't immediately tell them to rise, not because he had any desire to see people kneel, but because to do otherwise would be viewed by Hightons as a weakening of his authority. Early on in his reign, he had learned the hard way: behave as expected or deepen the risk of assassination.

A memory jumped into his mind of the day ESComm had found his father and taken him away. Jaibriol had been fourteen. ESComm had wrested his father from his world of refuge without knowing the man they found had a family. After that shattering day, Jaibriol's mother had hidden her children on Earth with one of the few people she trusted, Admiral Seth Rockworth. Then she had started the Radiance War. Almost no one knew she had done it to reclaim her husband. Jaibriol had ascended to his throne with the foolish hope that he could end the hostilities between the empires of his parents, but after ten years among the Aristos, he despaired that he would ever make headway.

Finally he moved his hand, palm down, permitting the aides to stand. Although their gazes were downcast, they caught his gesture. After they rose to their feet, he stood up and descended the dais, taking his time, studying the general and admiral. Both were tall, especially Erix Muze, who stood nearly eye to eye with Jaibriol when the emperor stopped in front of them.

"I am pleased," Jaibriol said. He wasn't; he liked neither of his arrogant joint commanders. But even if they loathed him, especially Barthol, at least they were more loyal than the previous two, who had kept trying to murder him.

Jaibriol motioned toward the closest bench. He didn't invite them to sit; such a direct comment from one Aristo to another would be a profound insult.

As soon as Robert saw Jaibriol lift his hand, he spoke with deference. "General Iquar and Admiral Muze, it would please the emperor if you would join him."

The three of them took their seats on the bench, Jaibriol on one end and his commanders in its middle. It was an awkward arrangement for a conference, but he had no intention of making this easy. He was tired of their delaying tactics. If he had to spend time in their mind-torturing presence, he wanted them off balance. He had discovered that the more uncomfortable he made the Aristos around him, the less likely they were to notice his discomfort, or his "penchant" for treating non-Aristos as if they were human.

Captain Vitar stationed himself next to Jaibriol, a stark reminder of the power wielded by the emperor, that he could command ESComm's billion-credit Razers as his private bodyguards. Vitar wore the face of a mechanical killing machine with no emotions. He didn't fool Jaibriol. His guards loved, hated, laughed, and wept like other humans. He sometimes had the odd sense that Vitar enjoyed intimidating Aristos he knew Jaibriol didn't like. The Razer would of course never do anything to suggest he harbored such inappropriate sentiments, so Jaibriol could never be sure. He had difficulty picking up moods from his guards because the extensive biomech augmentation to their brains changed their brain waves.

Barthol Iquar spoke the requisite formal phrases. "You honor the Line of Iquar with your presence, Esteemed Highness."

Erix spoke. "You honor the Line of Muze, Esteemed Highness."

Jaibriol inclined his head. In the convoluted Highton language, it meant he accepted their words without rancor, but without any particular encouragement, either. To Barthol, he said, "I understand you have acquired a new corporation."

"Indeed," Barthol said, cautious. "A good business. Furniture."

Good business, indeed. The general was leaving him no openings. No matter. Jaibriol had expected this. "Perhaps I might look at your inventory. I understand you have an excellent selection of tables."

Although neither commander showed a reaction, they knew what he meant. The peace table. Their negotiations with the Imperialate. He felt the spark of their anger even with his mental barriers up. They would have to live with it. The negotiations had been stalled for years, and he was heartily sick of their maneuvers to avoid the talks.

"I will have an inventory sent to you," Barthol said smoothly.

Jaibriol just sat, letting the silence lengthen. The tactic sometimes prodded Aristos to speak, as if they couldn't bear a hole in the convoluted webs of discourse they wove. These two were too well versed in Highton to show discomfort, but their moods trickled over Jaibriol: unease and anger. Neither had any desire for peace with the Skolians. Barthol also thought him a callow youth with peculiarities that bordered on intolerable.

After several moments, Jaibriol said, "I'm sure you know best what inventory would suit my interests. Perhaps the most knowledgeable of your people can assist my review."

The general's eyes were hard and clear, like the gems in the Carnelian Throne. "Of course, Sire."

"I would particularly like to see any unusual pieces." Jaibriol didn't say *Skolian,* but they knew. He intended to reopen the talks, if he could convince the Skolians, and he expected at least one of his joint commanders in attendance. Barthol had a close relation to Tarquine, as her nephew, but he harbored a greater antagonism toward Jaibriol than Admiral Muze.

"We are always happy to seek the betterment of the empire," Erix Muze said.

"It pleases me to know." Jaibriol didn't doubt he meant it. He also had no doubt that "betterment of the empire" didn't include negotiations with Skolians.

He dismissed the commanders with body language, a slight shifting of his weight, a glance to the side. Suddenly Robert was there, escorting the officers away. He had developed his ability to read Jaibriol's Highton gestures to an art.

Captain Vitar directed the other bodyguards using commands Jaibriol couldn't see, except for the lights flickering on his biomech arm and those of the other Razers. The captain had biomech limbs, nodes in his spine, bioelectrodes throughout his brain, and threads and high-pressure hydraulics networking his body. Yet when Jaibriol looked into his face, he saw a man.

After his commanders were gone, Jaibriol stood up and beckoned to Vitar. The guard came over, looming above even Jaibriol, and bowed. The conduits on his dark uniform glinted. Although protocol demanded that everyone except other Aristos kneel to the emperor, Jaibriol shared one trait in common with his predecessors on the throne: he preferred his guards on their feet and ready to defend his person.

"Vitar, do you like your name?" Jaibriol asked.

"Most certainly, Sire. It is an honor." Disappointment flashed in his gaze, though he quickly hid the emotion. "But if you wish to withdraw it, I will be honored to obey your wishes."

"No, I didn't mean that." Jaibriol rubbed his chin. "I just thought you might like to choose your own."

The Razer paused only a moment, but for someone with a brain as much biomech as human, it was a long time. Then he said, "I would never presume to such. But it is a most esteemed offer."

"It's not a presumption," Jaibriol said. "If you could pick any name, what would you choose?"

Vitar thought for a moment. "Hidaka. Sam Hidaka."

"All right. If you would like, I will call you Hidaka."

For one of the few times in the years Jaibriol had known him, the captain grinned in an all-out smile. "Thank you, Sire! You are most generous."

Jaibriol didn't feel generous, he felt like a cretin. He should have asked Vitar years ago what name he preferred. No, not Vitar. Hidaka. He would have to remember.

He regarded the Razer curiously. "It's an unusual name. Did you make it up?"

The captain shook his head. "It is the name of the founder and chief executive of the most successful coffee business on Earth." Then he added, "Coffee is one of the Earth people's greatest achievements."

Startled, Jaibriol smiled. He wondered what other Aristos would say if they knew his Razers admired or even knew about any aspects of cultures outside the euphemistically named Eubian Concord, which as far as Jaibriol could see had achieved "concord" only in the Aristos' united desire to subjugate the rest of humanity.

"Well, Hidaka, you have an excellent name," Jaibriol said. "Your men may choose names as well, if they wish."

The captain bowed. "You honor us."

Jaibriol couldn't answer. It wasn't an honor, it was appalling it had taken this long for him to offer the choice.

They left the hall then, and as Jaibriol walked through the black marble halls of his palace, he brooded. He wished his joint commanders were as straightforward to deal with as his guards. He doubted he would ever convince Barthol Iquar or Erix Muze to endorse his wish for peace. And without support of the military, he didn't see how any talks with the Skolian Imperialate could even succeed.

"Jeremiah Coltman," Dehya said.

Kelric looked up from the console where he was scanning files on army deployments. He and Dehya were in a room paneled in gold and copper hues. It was one of many offices that honeycombed the hull of the Skolian Orbiter space station used as a command center by the Imperialate.

"Jeremiad what?" he asked.

Dehya regarded him from her console, a slender woman with long hair, sleek and black, streaked with white, as if frost tipped the tendrils curling around her face. Translucent sunset colors overlaid her green eyes, the only trace she had of her father's inner eyelid. Kelric didn't have the inner lid either, but he had his grandfather's metallic gold eyes, skin, and hair, modifications designed to adapt humans to a too-bright world.

"Jeremiah Coltman," she repeated. "Do you remember?"

"I've no idea," he said, rubbing his shoulder to ease his stiff muscles. He had many aches these days; he hardly recalled the years when he had been bursting with youth and energy.

"That boy from Earth," Dehya said. "About a year ago we had trouble with the Allied Worlds over him."

Kelric searched his memory, but nothing came. **Bolt,** he thought, accessing his spinal node. **You have anything on him?**

His node answered via bioelectrodes in his brain that fired his neurons in a manner he interpreted as thought. **Jeremiah Coltman was detained on a Skolian world. I'm afraid my records are spotty.**

Kelric remembered then. It had come up the day Jeejon died. He recalled little from that time, and he had recorded nothing well in the long days that followed. Even now, nearly a year later, he avoided the memories. They hurt too much.

"I thought the man they locked up was an adult," Kelric said. "A professor."

"An anthropology graduate student." Dehya was reading from her console. "He spent three years on one of our worlds while he wrote his dissertation. Huh. Listen to this. They didn't throw him in prison. They like him so much, they won't let him go home."

Kelric turned back to his work. "Can't somebody's embassy take care of it?" It surprised him that she would spend time on it. Dehya served as Assembly Key, the liaison between the Assembly and the vast information meshes that networked the Imperialate in space-time—and in Kyle space. Physics had no meaning in the Kyle; proximity was determined by similarity of thought rather than position. Two people having a conversation were "next" to each other no matter how many light-years separated them in real space. It allowed instant communication across interstellar distances and tied the Imperialate into a coherent civilization. But only those few people with a nearly extinct mutation in their neural structures could power the Kyle web. Like Dehya. As Assembly Key, she had far more pressing matters to attend than a minor incident from a year ago.

"Ah, but Kelric," she said. "It's such an interesting incident."

Damn! He had to guard his thoughts better. He fortified his mental shields. "Stop eavesdropping," he grumbled.

She smiled in that ethereally strange way of hers, as if she were only partly in the real universe. "He won a prize."

"Who won a prize?"

"Jeremiah Coltman. Something called the Goldstone."

She glanced at her console. "It's quite prestigious among anthropologists. But his hosts won't let him go home to receive it. That caused a stir, enough to toggle my news monitors."

Kelric felt a pang of longing. Had he been free to pursue any career, he would have chosen the academic life and become a mathematician. He and Dehya were alike that way. Those extra neural structures that adapted their brains to Kyle space also gave them an enhanced ability for abstract thought.

"Why won't they let him go?" Kelric said. "Where is he?"

"Never heard of the place." She squinted at her screen. "Planet called Coba."

He felt as if a freighter slammed into him. Jeejon's words rushed back from that moment before she died: *You never told anyone where you were those eighteen years.*

"Kelric?" Dehya was watching him. "What's wrong?"

Mercifully, his mental shields were in place. He didn't think she could pick up anything from him, but he never knew for certain with Dehya; she had a finesse unlike anyone else. So he told the truth, as best he could. "It reminded me of Jeejon."

Sympathy softened her sculpted features. "Good memories, I hope."

He just nodded. His family believed he had been a prisoner during those eighteen years he vanished. He let them assume the Eubians had captured and enslaved him, and that he didn't want to speak of it. That was even true for the final months. But he didn't think Dehya ever fully believed it. If she suspected he was reacting to the name *Coba*, she would pursue the lead.

He had to escape before she sensed that his disquiet went beyond his memories of Jeejon. Dehya's ability to read his moods depended on how well the fields of her brain interacted with his. The Coulomb forces that determined those fields dropped off quickly with distance; even a few meters could affect whether or not she picked up his emotions.

He rose to his feet. "I think I'll take a break."

She spoke softly. "I'm sorry I reminded you."

His face gentled, as could happen around Dehya. She was one of the few people who seemed untroubled by his silences and reclusive nature. "It's all right."

He left the chamber then, his stride long and slow in the lower gravity, which was forgiving to his huge size. Alone, he headed back to his large, empty house.

II
A Debt To Life

Kelric sat in his living room with no lights except the gold designs on the walls. No sunlight slanted through the open windows, but the bright day diffused into his home. He had settled on the couch, almost the only furniture in the huge room.

He sat and he thought.

Coba. It had taken eighteen years of his life. What would it do to Jeremiah Coltman? Would the young man's unwilling presence stir that world as Kelric's had done, until its culture erupted into war? Compared to the Radiance War that had raged between the mammoth Eubian and Skolian empires, Coba's war had been tiny. But it ravaged its people. And he, Kelric, had caused it. Coltman was a scholar, not a warrior, but the youth's presence would still exert an influence.

Kelric spoke to the Evolving Intelligence, or EI, that ran his house. He had named it after an ancient physicist who had illuminated mysteries of relativistic quantum mechanics.

"Dirac?" he asked.

A man answered in a deep baritone. "Attending."

"Find me everything you can about Jeremiah Coltman."

Dirac paused. "He was born in Wyoming."

"What's a wyoming?"

"A place on Earth."

"Oh." That didn't help. "What about his graduate school?"

"He earned a doctorate from Harvard for his study of human settlement on the planet Coba. He spent three years working on a construction crew there while he wrote his dissertation. One year ago, a Coban queen selected him for a *Calani*. I have no definition of *Calani*."

"I know what it means." Kelric leaned back and closed his eyes. *Queen* was the wrong word for the women who ruled the Coban city-estates. They called themselves Managers. In Coba's Old Age they had been warriors who battled constantly, but in these modern times they considered themselves civilized. Never mind this atavistic penchant of theirs for kidnapping male geniuses.

Dirac continued. "Coltman's family and members of the Allied diplomatic corps have tried to free him."

"Any success?" Kelric asked.

"So far, none. He agreed to abide by Coban law when they let him live on their world."

"What about this award he won?"

"Apparently the Coban queen relented enough to send his doctoral thesis to his advisor at Harvard. The advisor submitted it to the awards committee. At twenty-four, Coltman is the youngest person ever to win the Goldstone Prize."

Kelric was grateful the fellow had received the honor, not because he knew anything about anthropology, but because it had caught Dehya's attention, which meant Kelric had found out about Coltman. It also gave him a reason to ask about the planet.

"What do you have on Coba?" Kelric asked. His outward calm didn't match his inner turmoil. He had avoided directly speaking that question for ten years, lest someone notice and want to know why he asked. As long as he seemed to ignore Coba, no one had reason to suspect its people had imprisoned a Ruby heir for eighteen years.

"Coba is a Skolian world," Dirac said. "Restricted Status. No native may leave the planet. They are denied contact with the Imperialate. The world has one automated starport, a military refueling post that's rarely used. Skolians who voluntarily enter the Restricted zone forfeit their citizenship."

Kelric waited. "That's it?"

"Yes." The EI sounded apologetic.

Relief washed over him. It was even less than he expected. Restricted Status usually went to worlds inimical to human life or otherwise so dangerous they required quarantine. The Cobans had *asked* for the status, and ISC had granted it because Coba was so inconsequential that no one cared.

Kelric's Jag starfighter had crashed on Coba after he escaped a Eubian ambush. The Cobans should have taken him to the starport. He would have died before they reached it, but the Restriction required they do it. Instead they saved his life. His legs had been pulverized by the crash, and the Cobans had healed him the best they could.

But their medicine had limitations; even with additional work done by his people two decades later, his legs would always bear the internal scars of those injuries.

On Coba, by the time he recovered, they had decided never to let him go. They feared he would bring ISC to investigate the Restriction. They had been right. That had been before he understood how the Imperialate could destroy their unique, maddening, and wondrous culture.

Kelric couldn't fathom why they let Coltman study them. He rose to his feet, and his steps echoed as he walked through the stone halls of his house, under high, unadorned ceilings.

His office had a warmer touch. Jeejon had put down rugs, dark gold with tassels. Panels softened the stark walls with scenes of his home world, plains of silvery-green reeds and spheres adrift in the air. In some images, the spindled peaks of the Backbone Mountains speared a darkening sky.

He sat at his desk, and it lit up with icons, awaiting his commands. He turned off every panel. Then he opened a drawer and removed his pouch, a bag old and worn, bulging with its contents. Often he wore it on his belt, but other times he left it here, in the seclusion of his private office. He undid its drawstring—

And rolled out his Quis dice.

The pieces came in many forms: squares, disks, balls, cubes, rods, polyhedrons, and more. Not only did he have the full set carried by most Cobans, his also included unusual shapes such as stars, eggs, even small boxes with lids.

Dice and Coba. They were inextricably blended. All

Cobans played Quis, from the moment they were old enough to hold the dice until the day they died. It was one giant game, the life's blood of a world. They gambled with Quis, educated with it, gossiped through the dice, built philosophies. The powers of Coba used it to gain political influence. For a Manager to prosper, she had to master Quis at its topmost levels.

Then there were Calani.

The few men honored as Calani were extraordinarily gifted at Quis. They spent their lives playing dice. They provided strategy for the Manager, a weapon she wielded in the flow of power among the Estates. Managers had ten to twenty Calani; together, they formed her Calanya. The stronger a Calanya, the more a Manager could influence Coban culture. Quis meant power, and a Manager's Calanya was her most valuable asset.

Only Calani owned jeweled dice. The white pieces were diamond; the blue, sapphire; the red, ruby. But Calani paid a steep price for the spectacular luxury of their lives. They remained secluded. They saw no one but the Manager and the few visitors she allowed. They swore never to read, write, or speak to anyone Outside the Calanya. Nothing was allowed to contaminate their Quis, for anyone who succeeded in manipulating their game could damage the Estate, even topple the Manager from power. Managers shielded their scholarly Calani from Outside influences with the single-minded resolve of their warrior queen ancestors.

To symbolize Jeremiah, Kelric chose a silver ball. He built structures around it and let them develop according to complex and fluid rules. His skill molded the structures, but the complexity of the game and its often unexpected evolution informed their design just as much. Calani and Quis: they created each other.

He had intended to model Coban politics and examine what they revealed about Jeremiah. Instead, the dice patterns mirrored the history of his own people. He wasn't certain what his subconscious was up to, but he let the structures evolve.

Six millennia ago, an unknown race had taken humans from Earth and moved them to the world Raylicon. Then they vanished, leaving nothing but dead starships. Over the centuries, using libraries on those ships, the humans had developed star travel. They built the Ruby Empire and established many colonies, including Coba. But the empire soon collapsed, stranding the colonies. Four millennia of Dark Ages followed.

When the Raylicans finally regained star travel, they split into two opposed empires: the Eubian Concord, and Kelric's people, the Skolian Imperialate. Skolians referred to Eubians as "Traders" because they based a substantial portion of their economy on the sale and trade of human beings.

Since that time, Skolia had been rediscovering the ancient colonies like Coba. The people of Earth had a real shock when they reached the stars: their siblings were already there, two huge and bitterly opposed civilizations. The Allied Worlds of Earth became a third, but unlike their bellicose neighbors, they had no interest in conquering anyone. They just sold things. In his more philosophical moments, Kelric thought neither his people nor the Traders would inherit the stars. While they were throwing world-slagging armies at each other, the Allieds would quietly take over by convincing humanity they couldn't survive without Allied goods. Imperial Space Command had an incredible ability to expand to new frontiers, but it paled in comparison to Starbytes Coffee.

Earth's success in the interstellar marketplace, however, depended on maintaining civil relations with Skolia and Eube. They obviously had no intention of upsetting their relations with the Imperialate over one graduate student. The moment Jeremiah had set foot on Coba, he had forfeited his rights as an Allied citizen and become subject to the Restriction.

Kelric blew out a gust of air. He had to get Jeremiah out of there, and do it without alerting anyone. The Restriction protected Coba's extraordinary culture.

And it protected Kelric's children.

He sat back, staring at the Quis structures that covered his desk. "Dirac."

The EI's voice floated into the air. "Attending."

Kelric knew if he continued to ask about Coba, someone might notice. His interactions with Dirac were shielded by the best security ISC had to offer. But he knew Dehya. If she became curious, she could break even his security. He was taking a risk. But it had been so long, and he had so little time left.

"I need you to find a Closure document," he said. "It was written ten years ago, just after the Radiance War." He leaned his head back until he was gazing at the stone ceiling. Outside his window, wind rustled in the dapple-trees like children whispering together.

"Did you arrange it?" Dirac asked.

"That's right," Kelric said. "I was serving on a merchant ship. The *Corona*." He had escaped Coba in a dilapidated shuttle that had barely managed to reach another port. He hadn't had credits enough even to buy food, let alone repair the aging shuttle. The job on the *Corona* had offered a way out.

"I have records of a vessel fitting that description," Dirac said. "Jaffe Maccar is its captain."

"That's it. I filed a Closure document with the ship's legal EI."

A long silence followed. Finally Dirac said, "I find no record of this document."

Maybe he had hidden it better than he thought. Either that, or it was lost. "It's encrypted," he said, and gave Dirac a key.

After a moment, Dirac spoke crisply. "File six-eight-three. Marriage to Ixpar Karn Closed. If Closure isn't reversed in ten years, Kelric Garlin Valdoria Skolia will be declared dead, and his assets will revert to his heirs. Ixpar Karn and two children are named as beneficiaries." The EI paused. "Your listed assets are extensive."

"I suppose."

"In one hundred eleven days," Dirac said, "Ixpar Karn will become one of the wealthiest human beings alive."

Even though Kelric had known this was coming, it rattled him. "Ixpar doesn't know."

"Do you wish me to cancel the document?"

"I'm not sure."

"You aren't dead," Dirac pointed out.

"If you cancel it, I'll be married to Ixpar again." It was a dream he desired, but it meant too much danger to her and his family. The Closure didn't become permanent until the end of ten years. It was usually done when someone's spouse vanished, to declare that person legally dead. Generally, the abandoned spouse invoked the Closure, not the person who had disappeared.

"Is marriage to Ixpar Karn a problem?" Dirac asked.

He thought of Jeejon. His marriage to her had been valid because of the Closure. She had been dead a year, but grief didn't end on a schedule. It receded, yes, but it crept up on you like a mouse under the table, until one day you looked down and saw it crouched in your home, watching you with pale eyes, still there after all this time. It was true, he had married Jeejon in gratitude. Maybe he had never felt the soul-deep passion for her that he had with Ixpar, but he had loved Jeejon in a quieter way. She had given up everything she owned to save his life, even believing he was deluded to think he was the Imperator. She had never expected anything in return, but he had sworn to stand by her.

Dirac spoke. "Sir, the three people named as your heirs live on Coba. I don't think it's legal for inhabitants of a Restricted world to inherit from a Skolian citizen."

"I'm the Imperator," Kelric growled. "If I say it's legal, it's legal."

"According to Imperialate law, that isn't true."

Kelric scowled at the ceiling. Unlike his officers, his EI had no qualms about contradicting him.

"Who is going to tell me no?" Kelric asked.

"That would be complicated," Dirac acknowledged. "May I ask a question?"

"Go ahead."

"Why set up the Closure?" The EI sounded genuinely puzzled, as opposed to an AI, which only simulated the emotion. "You aren't the deserted spouse."

"I was unprotected, in a volatile situation." Painful memories rose within him. "I left my children on Coba so they would be safe and taken care of in case anything happened to me. If I died, I wanted to make sure they and Ixpar inherited."

"Yet nothing happened to you."

He grimaced. "I was kidnapped and sold as a slave."

"Oh." Another pause. "Are you saying you became a Trader slave after you signed this document?"

"That's right."

"But the document is only ten years old. Less, in fact."

"Yes."

"It was my understanding the Traders captured you twenty-eight years ago. Not ten."

Kelric didn't answer.

"When you die," Dirac added, "this document becomes public."

"My heirs could hardly inherit otherwise." He had wrestled with that decision, knowing it would draw attention to Coba. As long as he could shield both Coba and his family, he would do so. But if he ever had to choose, his wife and children came first. While he lived, the Closure document would remain secret even if it defined him as officially dead. When he actually died and could no longer look after Coba, the will within the document would become public, ensuring his heirs had his name and the multitude of protections that came with it.

And yet . . . he could protect Coba now in ways he couldn't have imagined ten years ago when, as a desperate refugee, he had written that will.

Dirac suddenly said, "This Closure document gives a new twist to the Hinterland defenses."

Kelric stiffened. "I have no idea what you mean."

"The Hinterland Deployment. One of your first acts as Imperator ten years ago. The military presence you established in sector twenty- seven of the Imperialate hinterlands."

"It was vital," Kelric said. "We needed to stop Traders from using that region of space."

"No indications existed that they were using it," Dirac said.

Kelric's advisors had told him the same. He gave Dirac the same answer he had given them. "That was the problem. No one paid attention to that sector. Had ESComm set up covert operations there, we might never have known."

"This is true." Dirac waited a beat. "How interesting that the Coban star system is the most heavily guarded region of that deployment."

Damn. It was how he protected Ixpar and his children without revealing his attention to their world. "Delete that from your memory."

"Are you sure?"

"Yes."

"Deleted. You have sixty seconds to undo the deletion before it becomes permanent."

Kelric knew erasing parts of an EI's memory was ill-advised. It always lost associated data as well. Such deletions could have unexpected results. But erasing one small fact wouldn't cause trouble. Still . . . perhaps he should reconsider.

"If I don't cancel this Closure," Dirac added, "you are going to be destitute in one hundred and eleven days."

A voice called from another room. "Kellie?"

"For flaming sakes," Kelric muttered. "Dirac, end session." He got up and stalked out of his office.

A woman was standing in his living room. Roca. Gold hair cascaded down her body and curled around her face. She had the same metallic gold skin and eyes as Kelric, but it looked much better on her. In her youth, men had written odes to her beauty and songs lauding her grace. Hell, so had women.

He scowled at her. "My name is Kelric, Mother."

"My apologies, honey. I forget sometimes."

Honey was almost as bad. He wondered when she would notice that her "baby" had grown into a hulking monster who commanded one of the deadliest war machines ever created.

"Don't glare at me so," she added, smiling.

"I thought you were going to Selei City for the Assembly."

Her good mood faded. "That's what I came to see you about." She walked to his console and stood facing it, her palm resting on the surface, though he didn't think she was looking at anything.

He went over to her. "What's wrong?"

She looked up at him. "The Progressive Party wants to abolish the votes held by Assembly delegates with hereditary seats."

That didn't sound new. The Progressives considered it appalling that the Ruby Dynasty and noble Houses held seats even though no one had elected them. As Pharaoh and Imperator, Dehya and Kelric were among the Assembly's most influential members. Roca had won election like any other delegate and become Foreign Affairs Councilor. With her hereditary votes added to that, she was also a great force. Kelric's siblings all held seats, but their blocs were smaller. Each of the eleven noble Houses had two seats, but those were mostly titular, with few votes.

Kelric smiled wryly. "One of these days, the Progressives will call for eradication of the Assembly on the grounds that EIs instead of people should run the government. The Royalists will agree we should abolish the Assembly, but only so Dehya becomes our sole ruler. The Traditionalists will insist a woman command the military and stick me in seclusion. The Technologists will blow up the Assembly with hot-air bombs. Meanwhile, the Moderates will urge everyone to please get along."

Roca laughed, her stiff posture easing. "Probably." She leaned against the console with her arms folded. "The problem is, I think the Progressives can make headway this time."

He didn't see how. "Every time they introduce one of those brain- rattled amendments, the Royalists vote them down. Usually the Traditionalists do, too. Your Moderates don't care, and they're the biggest party. Given that Dehya and I are both Technologists, I doubt our own party would vote to weaken our influence."

She stared across the room. "It seems the deaths in our family offer them a political opportunity."

Kelric stiffened. He hated that he had gained his title through the deaths of his siblings. "It may offend them that I inherited Soz's votes when she died, and that she inherited them from Kurj, but they can't deny the law. The Imperator holds a primary Assembly seat." Although technically the military answered to the Assembly, the loyalty of ISC to their Imperator was legendary. He doubted the Assembly wanted to push the issue of whom the military would obey. The last time they had faced that question, ISC had thrown its might behind the Ruby Dynasty and put Dehya back on the throne. In the end, she had chosen to split her rule with the Assembly because she genuinely believed it was best for the Imperialate. But few people doubted that, if put to the test, ISC would follow the Imperator.

"They won't touch your votes," Roca said. "They aren't stupid." Her voice quieted. "It's your father's bloc. No one objected to my inheriting it after he died because they knew how it would look. But it's been ten years." She sounded tired. "Before he became Web Key, we had only two Keys, the positions you and Dehya now hold. Those two Keys powered the Kyle web. It was a fluke that your father's mind differed enough from theirs to add a third mind without killing them. Many people don't believe we can duplicate that achievement. They say those votes should cease to exist unless we find another Web Key."

Kelric swore under his breath. The Progressives had grounds for their objection. He had expected them to raise it years ago, and when they hadn't, he had grown complacent. They had bided their time until they could no longer be accused of traumatizing the widow or her grieving family. They had even waited a year after Jeejon's death, though Kelric had no direct connection with his mother's votes. Yes, they had been careful. He could see why Roca was worried. They might win.

He didn't want her to lose those votes. She was one of the Assembly's greatest moderating forces. Many citizens felt the Imperialate subjugated its people with militaristic occupations and harsh laws. Facing the relentless threat of the Traders, Kelric understood all too well the draconian measures instituted by previous Imperators. He had enough objectivity to admit that in defending the Imperialate, he was capable of acts many would consider oppressive. They *needed* temperate voices. Roca offered a counterbalance. The day he rejected that balance was the day he became a tyrant.

"You have a plan?" he asked.

"I'm going early to the session," she said. "See if I can sway votes. It would help if you attended in person. Spend time softening up delegates with me."

"I couldn't soften a pod fruit."

"You're damned effective when you want to be."

He glowered at her. "Doing what? I hate public speaking."

"I'm not asking you to speak in the Assembly." She smiled with that too-reasonable expression that always meant trouble. "I just plan to give some dinners. Small, elegant, elite. People consider it a coup to be invited. They will think it even more so if the Imperator attends. We wine them, dine them, and convince them to support us."

Kelric stared at her. "You want me to attend dinner parties with the Imperial court?"

"Yes, actually."

"I would rather die."

Exasperation leaked into her voice. "It's not a form of torture, you know."

"It's not?"

"Do you want to win the vote or not?"

I'm going to regret this, he thought to her. "Fine," he growled. "I'll do it."

"Good." Then she thought, *The Dinners will be fun.* **Gods forbid.**

Her sudden smile dazzled. *Which ones will forbid it?*

Kelric glared at her. He had grown up on the world Lyshriol, steeped in its mythology of deities for the moons, suns, and mountains. He was named after Kelricson, the god of youth, though he hardly felt young anymore. He had become more pragmatic after he left home, but deep inside, a part of him still remembered when he had believed those luminous stories.

All of them. He let his thought grumble. **Especially Youth.**

Roca laughed good-naturedly. *Maybe even even he will enjoy himself.*

After Roca left, Kelric returned to his office and gazed at the dice on his desk. He thought of his children on Coba, the only he had ever fathered. In standard years, his son would be twenty-six now and his daughter sixteen. Ixpar was forty-two. She wasn't the mother of either child; she had only been fourteen when Kelric met her, and twice that age when she married him. He had never been allowed to see his son, and he had known his daughter only a few months after her birth. The ache of that lack in his life had never stopped, even after all this time.

Kelric often wanted to go to them. Then he would remember the devastation he had wrought on Coba, how cities had roared in flames while windriders battled in the skies. He had brought death and ruin to their world.

He would die before he let that happen to his children.

III
The Guards

A natural arch of black marble domed the mausoleum. It was set in cliffs high above the city of Qoxire on the planet called Eube's Glory, named by Jaibriol's unsubtle ancestor, Eube Qox, the monumental egotist who had founded the Concord. The crypt had stood for centuries, sheltering the ashes of the Qox Dynasty.

No wall blocked Jaibriol's approach to the crypt; nothing separated the inner sanctum from the chill morning except a row of black columns. In some ways, the vaulted spaces reminded him of Saint John's Church in the Appalachian Mountains on Earth. Seth Rockworth had taken Jaibriol and his siblings there each Sunday during the two years they had lived with him. But Saint John's had filled Jaibriol with warmth, with its stained-glass windows, graceful arches, and wooden pews. For all the majestic elegance of this mausoleum, its black marble spaces felt cold.

Accompanied by his Razers, he walked between two

giant columns. Mist curled around the pillars and shrouded their tops. He pulled his jacket tighter, grateful for its warmth. With the climate controls in his clothes, he could survive almost anything, even a blizzard. But no climate system could protect him from the snowfall of his emotions.

Inside the mausoleum, light orbs glowed above him and dimmed after he passed. Pearly mist softened the marble statues and wreathed the orbs, giving them an ethereal quality, as if he had entered a realm of translucent life. The obelisks he sought stood together, two thin pyramids of marble, all slanted lines, no square corners. They guarded the ashes of a man and a woman: Ur Qox and Viquara Iquar.

His grandparents.

The stark monuments mesmerized him. The reign of Ur Qox had been a long one. His son—Jaibriol's father—had spent only two years on the throne, imprisoned by Viquara and her new consort while they ruled from the shadows.

Jaibriol turned away, struggling with his confused pain. He wasn't certain why he had come here. Leaning against the steep side of the obelisk, he stared into the shadows of the mausoleum. Fog brushed his face with its damp kiss, and he wiped his palm along his cheek, smearing the clammy moisture.

Viquara Iquar had died in the Radiance War. Some said she had stepped in front of a laser shot meant for her son. Had she saved his life? Jaibriol didn't understand why it mattered so much to him, but he needed to believe she had loved her son.

Her Ruby son.

Jaibriol's great-grandfather had sired Ur Qox on a

provider so he could breed a psion, an heir with a mind powerful enough to create a Kyle web. But the traits that created psions were recessive; a child had to get them from both parents. So Ur Qox had repeated the process, siring a son on one of his providers. She gave birth to a Ruby psion. Jaibriol's father.

Ur Qox had been no saint; Jaibriol had no doubt that if the emperor could have impregnated his empress with another woman's child and tricked her into believing it was her own, he would have done it to protect the secret. But no Aristo could carry a Ruby child. The baby needed a psion as its mother, and an Aristo could never be a psion; they considered the traits a weakness and deliberately kept the DNA out of their bloodlines. The fetus of a psion responded dramatically to its environment. Nurturing it in a lab or even within a surrogate proved difficult and clones were rarely viable. The stronger a psion, the greater the problems. Ruby psions were almost impossible to birth except through natural methods. Had Viquara Iquar tried to carry a Ruby child, it would have died. She had to have known her son was another woman's child. Yet she had never revealed him.

Jaibriol laid his hand against the obelisk. Its polished surface chilled his palm. He was aware of his guards in the shadows, tall and silent, like the marble edifices. Tendrils of fog drifted above him, obscuring the light spheres until they became luminous blurs, as if they were ghosts of the Qox dynasty that had lived and died before him.

"Could you love him?" Jaibriol whispered. "You called him son, and he called you mother." Only Viquara would ever know the truth.

And what of his grandfather? Jaibriol knew Ur Qox only through the eyes of his son, Jaibriol's father. Ur Qox had been a distant parent, chill in his affections. Although Ur had been half Ruby, none of the traits had manifested, for Aristo genes dominated. Ur Qox had been an Aristo. Yet he never harmed his son. He had isolated Jaibriol's father in seclusion to protect him, not only against other Aristos, but even from himself.

The solitude had left Jaibriol's father craving love. He had only been twenty-four at Jaibriol's birth, three years younger than Jaibriol was now. He had been the finest man Jaibriol had ever known, a loving parent who taught him more than he felt he could ever give his own child. He knew now why it mattered so much to him to believe his grandparents had loved their son. Jaibriol's father had lived with the specter of Aristo brutality embodied by his own parents, both of them epitomes of a Highton. For Jaibriol, it would be the reverse, for his child would receive the Ruby genes only from him. Not from Tarquine.

His heir would be an Aristo.

Kelric met Admiral Barzun in the Skolian War Room.

Consoles filled the amphitheater, and robot arms carried operators through the air. Far above, a command chair hung under a holodome lit with stars, so anyone who looked up saw it silhouetted against the nebulae of space. When Kelric worked here, coordinating the far-flung armies of the Skolian military, he sat in that technological throne. It linked him into the Kyle web, which stretched across human-occupied space. Any telop, or telepathic operator, could use the Kyle web, but only Kelric and Dehya could create that vast mesh and keep it working.

Chad Barzun was waiting on a dais in the amphitheater. Crisp in his blue Fleet uniform, he was a man of average height, with a square chin, a beak of a nose, and hair the color of grey rock. As one of Kelric's joint commanders, he headed the Imperial Fleet. Kelric liked him because Barzun spoke his mind, with respect, but he said what needed saying even if he knew Kelric might not like it.

Barzun had commanded the fleet that returned Dehya to the throne. The shock of that coup had paled, though, compared to her next action, when she returned half her power to the Assembly. On his own, Kelric would never have split the power, but he understood her reasons. The time for a dynasty as sole rulers of Skolia had passed. They needed the Assembly. But unlike before, the Ruby Dynasty now had equal footing with that governing body.

Chad saluted Kelric, extending his arms at chest level and crossing his wrists, his fists clenched.

Kelric returned the salute. "At ease, Chad."

The admiral relaxed. "My greetings, sir. Are you leaving soon?"

"Later today." Kelric grimaced. "Unfortunately."

Chad smiled slightly. "I don't envy you this vacation."

Kelric didn't envy himself, either, having to attend dinner parties with the Imperial Court. "I'm taking a few days alone first."

"Very good, sir." Chad's voice quieted. "Let yourself rest. Gods know, you've earned it."

"I'll try," Kelric lied.

They spent the next hour going over the Imperator's

duties, which Barzun would oversee in Kelric's absence. If necessary, Chad could reach him through the Kyle web. Given that he believed Kelric was taking a long-overdue vacation, though, Kelric knew he would make contact only in an emergency.

Later, Kelric rode the magrail to a secluded valley of the Orbiter. He limped across the gilt-vine meadows, past Dehya's house. Holopanels on her roof reflected the sky and Sun Lamp several kilometers above. The spherical Orbiter was designed for beauty rather than efficiency; half its interior was just a sky. He could see the tiny figures of people walking by the sun. If they looked up, they would see the ground with its mountains and valleys curving above them like a ceiling of the world.

He hiked up the slope to his house. Inside, his duffle was where he had left it, on the desk in his office. He took his dice pouch out of the desk and tied it to his belt. Then he went to a black lacquered stand in the corner. Resting his hand on its top, he slid his thumb over its design, the Imperialate insignia, a ruby triangle inscribed within an amber circle. The gold silhouette of an exploding sun burst past the confines of the triangle. The symbol of an empire. The Imperialate claimed it was civilized, but a heart of barbarism beat close beneath its cultured exterior.

Bolt, his spinal node, interjected a thought into his musing. *Kelric.*

He roused himself. **Yes?**

According to your schedule, you depart from docking bay six in twelve minutes.

Kelric pushed his hand across his close-cropped hair. He couldn't put this off any longer. With a deep breath, he tapped out a code on the sunburst insignia. A hum vibrated within the stand as if it had come to life after a long sleep, and a drawer slid out. His Coban wrist guards lay inside.

The ancient guards were crafted from gold. Their engravings showed a giant hawk soaring over mountains, the symbol of Karn, largest and oldest city-estate on Coba. He picked up one of the guards and snapped it open. The hinge worked, though he had left it untouched for a decade.

Kelric couldn't put on the guards, however. He already wore gauntlets. He brushed his thumb over the massive cuff on his forearm, a marvel of mesh engineering. He had found the gauntlets in the Lock chamber. His ancestors had lost the knowledge to create Locks, and his people had yet to recover it, but they could use the machines they found derelict in space. These gauntlets were part of that ancient technology. They provided him with a mesh node, a comm, and a means to link to other systems. He felt certain they had intelligence, probably beyond his ability to understand. He had worn them for a decade, yet he still didn't know how they had survived for five thousand years or why they let him use them.

He clicked open a switch on his gauntlet—and it snapped closed. He pried at the switch, but this time it didn't move at all. Trying to open the entire wrist section didn't work, either. Odd. The gauntlet looked normal: small lights glowed on it, silver threads gleamed, and the comm glinted.

Come off, he thought. He didn't want to damage it; the gauntlets could never be replaced. Destroying them might even be murder. **If you won't open,** he added, **I can't put on my wrist guards.**

Both gauntlets snapped open.

Kelric blinked. Apparently they liked his Coban guards.

A socket showed in the skin of his left wrist. Normally the gauntlet jacked into that socket so it could link with his internal biomech web. He took his Coban guard and clicked it around his wrist, lining up a hole in the gold with his wrist socket. Before he could do anything else, his gauntlet snapped around his arm and fitted to the Coban guard as if they had always been joined. Filaments wisped out from the gauntlet, protecting the soft gold.

"Huh." Kelric squinted at his arm. He cautiously snapped his second Coban guard around his other wrist. That gauntlet immediately closed, repeating the same procedure as the first.

Bolt, Kelric thought.

Attending, Bolt answered.

Why did my gauntlets do that?

I don't know. Bolt projected a sense of puzzlement.

Do you know why they wouldn't come off before?

Based on past incidents, I would say they believe it would endanger you to remove them.

What, by my standing in my perilous office? I might stub my toe.

It does seem far-fetched.

He touched the wrist guard. Its gold seemed warm compared to the silver and black gauntlet. **Can you find out why they did that?**

If you mean can I talk to them, the answer is no. But we exchange information all the time. I sometimes read patterns in their data. If I direct our exchange, with your wrist guards as the subject, I may glean some insights.

See what you can find out.

I will let you know.

He gazed at the lacquered stand. His Calanya bands still lay in its drawer, gold rings that could be worn on the upper arms as a sign of honor, if a Calani wished. They indicated his Level, the number of Estates where he had lived in a Calanya. Most Calani were First Levels. Attaining a higher Level was a matter of great negotiation, for what better way for one Manager to gain advantage over another than to obtain one of her Calani? His Quis held immense knowledge of her Estate, strategies, plans, everything.

Toward the end of his time on Coba, Kelric had lived at Varz Estate. His Quis had vaulted the already powerful Estate into world dominance, but his submerged fury had also gone into the dice. His life had been hell. Harsh and icy, the Varz queen had been a sadistic nightmare. By that time, Ixpar had ruled Coba, a young Minister full of fire. She had freed Kelric from Varz—and so provoked the first war Coba had seen in a thousand years.

I've an analysis of your gauntlets, Bolt thought.

Kelric put away his memories. **Go ahead.**

They consider whatever you plan to do dangerous enough that you need them for your protection. However, apparently they deem your wrist guards acceptable, even beneficial, to your needs or emotions.

His emotions? Even he wasn't sure how he felt. He stared into the drawer. One of his Calanya bands was missing. It had come off during his escape from Coba and probably lay buried somewhere in the ashes of Ixpar's Estate.

Kelric gathered the bands and packed them into his duffle. Then he left for the docking bay.

"Prepare for launch," Kelric said. The cabin of the ship gleamed, small and bright. An exoskeleton closed around his pilot's chair and jacked into the sockets in his spine.

As the engines hummed, Bolt thought,

Kelric didn't answer.

Mace, the ship's EI, spoke. "Bay doors opening."

A hiss came from around Kelric as buffers inflated to protect sensitive equipment in the cabin. His forward screens swirled with gold and black lines, then cleared to reveal the scene outside. Two gigantic doors were opening, their toothed edges dwarfing his vessel, and the rumble of their release growled through his ship. Beyond the doors lay the glory of interstellar space, its gem-colored stars radiant against the dust clouds and the deep black of space.

Bolt's thought came urgently. You must not leave without security.

I have it. Kelric laid his hand on the massive Jumbler at his hip. The gun had to be big; it was a particle accelerator. It carried abitons, antiparticle of bitons, the constituents of electrons. With a rest energy of 1.9eV, bitons and abitons produced nothing more than orange light when they annihilated. But that was enough. In the atmosphere, the beam sparkled as it destroyed air molecules; when it hit anything solid, the instability of the mutilated electrons blew apart the object.

One gun is not enough to guard the Imperator, Bolt thought.

The ship is armed. And I used to be a weapons officer.

Even so. You should have—

Bolt, enough.

With a great clang, the docking clamps released Kelric's ship. He maneuvered out of the bay, leaving the Orbiter along its rotation axis. The great notched edges of the doors moved slowly past, as thick as his ship was long. Communication between Mace and the dock personnel murmured in his ear comm. To them, the launch was routine. No one knew he was alone. He had told Najo, Axer, and Strava he was taking his other guards, and he told the others he would be with Najo, Axer, and Strava.

As his ship moved away from the Orbiter and through its perimeter defenses, Kelric spoke into his comm. "Docking station four, I'm switching off your network and onto the Kyle-Star."

"Understood," the duty officer replied. "Gods' speed, sir."

"My thanks." Kelric cut his link to the Orbiter, but contrary to his claim, he made no attempt to reach Kyle-Star, the interstellar mesh of communications designed to guide starships.

Bolt, he thought. **Download my travel coordinates to the ship.**

I don't think you should do this alone.

I've made my decision.

I'm concerned for your safety.

I appreciate that. Now send the damn coordinates.

You are sure you want to do this?

Yes! I'm also sure I don't want to argue with a node in my head.

Bolt paused. Then he thought, Coordinates sent.

"Coordinates loaded," Mace said.

"Good." Kelric took a deep breath. "Take me to Coba."

IV
Viasa

Jaibriol ran. Struggling for breath, he raced through tunnels of dark rock that absorbed the light. A void was gaining on him, drawing closer, closer. A talon grasped his arm—

"No!" Jaibriol sat upright in bed, his heart beating hard.

It was several moments before his adrenaline eased enough for him to breathe normally. "Father in heaven," he whispered—and then realized he had spoken in Iotic. When seeking comfort, he instinctively lapsed into his first language, though only Skolian nobility used it. Or he spoke English. He had converted to Seth's Catholic faith on Earth, finding refuge from his nightmares in the sanctuary of his adopted religion. The one tongue he never associated with succor was Highton, supposedly his "true" language.

Night filled the imperial suite. He had woken up alone, but it wasn't unusual; his wife needed only a few hours of sleep compared to his nine or ten. Although he could now manage with sleeping every other day, he had never truly grown used to the sixteen-hour cycle of this planet.

Cloth rustled across the room; with a start, he realized someone was sitting in one of the wing chairs. He didn't think it was an Aristo; he felt none of the pain their presences caused. He reached out mentally—and sensed Tarquine. He exhaled, his rigid posture easing. She was one of the few Aristos whose mind didn't injure him.

He spoke in Highton. "My greetings, wife."

"Did you have another nightmare?" she asked from the dark.

"It was nothing." He often dreamed he was trapped, and he probably would for as long as he remained emperor, which would be the rest of his life, however long that lasted.

The glint of her eyes was visible even in the shadows. "It's been a strange day."

"Strange how?" Jaibriol doubted he wanted to know, but he couldn't afford to be oblivious.

"It seems a major mercantile firm in Ivory Sector has experienced a sudden reversal of fortune. Odd, that."

Hell and damnation. What had she done? "What reversal?"

"The Janq Line that manages the firm has financial woes," Tarquine said. "Apparently their investments in several merchant fleets have collapsed." Her words flowed like molasses. "It seems these fleets were actually pirates. They preyed on Skolian space lines, kidnapping people to sell as providers. In Skolian space. Which of course we know is illegal."

What startled him wasn't that the Janq Line sent

pirates into Imperialate space; half the Aristo Houses had
fleets raiding the Skolians. But they were rarely caught.
Of all the ways Tarquine might have brought down the
Janq Line, he never would have expected this. For one, it
would be difficult to achieve, given how well Aristos
protected their fleets. More to the point, it was understood that no Aristo Line touched the "merchant" fleets of
another. If Tarquine had aided in the Janq downfall, she
had broken an unwritten law of her own people. Why?

"I'm surprised they were prosecuted," Jaibriol said.

"Well, the Skolians caught them in Skolian space with
Skolian captives. They had plenty of evidence."

He wanted to demand *How?* but she would never
admit any involvement, and he was certain no evidence
existed that could link her to the situation. The idea that
one of their own would leak such information to the
Skolians was anathema to any Aristo—except him. He
would have liked to throw all their "merchants" in chains.

He recalled his discussion with Tarquine about the
Ivory Sector corporations trying to corner the export market.
He spoke warily. "I find myself wondering if the Janq
corporation that suffered this setback was involved in the
consortium that hopes to attain a monopoly on the Ivory
mercantile system."

"Oddly enough," Tarquine said, "they seem to be the
major players. Or they were, before this fiasco. With their
affairs in such disarray, they've had to step back from
the mercantile venture. It appears the consortium will
collapse."

"Imagine that," Jaibriol said sourly. He had been
preparing for talks with them, to limit their monopoly. "So

negotiations with the Janq Line won't be needed after all."

"Apparently not."

"And of course you had nothing to do with it."

If she heard his sarcasm, she gave no hint. "Of course."

Jaibriol sometimes thought she was like a night-panther stalking the palace, sleek and dark, deadly in her beauty. She slipped among the corridors of power as if they were trees in a jungle, her form visible and then gone as if she had never been there. How or when she attacked, he rarely knew. Telling her to stop was like trying to catch a shadow, for no proof ever connected her to the results of her operations.

"Why are you sitting over there?" he asked. It gave him an eerie feeling, as if she would fade into the night, only to reappear later with no blood on her hands, but her lovely, feral eyes glinting with triumph.

Cloth rustled. Tarquine coalesced out of the shadows, walking toward him. She sat on the bed, sleek in her silken black nightshift. "Azile spoke with me today."

"Azile speaks with you many days." Azile Xir was the Minister of Intelligence, after all, and she the Minister of Finance. The fact that they didn't like each other didn't negate their need to work together.

"Some days," Tarquine said sourly, "his words are less sublime than others."

He rubbed his knuckles down her cheek. "*Sublime* is an overrated word."

"Particularly in the matter of reminders."

"Reminders?" He had no idea what she meant, and she had shielded her mind.

"About heirs," she said. "Ours, to be specific." Only a

hint of anger touched her voice, but from Tarquine, that was a great deal. "Or our lack thereof."

Jaibriol gritted his teeth. Azile wasn't the first to bring up the matter, not by far. No matter how young Tarquine looked or how good her health, she was well past the age when most women could conceive. She had eggs in cryogenic storage, but she would need the help of specialists to carry a child.

"I've learned to ignore hints about our nonexistent progeny," he said. "Sublime or otherwise."

"You need an heir, Jai. Our firstborn will also inherit my title as head of the Iquar Line." A fierce pride infused her voice. "We must both ensure our successions."

Jaibriol did not want to have this conversation. He had avoided it for years. He had spent his childhood surrounded by the warmth and love of his family, and that was what he had imagined for his children. Not the chilly world of Aristos. In his youth, he had looked forward to fatherhood, inspired by the example of his parents; now he never wanted heirs.

He said only, "It isn't safe here."

"We can protect our child. It is well known your father isolated you in your childhood." She waited a beat. "To protect you against assassins, of course."

"Of course." His palms felt clammy. Tarquine knew the truth about him. She kept his secret just as he kept hers, that she had altered her own brain so she could never transcend. It was a change Aristos considered unforgivable. If they knew, they would destroy her. It was also why Jaibriol had married her; she was the only Highton woman he could live with, for she would never transcend with him. It also gave him leverage over her to keep his secret. That over the years he may have fallen in love with his deadly wife was a thought he avoided, for he didn't know how to deal with the idea he could love an Aristo.

Tarquine knew his grandfather had secluded his father until adulthood because his father was a psion. The Qox Dynasty had wanted a Ruby psion among its ranks, someone who could wrest the Kyle web from the Ruby Dynasty. With Jaibriol's father, they finally succeeding in breeding the psion they wanted—and he rejected Eube. Instead, he sought out one of the few people like him: Soz Valdoria of the Ruby Dynasty. Jaibriol's mother.

He spoke in a low voice. "Our heir will be more you than me." It could never be a psion; Tarquine didn't have the genes. The child would grow up to transcend on the pain of his own father. It was a prospect too gruesome for him to contemplate.

"The longer we wait," she said, "the greater the chance one or both of us will die before the child reaches maturity, or even before its birth. Is that what you want?"

"No." He shifted his weight. "But I would rather have this conversation another time."

"We've avoided it for ten years."

"I know." He pulled her closer. "Tomorrow, Tarquine. We will talk about succession then."

She put her arms around his neck. "Very well. Tomorrow."

He drew her down to lie with him, deep into the silk sheets and the shadows of the night. But as he caressed her soft skin, he felt as if he were drowning. Tomorrow he would put her off again, as he had for years, but someday he would have to decide: sire an Aristo child or die without an heir and leave Eube in the hands of those who would seek to subjugate humanity.

Kelric played dice.

The cockpit of the Skolian scout ship curved around him in bronzed hues. He was traveling in inversion, which meant the speed of his ship was a complex number, with an imaginary as well as a real part. It eliminated the singularity at light-speed in the equations of special relativity. He could never go *at* light-speed, so he went around it much as a cyclist might leave a path to ride around an infinitely high tree. Once past the "tree," he could attain immense speeds, many times that of light. During such travel, his ship needed only minimal oversight, which meant he had little to do. So he swung a panel in front of himself and played Quis solitaire.

He built structures of the Trader emperor. Jaibriol the Third had only been seventeen when he came into power. Kelric could barely remember being that young, let alone imagine ruling an empire at that age. Jaibriol had compensated for his deadly lack of experience by marrying his most powerful cabinet minister, Tarquine Iquar. Kelric knew Tarquine. Oh yes, he knew her, far too well. While he had been serving aboard the merchant ship *Corona*, the Traders had captured it and sold him into slavery. Tarquine had bought him. If he hadn't escaped, he would still be her possession.

Uncomfortable with the memory, he shifted his focus to politics. His structures evolved strangely. They implied Jaibriol Qox genuinely wanted peace. Kelric found it hard to credit, yet here it was, in his Quis.

The peace talks had foundered years ago. He had represented ISC at those talks, a military counterbalance to Dehya. They made an effective team: she the diplomat and he the threat. But for it to work, they had to *get* to the peace table. He had hoped Roca might sway the Assembly away from its current intransigence and back to negotiations. If they and the Traders didn't hammer out a treaty, their empires were going to pound away at each other until nothing remained.

Patterns of the upcoming Assembly session filtered into his Quis. The structures predicted an unwanted result: his mother would lose the vote. He varied parameters, searching for models that predicted a win, and found a few. They relied on her ability to sway councilors outside of the session, with a greater chance of success if he helped her. Which meant he couldn't avoid attending her infernal dinner parties. That put him in a bad mood, and he quit playing dice.

Sitting back, he gazed at the forward holoscreen, which showed the stars inverted from their positions at sublight speeds. He could replace the map with a display of dice and play Quis with the ship's EI. It seemed pointless, though. He had taught it the rules, and it played just like him, but without creativity. For ten years, he had done almost nothing but Quis solitaire. He was starved for a session with a real dice player, a good one. He had wanted to teach Dehya, had even given her a set of dice, but then he changed his mind. She was too smart. When she mastered Quis, she could unravel his secrets from his play. He couldn't trust anyone with that knowledge.

On Coba, he had sat at Quis with many Calani, saturating

their culture-spanning game with his military influence until the war erupted. Ixpar claimed that capacity for violence had always been within her people, that in the Old Age, queens had warred with one another until they nearly destroyed civilization. Finally, in desperation, they subsumed their aggression into the Quis. He believed her, but he also saw what they had achieved, a millennium of peace, one that ended when he came to their world.

Kelric would never forget the windriders battling in the sky or Karn roaring in flames. In that chaos, he had stolen a rider and escaped. By then, he had known all too well why the Cobans wanted the Restriction. If he, only one person, could have such a dramatic effect, what would happen if the Skolian Imperialate came to Coba in full force? He had sworn that day to protect his children, Ixpar, and Coba.

Which was why he had to go back.

The voice droned on the ship's comm. "Identify yourself immediately. This world is Restricted. Identify yourself . . ."

The automated message kept repeating, an eerie reminder of the day, ten years ago, when Kelric had flown to this starport so he could escape Coba. It was the only warning anyone received, either in space or on-planet. The port was fully automated and usually empty. ISC didn't care who landed as long as they stayed in the port. Any Skolian who entered the Restricted zone, which consisted of the entire planet outside of the port, essentially ceased to exist. Kelric doubted anyone in ISC bothered to keep track, though. It would matter only if the Cobans held someone against his will. Unfortunately, they had done exactly that with him, for eighteen years. It had nearly killed him.

Had ISC discovered the Cobans had imprisoned a Ruby prince, they would have considered it an act of aggression subject to military reprisals. They would have put the Cobans under martial law, prosecuted the Managers involved, absorbed Coba into the Imperialate, and never realized until too late, if ever, that they had destroyed a remarkable culture. He had the authority now to prevent the military actions, but he couldn't stop his family from turning their relentless focus here if anyone discovered his interest—which they might if the port recorded his landing. So he wouldn't go to the port.

"Mace," he said. "Get a map of the Coban Estates from the port. Hide your presence from the mesh system there."

"Accessing." Then Mace said, "The files are locked."

"Use my keys." His security should top any port safeguards.

"I have the map," Mace said.

"They're keeping Jeremiah Coltman in a city called Viasa," Kelric said. "It's in the Upper Teotec Mountains, the most northeast Estate." He was fortunate the Viasa Manager had bought Jeremiah's contract. Kelric had never been to Viasa, and his inviolable seclusion in the Calanya of other Estates meant that none of Viasa's citizens had ever seen him.

"I've identified a city that fits your description," Mace said. "But it's called Tehnsa."

"Oh. That's right." He had forgotten. "Viasa is below Tehnsa, near Greyrock Falls and the Viasa-Tehnsa Dam."

"I have the coordinates," Mace said.

A holomap formed to Kelric's left, a dramatic image of the towering Upper Teotec Mountains. The winds in those peaks were brutal. His ship was a Dalstern scout, designed for flight in planetary terrains as well as space, but it would need guidance. At least Coba had aircraft beacons. Although their culture had backslid during their millennia of isolation, they had redeveloped some technology even before ISC rediscovered them. Their windriders were small but respectable aircraft.

"The dam has a beacon that can guide us," Kelric said.

"I can't find it," Mace said. "And this map is wrong. We're passing over what appears to be Tehnsa, but the map places it southwest of here."

Kelric frowned. Although Mace continuously updated the holomap, it could only calculate the changes as fast as the scout's sensors could provide data about the mountains.

"How are you handling the winds?" Kelric asked.

"So far, fine. They're increasing, though, as we go lower in the atmosphere." After a pause, Mace added, "This port map is appalling. It hardly matches the one I'm making at all."

"Can you find the beacon?"

"So far, no."

"Keep looking."

"I'm getting a signal!"

Relief washed over Kelric. "From the dam?"

"No. It's a mesh system."

What the blazes? "Cobans don't have mesh systems."

"It's from Viasa," Mace said. "Not a guidance beacon. It's a general comm channel."

He couldn't imagine where the Viasans had obtained equipment to produce such a signal. He toggled his long-range comm and spoke in Skolian Flag, which was used by his people as a common language to bridge their many tongues. He didn't want to reveal he knew Teotecan, the Coban language, unless it was necessary.

"Viasa, I'm reading your signal," he said.

No response.

"Mace, can you increase my range?" Kelric asked.

"Working," the EI said.

"Viasa, I'm receiving your signal," Kelric said. "Can you read me? I repeat, I'm reading your signal. Please respond."

Still nothing. The scout was lower in the mountains now, and peaks loomed around them.

The comm suddenly crackled with a man's voice, words that made no sense.

"What the blazes was that?" Kelric asked.

"He's speaking Flag," Mace said. "Very *bad* Flag. I believe he said, 'Know English you? Spanish? French?'" The EI paused. "Those are Earth languages."

Kelric wondered if he was speaking to Jeremiah. **Do I know any of those?** he asked Bolt.

I have a Spanish mod, Bolt replied. I can provide rudimentary responses.

Go, Kelric thought.

Bolt gave him words, and he spoke into the comm, grappling with the pronunciation. The Skolian translation glowed on one of his forward screens.

"This is Dalstern GH3, scout class TI," he said. "Viasa, I need holomaps. These mountains are much trouble. The wind make problem also."

"Can you link your computers to our system here?" the man asked. "We will help guide you down."

"Computers?" Kelric said, more to himself than the man.

"I think he means me," Mace said. "I will make the link."

Kelric spoke into the comm. "We try." At least he thought he said *we*. The translation came up as *I*. He continued to navigate, relying on Mace to map the terrain and feed data to his spinal node. He could hear winds screaming past the ship.

"I'm having trouble linking to Viasa's mesh," Mace said. "It's manufactured by Earth's North-Am conglomerate and is only partially compatible with ours."

Kelric shook his head, wondering if anyone existed who had escaped buying products from the Allied Worlds of Earth. Coba, though? He hadn't expected that.

The man's voice came again. "Dalstern, can you send your data in an Allied protocol?"

"Which one?" Kelric asked.

Symbols transmitted from Viasa appeared on Kelric's screen, and he immediately saw a problem. The Viasa system wasn't set up to deal with starships, only windriders. It was trying to specify his trajectory in a system defined on the planet, in coordinates only they used.

"Viasa, we are maybe close to what we need," Kelric said. "Can you transform the coordinate system you use into the Skolian standard system?"

More silence. Kelric hoped his Spanish was intelligible. What he wanted to say didn't match what was coming out. Mace translated his last sentence as *Can you send the equations that transform the coordinate system in your primary nav module to the system we use?* He hoped it made sense to the people in Viasa.

A peak suddenly reared up on his screens. With accelerated reflexes, he jerked the scout into a vertical climb. G-forces slammed him into his seat as he veered east and dropped past another crag with a sickening lurch. The scout leveled out and shot through the mountains.

"Gods," he muttered. He spoke into the comm. "Viasa, where is beacon to guide aircraft in these mountains?"

A woman answered in terrible Spanish. "Say again?"

"The warning beacon. Where is it?"

"Broken." Her accent didn't mask her suspicious tone. He had just revealed he knew more about Viasa than almost any offworlder alive.

The man spoke. "Dalstern, we have holomaps for you, but we still have a mismatch in protocols. We are working on it. Please stand by."

"Understood." Kelric wiped the back of his hand across his forehead. "Mace, how is our speed?"

"Too fast. The deeper we go in these mountains, the more complex the terrain. I can't recalculate the map fast enough."

Kelric leaned over the comm. "Viasa, I need maps."

"I'm sending what I have," the man answered.

"Received!" Mace said. A new holomap formed, centered on a magnificent waterfall that cascaded down a cliff. In the east, a pass showed in the mountains. With a rush of relief, Kelric veered toward that small notch.

"Dalstern, did that come through?" the man asked.

"I have it," Kelric said. "I pull up."

"Viasa should be beyond the cliffs," Mace said. "I don't have the landing coordinates yet."

Kelric grimaced at the thought of setting down in a mountain hamlet without guidance, on a field that was probably too small. "Maybe we'll see it when we get through the pass."

The holomap suddenly fragmented. In the same instant, Mace said, "I've lost the Viasa data stream."

Damn! Kelric spoke into the comm. "Viasa, we have problem."

"We too," the man said.

Sweat dripped down Kelric's neck. Mace was doing his best to reconstruct the holomap, but they needed more—

With no warning, a wall of stone loomed on his screens. Kelric had no time to be startled; Bolt accelerated his reflexes, and he swerved east before his mind grasped what he was doing. Cliffs sheered up on his starboard side as they leapt into the pass. Closer, too close! He careened away, but that brought him too close to the other side.

Suddenly they shot free of the cliffs. Ahead and below, the lights of a city glittered like sparkflies scattered across the mountains. The rest of the majestic range lay shrouded in darkness beneath the chilly stars. Bittersweet memories flooded Kelric, and incredibly, a sense of *homecoming,* all of it heightened by the adrenaline rushing through him. He had never seen Viasa, but he knew the way of life, culture, language, all of it. Until this moment, he had never let himself acknowledge how much he missed those years he had spent submerged in Calanya Quis. He had given up everything for that privilege: his freedom, heritage, way of life, even his name. It had almost been worth the price.

"We need a place to land," Mace said. "Or I'm going to crash into that city."

"They must have an airfield."

"I don't see one."

Kelric spoke into the comm. "Viasa, I need set-down coordinates."

The man answered. "We're working on it!"

Kelric could guess the problem. They didn't know starship protocols. The Cobans learned fast, but no one could jump from elementary physics to astronavigation in ten minutes. Jeremiah was an anthropologist. Although most college students learned the rudiments of celestial mechanics, he had no reason to know how to guide down a starship.

"I'm mapping a landing site," Mace said. "I'll try not to hit too many buildings."

Kelric spoke into the comm. "Viasa, I have no more time. I guess coordinates."

"Dalstern, I have it!" the man shouted. Holomaps of Viasa flared above Kelric's screens.

"Received," Kelric said. Then he realized he was going to career right over the origin of the signal, which meant he might hit their command center. "Suggest you get out of there," he added with urgency.

A sparkle of lights rushed toward the ship, and towers pierced the starred sky. A dark area ahead had no buildings. With a jolt, Kelric realized they had sent him to the Calanya parks, probably the largest open area in Viasa, even bigger than the landing field.

The Dalstern was dropping fast, past domes and peaked roofs. A wall sheered out of the dark and grazed a wing of the ship, sending a shudder through it. Gritting his teeth, Kelric wrestled with the Dalstern, struggling to avoid the Estate buildings.

The scout slammed down into the park and plowed through the gardens with a scream of its hull on the underlying bedrock. Trees whipped past his screen as the Dalstern tore them out of the ground. A wall loomed ahead of them, and he recognized it immediately, though he had never seen this one before. A huge windbreak surrounded every Calanya in every Estate, and he was hurtling straight at Viasa's massive barrier.

With a shattering crash, the scout rammed through the wall. Kelric groaned as the impact threw him against his exoskeleton. The ship came to a stop balanced on a cliff that sheered down beyond the windbreak. Debris from the wall cascaded across the front of the ship. His lamps revealed a spectacular view; the Teotec Mountains rolled out in fold after magnificent fold of land, a primal landscape of dark mists and snow-fir trees.

The Dalstern began to tip over the edge.

Kelric tore off the exoskeleton and jumped to his feet. So much for his plans to land discreetly.

"We don't have much time," Mace said. "I can take off now, but if I tip too far, I'm going down that cliff."

"Coltman will come," Kelric said, more to assure himself than Mace. Jeremiah was smart. If a way existed to reach the ship, he would find it. At least, Kelric hoped so. He cycled through the air lock and jumped to the ground, into a wild night, with the notorious Teotecan winds blasting across his face. Two people were running across the parks toward him, a tall woman and a husky man.

He knew the man.

Kelric froze. His hope of managing this without anyone recognizing him had just vanished.

Pounding came from the other side of the ship. Kelric ran around the fuselage and found a youth banging on the hull.

"You have to get out!" the young man shouted in Spanish.

Kelric reached him in three ground-devouring strides. He grabbed the youth's arm and swung him around. The fellow looked up with a start, like a wild hazelle caught in a hunter's trap.

"I come for man called Jeremiah Coltman," Kelric said in his miserable Spanish.

The man inhaled sharply. "I'm Coltman."

Kelric took his chin and turned his face into the starlight. His features matched the images. He lifted one of the man's arms and read the glyphs on the armband: *Jeremiah Coltman Viasa.*

Relief washed over Kelric. "So. You are. We must hurry."

The Dalstern creaked as it tipped further. Alarmed, Kelric took off, pulling Jeremiah with him as he ran for the air lock.

A woman's voice called in Teotecan. "Jeremiah, wait!"

Kelric spun around. The woman and man had stopped a short distance away. The woman's attention was on Jeremiah, but the man stared at Kelric as if he were a specter from the graveyard.

Kelric's hand fell to his gun—and Jeremiah caught his arm. The youth had courage to touch a man with a

Jumbler, the weapon of a Jagernaut, one of ISC's notorious biomech warriors. Had Kelric had less control of his augmented reflexes, Jeremiah's impulsive action could have just ended his young life.

"Please," Jeremiah said in Spanish. "Don't shoot them."

Kelric lowered his arm. Watching them, the woman came closer. She was tall and elegant, with a regal beauty. A thick braid dusted by grey fell to her waist. The man was about forty, and he wore three Calanya bands on each arm. Third Level. He had been a Second Level when Kelric knew him.

"Don't go, Jeremiah," the woman said.

The youth's voice caught. "I have to."

"Viasa has come to care—" She took a deep breath. "I have come to care. For you."

"I'm sorry," he said with pain. "I'm truly sorry. But I can't be what I'm not." He glanced at the Third Level, then back to the woman. "And I could never share you. It would kill me." He sounded as if he were breaking inside. "Oh God, Khal, don't let pride keep you apart from the man you really love. Whatever you and Kev said to each other all those years ago . . . let it mend."

"Jeremiah." The starlight turned the tears on her face into silver gleams.

The ship scraped and shifted position as if warning them, impatient in its precarious balance. Kelric spoke to Jeremiah in a low voice. "We have to go."

The youth nodded, his gaze on the woman.

"Good-bye, beautiful scholar," she said.

Jeremiah wiped a tear off his face. "Good-bye." Then he turned and climbed into the ship.

With one hand on the hatchway, Kelric stared at the Coban man. The Third Level looked stunned, but his gaze never wavered.

Kelric spoke to him in Teotecan. "Don't tell anyone. You know why."

The man inclined his head in agreement, silent as he kept his Calanya Oath.

Then Kelric boarded the scout.

V
Scholars' Dice

Jeremiah sat in the copilot's seat while Kelric piloted the Dalstern. The youth said nothing, but he didn't barrier his emotions well. His pain scraped Kelric's mind. Kelric pretended to be absorbed in his controls, giving the fellow as much privacy as they could manage in the cramped cabin.

An image of Jeremiah showed in a corner of Kelric's screen. The fellow hardly looked more than a boy. He wasn't tall, and his lean physique lacked the heavy musculature valued in Earth's culture. His rich brown hair was longer than most Allied men wore it. He had a wholesome, farm boy quality, and a shyness Kelric associated with scholars. Those traits might not have made him a male sex symbol on Earth, but Coba's women probably adored him. Quiet, brilliant, scholarly, fit but slender, neither too large nor too strong: he matched their most popular ideal of masculinity. Kelric had unfortunately fit another ideal, albeit one less common, the towering, aggressive male they wanted to tame.

It didn't surprise him that Jeremiah's armbands differed from those worn by most Calani. Kelric recognized them because his were the same. Jeremiah was Akasi, the Manager's husband. Making him a Calani without his consent was coercion, which meant the union could be annulled if Jeremiah wanted. Whatever the youth decided, Kelric suspected it wouldn't be easy for him.

Jeremiah sat with his eyes downcast, and Kelric busied himself with checks that didn't need doing. They were high enough now that the winds and abysmal port map didn't endanger the ship.

Eventually, when Jeremiah began to look around, Kelric spoke in his clumsy Spanish. "Are you all right?"

The youth answered in the same voice Kelric had heard over the Viasa comm. "Yes. Thank you for your trouble."

"It is not so much trouble."

"You could have been killed."

Kelric suspected the biggest risk had been to the Calanya park. He would find a discreet means to recompense the Viasa Manager for repairs.

"I have seen worse," Kelric said. "I expect to have beacon, though. It help that you know the transform for the coordinates." Without Jeremiah's quick thinking, he would have had to land blind. The Dalstern would have survived, but not whatever part of Viasa it hit.

"I was guessing," Jeremiah said. Mortification came from his mind. "Playing dice with your life."

Kelric wondered if the young man realized just what he had accomplished. "Such a problem take more than guesses."

"I was lucky."

Kelric's voice gentled. "You are not what I expect."

Jeremiah watched him with large brown eyes that had probably turned the women of Coba into putty. "I'm not?"

"The genius who make history when he win this famous prize at twenty-four?" With apology, Kelric added, "I expect you to have a large opinion of yourself. But it seems not that way."

"I didn't deserve the Goldstone." Jeremiah hesitated. "Besides, that's hardly reason for your military to rescue me."

"They know nothing about this." Kelric wasn't certain how much to tell him. "I take you to a civilian port. From there, we find you passage to Earth."

Jeremiah's brow furrowed. "At Viasa you spoke in Teotecan. You even knew how to read my name from the Calanya bands. How?"

Kelric thought of Ixpar, his wife, at least for one hundred and nine more days. He answered, but not in Spanish this time. He spoke in Teotecan. It had been ten years, but it came back to him with ease.

"It doesn't seem to bother you to speak," Kelric said.

Jeremiah's eyes widened, and he just stared at Kelric. It was a moment before he answered, this time in the Coban language. "Well, no. Should it?"

Kelric spoke quietly. "It was years before I could carry on a normal conversation with an Outsider." He used an emphasis on *outsider* only another Coban would recognize, as if the word were capitalized. Calani were Inside. The rest of the universe was Outside.

Jeremiah froze, his eyes widening. He shifted his gaze

to Kelric's wrist guards, and his jolt of recognition hit Kelric like mental electricity.

"You were a *Calani*?" Jeremiah asked.

Kelric took a gold armband out of his pocket and handed it to him. "I thought this might answer your questions."

Jeremiah turned the ring over in his hands, and his shock filled the cabin. "You're him." He raised his astonished gaze. "You're *Sevtar*. The one they went to war over."

Sevtar. Kelric hadn't heard the name in a decade. Sevtar was the dawn god of Coban mythology, a giant with gold skin created from sunlight. He strode across the sky, pushing back the night so the goddess Savina could sail out on her giant hawk pulling the sun.

"Actually, my name is Kelric," he said. "They called me Sevtar."

"But you're *dead*."

Kelric smiled. "I guess no one told me."

"They think you burned to death."

"I escaped during the battle."

"Why let them think you died? Did you hate Coba so much?"

Kelric felt as if a lump lodged in his throat. It was a moment before he could answer. "At times. But it became a home I valued. Eventually one I loved." He extended his hand, and Jeremiah gave him back the armband. Kelric ran his finger over the gold, then put the ring back into his pocket. Those memories were too personal to share.

"Some of my Oaths were like yours," Kelric said. "Forced. But I gave the Oath freely to Ixpar Karn. When I swore my loyalty, I meant it." He regarded Jeremiah steadily. "I will protect Ixpar, her people, and her world for as long as it is within my power to do so."

Sweat beaded on Jeremiah's forehead. "Why come for me?"

"It was obvious no one else was going to." Dryly Kelric added, "Your people and mine have been playing this dance of politics for years. You got chewed up in it." He touched his wrist guard. "I spent eighteen years as a Calani. Everything in me went into the Quis. I was a Jagernaut. A fighter pilot. It so affected the dice that the Cobans went to war. I had no intention of leaving you in the Calanya, another cultural time bomb ready to go off."

Jeremiah didn't seem surprised. After spending a year in the Viasa Calanya, he probably had a good idea how influential the Calani could be with their Quis.

"You knew Kev," Jeremiah said.

Kelric thought of the Third Level he had seen. "He lived at Varz Estate when I was there. Kevtar Jev Ahkah Varz. He called himself Jev back then, because people mixed up our names." As a Third Level, he had an even longer name, now. Kevtar Jev Ahkah Varz Viasa. He would be one of the most powerful men on the planet.

"Why did you tell him not to say anything?" Jeremiah asked.

Kelric wondered if he could ever fully answer that question, even for himself. "I don't want my family seeking vengeance against Coba for what happened to me. They think I was a POW all those years. I intend for it to stay that way."

Jeremiah's posture tensed. "Who is your family?"

Kelric suspected Jeremiah would recognize the Skolia

name. It was, after all, also the name of an empire. For most of his life, Kelric had used his father's second name because fewer people could identify it.

"Valdoria," Kelric said.

Jeremiah stared at him. Although he seemed to recognize the Valdoria name as belonging to an important family, he gave no indication he realized the full import of what Kelric had just told him.

"Maybe someday I can return here," Kelric said. "But not now. I don't want Ixpar dragged into Skolian politics unless I'm secure enough in my own position to make sure neither she nor Coba comes to harm." Wryly he added, "And believe me, if Ixpar knew I was alive, she would become involved."

Jeremiah smiled shyly. "Coban women are—" Red tinged his face. "Well, they certainly aren't tentative."

It was an apt description of Coba's warrior queens. Kelric couldn't bring himself to ask more about Ixpar; he didn't want to hear if she had remarried. So he said only, "No, they aren't."

"I thought I would never see my home again," Jeremiah said.

"Your rescue has a price. If you renege, you'll face the anger of my family. And myself." Kelric thought of his children, those miracles he had hidden within Coba's protected sphere. He could sense their minds like a distant song. No matter who might claim it was impossible over such distances, he felt his link to them even now, perhaps through the Kyle. They were happy. Well. Safe. He wanted them to stay that way.

"I'll never reveal you were on Coba," Jeremiah said.

"Good."

"But how do I explain my escape?"

Kelric smiled. "It's remarkable. You managed to fly a rider to the port on your own." He motioned at the controls. "I've entered the necessary records and had the port send a message to Manager Viasa, supposedly from you."

"So she will tell the same story?"

"Yes."

Jeremiah spoke softly. "I'll miss her."

Kelric thought of Ixpar, of her brilliance, her robust laugh, and her long, long legs. "Coban women do have that effect." Then he remembered the rest of it, how they had owned and sold him among the most powerful Managers. "Gods only know why," he grumbled. "They are surely maddening."

Jeremiah laughed softly, with pain. "Yes, that too."

Kelric hesitated. "There is a favor I would ask of you."

"A favor?"

"I should like to play Calanya Quis again."

The youth sat up straighter, as if Kelric had offered him a gift instead of dice with someone who hadn't done it properly for ten years. "I would like that."

Kelric pulled a table-panel between their seats as Jeremiah untied his pouch from his belt. The youth rolled out a jeweled set similar to Kelric's, though with fewer dice. Soon they were deep in a session, their structures sparkling in towers, arches, pyramids, and curves. Kelric could see why Manager Viasa had wanted the youth's contract even though Jeremiah had no formal training for a Calanya. His Quis had clarity and purity. He made creative moves. Kelric had no problem anticipating them;

Jeremiah had a long way to go before he mastered his gifts. Kelric could have turned his game around, upside down, and inside out. But he didn't. He didn't want to discourage the fellow.

With subtle pressure from Kelric's Quis, Jeremiah built patterns of his first years on Coba. During the day he had worked in Dahl, a city lower in the mountains, and at night he had worked on his doctoral thesis. He considered it an idyllic life. He never had a clue that Manager Viasa had noticed him during her visits to Dahl—until it was too late.

After a while, Kelric realized Jeremiah was trying to draw him out. So he let his life evolve into the dice. Twenty-eight years ago, his Jag fighter had crashed in the mountains, and the previous Dahl manager had rescued him. Ixpar had been visiting Dahl, a fiery-haired child of fourteen. Kelric later learned it was Ixpar who had argued most persuasively that they should save his life, though it would violate the Restriction.

When he had realized they never intended to let him go, he had tried to escape. But the crash had damaged his internal biomech web and injured his brain. While fighting to free himself, he had lost control of the hydraulics that controlled his combat reflexes and killed one of his guards. Desperate to save the other three, who had befriended him during his long convalescence, Kelric had crippled himself to stop his attack.

The Cobans had been terrified that if he escaped, ISC would exact retribution against their world that would make the guard's death look like nothing. They had been right. They should have executed him, but instead they sent him to the prison at Haka Estate. What swayed the Minister who ruled Coba to let him live? The arguments of her fourteen-year-old successor. Ixpar.

"Good Lord," Jeremiah murmured. "I never learned any of this in Dahl."

"I doubt they wanted it in your dissertation," Kelric said.

The youth regarded him with a look Kelric had seen before, that awed expression that had always disconcerted him. "The way you play Quis is extraordinary," Jeremiah said. "And you were holding back. A *lot*."

Kelric shifted in his seat. "It's nothing."

Jeremiah made an incredulous noise. "That's like saying a supernova is nothing compared to a candle."

His face gentled. "Your Quis is far more than a candle."

"Do you miss Calanya Quis?"

"Every day of my life."

"Perhaps you and I could meet sometimes—?"

Kelric wondered what Jeremiah would do when he realized he had just asked the Skolian Imperator to play dice with him. No matter. It was a good suggestion. But unrealistic.

"Perhaps," Kelric said, though he knew it wouldn't happen. He doubted he would see Jeremiah again after they parted.

"You know," the youth said. "It could work in reverse."

"What do you mean?" Kelric asked.

"Quis. We worry about Outside influence on Coba, but think how Coba might affect the rest of us." He gathered his dice back into his pouch. "They're so peaceful here. Imagine if they let their best dice players loose on all those barbaric Imperialate warmongers." He froze, his hand full of jewels, staring at Kelric as he realized he was talking to one of those "warmongers."

"I'm sorry," Jeremiah said, reddening. "I shouldn't—I didn't—that is, I didn't mean to offend."

"You didn't," Kelric said. He knew all too well how the Allied Worlds viewed the Skolian military. He also preferred peace to hostilities. In theory. In reality, he fully intended to build up ISC; they needed more defenses against the Traders, not less. But he wasn't blind. Jeremiah had reason for his views. Only a thin film covered the Imperialate's conquering soul. It gleamed, bright and modern, but it could rip all too easily and uncover the darkness under their civilized exteriors.

Aristos filled the conference room, their gleaming black hair reflected in the white walls. Jaibriol felt as if he would suffocate from the pressure of their minds. After ten years of guarding his mind, his defenses were mental scar tissue, gnarled and rough. He had to deal with the Aristos or they would destroy him, but he could manage it only by locking himself within layer after layer of soul-smothering mental defenses, until he felt as if he were dying from a lack of air.

He met often with his top Ministers: Trade, Intelligence, Finance, Industry, Technology, Diamond, Silicate, Foreign Affairs, Domestic Affairs, and Protocol. High Judge Calope Muze also attended the meetings at Jaibriol's request. Lord Corbal Xir came, too. Both Corbal and Calope had been first cousins to Jaibriol's grandfather, and until Jaibriol sired an heir, they were next in line to the Carnelian Throne, first Corbal, then Calope. It bemused Jaibriol that he, a man of only twenty-seven years, had two people over a century old as his heirs. At 141, Corbal was the oldest living Aristo.

Corbal's son Azile served as Intelligence Minister. In the convoluted mesh of Aristo Lines, Jaibriol was even related to Tarquine; she had been the maternal aunt of his grandmother, Empress Viquara. Except the empress hadn't truly been his grandmother. He couldn't fathom how his grandfather had convinced her to participate in that mammoth fraud, one that would tear apart the Qox dynasty if it ever became known.

With Jaibriol on the throne, Corbal had expected to rule from the shadows, with Jaibriol as the figurehead and Corbal hidden. But he had found the new emperor less malleable than he expected. Jaibriol had been painfully naïve, yes, and so unprepared to deal with Aristo culture he had practically signed his death warrant the day he asserted his right to succeed his father. But he had never been malleable. He and Corbal had existed in a constant state of tension since then.

The worst of it was, Corbal was the closest he had to a friend. His few pleasant memories among the Aristos came from dinners with Corbal, Azile, and Corbal's provider, a woman named Sunrise. Corbal never admitted he loved Sunrise or that he never transcended with her. Although many people knew he favored her, he hid the full extent his feelings, perhaps even from himself. He would never reveal such affection for a provider, for it was considered aberrant to love a slave.

Today, Jaibriol sat at the gold octagon table and listened to his advisors argue about reopening treaty negotiations with the Skolians. They disguised their maddeningly convoluted discourse as small talk. Corbal sat across from him, watching everyone with a scrutiny Jaibriol knew well, given how often Corbal turned it on him. Calope Muze sat next to Corbal, cool and aloof, shimmering pale hair curling around her face, her elegant features suited to a classical statue.

Calope had let her hair go white. So had Corbal. Tarquine had a dusting of white at her temples. Jaibriol knew they allowed the color to change because it gave them an aura of authority. When everyone had beauty and youth, those who also had age found subtle ways to accent their experience. Only Jaibriol realized their hair had turned white as a side effect of changes they made to themselves. They were the only Aristos he knew who had eliminated their ability to transcend. That it had taken more than eighty years for each of them to develop compassion was sobering, but it also meant Aristos had the capacity to be other than the sadistic monsters he had thought defined their essence.

Tarquine sat at Jaibriol's left, apparently relaxed, but he wasn't fooled. Although she didn't really want a treaty either, she saw advantages to settling matters with the Skolians enough to open up trade. New markets increased the wealth of Eube, which of course included her own prodigious assets. She was already obscenely rich; she needed more money about as much as Jaibriol needed rocks in his head. But she thrived on the machinations that increased her assets. She might even be willing to establish peace with the Skolians if she thought she could exploit the treaty for financial gain.

At least, she implied such in response to veiled inquiries from other Aristos about whether or not she thought they should do business with the Skolians. Yet incredibly, deep in the night when Jaibriol held her in his arms, he glimpsed another reason his barracuda of a wife didn't oppose the negotiations. For him. In the light of day, when passion no longer clouded his mind, he suspected he only interpreted her motives in a way that made him less lonely. But whatever the truth, she didn't fight him on the treaty.

Trade Minister Sakaar loathed the negotiations. Jaibriol had hoped Sakaar would support opening trade relations because it would increase export markets for Eubian goods. But Sakaar's Ministry dealt primarily with the slave economy, and the Skolians refused to discuss any trade as long as the inventories included humans. Jaibriol agreed with the Skolians, but he could hardly tell that to his Ministers, at least not if he wanted to survive.

All the people of Eube except a few thousand Aristos were slaves. The bulk of them, nearly two trillion, were taskmakers. They led relatively normal lives, some even achieving a certain amount of authority and prosperity. But none were free and all wore collars indicating they were property. It sickened Jaibriol that he owned Robert, his bodyguards, and most everyone on this planet, as well as several hundred others, but if he ever let that sentiment slip, the Aristos would turn on him with a vengeance. It wasn't only that the economic structure of their empire depended on the trade; they also considered it their supposedly exalted right to own anyone who wasn't an Aristo.

Providers, or pleasure slaves, were at the bottom of the slave hierarchy. Only a few thousand existed. They lived in incredible luxury, but they had no power. Aristos acknowledged only one reason for a psion to exist—to provide transcendence. Their attitudes about the torture they inflicted horrified Jaibriol, especially because they would do the same to him if they ever learned the truth.

"Paris is a decadent city," Azile was saying. "I have no desire to tour France again."

Jaibriol tried to focus on the discussion. Azile's comment referred to the Paris Accord, the unfinished treaty they had hammered out with the Skolians eight years ago, before the talks stalled. They had "met" on a neutral planet, Earth, which sided with neither Skolia nor Eube. No one actually went to Paris, of course; no one would risk putting so many interstellar leaders together in one place. Rather, they convened as holographic simulations through the Kyle web.

Jaibriol wanted to rub his aching temples. Or better yet, leave. But he didn't dare show any sign they would interpret as weakness. He hid his raging headache behind an icy Highton veneer. "Paris is one of humanity's most remarkable cities."

"Of course we esteem Earth," the Trade Minister said sourly. His hand rested on the table with his thumb and forefinger together, a sign that his real opinion opposed his words.

"We should visit our birthplace of our race," Jaibriol said. It was the closest he would come to stating his intent to resume the talks.

Corbal smiled slightly. "That would be an unusual

vacation party: the emperor of Eube, his empress, his ministers, the high judge, and a doddering old man."

Jaibriol almost snorted. Doddering indeed. Corbal was as hearty as they came. He considered his cousin. "We should ask my joint commanders to join us."

The Silicate Minister spoke, a stately man of about fifty. "I suspect the commanders of ESComm have more important matters to attend than jaunts to Earth."

Jaibriol regarded him with a decided lack of enthusiasm. He had never liked Highton discourse, and the Silicate Minister was less proficient at it than most Aristos, with the result that his comments grated even more than usual. He spoke coolly. "More important than attending their emperor?"

The Silicate paled, realizing the insult he had given. "One always esteems Your Glorious Highness."

Sakaar leaned forward. "The Allieds have a penchant for theft. It makes me leery of supporting their tourist economy."

Jaibriol would have laughed if they hadn't all been so serious. He could well imagine the Allied reaction if the Eubian emperor, his ministers, and his joint commanders all showed up for a vacation on Earth. Panic hardly began to describe it. But he understood Sakaar's meaning; the Allieds refused to return slaves who escaped into their territory.

"Perhaps they just need to know our position better on the matter," Jaibriol said.

Sakaar snorted. "Assuming we all agree on that position."

Tarquine spoke in her husky voice. "I'd wager that's an impossible assumption."

Iraz Gji, the Diamond Minister, gave a discreet laugh. Jaibriol wasn't certain why it surprised him that Aristos had a sense of humor; maybe because he never felt like smiling when they came near. But Gji always enjoyed a joke, especially at the expense of his foes, which seemed to include Minister Sakaar. Gji represented the Diamond Aristos, who managed the means of commerce for the empire, so he and Sakaar both dealt with trade. They often came down on different sides of an issue. Like Tarquine, Gji had no love for the Allieds or Skolians, but an avid interest in their spending power.

A buzz came from the comm button Jaibriol had set in his ear. As his ministers continued arguing, he tapped the button, appearing as if he were simply touching his ear.

Yes? He barely moved his throat. Sensors in his body picked up the muscular changes, translated them into speech, and sent it to his comm. He said only that one word: anyone who could contact him on his private comm didn't need the usual overblown honorifics and responses.

The voice of his aide Robert came over the comm. "Sire, we have a report on the Skolian Assembly I thought you would want to know immediately."

Foreboding stirred in Jaibriol. The Skolian Assembly was always doing things he didn't want to hear about, but this sounded worse than usual. *Go ahead,* he answered.

"They introduced a measure to eliminate the votes that Roca Skolia inherited from her late husband."

Jaibriol stiffened. Roca Skolia—his grandmother—was a leading moderate in the Assembly. If her influence weakened, so did his hopes for resuming any talks. He not only had to persuade his people; he had to convince the Skolians as well.

A vote like that can't pass, can it? he asked.

"Apparently it might." Robert sounded miserable. He was the only person Jaibriol knew who actually supported the idea of peace for altruistic reasons rather than economic gain.

It was the final blow in a miserable day. His ministers were going on about tourism and the supposed decay of Paris, and he wanted to shout in frustration. He braced his elbows on the table and pushed back his chair with an abrupt scrape of exorbitantly expensive wood against polished bronze tiles.

They all went silent. His jarring interruption wasn't technically unacceptable, since he hadn't spoken directly, but it balanced on the edge. He looked around at them. "This has been a most auspicious discussion." It hadn't, it had been an exercise in circuitous evasion, but the phrase would get him out of the meeting without irredeemably insulting anyone.

After the barest pause, while they absorbed his dismissal, they each nodded to him, some with a veiled hostility they had no idea he could detect. He rose to his feet, and with a rustle of black diamond clothes, everyone else stood around the table.

His advisors departed through the main entrance, an elegant horseshoe arch with bronze columns, leaving in groups of two or three as they continued to confer among themselves. Jaibriol headed for a hexagonal arch in the back of the room with Captain Hidaka and four of his Razer bodyguards.

Corbal was standing by the table, talking with the Protocol Minister. When he saw Jaibriol leaving, he excused himself from Protocol and started toward to the emperor. Tarquine immediately came over to Jaibriol, deftly inserting herself between him and Corbal. Hidaka didn't block her, but Jaibriol had the sense that if the captain had thought he didn't want to see his empress, the Razer would have intervened even with Tarquine. Hidaka was a remarkably courageous man.

Right now, Jaibriol didn't feel ready to deal with either Corbal or Tarquine. One he could handle, but not both. He nodded to his cousin in an accepted gesture of farewell. Corbal frowned, but he had no choice except to stay back. Tarquine walked at Jaibriol's side, her laserlike gaze smoldering at Corbal.

Within moments, Jaibriol and Tarquine were striding down a hall outside the conference room, flanked by Razers. As with everything built by Hightons, the corridor had no right angles; its walls curved into the floor and ceiling. The halls that intersected the corridor came at acute angles.

Eventually Jaibriol slowed down. "Damn tourists," he grumbled.

Tarquine gave a startled laugh. "Was that a joke?"

He slanted a look at her. "I'm allowed a sense of humor, my lovely wife."

Her lids half closed. "So you are."

He wasn't certain how to interpret her response. He had the feeling he fascinated her. Perhaps that was what kept her interested in him; she couldn't predict his behavior.

"What did you think of the meeting?" he asked.

"They will never agree to more talks."

"I could order them to do it." He didn't need all of them, just one of his joint commanders, Corbal, and the Intelligence and Foreign Affairs Ministers. And Tarquine, of course.

"Without their cooperation," she said, "the negotiations would be a disaster."

He knew it was true. "The Skolians probably won't agree anyway."

Tarquine drew him to a stop. "If you try to catch stardust, you will die from a lack of air."

"I won't give up."

"Then look to the Diamonds."

His brow furrowed. "The Aristo caste? Or the rocks?"

"Aristo." Her eyes glinted. "They failed in their attempt to dominate the Ivory export corporations, so they will be looking for new ventures. Perhaps even among the Skolians? Just think what a huge, untapped market our enemies offer."

He raised an eyebrow at her. "No doubt that market could benefit the Finance Ministry as well."

"Perhaps."

He knew she had probably figured out many paths to profit, like a fractal that became ever more intricate the more closely one looked at it. "I don't suppose you have an idea how to interest the Diamonds in supporting us."

She started walking with him again. "I'll think on it."

That didn't reassure him. Whenever she turned her prodigious talents to solving a problem, he never knew whether to be grateful or terrified.

VI
A Court of Rubies

The world Metropoli boasted the largest starport in all of the Skolian Imperialate, teeming with people and vehicles. Kelric's small scout ship went unnoticed in all the tumult, especially with his stratospheric clearances, which invoked veils of security most people had no idea existed.

He dulled the metallic sheen of his skin and hair so he appeared more his age. Then he donned clothes that made him look overweight. His passenger, Jeremiah Coltman, watched him with puzzlement, but he didn't push the matter. He would figure out the truth soon enough. Kelric avoided news broadcasts when he could, but his likeness was out there on the meshes. If Jeremiah worked at it, he could identify his rescuer.

They walked to the gate where Jeremiah would board a transport to Earth. The youth was wearing a blue pullover and "jeans" interwoven with mesh threads. He had purchased them at a store that sold Allied imports. Several women gave him appreciative glances, but no one otherwise paid attention to them. It amused Kelric that he could so easily hide in plain sight.

At the gate, Jeremiah offered his hand. "Thank you for everything."

When Kelric hesitated, Bolt prompted him. Put your hand in his and move it up and down.

Oh. That's right. He clasped Jeremiah's hand and shook until Jeremiah winced. Embarrassed, Kelric let go. He sometimes forgot to moderate his strength.

"You're sure you have enough funds?" he asked.

"You've been incredibly generous," Jeremiah said. "You must let me pay you back."

"It's nothing." Kelric didn't know the value of what he had given Jeremiah. He could multiply the amount by a million and it would still be insignificant to his estate. At least, that would be true for one hundred and eight more days. He had to decide what to do, or he would soon be penniless and officially dead.

A female voice spoke from the air. "Mister Coltman, please board the shuttle. We are ready to leave."

Jeremiah swung his new smart-pack over his shoulder and smiled at Kelric. "Good-bye. And good luck."

Kelric inclined his head. "You also."

After Jeremiah boarded, Kelric stood at a window-wall and watched the shuttle take off. *Good-bye,* he thought, to Jeremiah and to Quis.

But an idea was lurking in his mind. It had hidden in his subconscious, and now it crept into his thoughts like mist, blurring the outlines of his reality.

Had the time come to stop hiding Coba?

❖　❖　❖

When Kelric visited the world Parthonia, to attend Assembly sessions in person, he stayed at the Sunrise Palace. It was built of golden stone, with arched colonnades. Trees shaded its wings, silver-bell willows and ghost elms with pale green streamer-leaves draped from their branches. Three million people lived in Selei City far below, but this region of the mountains was off-limits except to guests of the Ruby Dynasty. Tomorrow, the Assembly would convene in the city; tonight, the elite of that legislative body had invaded the palace.

Kelric wore his dress uniform. After many studies, the ISC protocol experts had designed it from a dark gold cloth that glimmered. The sheen seemed superfluous to Kelric, but it thrilled the analysts who charted how his appearance affected the public. The tunic had a gold stripe across his chest, and a gold stripe ran up the trousers, which Protocol claimed accented the length of his legs. It wasn't clear to him why anyone would give a buzz in a battleship about the length of his legs, but his bewildered comments had no effect on their efforts. They polished his boots to a shine and fastened a dark gold belt around his waist, all the time rhapsodizing about how the uniform complimented his physique. It was mortifying.

He put off going downstairs as long as he could, but finally he descended the staircase that swept into the foyer of the Grand Opera Hall. Chandeliers dripped with sun-burst crystals, and gold shimmered on the walls. Guests filled the room, sparkling in their finery. Human servants rather than robots moved among them, carrying platters of drinks or pastries. So much for his mother's "small" dinner party.

As Kelric entered the Hall, he fortified his mental barriers until the emotions of the crowd receded. He was actually prodding his mind to produce certain chemicals. They blocked the neurotransmitters necessary to process the brain waves he received from other people. If he produced too many blockers, it damped his ability to think; at the extreme, to protect himself from Aristos, it could cause brain damage. But for a party, he needed only levels that were a natural and normal precaution.

A man carrying a tray of goblets bowed to him. With a self- conscious nod, Kelric took a glass of a gold drink that bubbled. He would have preferred Dieshan pepper whiskey.

A woman in a long green dress was talking to several people nearby. She glanced idly at Kelric, then froze with her drink raised, staring at him. It was odd. He lived here, after all. They were attending an affair hosted by the Ruby Dynasty; seeing a member of that dynasty shouldn't elicit surprise.

Everyone in her group was staring at him now. They bowed, all except the woman, who kept gaping, her face flushed. Then she jerked as if remembering herself and bowed as well. Bewildered, Kelric nodded to them and kept going.

After he passed the group, he glanced at himself. Nothing looked wrong, and he didn't think he had done anything strange, unless they noticed his slight limp. He eased down his defenses to search for clues, but the pressure against his mind increased, and his head throbbed. The moods of his guests swirled, too many to distinguish, a thick stew of emotions flavored by anticipation, curiosity, jealousy, avarice, boredom, and sensuality. Ill at ease, he reinforced his barriers until they muted the onslaught.

"I haven't seen you at one of these in ages," a man drawled.

Kelric tensed as he swung around. Admiral Ragnar Bloodmark stood there, idly holding a goblet of red wine. Tall and lean, with sharp features, he had an aura of menace, as if he were ready to strike. His dark coloring came from his Skolian mother and evoked a lord of the noble Houses, but his grandfather had actually hailed from a place called Scandinavia on Earth. Ragnar was a Skolian citizen, however. His impressive military record and seniority should have made him the top choice to head the Imperial Fleet. Kelric had never trusted him, which was why he had promoted Chad Barzun instead, and he doubted Ragnar would ever forgive him that decision.

Although Ragnar bowed, he somehow made the gesture mocking. Kelric had always wondered how he managed that, following Imperial protocols to the letter, yet projecting disdain rather than respect. If he meant it to bother Kelric, the ploy failed; Kelric had never felt any need to have people bow to him.

"My greetings, Admiral." Kelric kept his voice neutral.

"And mine." Ragnar watched him closely. "So you will attend the Assembly in person this time?"

"I imagine so." Kelric wondered if Ragnar was probing for clues about his vote. The admiral was a Technologist. Although Ragnar had supported Dehya's coup, Kelric had no illusions about his motives. He had helped her for two reasons, the first being because he thought she could win. He hid his second, but as an empath Kelric knew; Ragnar coveted the title of Ruby Consort and the power that came with it. That Dehya already had a consort didn't deter him. Kelric had no proof that Ragnar had plotted against her husband, nor would any tribunal accept empathic impressions as evidence; even if a way existed to verify them, they were too vague. But he had no intention of trusting the admiral.

"Your mother looks lovely," Ragnar was saying.

Distracted, Kelric followed his gaze. Roca stood across the hall in a sleeveless blue gown, talking with several councilors, her gold hair piled elegantly on her head. Diamonds sparkled at her throat and dangled from her ears. One man was paying especially close attention to her, and Kelric doubted his interest had anything to do with politics. He hated it when men noticed her that way. They were intruding on his father's memory.

"You're talkative tonight," Ragnar said. A laconic smile curved his lips. "As always."

Deal with it, Kelric told himself. He motioned at the crowd. "They all glitter tonight. But tomorrow in the Assembly, it will be a different story."

"The ballot on your father's votes comes up, doesn't it?"

Kelric shrugged. "Votes on the hereditary seats come up every year." He eased down his barriers so he could probe the admiral. "And always fail."

"Perhaps not this time." Ragnar had worked with Ruby psions for decades and knew how to shield his mind. He also wasn't an empath, which meant Kelric couldn't receive impressions from him as well as from a psion. Although Kelric felt his ambivalence, he couldn't tell if it was because Ragnar wasn't certain how to vote or because he doubted the vote would succeed.

"It would be unfortunate for our party if the vote passed," Kelric said.

Ragnar gave an incredulous snort. "It's ridiculous that a technology party supports hereditary rule within a democracy."

Kelric cocked an eyebrow. "Ridiculous?" Ragnar wasn't the only one to make that assertion, not by far, but most people didn't say it to Kelric's face. He saw their point perfectly well, but he had no intention of giving up his power.

"I apologize if I gave offense," Ragnar said.

Kelric doubted he felt the least bit apologetic. He sipped his drink. "It's only half a democracy."

"So it is." An image jumped into Ragnar's mind, his memory of Dehya in the command chair of an ISC flagship while a million vessels gathered in support of her coup. He had helped put her there despite his objections to her throne. His motives were purely self-interested; her ascendancy worked to his advantage if he backed her. However, he had no wish to support Roca's moderating voice in the Assembly. He wanted to conquer the Eubian Traders. Period.

Kelric couldn't keep up even his minimal link to Ragnar. His head was swimming from the flood of moods. He raised his shields, and the deluge eased.

A woman spoke at his side, her voice rich with the Iotic accent of the nobility. "So what are you two plotting?"

Kelric turned with a jerk, even more edgy. Naaj Majda had joined them. At six-foot-five, she commanded attention.

Gold braid glinted on her dark green uniform, and her belt had the Majda insignia tooled into it, a hawk with wings spread. Iron-grey streaked her black hair; she was almost eighty, but she looked fifty. As General of the Pharaoh's Army, she served as one of his four joint commanders. She was also matriarch of the House of Majda and a ranking member of the Royalist Party. In the interim after the war, following the death of Kelric's sister but before Kelric assumed command of ISC, Naaj had acted as Imperator.

She was also his sister-in-law.

Ragnar bowed to Naaj in perfect style and managed to make it even more sardonic than with Kelric. "My greetings, General." He raised his glass to her. "Oh, my apologies. You prefer the dynastic address, yes? Your Highness."

Naaj cocked an eyebrow at him. "Apology accepted." She knew perfectly well he was baiting her.

Kelric nodded to Naaj, and she nodded back, both of them excruciatingly formal. The House of Majda was the most powerful noble line, and thousands of years ago they had been royalty in their own right. Now their empire was financial, with holdings vast and lucrative. They had served the Pharaoh's Army since before the Ruby Empire and provided many of ISC's top officers.

Over forty years ago, Kelric had wed Naaj's sister—and lost her soon after to assassination. After the Radiance War, when Kelric had shown up to claim his title as Imperator, he had feared Naaj would refuse to relinquish either the title or the substantial Majda assets he had inherited from her sister. As Matriarch, however, she was honor bound to protect the widower of the former matriarch.

If not for that kin-bond, he wasn't so sure she wouldn't have tried to depose him.

She spoke with impeccable courtesy. "Your House does honor to your guests, Your Highness."

Well, that was safe. He gave a safe response. "We value the honor of your presence." He eased down his barriers, but Naaj was guarding her mind, and she blocked him.

"We were discussing my father's votes," Kelric said.

She inclined her head. "His memory lives with honor."

He returned the gesture. That seemed the extent of their ability to relate tonight: nods and platitudes about honor. At least she spoke with respect. Kelric's father had been a farmer from a relatively primitive culture, which had appalled the Royalist Party. Personally, Kelric would have far rather spent his time on a farm than in the royal court, but he could hardly tell Naaj that, not if he wanted her votes.

"We venerate his noble memory," Ragnar told Naaj, his eyes glinting.

"So we do." Her expression remained neutral despite his use of *noble* for a farmer. Kelric wondered why Ragnar bothered trying to bait her. No one could fluster Naaj.

As Naaj and Ragnar parried with barbs disguised as small talk, Kelric began to wonder if Ragnar provoked Naaj more than she let on, for her shields slipped, and Kelric sensed her mood in unexpected detail. She intended to back Kelric tomorrow even if he counseled peace. She preferred action against the Traders, but she would follow Kelric's recommendations even if her House wished otherwise—because she respected his judgment.

That floored him. She sure as hell hadn't felt that way

when he had assumed command of ISC. As the head of a conservative House, she followed ancient customs from a time when men were property and kept in seclusion. Modern Skolia had an egalitarian culture, and Naaj was too savvy to let her personal views destroy her career; she knew she had to deal with him as Imperator. But she had obviously doubted his leadership ten years ago. He hadn't realized how much had changed since then.

And you? he asked himself. *Do you see Coba the same way Naaj used to see you?* He had never considered it in that light.

"Good gods," a sensual voice said. "Kelric, what have you gotten into, caught by these two?" A woman with dark eyes and night-black hair was strolling up to them. Her glistening red gown could have been painted onto her prodigiously well-toned body. Ruby balls dangled from her ears, and her ruby necklace was probably worth more than a fully armed Starslammer warship.

Naaj gave the woman a dour look. "You're out of uniform, Primary Majda."

"So I am, cousin." The woman, Vazar Majda, smiled lazily, with the ease of someone who was both off duty and out of Naaj's line of command. A former fighter pilot, Vazar now served in the upper command echelons of the Jagernaut forces, or J-Force.

Ragnar bowed to Vazar, and this time he even looked as if he meant it. He raised his goblet. "You're stunning tonight, Primary Majda."

"Thank you, Admiral," Vazar said. With a wicked gleam in her eyes, she grasped Kelric's arm. "I'm rescuing this golden apparition from you two." Then she dragged him away.

Laughing, Kelric tried to extricate his arm. "Vaz, you'll give people ideas about us."

"Oh, they'll get them anyway." She drew him through an alcove and onto a balcony above the palace gardens. Out in the balmy night air, she closed the doors and sagged against the wall. "Gods, I thought I was going to suffocate in there. How can you stand these parties?"

He leaned against the wall and smirked. "That's a good question. The place is teeming with my sisters-in-law."

"Given all the brothers you have, that's no surprise." Her smile faded. "Had."

Kelric's mood dimmed. He had lost a sister and a brother in the Radiance War. Soz and Althor. Althor had been married to Vazar.

"Ragnar is right," he said, offering her a less painful subject. "You could be a lethal weapon in that dress."

Mischief returned to her eyes. "What about you, eh? Roca's greatest weapon, her gorgeous, powerful, bachelor son."

Kelric grimaced at her. "ISC needs an entire protocol division to make me look this way." He grinned as a wicked thought came to him. "We should set them loose on the Trader emperor. He'll surrender just to make them go away."

Vazar's laugh rumbled. "I imagine so." Then she said, "Roca wants you to sway votes."

He couldn't let that opening go by. "What votes?"

"That's why we're all here, isn't it? If the Assembly eliminates your father's votes, your mother loses power."

Well, that was blunt. It was one reason he liked Vazar; she didn't play at intrigue. He lowered his barriers. It wasn't as painful out here, where distance and several walls muted the torrent from the Opera Hall. He probed at her mind.

"The drawbridge is up and the moat full of sea monsters," Vazar said. "You can't come in."

He squinted at her. "What?"

"You've a luminous, powerful mind, Kelric, but subtlety was never your strong point. Quit snooping."

He lifted his goblet to her. "I was knocking at the door."

She stood against the wall, facing him, curved and deadly in her glittering red dress. "If you want to know how I plan to vote, the answer is 'I don't know.'"

Damn. Her Assembly seat was hereditary. How could she not know her position on a ballot that jeopardized her own votes?

"I didn't realize a question existed," he said.

"I'm not Naaj. There's a reason I'm a Technologist instead of a Royalist." She shook her head. "If anyone should wield those votes, it's Roca. But should we concentrate so much power in unelected seats? Even without them, she's one of the most influential councilors in the Assembly."

Kelric's voice cooled. "That's right. She earned it through election."

"No one elected her to your father's votes."

"Better her than anyone else."

"Why should *anyone* have them?"

He spoke quietly. "My mother lost two sons and a daughter in the Radiance War. The Traders captured and tortured her husband, several of her children, and herself. She more than any of us should hate them. And believe me, she's capable of it." He knew Roca's darker side, the

anger she wrestled with, but when she walked into the
Assembly Hall, she put it behind her. "Yet *she* counsels
peace, now that we have a Trader emperor who claims he
will negotiate with us."

"She's an invaluable voice of moderation," Vazar said.
"But if we reaffirm that power for Roca, what happens
when the next person wants it? And the next?" Her gaze
hardened, reflecting the pilot who had become infamous
in battle. "And maybe moderation is the wrong counsel."

He couldn't argue. Sometimes, when his anger or grief
became too great, he wanted to launch his war fleets and
destroy the Traders, even knowing his forces and theirs
were too evenly matched to ensure any outcome but
misery.

"If we don't negotiate peace," he said, as much to himself as to Vazar, "this hostility will never end. Do you want
a thousand years of war?"

Vazar pushed back her hair. "No." She stared down at
the gardens. "Have you talked to Brant?"

He followed her gaze. In the garden below, Brant
Tapperhaven was walking with a woman. As head of the
J-Force, Brant was another of Kelric's joint commanders,
and like most Jagernauts, he had a fierce streak of
independence. He also abhorred the idea of inherited
votes. Kelric was glad Brant didn't hold an Assembly seat;
he might have gone against Kelric tomorrow.

"We've discussed it," Kelric said, and left it at that.

"Who is that girl with him?" Vaz asked.

"I don't know." He watched the couple stroll under
colored lamps strung from silver-bell willows. The woman
was lovely with her dark hair and sensual grace. She

reminded Kelric of Rashiva, the Manager of Haka Estate on Coba. Haka ran the prison where he had spent one of the worst years of his life, after he killed his guard trying to escape. Then Rashiva had taken him out of prison and made him her Calani and husband, under coercion. It had outraged the Minister who ruled Coba, for Haka was an antagonist of the Ministry, whereas Kelric's former Estate, Dahl, had been the Ministry's strongest ally. Within a year, the Minister had pardoned him and he had no choice but to return to Dahl.

They had never allowed him to see Rashiva again, but seven months later, she had given birth to a son. She claimed the boy was premature, the son of another man, but rumors spread about his violet eyes, a color never before seen on Coba.

The same color eyes as Kelric's father.

Something was building within Kelric, something ten years in coming. He kept hearing Jeremiah's words: *They're so peaceful here. Imagine if they let their top dice players loose on all those barbaric Imperialate warmongers.*

Watching the woman in the garden, he spoke quietly. "She looks like my ex-wife." It was the first time he had mentioned anything about his life on Coba to any Skolian. It felt as if alarms should blare or bells toll.

"You think so?" Vaz peered at the woman. "Corey wasn't that pretty." She flushed and quickly added, "I mean no offense to her memory."

"I know. None taken."

She gave him an odd look. "Why would you call my cousin Corey your ex-wife? You two were married when she died."

Softly he said, "I wasn't talking about Corey."

"Who else could you mean?"

Ten years of caution, ten years of silence: he couldn't break it so easily.

"We should go back inside," he said.

Vaz was watching him intently. "All right." For now she let it go.

But he knew her silence wouldn't last.

VII
The Gold Die

Jaibriol ran hard, his feet pounding the dirt path. Above him, the sky vibrated in the blue-violet splendor of the high mountains, streaked with wispy clouds. Six tiny moons glittered in different phases, but none of the big ones were visible. Even this high above the coast, in the crystalline silence of the mountains, he could hear the thundering tides ripped from the ocean by those moons and hurtled against the shore far below.

Although the thin air up here bothered most people, Jaibriol enjoyed the challenge. Hidaka ran with him. Given all his augmentation, the Razer wasn't the least bit out of breath, which could get annoying, but Jaibriol would far rather exercise with him than with another Aristo. He reveled in the sheer joy of running in the clear, cold morning. His doctor claimed his body was a tuned instrument in its prime, bursting with health. He didn't know about that, but he felt as if he could live forever.

A hum came from the comm plug in his ear. Loping along, he said, "Yes?"

"Sire, it's Robert. Are you all right?"

"I'm fine. Why wouldn't I be?" Surely Robert didn't think jogging a few kilometers would harm him.

"The Amethyst Wing of the palace blew up," Robert said.

"*What?*" Jaibriol came to an abrupt stop. Hidaka halted next to him, and his other three guards stopped behind and before them.

"A pipe detonated under the Columns Hall," Robert said. "The section with the gold tiles and black pillars. The columns shattered on the floor and the walls collapsed."

Good Lord. Had someone attacked the palace? Remarkably, it had actually been several years since anyone tried to assassinate him or any of his advisors. "Was anyone hurt?"

"No one," Robert said. "The hall was empty."

Jaibriol didn't see why anyone would bomb an empty hall. He glanced at Hidaka, who was undoubtedly wondering why the emperor was talking to thin air. Jaibriol tapped his ear and mouthed *Robert,* and Hidaka nodded.

"Is security checking it out?" Jaibriol asked.

"I called them immediately," Robert said. "They're making sure it's safe for the repair teams. And for you, of course."

"Good," Jaibriol said. "I'll be down as soon as I change."

Jaibriol stood in the ebony and gold hall, half hidden by a column that hadn't fallen, and watched the repair crews. Gilded dust swirled and mounds of glinting rubble were piled everywhere. The techs were calculating the cost of the robots they would need to replace those destroyed in the blast. More durable and less emotional than human beings, the robots needed neither sleep nor food. When Jaibriol realized the techs would have rather lost taskmakers than robots, bile rose in his throat. They ranked a machine above a human.

With Robert at his side, he resumed his walk through the hall, past crushed marble and melted gold, as much to escape the techs as to survey the damage. The dust would have bothered his nose, so he was glad his updated nanomeds neutralized its effect. Hidaka stayed with them, tall and silent, towering over even Jaibriol. The other three guards went ahead or behind them.

"Any report yet on why this happened?" Jaibriol asked.

Robert had his hand cupped around his ear where he was wearing a comm. "A pipe exploded." He paused, listening. "A pressure differential in the gas it carried may be the culprit."

Jaibriol stepped over chunks of a fallen column, a mess of gleaming marble shot through with jagged cracks. "That wouldn't cause a blast this big."

Robert nodded his agreement. "But security has found no trace of a bomb."

"Was anyone scheduled to be here?"

"Not a soul."

Jaibriol didn't like it. In his experience, nothing ever happened in the palace without reason, because someone was plotting this or that, anything from humbling a rival to seeking their demise. "Let me know as soon as you find out more."

"I will, Sire."

As they continued through the wreckage, Jaibriol's unease grew. He would have to ramp up his defenses even more; in the relative calm of the past few years, he had almost become fatally complacent.

People overflowed the Amphitheater of Memories where the Skolian Assembly met. Tiers of seats rose for hundreds of levels; above them, balconies held yet more people. Delegates filled the amphitheater, and images glowed at VR benches where offworld representatives attended through the Kyle web. Controlled pandemonium reigned as thousands conferred, bargained, and argued, all the gathered powers of a civilization struggling find an accommodation between dynastic rule and democracy.

Kelric sat at the Imperator's bench with Najo, Axer, and Strava standing on duty. They hadn't stopped scowling at him since they had discovered he took his "vacation" with no guards.

A dais was rising in the center of the amphitheater. The Councilor of Protocol sat at a console there, preparing to call the vote. Tikal, the First Councilor of the Assembly, and so the elected leader of the Imperialate, waited at a podium. Dehya was standing next to Protocol's console, gazing out at the amphitheater. On principle, Kelric would have preferred Dehya attend through the web; that way, his people could protect her even better than the stratospheric level of security he already had in place. But he knew why she came in person. Although she was one of the savviest people here, her waiflike face and small size made her appear fragile. It inspired protective instincts in people and helped counterbalance his presence, which many people found alarmingly militaristic.

The session had started only an hour ago, and already the debate regarding his mother's voting bloc had finished. Few speakers had commented. Those who did, including Naaj Majda, orated eloquently in Roca's favor. The lack of counterarguments didn't fool Kelric. No one wanted to speak openly against the Ruby Dynasty. Unfortunately, their reluctance only went so far; it wouldn't stop most of them from voting against her even in an open ballot. He could see Roca on his screens. She sat across the amphitheater, appearing relaxed at her console with a composure that he doubted came easy today.

The number of votes a delegate held depended on the size and status of the populations that elected them, or in the case of hereditary seats, on the power of the family. As populations fluctuated, so did the voting blocs, continuously updated. No one ever knew exactly how many votes everyone had, though they could estimate it with good accuracy. The Ruby Pharaoh and First Councilor held the largest blocs. The next largest went to Kelric, then to the councilors of the Inner Circle: Stars, Intelligence, Foreign Affairs, Finance, Industry, Judiciary, Life, Planetary Development, Domestic Affairs, Nature, and Protocol. For the First Councilor, Ruby Dynasty, Inner Circle, and Majdas, the size of their blocs depended on a complicated and oft-debated algorithm that took into account their political influence as well as the populations or hereditary position they represented.

Protocol spoke into her comm. "Calling the vote."

The words flashed on Kelric's screen. They also came over the audio system, almost lost in all the noise. She waited while people quieted. Then she said, "The measure is this: The voting bloc of the Web Key should cease to exist until another Web Key ascends to the Triad. A vote of Yea supports abolishing the bloc: a vote of Nay opposes the measure."

She called the roll, starting with the delegates of lowest rank, who had the fewest votes. Their names appeared on Kelric's screen, their *Yea* or *Nay*, the number of votes they carried, and the overall tally. The results also showed on a large holoscreen above the dais.

Bolt, Kelric thought. **Project the outcome based on the current results and your expectations for delegates who haven't yet voted.**

Your mother will lose, Bolt answered.

Damn. At the moment, the tally favored Roca. Most of the noble Houses had already cast their ballots, though, and they supported her. Ragnar's name came up—and he voted against her. Kelric gritted his teeth as her edge shrank. The vote continued inexorably, and when it turned against Roca, murmurs rolled through the hall. Kelric heard a snap, and pain stabbed his palm. Startled, he looked down. He had gripped the console so hard, a switch had broken and jabbed his hand.

"Cardin Taymor," Protocol called.

Kelric glanced up, at a loss to recognize the name.

She's new, Bolt informed him. From Metropoli. Given her record in their Assembly, she will undoubtedly vote Yea. He accessed Kelric's optic nerve and produced an image of Taymor. Kelric blinked; she was the woman in the green dress who had done a double take last night when he walked into the party.

His screen flashed with Taymor's vote: *Nay.*

Hah! Kelric grinned. **You calculated wrong.**

Perhaps I had too little data. Bolt paused. Or maybe your protocol analysts know what they are doing better than you think. She did seem taken with you.

Dryly Kelric thought, **Thanks for your confidence in my intellect.**

Voices rumbled in the amphitheater; apparently Bolt wasn't the only one who had misjudged Taymor's intent. Coming from the most heavily populated world in the Imperialate, she wielded an impressive bloc. The tally swung back in favor of Roca.

Update, Bolt thought. I now project you will win.

Kelric exhaled. The broken switch fell out of his hand and clattered onto the console.

As the vote continued, the tally fluctuated, but remained in Roca's favor. Two of Kelric's brothers had attended: Eldrin, his oldest sibling and the Ruby Consort; and Denric, who had earned a doctorate in literature and now taught children on the world Sandstorm. Both voted with Roca, and she cast proxies for Kelric's other siblings, also in her favor.

Then Protocol said, "Vazar Majda."

Across the amphitheater, the Majda queens were sitting at their consoles, tall and aristocratic. Only their women held Assembly seats; even in this modern age, they followed ancient customs that forbade their men to inherit power.

When Earth's people had finally discovered the

Imperialate, they had scandalized the noble matriarchs of Skolia. Apparently on Earth, men historically held more power than women. The matriarchs claimed this was why it had taken Earth's people so long to reach the stars. They asserted that if women had been in charge, Earth would have achieved that pinnacle of technology thousands of years earlier. Their arguments conveniently ignored the fact that their ancestors had developed star travel because they had starships to study.

Earth's annoyed males responded by pointing out that Earth had achieved a far greater degree of peace than the Imperialate, which surely had to do with the fact that bellicose, aggressive women had been in charge of the Imperialate rather than peaceful men. Naaj Majda hadn't understood why Kelric found this so funny. She even acknowledged the Earth men had a point. Kelric told her to go read Earth's military history.

By the time Earth and Skolia discovered each other, both had evolved toward equality, though men still tended to hold more power on Earth and women more among the Skolians. The Traders had always been egalitarian; they enslaved everyone equally, male and female alike.

The way the Majda queens secluded their princes reminded Kelric of the Calanya on Coba. He had lived in over half of Coba's cities, yet he knew almost nothing about them, for he had spent almost his entire time in seclusion. He had never done anything as simple as buy a sausage at market. They had imprisoned him in luxury as if he were a ruby die locked in a treasure box, withholding something far more precious than all the wealth they had lavished on him—his freedom.

Protocol's words came over the audio system. "Vazar Majda, does your console have a problem?"

With a start, Kelric realized Vazar hadn't voted.

Her answer came over the audio. "No problem."

"Please place your vote," Protocol said.

Why isn't she responding? Kelric asked Bolt. He could see her arguing with Naaj.

I don't know, Bolt thought. However, my projection of your win assumes the Majdas support you.

He didn't believe Vazar would go against them. But she had worried him last night.

"Vazar Majda, you must respond," Protocol said.

The buzz of conversation in the amphitheater died away. Such a wait was unprecedented. Then Kelric's console flashed—like a punch to the gut.

Yea.

Voices swelled as the tally swung solidly against Roca. Naaj's face was thunderous. Protocol called her next, and she struck her console with her adamant *Nay*, negating Vazar's vote. Then the Inner Circle voted—and doubled the tally against Roca. Roca went next and took a huge bite out of their gains.

"Kelric Valdoria," Protocol said.

He stabbed in his answer, and it flared on his screen. *Nay*. The tally careened toward a balance, almost evening the sides.

Two voters remained: the Ruby Pharaoh and First Councilor. Their blocs were almost identical, but Dehya always had a few more votes— because she had staged the coup that deposed Tikal. Her decision to rule jointly with him had been contingent on those extra votes, and with them the ability to break a deadlock.

"First Councilor Tikal," Protocol said.

His answer was no surprise: *Yea.* The tally shifted firmly to his side, and the amphitheater went silent as if the Assembly were holding its collective breath.

"Dyhianna Selei," Protocol said.

Dehya's vote flashed: *Nay.*

The tally careened toward Roca's side. When it finished, the result glowed in large red letters above the amphitheater.

By a mere six votes, Roca had lost.

Kelric brooded in the Corner Room, an alcove well removed from the amphitheater. Someone had shoved a divan in a corner, so he sat on it with his back against the wall and his legs stretched out along its length. A line of blue and white glyphs bordered the wall at shoulder height, more artwork than words.

Leaning his head back, he closed his eyes. He was clenching his Quis pouch, and dice poked his hand through the cloth. He told himself today's vote didn't matter. If anything, it strengthened his position as Imperator. But he feared it boded a more intransigent Assembly and a future of greater hostilities with the Traders, the Allieds, even his own people.

A creak broke the silence. As Kelric opened his eyes, the antique door across the room swung inward on old-style hinges designed for aesthetics rather than practicality. A slender man with curly blond hair stood in archway. Beyond him, Kelric's bodyguards were talking to another guard in Jagernaut leathers. Kelric's visitor came in and closed the door.

"My greetings, Deni," Kelric said.

Denric, his brother, crossed the room. "It's good to see you."

Kelric felt the same way. He saw Denric only a few times a year. When had that streak of grey appeared in his brother's hair? Denric had always seemed young, though he was a decade older than Kelric. Perhaps it was his boyish face or small size compared to his towering brothers. Or maybe it was his idealism, his belief he could bring about a more peaceful universe by schooling young people. Kelric suspected the universe would resist tranquility regardless of how well its inhabitants educated themselves, but that had never decreased his admiration for his brother. Denric had taken a teaching post that paid almost nothing in an impoverished community and dedicated his life and personal resources to its youth.

Denric settled into an upholstered chair and swung his feet up on the footstool. "Well, that was certainly a rout."

"We only lost by six votes," Kelric said. "That hardly qualifies as a rout." Not that it made him feel any better.

Denric considered him for long enough to unsettle Kelric. Then his brother said, "I suppose for you, it has advantages."

"You think I *wanted* that to happen?"

"It supports you." Denric's voice was atypically cool. "It will help you continue to build up the military beyond our needs and to increase ISC control over our people."

Kelric couldn't believe he was hearing this from his own brother. "You ought to know me better than that."

"I thought I did." Denric shook his head. "But sometimes it seems like I hardly know you at all. You've become so focused on ISC, people are comparing you to Kurj."

Kelric stared at him. People had called Kurj a *dictator.* Yes, Kelric physically resembled him. Even their names were similar. But he had little else in common with his half-brother.

"If I don't build up ISC," Kelric said harshly, "the Traders will conquer us. Then we'll all be slaves."

Denric gave him an incredulous look. "So you need military threats against our own people?"

"Of course not."

"Which is why all our worlds have such a strong ISC presence."

"It's to protect them." Kelric eased down his shields. **We have to be ready. If the Traders attacked today, we would lose.**

Denric's cultured thoughts came into his mind. I had heard nothing of our situation being that bad.

It is hardly something I want to broadcast.

Then why don't they attack us?

They probably don't know they can win. After a moment, Kelric added, **Or maybe this emperor of theirs genuinely desires peace.**

Maybe. Denric didn't hide his doubt.

Kelric's head throbbed from the contact. Releasing the link, he shielded his mind and exhaled as the ache in his temples receded. He doubted psions could survive without the ability to raise shields. The onslaught of emotions could drive a person insane.

Kelric thought of his only face-to-face meeting with the

Trader emperor. He had felt certain Jaibriol the Third was an empath, though Aristos supposedly lacked the "contaminating" genes that created a psion. The youth protected his mind well; only a Ruby psion would have guessed. Maybe this emperor had reasons no one expected for wanting connections with Skolia.

The door opened again, and this time Dehya stood framed within its arch. Yet more black-clad bodyguards had gathered outside, dwarfing her delicate form. They were human components in the myriad of defenses that protected the dynasty, especially the Dyad.

"Well." Denric pulled himself out of his chair. "I'll leave you two to talk."

A smile touched Dehya's face. "My greetings, Deni."

He swept her a gallant bow. Court etiquette didn't require he do so with his own family, but he always treated Dehya that way. Straightening up, he winked at her. "Don't intimidate my little brother."

Her laugh was musical. "I'll try not to terrorize him."

After Denric left, closing the door behind him, Kelric smiled at his aunt. "I'm quaking in my boots."

Dehya dropped into the chair, taking up much less of it than Denric had done. "Roca isn't happy."

That had to be an understatement of magnificent proportions. "She's still one of the most influential voices in the Assembly."

Dehya regarded him wearily. "It isn't only the vote. She believes Vazar betrayed us. She used words that—well, let's just say it was language my sister the diplomat rarely employs."

"I don't blame her." Yet for all his anger, Kelric knew

Vazar too well to call her decision a betrayal. "Vaz follows her conscience, not anyone's political agenda."

The door slammed open and Roca stalked into the room. "She dishonored him." She closed the door with a thud. "She *inherited* Althor's votes. Now she disrespects his memory."

"I doubt she sees it that way," Dehya said.

"Why aren't you angry?" Roca demanded.

Dehya grimaced. "I'm worn out with being angry. It seems to be a constant state where the Assembly is concerned."

Roca scowled at Kelric.

"What?" he asked.

"First Denric, then Dehya, now me. What is this, we must come to petition the mighty Imperator?"

"Why are you angry at me?" he asked.

"You spoke to Vaz last night."

"I speak to Vaz all the time."

"Did you encourage her to change the vote?"

"You think I *plotted* this with her?"

Roca met his gaze. "Did you?"

"No." He barely controlled his surge of anger. "I can't believe you would even ask."

"Her vote benefits you."

"For flaming sakes," Kelric said. "If I had wanted to vote for the damn ballot, I would have."

"Having Vaz do it makes her the traitor." Roca's gentle mental tap came at his mind, at odds with her tense words. *Kelric?*

He crossed his arms and strengthened his mental shields.

Kelric, come on. Her thought barely leaked through.

She wanted to talk? Fine. He lowered his barriers and let his anger blast out. **You have no business accusing me.**

Roca took a step back and her face paled. *I know.*

So why the bloody hell say it?

It was Dehya who answered. *We think someone has compromised security.*

What? Is this supposed to be a test?

Roca winced at the force of his thought *Yes. If we argue and rumors of strife within the Ruby Dynasty spread, it implies a leak in our security.*

He was the one who oversaw security. If they trusted him, they would have told him. **Why didn't you warn me?** This time, though, he moderated his thought so its power didn't blast them.

We had to make it convincing, Roca thought.

She had a point; he was a terrible actor. But they were testing him, too, regardless of what she claimed. He gave her a dour look. **Did you ask Denric to challenge me?**

Surprise came from her mind.

Although that troubled Kelric, he knew Denric had never been easy with the military. **The problem isn't Vazar. The Assembly doesn't like our hereditary seats. If they could remove them all, they would.**

Roca crossed her arms. *After all this, I can't believe they still expect us to do the Promenc*

Kelric couldn't either, but he had always felt that way. Every seven years, the Assembly asked the Houses to walk in a ceremonial promenade. The public loved it, which was why the Assembly promoted the whole business, because it inspired the public to love them, too.

We can refuse, he thought.

I'd like to. Roca uncrossed her arms. *But it would make us look ill-tempered.* She resumed pacing. *I need to talk to Councilor Tika.*

Dehya glanced at Kelric with a slight smile. *I think we should let her loose on the Assembly to work her magic.*

Maybe she'll convince them to take another vote. Aloud, in case someone actually was eavesdropping, he added, "If you believe I plotted with Vaz, you should, uh, leave." He winced at his dreadful acting, and a swirl of amusement came from Dehya.

"Very well," Roca said. "I will." With that, she swept out of the room. In the wake of her departure, the chamber seemed smaller.

Dehya sat back in her chair. "She won't stay angry."

Kelric just shrugged. He was still simmering.

"I spoke to Vaz before I came here," Dehya added.

He hadn't caught *that* from her mind. He always kept his shields partially up when he mind-spoke with her, though; she had more mental finesse than he would ever manage, and he didn't want her to learn too much from him.

"About the vote?" he asked.

"She didn't want to discuss it," Dehya said. "I think she's as upset with herself as we are."

Kelric scowled. "That didn't stop her from doing it."

She told me something peculiar, Dehya thought.

Wary, he let her see only the surface of his mind. **Peculiar how?**

Her answer had an odd stillness. *That you had an ex-wife.*

Kelric was suddenly aware of the dice pouch in his hand. **I do.**

I thought providers were forbidden to marry. Her thought was muffled.

They are.

Then how could you have had a wife?

He couldn't respond.

Kelric? Dehya asked.

His answer came like a shadow stretching out as the sun hovered above the horizon. **I wasn't with the Traders all those years.**

Neither her posture nor her face betrayed surprise, but it crackled in her mind, not from what he told her, but because he finally admitted what she had always suspected.

Kelric couldn't explain. He had been married against his will too many times. Jeejon was the only woman *he* had ever asked. He had been bought, enslaved, kidnapped, forced, and otherwise had his life arranged, often with no regard to his own preferences. He had never perceived himself as pleasing, but apparently women found him so, enough even to do something as mad as launch a thousand windriders in war over him. He didn't understand why.

But gradually he had come to understand his responses. If a woman treated him well, he became fond of her even if he resisted the emotion, as he had with Rashiva who had forced him into an unwanted marriage. As an empath, he thrived on affection. The better his lover felt, the better he felt. All psions experienced that effect to some extent, but for him it seemed unusually intense. The more he gave his lover, the more she gave back. When she desired and cherished him, he felt those emotions. So he sought to make his lover happy. He liked to see her smile, hold her, laugh with her, pleasure her. Her contentment became his.

It wasn't love, though. When he truly loved a woman, it blazed inside him, until she became imprinted on his heart, even his soul. In his seventy years of life, only two women had seared him with that mark. Ixpar would always be his greatest love, but it had taken him years to realize—for she had come second, when he had believed he could never feel such passion again. She had waited, giving him the time he needed, knowing his ability to love had been crippled, leaving emotional scar tissue in his heart.

The words wouldn't come for him to tell Dehya. So instead he lowered his barriers and formed an image in his mind.

Savina.

She had brought sun into his life. She laughed often, and her yellow hair framed an angelic face. She had stood only as tall as his chest, but that never stopped her from doing outrageous things to him: climbing the tower where he lived and hanging on a rope while she proclaimed her love; carrying him off, up to a ruined fortress; getting him drunk so she could compromise his honor in all sorts of intriguing ways. Somewhere in all that, their play had turned to love, and it had changed him forever.

Kelric couldn't bear the memory. He hid it deep in his mind.

"Saints almighty," Dehya murmured. "What *happened* to you?"

He just shook his head.

After a silence, she said, "Do you want to be alone?"

He nodded, staring at his dice pouch. He listened to the sound of her retreating footsteps and looked up just as she set her hand on the crystal doorknob.

"Do you remember," Kelric said, "when I asked you to make copies of my dice?"

She turned to him. "I still have them."

"Tonight, at home, will you join me for a game of Quis?"

"Quis?"

He shook his pouch, rattling the dice. "This."

Surprise jumped into her expression. "I would like that."

He said no more. That had been enough. Maybe too much.

After Dehya left, Kelric poured his dice onto the divan. He picked up the gold ball. He almost never used it. For him, it symbolized one person. Savina. She had been an empath, a mild talent, but she carried all the genes. Living with primitive medical care, in a place with infant mortality rates higher than on almost any other settled world, Savina had brought an empath into the world. Incredibly, the baby girl had survived the agonizing birth.

Not so for Savina. She had died in Kelric's arms.

On a distant world, protected by the inimitable Hinterland Deployment, a child with gold eyes was growing to adulthood. She had been born of Kelric's greatest sorrow, but she was an even greater treasure, hidden by the Restriction and by one of the greatest military forces known to the human race.

VIII
Sunsky Bridge

"Peace talks be damned!" Corbal faced Jaibriol across the glossy black expanse of the desk in Jaibriol's office. "With this vote, the Skolians have made their intentions clear. They intend to ramp up hostilities, not flaming chat with us in Paris."

They were on their feet with the desk between them. It was as if they stood within the void of space; today, the walls of emperor's office gleamed with nebulae, and blue points of light glowed in the cobalt floor. A sapphire lamp hung from the domed ceiling. The entire room felt as cold and distant to Jaibriol as any hope for the negotiations.

"The vote was a protest against hereditary rule," he said. "Not peace."

Corbal's red gaze didn't waver. "It was a vote to give Imperator Skolia more power."

Jaibriol stiffened. He could never live up to Tarquine's memory of Kelric, the man who had been her provider and lover, who had escaped from her habitat, shredded her security, and infiltrated one of the largest military complexes in Eube, the Sphinx Sector Rim Base. The Lock that ESComm had stolen from the Skolians was in that complex. Kelric had used it to join the Dyad—to become a Key, which only a Ruby psion could do. Now he was the Imperator. The Military Key. The Fist of Skolia.

Compared to Kelric, Jaibriol had no doubt he seemed young, callow, and inexperienced. Tarquine claimed she no longer wanted Kelric, but Jaibriol didn't believe her. He could never compete with a legend.

Only Corbal and Tarquine suspected Jaibriol could also use the Lock. Except no one would ever use it again, for Kelric had killed it, or whatever one did to deactivate a singularity where Kyle space pierced their universe. Jaibriol had found Kelric in the Lock that day—and he had let the Imperator go free, an act many would consider treason. *Meet me at the peace table,* Jaibriol had told him. But the Paris Accord had fallen apart and now Kelric had even more power. Enough to conquer Eube? All Jaibriol saw was the long, slow dying of his dream.

He sank into his high-backed chair, put his elbows on his desk, and leaned his head in his hands. He was so very tired, a bone-deep exhaustion that sleep never cured. The longer he lived among the Aristos, the more hopeless it seemed that they would ever deal with the Skolians, a people they didn't consider human. They weren't capable of understanding why Skolians abhorred the Concord. After all, Eubian taskmakers had a high standard of living. It took no genius to see why Aristos maintained it; only a few thousand of them controlled two *trillion* taskmakers. The Aristos didn't care about the soul-parching effects of that control, how they crushed the spirit of those who resisted them. The slagged remains of several worlds served as testament to how far Hightons would take their reckoning against definace.

But no sane Aristo wanted genocide. They knew perfectly well that too much repression inspired rebellion. Taskmakers formed the backbone of civilization; even a fool could see that keeping them satisfied worked better than oppression. Aristos might be arrogant, amoral, and without compassion, but they were never stupid. They ensured their taskmakers lived good lives—as long as they obeyed.

Providers were another story. Aristos believed they had one and only one purpose: to please Aristos. In their twisted world view, torturing providers "elevated" those slaves to a higher form of existence. But the Aristos knew the truth, no matter how much they masked it with the convolutions of their speech. It was why Corbal hid his tenderness toward Sunrise; his love for her threatened the fabric of an empire. Lurking in every Aristo's mind was the specter that one day their slaves would rise against them, not a city, a world, or a star system, but all of them. Trillions. Then nothing could stop the fall of Eube.

Jaibriol lifted his head to regard his cousin. "We will deal with the Skolians as we must."

Corbal was studying him. "Never show signs of weakness. Your enemies will devour you."

Jaibriol just stared at him, and wondered if he could ever resurrect his dream.

Dehya sat at the round table with Kelric, and they each

rolled out their dice. While the rest of the Assembly slept, celebrated, or brooded, the Dyad played Quis.

Words had never been Kelric's forte, so instead of explaining the rules, he showed them to her. He placed a regular tetrahedron, a ruby pyramid, in the center of the table. Then he waited.

Dehya looked from the die to Kelric. When he continued to wait, she smiled slightly, then took a gold pentahedron and set it next to his piece.

That surprised him. Did she know she had started a queen's spectrum? She had probably studied records of his solitaire games, trying to figure them out. Building a spectrum against an advanced player was difficult. An augmented queen's spectrum was almost impossible; to his knowledge, he was the only person who had done it in Calanya Quis.

He rubbed his fingers, which ached with arthritis even his nanomeds couldn't eliminate. Then he set a yellow cube against her die. She followed with a green heptahedron. Well, hell. She *was* making a spectrum.

Kelric played a sapphire octahedron. "My game."

She looked up at him. "You can win Quis?"

He grinned. "Of course. You're lucky we aren't betting; you would owe me ten times whatever you had risked."

Dehya cocked an eyebrow. "Why should I believe you won?"

Despite her outward skepticism, he could tell she was enjoying herself. It was the advantage of being an empath; it helped him learn gestures, body language, and expressions until interpreting them became second nature. He could read Dehya even when she shielded her mind.

He tapped the line of dice. "These increase in rank according to number of sides and colors of the spectrum. Five make a queen's spectrum. Three of the dice are mine and two are yours. That means I have advantage. So I win."

"I was helping you, eh? If you start the spectrum, you win no matter what."

"You can block my moves." He took his dice and slid hers across the table. Then he set an amethyst bar in the playing area. "Your move."

"Are we gambling?"

"If you would like."

She laughed softly. "Ah, well, you made up the rules, I don't know them, and you've been playing for decades. I *don't* think I want to bet." She set her amethyst bar on top of his.

Kelric stared at the bars, frozen. He felt her amusement fade to puzzlement. Finally, still not looking at her, he said, "I didn't make up the rules."

"Who did?" Her voice had a waiting quality.

He set a diamond sphere near the structure. "Your move."

She waited a while. When he said nothing else, she said, "Spectrums go by color, yes?"

He glanced up. "That's why they're called spectrums."

"And white is all colors, as in light."

"Yes!" She was going to be formidable at Quis. He wondered if she realized he had used the diamond ball, the highest ranked piece, to symbolize her. Dehya wasn't hard like a diamond, but its strength fit her, as did the way it refracted light into many vivid colors.

She set a gold dodecahedron apart from the other dice. *Interesting.* The dodecahedron came next in rank after the sphere. What did she mean? Possibly nothing. He could never tell with Dehya, though; her complex, evolving mind often startled him.

He set down an onyx ring, one of his symbols for himself. She thought for a moment, then balanced a topaz arch so it connected the diamond ball and gold dodecahedron.

"That's a sunsky bridge," Kelric said. "It suggests a cooperative venture."

She tapped the gold dodecahedron. "Roca." Then she touched the diamond ball. "You."

He regarded her curiously. "Why assign names to the dice?"

"I've watched you play. Your structures evolve. It's almost as if they have personalities."

It gratified him that she understood. "They tell stories. Or make the story. The dice shape events as much as portray them."

"I don't see how gambling can spur events." With a wry smile, she added, "Except to lower my credit account."

Kelric waved his hand. "Gambling is for Outsiders. It isn't true Quis."

"Then what do you do with it?"

He leaned forward. "Suppose everyone played. Everywhere. Throughout the Imperialate."

She was watching him closely. "And?"

"I put my stories into my Quis when I sit in sessions with other people. Then they play with others. The better designed my strategies, the more it affects their Quis, and the more they pass on my intentions."

"So your effect spreads."

"Yes."

"And if, say, Vaz Majda played Quis, you might affect her opinions with your influence."

Good! She understood. "But other people also input stories. Ragnar might build patterns of war. Councilor Tikal would focus on politics. Naaj would bring in heredity. Their input goes to the public, who all play Quis. Everyone affects the game, but most people don't play well enough to do much beyond accepting, refusing, or transmitting ideas."

Her voice took on a careful quality. "And when everyone is playing Quis this way, what do you call your world?"

He knew what she was asking: where had he spent all those years? He gathered his dice and put them in his pouch. "Thank you for the game."

She started to speak, but whatever she was going to say, she let it go. Instead she asked, "Who won?"

"Both of us."

"So you and I, we don't gamble."

Calani and Managers never do. But he kept that thought shielded from her. "With you, I would rather work together."

She met his gaze. "So would I."

He stood and bowed. "We will play again."

Dehya rose to her feet. "I hope so." Her thoughts swirled with unasked questions, and he knew if he let down his barriers, they would flood his mind. But she didn't speak. Perhaps she knew he couldn't bring himself to answer.

Not yet.

IX
Plaza of Memories

Jaibriol unexpectedly found Sunrise.

He went to the opulent wing of the palace where Corbal lived. His cousin stayed there when he wasn't seeing to his business affairs or meddling in Jaibriol's life. Hidaka came with Jaibriol, along with three Razers who were like extensions of the captain's biomech-enhanced mind.

His unannounced visit shook up the taskmaker who looked after Corbal's suite. She and her husband had served the Xir Lord for decades. She was trembling as she knelt to Jaibriol, and tendrils of her auburn hair wisped around her face.

"Please rise," Jaibriol said, far more gently than Hightons were supposed to speak to taskmakers.

She rose to her feet, her gaze downcast. "You honor us with Your Most Glorious Presence, Your Highness."

Jaibriol winced. He had managed to stop his staff from talking that way, but everyone else did it regardless of what he said. He just nodded and walked into the living room of Corbal's suite. Plush cushions were scattered across a carpeted floor that sparkled with holographic tips on the pile. Blue-lacquer tables shone and the walls gleamed blue. The room glistened.

With a start, Jaibriol realized someone was sleeping on a large pillow in one corner. It was Sunrise, Corbal's provider. She lay curled on her side with her eyes closed in her angel's face. Her hair fell across her body in glossy waves, as bright as a yellow sun. She wore nothing more than a scant halter of gold chains, with sapphires that barely covered her enlarged nipples. A gold chain around her hips held the gold triangle of her G-string. She was lushly, voluptuously desirable, full and round where Hightons were lean.

Jaibriol stopped, his face heating. Even while she slept, her contentment soothed. He blocked her, not because he didn't appreciate the healing balm of her mind, but because if she awoke, she might suspect him. Sunrise was a powerful empath, able to detect far more than most Aristos realized.

Jaibriol never knew how to act around her. He had spent the first fourteen years of his life with only his family. On Earth, he had been shy around girls, unsure how to behave. As emperor, he had slept with a provider once, a sweet, silver girl who had taken his virginity and left him with a treasured memory. Then he had married Tarquine, and he hadn't touched any other woman since.

He spoke self-consciously to Hidaka. "I'll come back later. Lord Xir doesn't seem to be here." Corbal obviously had been, though, given Sunrise's state of dress, or lack thereof. He felt like an intruder.

A deep voice came from behind him. "Your Highness?"

Jaibriol turned with a start. Corbal's son Azile was walking through the archway and unfastening a long coat, which he wore over a silk shirt and elegant slacks. His cheeks were red from the wind, which probably meant his flyer had just landed on the roof of the palace.

Jaibriol inclined his head to his Intelligence Minister, his closest kin after Corbal and Calope Muze. He used the minimalist Highton greeting appropriate for family. "Azile."

The older man bowed. "You honor my father's home."

"I came to talk to him." Jaibriol indicated where Sunrise slept. "But I didn't want to wake her."

Azile glanced idly toward the corner, then did a double take. His startled, instinctual response was so intense, Jaibriol felt it despite the muting effects of his shields. Azile sensed Sunrise's unprotected mind, but in a far different manner than Jaibriol. In that instant, the desire to transcend hit Azile so hard, an image jumped into his thoughts of Sunrise crying in pain.

Bile rose in Jaibriol's throat. How the blazes could Azile desire to hurt her that way? He wanted to throw his Intelligence Minister across the room.

The blood drained from Azile's face. Shock surged from his mind, and a deep loathing for himself. He spun around and strode from the room through a smaller archway. Jaibriol watched in amazement, not because it offended him to have his cousin walk out, not even because it was a crime to leave the emperor's presence in such a manner, but because he had never felt such remorse from an Aristo capable of transcending. Azile was only in his fifties, much younger than Corbal or Tarquine had been when they changed.

When Hidaka motioned for two of the Razers to go after Azile, Jaibriol held up his hand, stopping them. Then he followed his cousin into a small alcove stocked with liqueurs. Azile was leaning on a counter, his face ashen. As Jaibriol entered, the Intelligence Minister jerked up his head and comprehension of his trespass against the emperor flooded across his face.

"Your Highness!" Azile straightened up abruptly. "Please accept my most humble apology."

"Accepted," Jaibriol said, sparing Azile an arrest. He had never seen his cousin disturbed this way. Sweat sheened Azile's forehead. Could he be more like his father than Jaibriol had realized? He knew Azile transcended; even now, with his shields full strength, he sensed the crushing pressure of Azile's mind.

"One might be distracted by many things," Jaibriol said, probing. "It is always my hope that my kin are well and serene."

Azile inclined his head to the right, indicating gratitude at Jaibriol's response. "Most serene, Your Highness."

"I'm pleased to hear it." Jaibriol studied him. "Tell your father I visited."

"Certainly. It will be my pleasure to serve the throne."

Jaibriol doubted it; he knew Azile disliked him. But maybe this was a start toward better relations between the two of them.

Jaibriol found Tarquine at a crystal table in the Atrium, surrounded by lush trees, with sunlight filtering over her from the polarized glass of the ceiling and walls.

"My greetings, husband." She was spearing sea delicacies in a porcelain dish using a sharpened ivory prong.

"Tarquine." He sat down, preoccupied with his thoughts.

She studied him for a moment. "Distraction becomes you."

Jaibriol had no idea how to take that, which he told her in suitably convoluted Hightonese. "I would never say incomprehensibility becomes you, my lovely wife, since you are always comprehensible, but should that ever change, I'm sure it would reflect just as well."

Tarquine smiled, a slow curve of her lips. "I do believe I've just been insulted."

Jaibriol grinned at her. "Never."

She blinked, staring at him.

"Astonishment also becomes you," he added amiably.

"'They say his smile is like the sun that rarely rises,'" she murmured. "Carzalan Kri wrote that in one of his poems."

"You think my sun doesn't rise enough?" Jaibriol supposed it was true. He rarely felt like grinning at anyone.

"It's another sign of your distraction," Tarquine decided.

He took a tobin-plum out of a bowl and bit into the pale blue fruit. "This is good."

"Indeed."

He gave her a dour look. "If Highton words were a form of nourishment, that one would have no nutritional value at all."

She sat back, relaxed, regarding him as if he was a rare and valuable acquisition. "You look well today."

"Don't do that."

"What? Compliment you?"

"Look at me like I'm your dessert."

Her smile turned sultry. "My dessert was never so sweet."

Jaibriol wanted to groan. Sweet, indeed. He was an emperor, not a slice of cake.

"I've been wondering something," he said.

She regarded him curiously. "And what could that be?"

"Is it unusual for a man to feel affection toward his father's provider? I don't mean desire. More like kinship."

"Not particularly." She swirled a melon-shrimp around in the sauce on her plate and took a bite.

He sat back, thinking. "Perhaps Azile was affected by something else."

"An intelligence matter, I would imagine."

He knew she was fishing to find out if his comment connected to Azile's work as Intelligence Minister. Her mind never rested when it came to politics.

"It's Sunrise," Jaibriol said.

"Providers always affect Aristos." Tarquine finished her melon- shrimp. "I'm told she has a high Kyle rating."

"I wouldn't know," he lied.

She spoke quietly. "Corbal values the dawn. He would never let its radiance dim."

Jaibriol knew she was right. Despite Corbal's attempts to disguise his affection, Tarquine had long ago realized how he felt about Sunrise. She was the radiance in his life.

"It's always intriguing when people act out of character," Tarquine said. "Don't you think?"

Jaibriol stiffened. "No."

She was probing about Azile, which meant she was

thinking of looking into the matter. He didn't want her investigating his Intelligence Minister, at least no more than usual. He had no doubt she and Azile kept dossiers on each other. But he had managed to keep their mutual ill will at bay.

He sincerely hoped it stayed that way.

Sunlight flooded Selei City on the planet Parthonia. Skyscrapers pierced the lavender sky, which had never taken on the bluer hue intended by the world's terraformers. The mirrored buildings reflected clouds as if they were part of the sky. Kelric strolled across a plaza tiled with blue stone. Government officials walked in pairs and trios through the area, their executive jumpsuits glossy in the sunshine. They gave Kelric and his heavily armed guards a wide berth.

Kelric was always aware of the stronger gravity here and its effect on his heavy build. He felt slowed down, and he fatigued more easily. The beautiful weather contrasted with his mood. He had no desire to attend the Assembly after yesterday's loss. But the sessions continued regardless of his mood. At least he could escape during this break.

"Nice day," Strava commented as they strolled along.

"It is." Kelric needed to say no more. It was one reason he liked these guards. They were as taciturn as he.

He stopped at the plaza's fountain, a jumble of geometric shapes with water cascading over them. It looked like a big pile of wet Quis dice. What would happen if he introduced Quis into Skolian culture? It could just become a fad, but he knew it too well to believe that. Quis would fascinate his people. Scholars would write papers on it. Gaming dens would proliferate. Schools would teach it. The game was too powerful to fade away.

Maybe it would even spread to Eube. The Coban queens had sublimated their aggression into Quis. He doubted it could affect the Traders as much, but even a small change might get the stalled treaty negotiations back on track.

A silver spark flashed in Kelric's side vision.

Combat mode toggled, Bolt thought.

What the hell? Kelric spun around as his body toggled into combat mode and accelerated his motions.

Najo shoved him to the ground, and Strava and Najo threw themselves across Kelric as he hit the pavement. Axer stood over them with his feet planted wide, firing, his massive Jumbler clenched in both hands. He swept the beam across the plaza with enhanced speed, his reflexes powered by the microfusion reactor within him. Strava and Najo were shooting as well, even as they protected Kelric with their bodies. Sparks glittered in the air, and when the beams touched ground, it exploded in bursts of orange light. Debris flew and dust swirled around the fountain.

Kelric lay with his palms braced on the ground, tensed like a wire drawn taut. He wanted to throw off his guards and vault to his feet; it took a great effort to stay put and let them do their job. His enhanced vision picked out projectiles headed toward him and also their demise in flashes of light.

After an eon, his bodyguards stopped firing. The air had the astringent smell of annihilated bitons, and sirens blared throughout the plaza. Engines rumbled overhead as military flyers soared through the sky.

"Imperator Skolia?" Najo asked, getting to his feet. "Are you all right?"

Kelric pushed up on his elbow. "I'm fine. Are we clear?"

"Looks like it," Strava said. She was kneeling over him, her calves on either side of his legs while she surveyed the ruined plaza. Najo scanned the area with his gauntlet monitors, and Axer was speaking into his wrist comm.

Kelric stabbed a panel on his own gauntlet. "Major Qahot, what the hell is going on?"

The voice of his security chief came out of the mesh. "The shooters are dead, sir," he said. "It doesn't look like they expected to survive."

"Suicide assassins," Kelric said.

"Apparently. Are you all right?"

"I'm fine," he growled. "I want to know how the blazes they got in here." The Assembly drew delegates from all over Skolia. Some attended through the web, but many gathered in Selei City. ISC had ramped up security so high, they should have known if anyone within a hundred kilometer radius even breathed oddly.

Strava climbed to her feet, freeing Kelric. He stood up and spoke quietly to his bodyguards. "Thank you."

Najo inclined his head, and Strava lifted her hand in acknowledgment. Axer was getting updates on his gauntlet and probably his ear comm, too. ISC police were already combing the plaza, and no doubt every nearby building. The flyers overhead gleamed gold and black, reflected in the mirrored skyscrapers.

Kelric finally let himself absorb that he had almost died.

"They never had a chance," Major Qahot said, pacing across the security office beneath the Assembly Hall. A stocky man with bristly hair, he moved as if he were caged, unable to break free until he solved the mystery of Kelric's attackers.

People filled the room, officers, aides, guards. And Roca. Kelric had arranged to have Dehya and his brothers transferred to safe houses, as well as the First Councilor and Inner Circle. Roca, however, refused to leave. His people would take her if he ordered it, but he knew it would antagonize her. For now, in the depths of this secured command center, he let her stay. She stood by a wall, listening while his officers investigated the attempt on his life. Kelric sat at a console that monitored the Assembly Hall, Selei City, the countryside, even orbital traffic. From here, he could access any system on the planet.

"The assassins could never have reached you," Qahot said as he paced. "Their clothes were shrouded against sensors, but the moment they drew their weapons, it triggered alarms all over Selei City. Their shots would never have hit home."

Roca spoke, her voice like tempered steel. "They should never have gotten close enough to shoot."

Perspiration beaded on Qahot's forehead. "It won't happen again, Your Highness."

"Imperator Skolia." Strava spoke from her seat at another console. "We've identified the security hole that let the assassins slip their guns by our systems."

"A hole?" Kelric said. "How did that happen?"

"It migrated from another system." She was reading from one of her screens. "The Hinterland Deployment."

Kelric froze. The Hinterland Deployment guarded Coba. "How could it affect us? That's a different region of space."

She rubbed her chin as she studied the data. "It's odd. A few bytes are missing from a security mod in the Hinterland codes. Almost nothing. But the hole propagated to other systems." She looked up at Kelric. "The mesh-techs couldn't locate the cause, but they're patching the hole."

It was all Kelric could do to remain impassive. One little hole in Hinterland security. Just one, but it had spread. Because it hadn't been properly coded. Because it should never have existed. Because he had made it in secret.

Kelric had told Dirac to "forget" Coba was the focus of the Hinterland Deployment. He should have known better. The deletion had ended up drawing far more attention than if he had done nothing. Hell, it had nearly killed him.

"Keep me apprised of their progress," he told Strava.

"Will do, sir."

He swiveled his chair to Axer, who was standing by a console with his hand cupped to his ear as he listened to his comm. "Do you have anything on the three assassins?" Kelric asked.

A frown creased the broad planes of the guard's face. "They were delegates in the Assembly. The police found records in their quarters."

His careful expression didn't fool Kelric. His guards shielded their minds and didn't talk much, but he knew them well. Axer was worried.

"What do you have on them so far?" Kelric asked.

"They feared what would happen if Councilor Roca lost the vote." He glanced at Kelric's mother. "I'm sorry, ma'am."

"Why would they fear the vote?" she asked. "Their seats aren't hereditary."

"Apparently they thought it gave Imperator Skolia too much power and you too little."

Kelric stared at them. "They would assassinate me to support my mother?"

Roca's voice hardened. "Then they deserved to die."

Don't, Kelric thought to her.

No one tries to murder my child and gets away with it.

Kelric recognized her cold fury. Normally she was a gentle woman, but threats to her family brought out a ferocity that startled even him. He thought of his ordeals on Coba. Had she known, she would have retaliated against the Cobans. And if today's assassination had succeeded? Roca was next in line to become Imperator. It was among the more bizarre ramifications of their extended lifespans, that a parent could be her child's heir. She didn't want the title; she was trained to succeed Dehya as Assembly Key. But she was better qualified as Imperator than Kelric's siblings, and only a Ruby psion could join the Dyad.

Had Kelric died, the Closure document would have released to the authorities as soon as the news became public. ISC would have gone to find Ixpar and his children.

He had always known that could happen, but when he had written his will, he had seen no other choice.

Kelric? Roca's forehead furrowed. *You think I will retaliate against the families of the assassins?*

Startled, he strengthened his shields. At least his defenses had been strong enough that she misread his thoughts. **Let the courts deal with it.**

She regarded him impassively.

I mean it, Mother. Let Legal handle this. He was aware of his guards watching. They had probably figured out he and Roca were mentally conversing. As Jagernauts, they were psions, but if even Roca picked up so little through his shields, it was unlikely they would get anything. They had nowhere near her mental strength. Kelric had become a master at hiding from his family, but he was worn out by cutting himself off that way.

Security suspected something was up, Roca thought. *But not this.*

So you really were trying to start a rumor yesterday.

Yes. To trace its source.

Apparently its source found us first.

Roca exhaled. *It seems so.*

Kelric glanced at Qahot, who was leaning over a console to read its screen. "Major, do we have leads on who the assassins were working with?"

Qahot straightened up. "So far, it looks like only those three were involved. Records of their correspondence indicate they've grown disaffected over the years." Then he added, "Yesterday, one of them told another delegate you should be 'voted out' of your seat permanently."

It was a sobering response. Kelric had known the Imperator wasn't well-liked, but he hadn't thought anyone wanted him dead. Had he lost sight of his humanity in the performance of his duties?

Axer was watching his face. "Sir, they were fanatics. No matter what you did, they would have objected. It was the office of Imperator they opposed. Not the person."

Kelric knew Axer meant well, and it was one of the longer speeches his guard had ever made to him. But he suspected the assassins protested the man who held the title as much as the title itself. He had to do his job, even if people hated him for it. He nodded to his guard, then spoke to Qahot. "Do checks on all the Assembly delegates and their aides. Make sure no one else was involved."

"Right away, sir," Qahot said.

A door across the room opened to admit a Jagernaut in black leathers. Vazar. She strode to Kelric's console. "Primary Majda reporting, sir."

Kelric stood up, regarding her coolly. "Are my joint commanders safe?"

"Yes, sir." Her posture was ramrod straight. "General Majda and Primary Tapperhaven have left Parthonia. Admiral Barzun is on the Orbiter. General Stone is on Diesha. All are under increased security."

"Good," he said. Her tension practically snapped in the air. Yesterday she had voted against the Ruby Dynasty; today she was tasked with protecting their interests. Neither of them missed the irony. He went around the console to her and spoke in a low voice only she could hear. "You're on duty here until I get back. Don't disappoint me."

She met his gaze. "I won't, sir."

He felt her mood: regardless of her vote, she would protect his family with her life. As angry as he felt toward her, he had to respect the integrity that spurred her to choose what she believed was right even when she knew it would alienate him and imperil her own Assembly seat.

Kelric beckoned to Roca, and she left the command center with him and his guards. Her anger at Vaz simmered, but she said nothing. She rarely spoke aloud to him when he was dealing with ISC, and he had realized she didn't want to appear as if she were interfering with his authority. He doubted she would, but he appreciated the consideration. The Assembly needed more of that sensitivity she brought to the table, not less.

Her bodyguards were outside, three instead of the usual two. They fell into formation around Kelric and Roca, along with Najo, Strava, and Axer. They all walked down the metallic tunnel deep below Selei City.

"With supporters like those assassins," Roca said in a low voice, "I don't need enemies."

"It's not your fault," he said.

She glanced at him. "You're a damn fine commander, Kelric. Don't let what happened today make you believe otherwise."

He rubbed his neck, working at stiffness his nanomeds couldn't seem to ease. "Doubt is good for the soul."

"I'm just so immensely grateful you're all right."

"I, too," he said wryly.

Her normally dulcet voice turned icy. "Everyone involved with this attempt against your life will pay."

She reminded him of the clawcats that prowled the Teotec Mountains on Coba. "Let the courts deal with it."

"Of course."

Kelric didn't trust *that* answer. She never gave in that easily. He knew she wouldn't rest until they had caught everyone connected with the attempt on his life.

The assassins had forced him to face certain facts. If he died and Roca became Imperator, then at the same time she was taking command, the Closure document would come to light. And he would no longer be alive to protect Coba.

X
King's Spectrum

Jaibriol sat sprawled on a sofa in the sitting area of his bedroom, his eyes closed. His mind brimmed with the bittersweet memories that crept up on him when he didn't fill his days with enough work to make him forget. Tonight he remembered how his mother had brought him and his siblings to Earth, deep in the night, to a starport in Virginia. She had asked Admiral Seth Rockworth to meet them, and he had been waiting.

Seth had looked after Jaibriol, his sister, and his two younger brothers for two years—while their mother waged war against their father's empire. They had lived in a gorgeous area of the Appalachian Mountains. Everyone had known Jaibriol as Jay Rockworth. He could have gone by Gabe; some historians believed his name derived from *Gabriel*. But it felt wrong to call himself after an angel when he descended from Highton Aristos. No one who knew him had dreamed he had a claim to both the Carnelian and Ruby thrones.

The loneliness of those days had weighed on him, for he could never acknowledge his parents. But it had also been a gentle time when he made friends, went to school, played sports, attended church, and had the closest he would ever come to a normal life. He and his siblings had cared deeply for Seth. Their mother had taken them to the retired admiral because he had been the Ruby Pharaoh's first consort, an arranged union that established a treaty between Skolia and the Allied Worlds. That he and the pharaoh later ended the marriage hadn't dissolved the treaty. Although technically Seth was no longer a member of the Ruby Dynasty, Jaibriol's mother had trusted him, enough to leave her children and their secret in his care.

Jaibriol didn't know what had happened to his sister and brothers; he had been offworld when he claimed his throne, and they had been on Earth. He had searched the meshes for them and found nothing. He feared to investigate too far, lest he endanger them with his attention, but he mourned the loss of their companionship as much as he grieved for his parents.

Tarquine had erased the few images of him on the meshes from that time on Earth. He hadn't looked Aristo then, with gold streaks in his hair and brown contacts that covered his red eyes. She wanted no questions. Not long after their marriage, she had cracked his secured medical files and discovered he had the same nanomeds in his body as Kelric. Roca Skolia had passed the meds to her children in her womb, and Jaibriol inherited them from his mother. From that, Tarquine had deduced the truth. Only she could have found that damning shred of evidence because she had owned, ever so briefly, a member of the Ruby Dynasty.

Tarquine had destroyed the files.

Why she protected him, Jaibriol didn't know, though surely it was because he held a similarly damning secret about her, that she no longer transcended. It seemed impossible it could be because she loved him.

Slumping back on the sofa, he put his feet on the table in front of him. Gold and midnight blue brocade glimmered on the sofa and the wing chair at right angles to it. Far across the suite, his canopied bed stood on a dais. The bedroom gleamed, gilt and ivory, with blue accents and tiered chandeliers.

His guards were outside. This bedroom suite was one of the few places with enough safeguards to allow him privacy even from his formidable Razers. They were infamous for their supposedly inhuman nature, but Jaibriol wondered, especially about Hidaka. He felt certain the guard knew when he wanted to be alone and when he wanted visitors, and did his best to ensure Jaibriol's wishes were met. Why Hidaka would care, he had no idea, but he appreciated the results.

His wrist comm buzzed. Lifting his arm, he said, "Qox."

One of his guards answered. "Robert Muzeson is here, Your Highness. Shall we let him in?"

"Yes, certainly," Jaibriol said.

As Jaibriol sat up, the arched door to the entrance foyer opened. Its corners were curved, avoiding the right angles Aristos abhorred. Squared-off corners, like direct speech, were for slaves. Aristos considered abstraction elevated; Jaibriol considered it maddening.

Hidaka escorted Robert inside and bowed deeply to Jaibriol.

"Thank you," Jaibriol told the guard. Then he added, quietly, "For everything, Captain."

For an instant something showed on Hidaka's face. Shock? Jaibriol wasn't certain. He tried to pick up a mood from the captain, but he couldn't read the Razer's mental processes, which had been substantially altered by the extensive biomech in his brain.

After Hidaka withdrew, Jaibriol motioned Robert to the wing chair. "Relax, please."

"Thank you, Your Highness." Robert settled in the chair and leaned back, though he wasn't truly relaxed. Jaibriol slouched on the sofa, his long legs on the table. He knew it wasn't regal, but he really didn't care.

Robert looked as professional as always, a fit middle-aged man with brown hair. He dressed in elegant clothes of muted colors with peculiar names like *ecru*. To Jaibriol, it just looked like pale brown. Robert didn't have the stunning appearance of his father, Caleb, but from what Jaibriol had gathered about Caleb's life before he came to the palace, those good looks had brought him only grief. He had been a provider for Robert's mother. Now Caleb spent his days painting, as he had done before he was sold as a slave.

Jaibriol exhibited Caleb's work in one of the palace galleries. He never considered his patronage a favor; Caleb had great talent and was developing a well-deserved renown. The gratitude Robert and his father expressed made him want to crawl in a hole. How could they thank him? He *owned* them. They wore slave cuffs on their wrists and collars threaded with picotech that included ID chips and security monitors. They ought to hate him. Maybe they felt that way about other Aristos; he had certainly sensed it in Caleb. But never about him.

Right now, he sensed calm from Robert. Although Jaibriol could pick up moods, he couldn't always tell *why* a person felt that way. The emotions might be vague or mixed together. He received the clearest impressions from other psions. As a telepath, he might glean hints of a person's thoughts, but only if they were strong, well-articulated, and on the surface of the mind. Even to do that, he had to lower his barriers. He could mind-speak only with his family. One of the many reasons he appreciated Robert was because very little ruffled the aide. He wasn't a psion, so Jaibriol didn't have to shield his mind, and Robert's even temper often eased Jaibriol's agitated moods.

"Do I have any appointments?" Jaibriol asked. He had slept last night, so tonight he would work.

Robert unrolled his mesh film onto a board in his lap and read from the screen. "Nothing for the next three hours. A report came in on that explosion in the Amethyst Wing."

Jaibriol leaned his head against the headrest on the sofa and closed his eyes. "What caused it?"

"That's the rub of it, Your Highness. They found nothing wrong with the pipes and no indication of explosives."

Jaibriol opened his eyes. "That makes no sense."

"It doesn't appear to, no." Robert squinted at his screen. "It says here that about three centimeters above the pipe, space imploded. The surrounding region of space-time collapsed into the hole left behind in the, uh, weave of space and time." He looked up to meet Jaibriol's incredulous stare. "I'm sorry, Sire. That is what it says."

"They expect me to believe it?" Maybe they thought he was an idiot. "How would repair techs know that?"

"They forwarded a report to Professor Quenzer in the physics department at Qoxire University," Robert said. "Her research team came to examine the blast area and data. They are the ones who proposed the theory."

"Oh." Although Jaibriol knew very little about physics, even he had heard of the renowned Quenzer group. If they said space was falling apart, he would have to take them seriously. "It's an odd theory." To put it mildly.

"That's not all," Robert said. "Three other explosions took place, one on this planet, one in space, and one on a starliner in Sapphire Sector."

Jaibriol swung his legs off the table and sat up straight. "All like the one here?"

"It appears so."

"Was anyone hurt?"

"Several people on the liner had to be treated for minor injuries they sustained during a hull breach. But the situation was contained without any serious problems."

"What about the second blast here?"

"It happened in the Jaizire range." Robert looked regretful. "I'm afraid it destroyed a portion of one of your mountains."

Jaibriol loved the peaks and their wild, primordial forests, but he would far rather lose a mountain than people. "Why would space implode in four different places? It sounds crazy."

"No one seems to know," Robert said.

"Do they think it will happen again?" The prospect of space falling apart that way was just too eerie.

"They don't know that, either."

"Well, have them investigate it. The physicists, I mean." Jaibriol rubbed his eyes. "I want to know why it's happening."

Robert bent over his mesh screen. "I will see to it."

Jaibriol hesitated. "I have a question for you, Robert."

His aide looked up. "Yes, Sire?"

"Did I say something strange to Hidaka just now?"

"I don't think so. Why do you ask?"

Jaibriol felt odd, asking if he had offended his biomech guard. "He seemed taken aback when I thanked him."

Robert's puzzlement vanished. "You didn't trouble him, I'm sure. Surprised him, perhaps."

"Why?"

"You thanked him."

Jaibriol waited. When his aide said nothing more, he spoke wryly, "Aristos do say thank you, you know."

Robert met his gaze. "Not to machines."

"He's not a machine. None of them are."

Robert didn't answer. They both knew that not only would other Aristos disagree, they would find Jaibriol's statement offensive, a threat even. If they started acknowledging their slaves as human, their carefully crafted worldview would crumble. They had far too much power and wealth at stake to let that happen.

A beep came from Robert's mesh. Peering at the screen, he flicked his finger through several holoicons. "I'm getting a message for you." His eyes widened. "Good gods."

Jaibriol leaned forward. "What is it?"

Robert looked up, his face pale. "Someone tried to kill Imperator Skolia."

Hell and damnation. "Who did it?" Jaibriol could guess. "Someone who didn't think the Imperialate military should have as much power as the Assembly handed him with that vote, yes?"

Robert scanned the screen. "It looks that way. His people aren't releasing much information. The attempt took place in public, though, and monitors in the area recorded it."

"So they can't hush it up," Jaibriol said, shaken. He had almost lost another family member. "He's all right, isn't he?"

Robert looked up with a start, then caught himself and said, "According to these broadcasts, he's fine."

Jaibriol didn't need to ask Robert why he gaped. A normal Eubian emperor, upon learning that his greatest enemy had suffered a murder attempt, wouldn't seek assurance his foe was all right.

"They would claim everything is fine no matter what," Robert said. "It does look true, though." He indicated his screen, and Jaibriol leaned over to peer at it. The news holo showed Kelric climbing to his feet in the middle of a plaza, surrounded by three huge Jagernauts with gigantic black guns.

"So," Jaibriol said. As much as he wished the specter of Kelric Skolia would disappear from his life, or at least his wife's memory, it relieved him to see his uncle well. Of course, that assumed the broadcasts told the truth.

"Imperator Skolia doesn't have an heir," he said. "If he dies, it will destabilize the Imperialate."

"His mother is his heir," Robert said.

Jaibriol didn't want to think about succession in the Ruby Dynasty, because it meant considering the death of people his mother had loved. He had never met her family, but through her, he felt as if he could love them as well, given the chance. It would never happen; they would probably rather see him dead first. And no matter how uncomfortable it made him, he had to consider the ramifications should any of them die.

"If Roca Skolia became Imperator," Jaibriol said, "she might be more amenable to the talks."

"If Roca Skolia became Imperator," Robert said flatly, "she would destroy the galaxy to avenge the murder of her child."

Jaibriol couldn't argue with that. She might be moderate politically, but rumor claimed she was fiercely protective of her family. The ferocity didn't surprise him in the least. Her daughter—Jaibriol's mother—had been the same way.

The emperor shook his head. He didn't want to imagine the consequences if Kelric took the mandate offered to him by that vote. Jaibriol knew that going to war against his own family would destroy him.

It had been ten years since Kelric walked in the desert of Coba. Hot wind tugged his leather jacket and the pullover he wore underneath. Gusts pulled at the Talha scarf hanging around his neck. Woven from coarse white and black yarn, the Talha resembled a muffler, with tassels along its edges.

Carrying his duffle, he walked down the sand-scoured

street of the starport. Najo, Axer, and Strava stalked at his side, sleek and lethal, each with the bulk of a Jumbler on his or her hip. They scanned the area continually and monitored it with their gauntlets. They weren't happy about this trip, even less so because he had told them almost nothing of his intentions.

They encountered no one. The place consisted of a few wide streets bordered by unused buildings. Robots kept the tiny port in shape, and travelers rarely visited. Nothing more than a low wall surrounded the base; beyond it, desert stretched in every direction, punctuated by sand dunes mottled with spiky green plants, and by bluffs streaked with red and yellow layers of rock. It reminded Kelric of ballads his father had sung about a starkly beautiful desert that separated the world of mortals from the land of the two sun gods.

They soon reached a wide gap in the wall. A pitted windrider stood beyond it, partially buried in drifts of sand. That was it. No gate. Nothing. On this side, they were Skolians; on the other, their citizenship ceased to matter. Even knowing that, his guards didn't hesitate to walk with him into the Coban desert. Restricted territory.

Kelric spoke into his gauntlet. "Bolt, connect me to the port EI." He could have thought the command to his node, but he wanted his guards to witness what he had to say.

Bolt's voice came out of the mesh. "Connecting."

The EI that ran the port spoke. "ISC-Coba attending."

"ISC-Coba," Kelric said, "I'm sending you some codes. Use them to access the Kyle web and contact the EI called 'Dirac' on the Orbiter space station."

"Understood," ISC-Coba said.

Najo watched him with that uncanny ability of his to seem utterly still. Strava rested her hand on her Jumbler while she scanned the desert. Axer was checking the area with his gauntlet.

"Contact made," ISC-Coba said.

Dirac's rich baritone rumbled. "My greetings, Imperator Skolia."

Kelric gazed north to mountains that reared against the pale sky. It had been so long. "Dirac, how many days until my Closure becomes permanent?"

"Ninety-seven," Dirac said.

Najo stiffened, his eyes widening. Axer raised his head, and Strava snapped her attention back to Kelric. Learning he would be legally dead in ninety-seven days had to be unnerving for the people tasked with ensuring he stayed alive.

Kelric turned toward the nearby windrider. It was painted like a giant althawk, with red wings and a rusted head that had once gleamed. The landing gear resembled black talons, or it would have if he could have seen under the sand dunes drifted around the aircraft.

"Dirac," he said. "Cancel the Closure."

A pause. "Cancelled," Dirac said.

Najo started to speak. Kelric didn't know how he looked, but whatever Najo was about to say, he changed his mind. Axer and Strava exchanged glances.

"Closing connection," Kelric told Dirac.

"Orbiter connection closed," ISC-Coba stated.

"ISC-Coba," Kelric said. "Verify my identity."

"You are the Imperator of Skolia."

Kelric stopped then, unable to take the final step. He tried to go on, but no words came.

"Do you have a command?" ISC-Coba asked.

"Yes." He took a deep breath. "Change the status of this world from Restricted to Protected."

"That requires a review by Imperial Space Command."

"I'm the Imperator. That's review enough."

Silence.

In truth, Kelric knew of no cases where ISC had altered a world's status without a review. The process could take years. However, nothing prohibited him from doing it. In theory.

Then ISC-Coba said, "Status changed."

Kelric exhaled. A human probably would have protested. "End communication."

"Connection closed," Bolt said.

Najo spoke. "Sir, to protect you, we need to know what's going on."

Kelric indicated the mountains. "We're going to a city up there. The air is even thinner than here, so use caution in any exertions. The food varies from irritating to toxic, at least to us, but our nanomeds can deal with it. Boiling the water helps. For a short stay, we should be all right." Eighteen years here, with his meds failing, had nearly killed him. By the time he had left, he had been dying. His capture and subsequent escape from Trader slavery had worsened the injuries to his body and biomech, until he had gone deaf and blind, and lost the use of his legs. Jeejon had given up everything she owned to get him help; without her, he wouldn't have survived.

A wave of grief hit Kelric. He remembered what Jeejon

had told him just before she died: *Someday you must finish that chapter of your life you left behind for me.* It was true, but he had needed this year to say good-bye to her.

Kelric looked out over the desert. **Be well, love.** He sent his thought into the wind, across the sands, as if it could float into the pale sky, to the stars and beyond, until it reached her spirit.

"Sir, I don't understand," Strava said. "Why are we here?"

Kelric continued to gaze at the desert. "So I can see the city. Walk down a street." He turned to them. "Buy a sausage at market."

They regarded him with bewilderment.

Finally Axer said, "What are the threats?"

"To me?" Kelric asked. The greatest threat here was him, to Coba.

"Yes, sir."

Kelric answered wryly. "People in the city might gawk at my metallic skin. They will probably stare more at you three, with those Jumblers. Their city guards just carry stunners."

"You seem to know this place," Najo said.

More than I ever admitted, he thought. The sight of the land, the smell of the air, the feel of the wind: it was achingly familiar. "I spent eighteen years here," he said.

"Gods above," Strava said. "Sir! Is this where—"

Kelric held up his hand. "None of you can talk about this without my leave." He had known them for years and trusted them, at least as much as he trusted anyone. But he had left a trail this time, and if and when questions arose, he wanted to be the one who responded.

"We won't say anything," Najo told him. Axer and Strava nodded their agreement.

"I'm not sure what will happen at the city." Kelric rolled a tassel of his Talha between his fingers. "For personal reasons, I may find it hard to speak. You won't know the language. It has roots in common with ours, but it has evolved in isolation for thousands of years. Your nodes can analyze it and eventually provide translations, but at first it may sound like gibberish."

"What hostiles should we be aware of?" Axer asked.

Kelric would have laughed if this hadn't hurt so much. "These people are peaceful. Treat them gently."

"We need a flyer to reach the mountains," Strava said.

Kelric indicated the windrider. "I flew that here ten years ago. If it still works, we can take it to Karn."

"Karn?" Najo asked.

Softly Kelric said, "My home."

The voice on the radio sent a chill up Kelric's spine. The woman spoke in normal tones—in Teotecan. "Sky Racer, I've received your ID. Are you new here? I don't recognize your codes." She paused. "Or your accent."

"It's an old windrider," Kelric said, self-conscious about his rusty Teotecan. "And I haven't been to Karn in years."

"Welcome back." She sounded wary.

"My thanks." Talking to an Outsider was strange. Keeping an Oath of silence for so many years had reinforced his taciturn nature. As Imperator, he had to overcome his reticence to speak, but being here brought it back. In all his time on Coba, he had never had a conversation like this. Piloting a rider wasn't that different from the antique aircraft he flew as a hobby, and he had overheard pilots during his trips as a Calani, so he had an idea of protocols. But this felt surreal.

"Request permission to land," Kelric said.

"Go ahead," the woman said. "Lane Five."

Quis patterns appeared on his screen, providing directions. In the copilot's seat, Najo peered at the symbols, his brow furrowed. Axer and Strava had the two seats in back, and Kelric felt them concentrating on his Teotecan. He could have translated, but he wanted the privacy of his adopted language for a little while longer.

He spread the wing slats of the great metallic hawk and circled the airfield, fitting into the pattern of two other riders. At most Estates, he would have been the only one; Karn, however, had the largest airport on Coba. The woman in the tower tried to draw him into conversation, but he remained noncommittal. She was more curious about a man piloting a rider than about his accent.

Kelric landed reasonably well, though the craft bounced a couple of times. While his guards unstrapped from their seats, he went to the locker in the back. He hung his jacket on a seat. As he pulled off his shirt, a surge of pleasure leaked around Strava's mental shields, which she immediately clamped down. Facing away from her, Kelric smiled. Her appreciation of her shirtless commander embarrassed her far more than him.

He removed his duffle from the locker and donned the white shirt with loose sleeves he had packed. It matched the ones he had worn here, even the embroidery on the cuffs. Next he took out his armbands. For a moment he stood, staring at the engraved circles of gold. Finally he slid them on his arms. They felt strange. He almost took them off again, then decided that for this one day he would wear these signs of his former life.

He shrugged back into his jacket, in part against the chill winds of the Teotecs, but also to hide his bands and gauntlets. His dice bag hung from his belt and his Talha around his neck. Seeing the scarf, people would assume he came from Haka Estate, which was far from Karn in both distance and culture. It would, he hoped, account for his accent and bodyguards. He didn't have the dark coloring of the Haka- born, so he obviously wasn't native to that shimmering desert land. People would probably assume that was why he neither covered his face with the Talha nor wore a robe. In this age, only Haka men went robed. And Calani. But of course no sane person would believe that even a guarded Calani would be out on his own.

Finally they disembarked from the rider. He stood on the tarmac with his guards, wind tugging his clothes, surrounded by spectacular scenery. To the west, the Teotec Mountains rolled out in forested slopes; to the south and east they dropped down in endless ripples of green. The city jumbled north of the port, and the Upper Teotecs towered starkly above it. Clustered beneath those peaks, Karn basked, yellow and white in the morning sunshine from a cloud-flecked sky.

The lane of blue and white cobblestones was as familiar to Kelric as a picture seen a thousand times but never touched. He walked with Najo, Strava, and Axer, marveling at the city he had lived in, yet never experienced. Shops crowded both sides of the street, and wooden signs hung from bars above the doors, creaking in the wind. He passed glassblowers, potters, butchers, and dice makers.

The pure mountain air, exhilarating in its clarity, stirred memories edged with beauty and pain. After Savina had passed away, he had ended up at Varz Estate, even higher in the Teotecs. The Varz queen had been a nightmare. She had forced him into a marriage the day after Savina died, respecting neither his grief nor his need to see his child. He hadn't known which was worse, the physical brutality of her obsession with finding ways to hurt and control him, or the cruelty she could inflict with words. His repressed fury had saturated the Quis and roused the sleeping dragon of violence the Cobans had so long submerged.

It had been more than a year before Ixpar brought him to Karn. In the exquisite serenity of her Calanya, he had begun to heal, but it had been too late by then. His influence had saturated the Quis for nearly eighteen years. Nothing could have stopped the war.

A pack of boys burst out of a side lane, laughing and calling to one another. They gaped at Kelric but kept going, jumping over invisible obstacles with shouts of delight.

"Happy kids," Najo commented.

Kelric couldn't answer. His memories brought such longing. He *missed* Coba. Despite everything he had gone through on this world, he had also spent the best times of his life here.

He knew the location of the market only from maps he had studied as a Calani, and he wasn't sure he could find it. He heard it first, a rumble of voices in the street. The lane crooked around a corner and opened into a bustling plaza like a tributary feeding a great lake. Merchants, stalls, and customers thronged the area. Buildings two or three stories high bordered it, many with balconies. Chains adorned with metal Quis dice hung from their eaves, clinking in the ever- present wind. A tumult of voices poured over him like Teotecan music. So much color and vibrancy and *life*.

"Too many people," Axer said, his hand on his holstered gun.

Kelric barely heard. He walked forward and Cobans flowed around him. Merchants called out wares; children ran and hopped; street artists sang, fiddled, or acted out skits. He looked around for a sausage stand. In the first Quis game he had ever played, the Dahl Manager had bet him one tekal, "enough to buy a sausage in the market." He had owed her Estate that tekal for twenty-eight years. He didn't know the cost of a sausage now, though, besides which, he had no Coban money.

Although people noticed him, they paid less attention than he had expected. Just as he started to relax, a lanky woman in the red and gold of the City Guard stared hard at him. Then she spun around and strode across the plaza.

"Not good," Strava said, watching the woman.

"She knows we're out of place," Najo said. "She's going to tell someone."

"Probably at the Estate." Kelric indicated a fortress of amber-hued stone high on a hill across the city. "The Manager lives there." He might soon see Ixpar, perhaps his children. Just as he had needed time alone after Jeejon had died, so now he needed to prepare; in matters of emotion, it always took him time to adjust. Before he faced Ixpar, he wanted to know how it felt to be part of Coba in a way he had never known when he lived here.

Strava was studying him with that penetrating gaze of hers. "What is a Manager?"

"The queen of a city-estate," Kelric said. "The Manager of Karn, this city, is also the Minister. She rules Coba."

Najo tensed. "Does she pose a danger to your person?"

Danger indeed. He wondered how such a funny question could hurt so much. "No," he said. The only danger was to his heart.

Nearby, a man was sitting against the yellow-stone wall of a shop. He wore fine clothes: a well-tailored white shirt, suede trousers with gold buttons up the seams, and suede boots. His air of confidence evoked a king in his milieu. Quis dice were piled on his low table.

"Someone you know?" Strava asked.

"I've never seen him before," Kelric said.

A woman had sat down at the table, and a crowd was gathering. Kelric stayed back and acted like a Haka man, never smiling. With so many people around, he absorbed a sense of their moods even through his shields. They found him exotic, but he didn't think anyone realized he was more than a visitor from a distant city. Although his guards disconcerted people, no one seemed to realize the Jumblers weren't just big stunners.

The man at the Quis table cleared off his extra dice, and the woman rolled out her set, all their pieces carved from wood. The two players were talking, setting a bet that involved many coins and goods. When they finished, the woman opened the game by playing a blue cylinder.

Conversations drifted around Kelric from the crowd.

"I heard she came all the way from Ahkah to challenge him," a man was saying.

"His reputation is spreading," a woman replied.

"I can't figure why he isn't in a Calanya," another woman said. "Everyone says he's good enough."

"Maybe he has some problem," someone else said.

A man snorted. "Right. A problem with living in a cage."

"Why go in a Calanya?" another man said. "He's making pots of coins here, and he doesn't have to abide by an Oath straight out of the Old Age."

"Did you hear about the offworld Calani in Viasa?" a woman asked. "Viasa Manager kidnapped him, just like in the Old Age."

"Heard he was good-looking," a second woman said.

A third one chuckled. "You want to carry one off, too?"

The other woman bristled. "I don't need to kidnap a man to get a husband."

"You haven't heard?" a man said. "The fellow escaped."

"He did not," a woman said.

"Play Quis with someone from Viasa," he countered. "It's in their dice. Stole himself a windrider and whisked off."

Kelric listened as people embellished Jeremiah's tale. Manager Viasa had built her cover story well; he heard no hints of his own involvement. So he returned his focus to the game. The players competed rather than studying problems or plotting the ascendance of their Estate. They were opposed rather than aligned. It reminded him of the Quis played among Managers, but on a less intense scale, for fun rather than politics.

Both players surely rated the title of Quis Master. They built towers, arches, stacks, bridges, rings, claws, and more. Whenever one gained advantage, the other wrested it back. The man was probably the better player, but the woman seemed more experienced. They vied solely for advantage, without the complexity of Calanya Quis. Kelric had no doubt the man would thrive in a Calanya: he had the gift. He would find such Quis far more satisfying than anything Out here. That he chose freedom despite the price it exacted—never to play true Quis—hinted at far-reaching changes in Coba's social structure.

Suddenly the man grinned. "My game."

"What?" The woman looked up with a start.

Murmurs rolled among the crowd. "He hasn't won . . ."

"His tower has more dice then hers . . ."

"She collapsed his tower . . ."

"But look! He hid an arch."

Axer spoke to Kelric in a low voice. "Do you have any idea what these people are saying?"

"They're arguing over the game," Kelric said, intent on the dice. The man had bridged several structures with an elegant arch, increasing their worth enough for him to claim victory. He had managed it despite his opponent's vigilance because he used dice of a similar color to the surrounding pieces, so it looked as if he were creating lesser structures. A camouflage.

The woman ceded the match, and applause scattered as people slapped their palms against their thighs. After arranging to pay her debt, the woman stood and bowed with respect to the Quis Master. Then she went on her way.

Kelric walked forward.

The gleam in the man's eyes when he saw Kelric was the same as in any culture on any planet, the calculation of a master sizing up a rube. Kelric temporarily eased down his barriers. With so many people at market, it was hard to distinguish moods, but he gathered the man didn't see him as a challenge. Good male Quis players were in a Calanya. He also associated Kelric's large size with low intelligence. The crowd that had watched the last game was dispersing.

"Have a seat," the Quis Master said. "I'm Talv."

As Kelric sat down, he wondered if he had somehow let on that he didn't know market-style Quis. He had never learned to gamble, and he had played nothing but Quis solitaire for ten years. He wasn't certain he could beat Talv. But if he could win a few tekals, he could buy a sausage and indulge his admittedly whimsical desire to repay his old debt.

Talv glanced at the pouch on Kelric's belt. "You've brought your set, I see." He started to remove his extra dice.

Kelric knew if he rolled out jeweled Calanya dice, the game would end before it started. As much as a Quis Master might want to challenge a Calani, he would never risk the ire of a Manager. So he indicated Talv's extra dice. "I prefer those." Speaking with an Outsider was even harder when he was about to play Quis. "Your extra set."

"Are you sure?" Talv yawned. "Most people find it easier to use their own dice. They will be more familiar to you."

It was, of course, something any child knew. "Yours will be fine," Kelric said.

"All right." Talv smirked at him. "What shall we bet?"

"How much for a sausage?"

"A *sausage*?" Talv wasn't even trying to hide his disdain. "One tekal."

So. Same price. "Let us play for two tekals."

Talv shrugged. "Oh, all right. You can start."

"Shouldn't we draw dice?" Going first was an advantage.

"If you insist." Talv pulled a disk out of his pouch and handed over the bag. Kelric took out a lower-ranked piece, a flat square.

"Your move," Kelric said.

"So it is." Talv set a red pyramid in the playing area. He seemed bored, but Kelric could tell he believed the game would be over fast enough to make the tedium bearable.

A sense of *opening* came to Kelric. After so many years of solitaire, sitting here made him feel . . . expanded. It hadn't happened with Jeremiah or Dehya, but he had held back in those games. Now he envisioned a myriad of elegant patterns stemming from that single die that Talv had placed. He set down a grey pyramid with curved sides.

Talv looked up at him. "If your die doesn't touch mine, you aren't building a structure."

"I know," Kelric said.

"Are you sure you want to play that piece?" Talv said. "Nonstandard dice are difficult to use."

Kelric was growing irritated. Calani never disrupted a session, especially not with unasked-for Quis lessons. "It's your move."

"Suit yourself." Talv set down an orange pentahedron. Kelric saw his intent: a queen's spectrum. Few players could manage them; they were too easy to block. Kelric had slipped one past Dehya because she hadn't known the rules, but he wouldn't be that lucky with her again. To succeed against someone who knew Quis, Talv either had to camouflage the spectrum or else hope his opponent was too stupid to see it. He hadn't bothered with a camouflage.

Kelric had met only one other player who could consistently build a queen's spectrum in high-level Quis: Mentar, the Fourth Level at Karn Estate, the elderly widower of the previous Minister. Mentar's Quis had fascinated Kelric. Ixpar had claimed that when he and Kelric played dice, the world shook.

This callow player was no Mentar. Kelric slid an aqua piece against the orange die, disrupting the spectrum. Talv grunted and placed a yellow cube. So. He was trying to recover by turning his spectrum at an angle. Kelric blocked him with an ocher cube.

"Huh." Talv rubbed his chin. He set down a green die, again turning his spectrum.

Enough, Kelric thought. He bridged Talv's pyramid and his own cube with an arch. The cube had a higher rank, so the advantage went to Kelric. He had no idea what points went with it, but he doubted he had enough to win. And indeed, Talv continued playing. Good. Kelric didn't want to stop; he was envisioning an exquisite design with the dice. His Quis thoughts pleased him, and he set about making them reality.

Talv became quieter as they played. His sneer vanished, and he spent more and more time considering his moves. Then he began to sweat.

Kelric built for the sheer beauty of it. Dice spread in

patterns of platonic solids, and geometric elegance covered the table. After a while, Talv stopped sweating, and his game took on a new quality, as if he were appreciating a work of art. When he quit fighting Kelric, he became a better Quis partner. The structures flourished.

With regret, Kelric pulled himself back to here and now. As much as he would have enjoyed playing for hours, he had business to attend. He set down a white sphere. When Talv started to place a ring, Kelric spoke quietly. "It's my game."

Talv lifted his head like a swimmer surfacing from a dive. "Your game?"

A woman behind them said, "I don't believe it!"

Startled, Kelric looked around—and froze.

People.

They had crowded around, more even than for the last game. The woman who played before, the other Quis Master, was gaping at the table. Others looked from her to the board with bewildered expressions.

"What is it?" Talv said.

Kelric turned back to him. He tapped a line of dice that wound across the table, around and through other structures: grey, orange, gold, yellow, yellow-green, green, aqua, blue, indigo, purple, and finally the white sphere.

Murmurs swelled in the crowd. Talv stared at the structure for a long time. Finally he lifted his gaze to Kelric. "I don't think I've ever heard tell of anyone, even the highest of the Calani, building a grand augmented queen's spectrum."

XI
Hawk's Queen

Murmurs spread through the crowd like the hum of dart-bees swarming together. Kelric hadn't intended to draw attention; he had become too caught up in the game. He had to admit, though, it was a good spectrum.

He inclined his head to Talv. "You play well."

"I had thought so," Talv said. "Now I know better."

"You have talent. It's wasted on market Quis."

Talv's voice heated. "You won't lock me in a Calanya!"

"Find other ways to use your talent," Kelric said. "Join the Minister's staff. Work your way up in the Estate Quis."

Talv snorted. "In case you haven't noticed, I'm the wrong sex."

"No laws forbid it."

"Sure they do," Talv said. "They're just unwritten."

"So break them."

"Who *are* you?"

Kelric smiled slightly. "I believe you owe me two tekals."

Talv squinted at him. "Just two?"

"That was the bet."

Talv shook his head, but he handed over two coins. Kelric turned the copper heptagons over in his hand. One side showed a Quis structure, a nested tower that symbolized protection. The other had the portrait of a regal queen.

"That's Ixpar Karn," Kelric said.

"Haven't you ever seen a tekal before?"

He looked up to see Talv watching him oddly. Kelric rose to his feet. "Thank you for the game."

"The honor was mine." Talv stood as well. "That was Quis like nothing I've ever played or even heard of in a Calanya."

It was the highest compliment among Quis Masters. Kelric nodded to indicate honor to his opponent. His guards gathered around him, and he could tell they wanted him away from this attention. He left the table, and people stepped respectfully aside as he walked through the crowd. He felt their awe and curiosity.

Kelric went deeper into the market until he lost himself among the crowds. A familiar aroma teased his nose, wafting from a stall with yellow slats. A sausage merchant stood behind the counter, a plump man with a white apron pulled across his large belly. He beamed as Kelric paused. "What can I get for you, Goodsir?" He motioned at sausages hanging from the rafters. "I've the best spiced-reds from here to Haka."

Kelric indicated a fat specimen. "Kadilish."

"Ah! A man after my own tastes." The merchant wrapped the sausage in waxy paper, accepted Kelric's tekal, and handed over the purchase as if it were the most natural thing to do. For him, it was. To Kelric, it was another watershed.

"Sir," Najo said, his voice uneasy.

Kelric looked up at his worried guard, then turned in the direction Najo indicated. Across the plaza, a street opened into the market. Far beyond it, on its distant hill, the Estate glowed amber in the sunlight. Someone was entering the plaza from the street. Many someones. They came in formation, all wearing the uniform of the City Guard, and they were headed straight for him.

Strava stepped closer, and Kelric was aware of Axer behind him and Najo, tall and solid. He had no idea if the City Guard members approaching him suspected his identity, but if they did, and if Ixpar had sent these guards, then she might well hate him for bringing his people to her world. He had no reason to think she wanted to see him.

Najo, Axer, and Strava drew their guns, the black mammoths glittered harshly in the streaming sunlight, a forbidding contrast to the small, light stunners worn by the Coban guards. Then Najo sighted on the group coming across the market.

Kelric grabbed his arm. "Don't harm them!"

All three of his bodyguards waited, poised and ready. It was in that instant that Kelric realized who walked in the center of the approaching retinue. She had to see the monstrous guns his guards had drawn, but she kept coming without hesitation. She was tall even among Cobans, and her hair blazed like fire, pulled loosely into a braid. Her suede trousers did nothing to hide the muscular lines of her long, long legs. She had a powerful beauty, wild and fierce under a veneer of elegance—a face that could inspire armies and conquer a world.

For Kelric, time slowed down. In this crystalline moment, he thought the two of them would be here forever. She came closer, closer still, and then she was in front of him, her gray eyes filled with incredulity. He had thought of a million words for this moment, planned for days. Seasons. Years. Now the words left him.

"Kelric?" she whispered.

She was one of the few Cobans who had known him as Kelric rather than Sevtar. Seeing her filled him with an emotion he couldn't define, jagged and painful and miraculous. They stood together as if they were inside a bubble, and he wanted to touch her, feel her cheek, her hair, her lips, but he feared to move, lest it burst this tenuous sphere.

He spoke in a voice rough with the feelings he couldn't express. "My greetings, Ixpar."

XII
The Last Band

"It cannot be!" Ixpar reached into her pocket and drew out a half- melted ring of gold. She held it up so he could see the remains of his twelfth armband. "This is all that remains of Kelric Valdoria."

He pulled up his jacket cuff and uncovered the wrist guards embedded in his gauntlets. It astonished him that his hand didn't shake. "These, too."

Ixpar stared at the heavy gold for a long moment. The engraving of a hawk soaring over mountains gleamed in their ancient engravings. Then she looked up at him and spoke in her husky voice, so familiar to him and yet also so new.

"If the god of the dawn has come seeking vengeance," Ixpar said, "I entreat him to reconsider."

"Vengeance?" He blinked. "For what? My shattering Coba?"

Moisture gathered in her eyes. "Ten years is a long time."

Too long. He wanted to say so much, but he could neither move nor speak. It was several moments before he found his voice again, at least enough to ask the question that was always with him. "My children?"

Her face gentled. "They are well."

Softly he asked, "And who came after me?"

"After?" She seemed as lost for words as him.

He forced out the question. "As your Akasi."

"None now."

"You have no husband?"

"I thought not." Her voice caught. "It seems I was wrong."

A sense of homecoming came over him then, more than he had felt since he set foot on her world. He took her into his arms and embraced the wife he had never expected to see again. She stiffened, and his bodyguards loomed around them. Gods only knew what they thought.

Then Ixpar exhaled and put her arms around him, leaning her head against his. He held a stranger, yet he recognized her curves and strength, the sensual power of her body. If he had erred in coming here, it was too late to turn back.

In this incredible instant, he didn't care.

XIII
Space-time Enigma

The fifth implosion happened in Sphinx Sector, in deep space. Jaibriol heard about it while he was dining with Iraz Gji, the Diamond Minister, and Gji's wife, Ilina. Gji and Ilina were impeccable Aristos, their black hair glittering in the cool light, their eyes a clear, crystalline red. Just like Jaibriol. He had even become used to seeing himself that way. In his youth, gold had streaked his hair. Never again. Now he looked the perfect Highton.

Jaibriol had expected Tarquine to join them, but she had vanished, he had no idea where. He had no intention of admitting he couldn't keep track of his empress, so he asked his cousin Corbal to join him instead, to make her absence less noticeable.

They relaxed in the Silver Room, a parlor with holoscreens for walls and plush divans where they could recline, sipping wine and watching the broadcast about the implosion. A taskmaker read the news, which meant she could speak as directly as she pleased; indirect speech was only required from Aristos with other Aristos.

"Space-time ripples have spread outward from the disturbance in every direction," she said. "It is by far the most extreme of the five events."

Jaibriol grimaced as he listened, stretched out on his divan. If this last blast had happened here, it sounded like it could have destroyed the palace and the surrounding coast.

"As to why the disturbances are occurring," the broadcaster continued, "scientists postulate that the fabric of space-time has weakened in the region of space where an implosion takes place."

"Weakened?" Gji asked, incredulous. "That's like saying the sky or the air weakened. It makes no sense."

Jaibriol sat up, swinging his feet to the floor while he touched a finger-panel on his wrist comm.

Robert's voice came out of the mesh. "Muzeson, here."

"Robert, get me the head of the team at the university studying this implosion business," Jaibriol said.

"Right away, Your Highness."

"Odd little events, aren't they?" Ilina said languidly. She was lying on her divan, sleek in a black diamond bodysuit that fit her like a second skin. She sipped her Taimarsian wine. "Perhaps a Highton sneezed and his exhalations shook up space."

Her husband laughed, relaxed in a lounger. Although he had drunk several glasses of wine, he hardly seemed affected. Either he held his liquor remarkably well or else meds in his body kept him from becoming intoxicated. "Such exhalations would surely do more than shake space, eh?" Gji said. "Perhaps they could cause a black hole such as the one at the center of the galaxy."

Jaibriol didn't know whether to be astounded or exasperated. Eube and Skolia might be on the verge of war, assassination attempts threatened to destabilize the Imperialate, space-time was falling apart, and all they could talk about was the purported superiority of Hightons, even to the extent, it seemed, of causing galactic formation. He had learned to deal with Aristos, but sometimes it truly taxed his diplomatic skills.

The feeling was probably mutual. He knew Gji and Ilina were irritated that he hadn't offered them providers as part of tonight's entertainment. He had no intention of letting them transcend with the slaves he had inherited from his grandfather. By not doing it, he weakened his standing with them, but good Lord, he couldn't let them torture the people in his care. He hadn't lost that much of his soul.

Most Aristos considered him eccentric, particularly in his avoidance of providers. True, fidelity to one's spouse was expected; in castes where heredity and genetics meant everything, adultery brought high penalties. But that didn't preclude Aristos doing whatever they wanted with providers. Such slaves weren't considered human. It baffled Aristos that Jaibriol eschewed the pleasure girls offered to him and instead preferred his wife.

What stunned Jaibriol most, though, was that Tarquine did the same for him. She refused to discuss the matter, yet during nine years of marriage, she had never to his knowledge taken a provider. He told himself she made that choice for him and not because no one could measure up to Kelric. Sometimes he almost believed that.

Corbal was reclining on his divan as he watched the broadcast, which had shifted into a scientific discussion about bubbles frothed in space-time. "Who would have thought," he mused, "that carbonation could be such a problem?"

Jaibriol smiled, just slightly, as supposedly befitted the emperor. He was aware of Gji watching him with a speculative gaze. When he glanced at the Diamond Minister, Gji bowed his head to indicate respect. Jaibriol tried to probe his mind, but as soon as he relaxed his defenses, the pressure from Gji and Ilina swamped his empathic reception. He wanted to flee the agony of their presence, and he had to force himself to keep his barriers down. Gji's ire at what he considered Jaibriol's lack of hospitality came through strongly, and also a hint of something else. Suspicion? Something to do with Corbal.

The pain was unbearable. Jaibriol gave up probing and raised his barriers. He knew some Aristos suspected Corbal of showing too much affection for Sunrise, his provider. He didn't think Gji's concern involved Corbal's private life, though. Whatever disturbed Gji went a lot farther than Sunrise.

Jaibriol's comm crackled, and Robert's voice came through. "Sire, I have Professor Cathleen Quenzer on comm."

"Put her through," Jaibriol said.

A woman spoke. "My honor at your esteemed presence, Your Highness."

Relieved to speak with a taskmaker, Jaibriol slipped into direct speech. "Doctor Quenzer, what is going on with these implosions?"

"We just received word of the fifth," she said. "We are optimistic it will provide us with more information."

Apparently she was used to dealing with Aristos; that sounded like Hightonese for *We don't have a clue*.

"Why do they keep happening?" he asked.

She spoke carefully. "Think of space-time as cloth. It's fraying in some places. When it gets too thin, it rips, and we register that as an implosion."

"But why is it happening?"

"We're working nonstop to understanding the causes."

Jaibriol knew she wasn't going to admit to the emperor that she didn't know. He doubted the scientists would believe he had no intention of taking punitive steps if they didn't give him immediate answers. His predecessors had unfortunately ensured that such an atmosphere reigned in Qoxire. So he just said, "Keep me informed."

"Absolutely, Your Highness." She sounded relieved.

After Jaibriol signed off, Corbal said, "It would hamper repairs in the Amethyst Wing if the damage spread."

Jaibriol wasn't exactly sure what Corbal meant, but he thought his cousin was asking if they expected more implosions in the palace. So he said, "One can never be certain."

Gji had his full concentration on Corbal, with a hardness in his attitude he hadn't shown before. "It would certainly hamper repairs to spread damage, whether in a palace or an entire sector of space."

Corbal met his gaze with a guarded expression. "Indeed."

Jaibriol wondered what Minister Gji thought Corbal had done. He didn't think Corbal knew, either. It apparently had some link to a repair. Probing, Jaibriol said, "In the end, though, repairs usually have the desired effect. Improvement."

Gji took a sip of his wine. "Assuming the need for them didn't cause a grounding elsewhere."

Grounding? What the blazes—

Then it hit Jaibriol. Gji meant the scandal with the Janq pirate fleet. The grounding of the Janq ships had dealt a fatal blow to the Ivory Sector mercantile coalition. For some obscure reason, Gji believed Corbal had something to do with that fiasco.

Jaibriol took a swallow of the wine he had barely touched. Then he said, "One could always go to sea somewhere else." It seemed glaringly obvious to him; if they quit trying to sell Skolians *as* Eubian goods, they could sell Eubian goods *to* Skolians.

"Sailing to new shores can be a risk," Gji said cautiously. He seemed uncertain how to interpret Jaibriol's remark.

Ilina waved her hand. "Oh, sailing is a pleasure. I do love cruises. Perhaps, Your Highness, you know of some good ones."

"I wonder if we might try new routes," Jaibriol said.

"One can always look," Gji said. He glanced from Corbal to Jaibriol. "However, no reason exists to give up the old." An edge had entered his voice, and in Highton, that had layers of meaning, none of them good.

Corbal was as cool and as unreadable as always, so Jaibriol fell back on his advantage that no other Aristo shared; he probed Corbal's mind. He couldn't lower his barriers much, but it was enough to sense that his cousin understood his idea about trade with the Skolians far better than he let on—and that Corbal didn't like it at all.

With Gji and Corbal both on edge, Jaibriol suspected that if he pushed the idea now, they would reject it. So he said only, "Indeed," relying on that annoying but useful all-purpose word.

Then Jaibriol changed the subject by appearing not to change the subject. "These implosions add many layers to the idea of giving up the old," he said. It meant absolutely nothing, but what the hell. It would distract their attention while they tried to puzzle it out.

Corbal slanted a look at him. "I should not like to see space imploding everywhere, like bubbles popping in froth. Or words."

Jaibriol almost laughed. He knew Corbal meant his words were froth, which was quite true at the moment. "That would be strange," he said. "Five events already, from here to—"

Then he stopped, as the realization hit him.

He knew where the implosions were headed.

Kelric stood with Ixpar by a high window that overlooked Karn. Houses clustered along the streets and down the hills, and plumberry vines grew in a profusion of purple and blue flowers, climbing walls and spiraling up street lamps. So many times he had stood savoring the view from this window.

"I'd forgotten how beautiful it is here," he said.

Ixpar was leaning against the wall across the window from him. "I never did."

He turned to find her looking at him, not the city. She had that quality he remembered well, a serenity that came when she wasn't preoccupied with politics or war. Soon she would be pacing and planning again, her agile mind occupied with affairs of state. But she let him see this reflective side she showed so few people, indeed that few knew existed. She had always been compelling, but the years had added a maturity that made it difficult to stop gazing at her face.

"You look good," Kelric said.

Her expression gentled. "To see you again is a miracle." Then her smiled faded. "But I fear your reasons for coming. What happens now? Will Skolia retaliate against Coba?"

"I won't allow it."

"You can't stop the Imperator."

Softly he said, "Yes, I can."

Her posture stiffened. "You said otherwise ten years ago."

It was hard to tell her. Once she knew what he had become, this bubble that held them would disintegrate. So he said only, "The Imperator has changed the status of Coba."

"We no longer have the Restriction?"

"As of this morning, no. Coba is Protected."

She clenched the window frame, and her face paled. "What does it mean?"

His words were coming out all wrong; he had meant to reassure her, not cause alarm. He tried again. "In some ways it's like Restriction. A Protected world is even harder to visit. But you decide who comes here. You control what happens. And your people now have Skolian citizenship."

She stared at him. "Why would your brother do this thing?"

"He didn't."

"Then who did?"

The world was too quiet. Muffled. His voice seemed far away. "Me."

For a long time she just looked at him. Finally she spoke in a low voice. "Do I say Your Majesty? Or Imperator Skolia?"

Heat spread in his face. "Call me Kelric. Hell, Sevtar."

She started to answer, then stopped as if she had glimpsed something truly strange. "Am I your wife by Skolian law?"

He thought of the Closure he had cancelled. "Yes."

"Doesn't that make me the Imperator's consort?"

The answer welled up within him, one word he had waited so long to say. "Yes."

"Winds above," she murmured. "I am honored. But Kelric, that changes nothing. Your empire can still destroy us."

He knew she would never have allowed Jeremiah Coltman to study them if she had felt all offworld influence would bring harm. "Change *will* come. You can't hide forever. Must it be for the worse?"

Her gaze never wavered. "We would be just as wrong to deny the danger now as we were when we took you into the Calanya."

Kelric knew her fear. He shared it. Then he thought of the Assembly vote that had strengthened his position. "I control ISC now. My influence becomes more established every year. I can set it up so no Skolian ever sets foot here." He struggled for the words. "A parent has to let a child become an adult. Coba can't live protected all its life."

She regarded him dourly. "We are not children."

He suspected he would make it worse if he continued these inarticulate attempts to express himself. So he said, "Play Quis with me."

❖ ❖ ❖

Ixpar placed the first die.

They sat at a table by the window and played dice at its highest level. Ixpar had always been brilliant, and the years had added even greater depth to her Quis. She wove patterns of other Managers into her structures, other Calani, other Estates. She synthesized a world into her Quis with a virtuosity that took his breath. Her patterns spoke of how the war had drenched Coba in violence and ruin. The recovery had taken years, but they were healing. He would destroy their hard-won stability.

Kelric molded the structures to portray positive off-world effects. New technologies. Better educations. Health care. The mothers of his children had received nanomeds from him and passed them to his son and daughter; they would all live longer, healthier lives as a result. All Cobans could have those advantages. He wove patterns of Jeremiah; in allowing an offworlder here, Ixpar had dared take a chance. He had expected Jeremiah to create turmoil, but the youth's Quis had told another story, how he benefited Coba.

Ixpar turned his patterns into comparisons of Skolia and Earth, symbolized by Kelric and Jeremiah. One aggressive and large; the other gentle and scholarly. One overwhelming; the other seeking friendship. Jeremiah would never hurt anyone; Kelric was the military commander of an empire.

He saw himself through her Quis and wasn't sure he knew that man, one with great strength of character, but also one who wielded a power so immense, he could crush them without realizing it. He created patterns showing her how he would work with the Managers of Coba. He would sit at Quis with them. Ixpar's eyes blazed as she played fire opals, garnets, rubies. Angry dice. Never would she agree to have her Calani play Quis with other Managers! Her vehemence startled him. That he sat in the Assembly as Imperator—*that* she could deal with. But for him to reveal his Quis to other Managers went against every principle she held true.

So he showed her harsher reality: someday the Imperialate *would* find Coba. Without his intervention, it could do them great harm. Or perhaps, despite his best attempts to prevent it, the Traders would conquer her world and enslave her people. Coba should join the interstellar community on their terms. They should open or close their world according to *their* choice. They needed a gatekeeper. Him.

Ixpar countered with jagged patterns of destruction, of his life on Coba and the upheavals that followed. Her dice never accused, never damned. She blamed Coba. But he knew the truth. He had left terrible wounds here.

Kelric paused, subdued. This intense session, with someone he hadn't seen for ten years, drained him. She believed that to protect Coba, they should strengthen its isolation until they could survive even if he died. He took a breath and continued the session. With the utmost care, he molded new patterns. All the finesse he lacked in the blunt power of his mind and body, he put into his dice. He had been a prisoner before, on Coba, with neither the understanding nor opportunity to control his effect on the Quis. Now he and Ixpar had that knowledge. Together they could make a better world.

Her Quis called him idealistic. Her patterns revealed the deep differences between his people and hers, his way of life and that of Coba. Skolia would saturate the Quis until it swamped Coba's unique, irreplaceable culture.

It doesn't have to be that way, he answered. He sifted a new idea into his dice: Quis was like the mesh his people had created in Kyle space. To open a gate to the Kyle, they needed only a telop, or telepathic operator. The most gifted telops managed the star-spanning net that wove the Imperialate into a coherent whole. The Dyad created and powered that mesh.

Quis was a web. It, too, linked a civilization. Cobans communicated and took information from the world-spanning game; the more adept players acted as operators; the rare geniuses who dedicated their lives to Quis defined its highest levels. The best players read moods, even thoughts, from the dice. With both Quis and the Kyle, it became hard to tell where the web left off and the mind began. Intellect and emotion; technology and art; communication and intuition: it all blended. If Coba and Skolia combined their remarkable cultures, with care, they could achieve great marvels. At their best, they could produce a civilization greater than the sum of the two alone.

And at their worst? Ixpar asked.

He made no false promises; she could pick up nuances in his Quis he never meant to reveal. She knew his doubts, which had never left him. But she would also recognize his belief that he could protect Coba. She would have to choose which to trust.

Their session lasted hours. He had to return to Parthonia,

yet long after he should have left for the starport, they continued to play. Their guards kept anyone from disturbing them. The people of Karn surely knew by now their Minister was playing Quis with a Calani returned from the dead. Windriders would carry the news to other cities.

Within days, all Coba would know: the Minister had sat at Quis with the Imperator.

Afternoon had melted into evening by the time Kelric and Ixpar pushed back from the table. He stood up, his joints creaking. "A good session," he said. More than good. It was worth ten years of solitaire.

"So it was," Ixpar murmured. She rose to her feet, and they stood together at the window above Karn. Long shadows from the mountains stretched across the city.

Leaning against the wall, Kelric gazed across the window at his wife. She looked as fit today as ten years ago. And as erotic. Quis with her had always had a sensual undercurrent.

"It's been a long time," he said.

She regarded him with smoky eyes. "Too long."

Kelric heard the invitation in her voice. He grasped her arm and drew her forward, into his embrace. But she resisted, her palms against his shoulders.

"I have a thing to say," she told him. "You should know."

That didn't sound good. "Know what?"

"I remarried."

Kelric stiffened. Had he misinterpreted her mood? His voice cooled. "You said you had no Akasi."

"I don't." Sadness touched her voice. "He passed away."

"Oh." *Idiot*, he told himself. "I'm sorry."

"It's been several years." Her face was pensive. "After the war, the Council felt I should remarry. As expected."

As expected. By law, the Minister had to marry a Calani, preferably the man with the highest level among the suitable candidates. "You mean Mentar?" As the previous Minister's consort, the Fourth Level had been more than twice Ixpar's age.

She nodded. "Together, he and I knew more of the Quis than anyone else alive. We had much in common."

He heard what she didn't say. "Did you love him?"

"I always had great affection for him."

"More as a father figure, I thought."

"I loved him." She paused. "In a quiet sort of way."

Kelric told her about Jeejon then. When he finished, Ixpar spoke with pain. "We have each done as we should. But sometimes, I wish . . . we hadn't lost so much."

"I, too," he said.

Ixpar took his hand. Then she led him to a private door of the Rosewood Suite.

That evening, in the last rays of gilded sunlight slanting through the windows, they lay in the rosewood bed where they had loved each other so many years ago. Outside, in the city below and the world beyond, life continued, people working, bargaining, playing Quis. Beyond Coba, stars shone, worlds turned in their celestial dance, and ships streaked among the settlements of thriving humanity. They were all oblivious to two people, neither of them young, who had lost so much in their lives, but for a brief time in each other's arms, found a bittersweet happiness.

XIV
Cathedral

Jaibriol was working at his private console when Tarquine strolled into their bedroom. Her windblown hair was tousled around her shoulders, and she had on a violet jumpsuit and boots suitable for weather far colder than here in the seaside capital.

"Where have you been?" Jaibriol asked.

She came over and leaned down to kiss him. "My pleasure at your company as well, my esteemed husband."

"Tarquine, don't."

She straightened up, her face composed as if she had just been out for a moment rather than slinking into the room three hours late. "You look tired. Perhaps you brood too much."

Jaibriol sat back and crossed his arms. "And I imagine you must be hungry, my dear wife, since you missed dinner."

She went to the antique wardrobe against the wall and took out a silken black nightshift. "I'm sure I'll satisfy my hunger," she murmured.

205

Jaibriol flushed, and tried not to stare as she changed into the shift. She had a beautifully toned body, long and lean, with flawless skin and legs that could wrap around him in ways that right now he didn't want to think about.

"I'm not as distractible as you think," he said, though she never deliberately played such games. Just being herself, she affected him even after ten years, perhaps more now that he knew what waited for him under the velvet bedcovers. But he couldn't let her sidetrack him. "Where were you tonight?"

She smoothed her shift into place around her thighs. "You could have asked Corbal to that dinner with Minister Gji." Her gaze darkened. "I'm sure he would have been pleased to join you. He's always happy to insinuate himself."

"He's my kin. And as a matter of fact, I did ask him."

"You trust him too much."

"Do I now?" He narrowed his gaze. "For some inexplicable reason, the Diamond Minister seems to think our good Lord Corbal is responsible for exposing the Janq merchant fleets as pirates."

Her response was barely detectable, just a quirk of her eyebrow. But Jaibriol noticed, and he dropped his barriers in time to catch a flicker of her hidden emotions. She hadn't expected him to figure out the business about Corbal.

Tarquine came over with that slow walk of hers that made his throat go dry and sweat break out on his brow. At times like this, he thought she ought to be required to register it as a deadly weapon.

She leaned against the console, her gaze languorous. "You seem flushed."

Jaibriol spoke coolly. "Corbal Xir is one of the savviest people I know. He's too smart to let someone divert blame to him for something he didn't do. No one could manage it." He paused. "Almost no one."

"I wouldn't know."

"No, of course not. You never do." He stood up, facing her eye to eye. "Don't undermine my advisors."

"You worry too much."

"I mean it, Tarquine." Married to her, he would be a fool not to worry. "And where the hell were you tonight?" Perhaps direct speech would startle her into an admission.

It didn't work. Her lips curved, and her lids lowered over her tilted eyes. "Such passionate language."

Jaibriol couldn't get anything from her mind except arousal. Over the years, she had learned to shield her thoughts, but at the moment, she wasn't trying. Knowing he excited her that much was more stimulating than any seduction. Hightons were supposed to marry for political or economic reasons, not passion, but with Tarquine, he was never sure about anything. She kept him forever off balance.

He turned and walked away from her. Unfortunately, that meant he was approaching the bed, which led to the obvious train of thought. Even as he tried not to imagine her body stretched across the sheets, he caught a hazy, sexualized image from her mind: himself, his eyes full of desire, his muscles straining against her as they made love. He almost groaned aloud. He had to get a grip.

Jaibriol swung around. "You set him up."

"Him?" Her gaze went up his body, and he remembered he had on only his trousers and a shirt open at the neck, not even his shoes. And of course, the more direct the speech between lovers, the more erotic the invitation.

"Corbal," he said, flustered. "You set up Corbal."

"How could I do that? I had no idea you would invite him in my stead."

"Like hell."

She frowned at him, and her exasperation felt real, though he wasn't certain if his claim about Corbal caused it or his insistence they keep talking instead of going to bed.

"Jai, I went to a meeting with the chief executive officers of the Onyx Sector textile guilds," she said. "It lasted longer than I expected."

He felt as if he had run into a wall. Such meetings were her job, after all. After a moment, he said, "Was it productive?"

"As much as ever, I suppose." She tilted her head. "What about your dinner with Gji?"

"I set the groundwork for suggesting trade relations with the Skolians." He shrugged. "We'll see." She would figure out soon enough the dinner had gone nowhere.

She glanced down at his console. "You're studying physics?"

"Just those implosions." He came back and touched a panel. A holomap formed in the air showing the locations of the five events. Although they were scattered in space, they lay roughly in a line, the most recent on the edge of Sphinx Sector. It was a long way from the Sphinx Sector Rim Base, but if they veered in their path, they would go through that military complex. He was convinced they were headed in that direction, though where the next implosion would occur, if it did at all, he had no idea.

The Lock was at the SSRB. Jaibriol had met Kelric there ten years ago, just after the Imperator killed the singularity. Now he wondered if Kelric had simply put it to sleep.

Maybe it was trying to wake up.

Tarquine trailed her finger over his lips. "If you relaxed more, you would worry less."

Jaibriol gave up trying to resist then and pulled her against him. As he closed his arms around her, she kissed him, her lips full and hungry. With a groan, he drew her to the bed, and they tumbled onto the velvet covers. He dragged off the shift she had so recently donned, ripping it apart. He was barely aware of her undressing him. She was fire and ice, tempting him into the depths of her passion, until he lost all sense of himself and melded with her, body and mind.

And when they lay sated and tangled in the rumpled sheets, he wondered if he had also lost part of his soul to her.

On the world Parthonia, Kelric waited in the Cathedral of Memories. Its sweeping wings graced Selei City, where elegant towers rose into the lavender sky. He gazed out a one-way window with a gold tint from its polarization. Like him, perhaps? Metal man, people said. A war machine.

Years ago on Coba, a friend had taught Kelric an ancient phrase that the fellow said was more about people than metal: "Iron chills whatever life it can hold, but never frozen is the touch of gold." In the times when Kelric wondered if he had lost his humanity as Imperator, he reminded himself of that saying. At least one person had seen him as warm rather than the case-hardened warlord.

The Royal Concourse, a wide path of white stone, led from the cathedral steps outside to an open-air coliseum about half a kilometer away. Metallic dust sparkled in the walkway, tiny nanosystems that monitored pedestrians, just as ISC security monitored every micron of the city. People lined the concourse and thronged the coliseum. Sunlight streamed everywhere, vendors sold food, and military police paced among the crowds. Breezes stirred flags with the Imperialate insignia on tall poles in front of the coliseum.

The Promenade was among the most popular Skolian festivals. A person needed stratospheric connections to obtain a ticket. But the spectacle would be broadcast throughout the Imperialate, and people everywhere would celebrate. Kelric hoped they enjoyed themselves. As exciting as it might be for the rest of the universe, it was excruciating for him and his security teams.

A door swooshed behind him, and he turned to see Najo, the captain of his bodyguards. The Jagernaut crossed the chamber and saluted, arms out, wrists crossed, fists clenched.

Kelric returned the salute. "Any news from the port?"

"Nothing, sir." Sympathy showed in his eyes. "I'm sorry."

Kelric felt heavy. He wanted to withdraw from the too-bright day and sit in private. He couldn't, so he just said, "Thank you."

"They still might come."

"Perhaps." But Kelric knew it was too late for Ixpar to change her mind. He had failed to convince her.

Ten days had passed since his trip to Coba. Ixpar had declined to return with him, and he hadn't even had a chance to meet his children yet. He wanted them all by his side so much it hurt. But the day he had sworn his Calanya Oath to Ixpar, he had vowed to protect her Estate. He would keep his Oath. Just as he had spent all those years secluded in a Calanya, so now he would do the same for Coba, secluding a world.

Music filtered from outside into the chamber where Kelric stood. It was the Skolian anthem, "The Lost Desert." Its rapturous melody could lift the spirit, but its bittersweet quality often brought people to tears.

The House of Jizarian began the Promenade. A man announced them, his voice resonating from spinning orbs that floated above the concourse and coliseum. As the music shifted into the brighter theme of their House, the Jizarians poured out of the cathedral. Children ran down the steps and onto the Concourse. The adults followed in traditional costume, the women in red silken tunics and trousers, the men in shirts and trousers sewn with glinting threads. Their hair gleamed, mostly dark, but a few with lighter coloring. Kelric even saw a redhead.

The matriarch came last, normally with dignity and age, but this one was barely twenty-four, full of exuberance and vim, having inherited her title when her mother passed away several years ago. Her hair bounced about her shoulders as she waved to the crowd. The spectators cheered and threw flowers as the Jizarians nobles walked the concourse.

"An attractive House," Najo said. "Vibrant."

"So they are," Kelric said, intent on his console. Everything looked secure. He had an odd feeling, though, like a pressure on his mind. He checked the room where his family waited: Dehya, Roca, his siblings and their families, including children. It hurt to see them. In all his time on Coba, he had never been allowed to share in the lives of his children, nor did it seem now that it would ever happen.

Najo was watching his face. He spoke quietly. "They are happy and well, sir. Safe."

Kelric couldn't answer. He knew Najo didn't mean his brothers and sisters. His guard was too perceptive, and Kelric didn't think he could talk about it, not now, maybe never.

Outside, the Jizarians were entering the coliseum. The House of Nariz left the cathedral, a small family of moderate lineage in conservative dress, dark pants and blue shirts. The Akarads came next, a line of merchants with thriving fleets. The men wore red-brown robes over their clothes, but in a casual manner, letting them billow behind them in the breezes. The Shazarindas followed, less strict in their demeanor, wearing a great deal of yellow.

Kelric shifted his weight, restless and unsettled. He cycled through views of the city and countryside. Then he paged his intelligence chief in the orbital defense system.

The chief's voice came over the comm. "Major Qahot." She was the sister of the Qahot who worked for Kelric down here; together, they formed an inimitable security team.

"Any problems?" Kelric asked.

"None, sir. Is anything wrong?"

"No. Nothing." Kelric wished he knew what bothered him.

Outside, the women in the House of Kaaj were descending the cathedral steps. Just the women: they kept their men secluded. In their traditional garb, they resembled ancient Ruby warriors, with leather and metal armor, curved swords at their hips, and glinting spears. In real life they ran robotics corporations, but right now they reminded Kelric of paintings he had seen of Old Age queens on Coba.

He spoke into the comm. "Qahot, let me know if you notice anything strange."

"Aye, sir." She paused as voices spoke in the background. Then she said, "We had an unauthorized ship request to land about an hour ago."

Kelric tensed, afraid to hope. "Who? And why?" He had left authorization for Ixpar, but the Coban port and its ships were decades out of date. Maybe security here hadn't recognized the codes. Maybe Ixpar hadn't realized that. Or maybe he was raising futile hopes within himself.

"They're tourists," Qahot said. "They didn't realize the festival is off-limits. We have them in custody, five men and six women, name of Turning. We're running checks."

"Did any of the women give her name as Ixpar Karn or ask for me?"

"No, sir," Qahot said. "Are you expecting someone?"

"No, not really." Kelric pushed down his disappointment. "Keep checking them out. Let me know if anything comes up."

"Yes, sir."

Outside, the Vibarrs were striding toward the coliseum. Their late matriarch, an aggressive powerhouse, had broken with tradition and named her son as her heir. Now he led the House, all bankers and lawyers and wildcatters, secure in their power and wealth. The Rajindias came next, the House that provided ISC with biomech adepts, the neurological specialists who treated psions. They were fierce, but less so than the hawklike Kaajs.

Hawk.

Insight came to Kelric like a rush, as a fire might flare at a campsite. Turning. *Tern.* A bird, yes, but they had the wrong one, probably because of language differences. Not *tern. Hawk.*

He spoke into his comm. "Qahot?"

"Here, sir," the major said.

"The leader of those tourists—is it a woman?"

"Yes, sir."

"With red hair?"

"No, sir."

Disappointment flooded over Kelric, even though he had kept trying not to hope.

Then Qahot added, "Her hair is orange. Like copper."

Kelric exhaled, long and slow, absorbing her words. Then he said, "I want to talk to her."

When the Majdas walked the Concourse, they left no doubt who dominated the noble Houses. With their black hair, high cheekbones, and great height, they embodied the quintessential Skolian aristocrat. Most of the women wore uniforms, primarily the dark green of the Pharaoh's Army, but also the blue of the Imperial Fleet. Vazar strode

along in her Jagernaut leathers, skintight black with glinting silver studs.

The Majdas also secluded their princes. But the same
indomitable will that infused their women manifested in
the men. More than a few of their brothers and sons had
defied tradition. They walked with the House, professors,
architects, scientists, artists, and military officers, tall and
imposing.

Naaj came last. Queen of Majda. She neither waved
nor smiled. She simply walked. It was enough.

Najo stood with Kelric at the window. "Impressive."

Kelric smiled dryly. "They've raised it to an art."

Then the announcer said, "The Ruby Dynasty."

A deluge of children flooded out of the cathedral,
Kelric's nephews and nieces, grandnephews, grandnieces,
and on down the generations. They waved enthusiastically
at the crowd, who cheered their approval of the dynasty's
beautiful progeny. Kelric had intended that effect; the
more his young kin charmed the public, the better. It was
good public relations.

His siblings came next, first his sister Aniece, small and
curved, with dark curls and gold eyes. Her husband Lord
Rillia walked at her side. Kelric's brother Shannon followed,
a willowy Blue Dale Archer with a bow and quiver on his
back. Then Denric the schoolteacher. Soz should have
been next; since her death, they had left a gap in the
Promenade, in her honor.

After a moment, Havryl walked down the steps, his
bronzed hair tossing in the wind, his toddler nestled in the
crook of his arm. His wife came with him, holding their
baby. Kelric's brother Del and his sister Chaniece, who

were twins, would have followed, but they had stayed home, tending to the family duties. Another lull came in the Promenade, in honor of Althor, who had died in the Radiance War.

A hum sounded behind Kelric. He turned to see that Najo had moved to the door.

"Sir?" Najo looked at him with a question in his gaze.

Kelric nodded as if he were ready, though he wasn't and might never be. But he had set these events in motion and he would never turn back.

Najo tapped his gauntlet and the door shimmered open. A woman stood in the archway. She had piled her hair on her head and threaded it with blue beads. Her leather and bronzed clothes evoked the warriors of her ancestors, and a keen intelligence filled her gaze.

As Kelric crossed the chamber, the tread of his boots on the tiles seemed to echo. He stopped in front of her, trying to absorb that she stood *here,* out of context with every memory he had of her, in a place he had never expected to see her.

"Ixpar." For him, that one word, at this moment, held more meaning than he could sort out. He knew only that his life had improved immeasurably.

She inclined her head. "My greetings."

He indicated the window. "Will you join me?"

"It would be my honor."

He felt painfully formal. He knew her so well, yet he barely knew her at all. As they reached the window, exclamations from the crowd swelled over the monitors. With Ixpar at his side, Kelric turned to look out the window.

A woman was descending the steps, a vision in rose-hued

silk that rippled around her figure. The announcer said, "Roca Skolia, Foreign Affairs Councilor."

"That is your mother?" Ixpar asked. When Kelric nodded, she said, "No wonder."

He glanced at her. "No wonder what?"

Her voice had that smoky quality. "No wonder you were the man whose face launched a thousand windriders into battle."

He crooked a smile at her. "What, it scared them that much?"

"Hardly," she murmured.

It didn't surprise him that she knew the tale of Helen of Troy from Earth's history; she would never have allowed Jeremiah to study Coba if she hadn't first studied him and his people. Kelric took her hands. "It's not too late to change your mind." He needed her to be sure she wanted this.

She spoke quietly. "I thought a long time before I boarded that ship in the port. Is this a mistake? No clear answer shows itself when I project futures with my Quis. Some patterns evolve into ruin. Others are incredible. Even beautiful." She stopped. He waited, and finally she said, "The time comes when we must take a risk. To decide our own future."

An odd silence fell over the room, coming from outside. Kelric hadn't realized how noisy the crowds were until they quieted. He glanced at the window—and froze.

A robed and cowled figure with four guards stood at the top of the cathedral steps. A Talha scarf wrapped around his head within the cowl, hiding his face, except for his eyes.

Kelric shot a look at Ixpar.

She answered his unspoken question by saying, simply, "Yes."

His emotions swelled, too jumbled to untangle. He stared at the robed figure. "I can't see him."

"He's never gone in public without robes," Ixpar said. "He's never even left the Calanya."

Dismay surged within him. "I would never force—"

She set her hand on his arm. "He *wanted* to come." Dryly she added, "Manager Varz was the one who balked. It took a lot to convince her."

It didn't surprise Kelric. It stunned him that she had allowed her Calani to travel at all, let alone off the planet. Apparently the current Varz Manager was more human than the monster he had known.

The announcer hadn't spoken; he was probably reading whatever notes Kelric's officers had delivered to him when the geneticists finished their tests. Kelric had ordered the tests the moment Ixpar told him who had come with her. He could almost hear the question whispered among the spectators. *Who is that?* It had been Kelric's question as well, for twenty-eight years. Finally he would have an answer.

With firm motions, the man pushed back his hood and pulled down his Talha. Kelric doubted anyone watching right now except he and Ixpar understood the significance of that action. A Hakaborn prince never showed his face to the public.

The man had large eyes. Violet eyes. His curly hair was as dark as the Hakaborn, but it glinted with metallic highlights. He stood tall and strong, his head lifted. He had a strange look, though, as if he were about to step off a cliff. Kelric knew the courage it took for him to do this, he who had surely never expected even to leave seclusion, let along walk before trillions on an interstellar broadcast. It was a quieter bravery than the dramatic acts of the Jagernauts Kelric had known at that age, but that made it no less real.

Then the announcer said, "Jimorla Haka Varz Valdoria."

Startled voices erupted among the crowd, and Kelric released a silent exhale. To use the Valdoria name at this point in the Promenade identified Jimorla as his child, as binding a declaration as any legal document. He had hoped and believed it for so long, but he had never been sure. Jimorla wasn't a Ruby psion, so he couldn't use the Skolia name, but he was Kelric's firstborn in every other aspect and would take his place in the line of succession to the Ruby Throne.

Jimorla visibly braced his shoulders. He descended the stairs with his guards and strode along the Concourse, his robe billowing out behind him. For the first time, a Calani walked openly on another world. Coba—and Skolia— were changed forever. Quis would come to the Imperialate.

A strained voice interrupted his thoughts. "Sir," Najo said.

Kelric turned to see Najo standing by the console, which blazed with lights. Najo had that same expression he had worn when Kelric revealed he had spent eighteen years on Coba, the look of a man who knew he stood witness to the making of history.

"People are trying to contact you," Najo said.

"Who?" Kelric could guess: the leaders of an empire. They had just learned they had a new crown prince.

"The First Councilor of the Assembly," Najo said. "General Majda, Admiral Bloodmark, Primary Tapperhaven, your mother, your brothers, your sister, the gene team you summoned, and several councilors of the Inner Circle."

Kelric noticed the list didn't include Dehya. She had just discovered the existence of a prince who preceded her own son in age, yet she waited. She understood Kelric in a way few others could.

"I imagine they're surprised," Kelric allowed.

Najo looked as if he considered that a monumental understatement. But he said only, "Yes, sir."

Kelric wasn't ready to talk. He wanted these moments for himself. "Tell them I'll contact them after the Promenade."

Voices surged outside. Startled, Kelric turned back. A young woman had appeared at the top of the cathedral stairs—a girl whose skin, hair, and eyes shimmered gold.

The announcer said, "Roca Miesa Varz Valdoria—" He took a breath that everyone on thousands of worlds and habitats in three empires would hear, a sound that would become another page of history. Then he added, "Skolia."

Until that moment, Kelric hadn't been one hundred percent certain. By using the Skolia name, the announcer verified what he had always believed: his daughter was a Ruby psion.

Someday she would take her place in the Dyad.

She descended the steps alone, but the defenses of an

empire protected her. Her true name was Rohka, the Coban version of Roca. Kelric felt as if he were sundering in two. Rohka, the miracle he and Savina had given life sixteen years ago, had come into the world as her mother died. The hours Kelric had spent cradling his infant child in his oversized arms had been the only light in his grief-shattered life. He would be forever grateful to Ixpar for freeing him from Varz, but he had mourned, too, for the Varz Manager had retaliated by denying him his child.

Jimorla had reached the coliseum, and officers ushered him to the area reserved for the Imperator's children. He was the first person to sit there in a century. On the Concourse, Rohka's stride never faltered, though Kelric recognized the overwhelmed look she tried to hide. He had seen the same expression on her mother's face when Savina felt daunted but refused to let fear diminish her spirit.

Welcome, Kelric thought to his children. They couldn't reply; even if they had known how to interpret mental input, they were too far away. He didn't even know if his son was an empath or had the rarer telepathic traits Kelric shared with his family.

And yet . . . he felt certain a man answered, distant but clear, the thought in Teotecan: *It is my honor.*

A girl's thought suddenly resonated in his mind, young and raw, untrained but full of power. ***And mine, Father.***

The speaker said, simply, "Kelric Skolia, Imperator of Skolia, and Ixpar Karn, Minister of Coba."

Kelric and Ixpar descended the cathedral steps together. The crowds had cheered the Houses and Ruby

Dynasty. They were silent now, whether in shock or respect, he didn't know. He had never been comfortable in public displays; he preferred to stay in the background. But he had waited ten years for this—no, twenty-eight. That was when he had first seen Ixpar, as he awoke in a sickroom on Coba with the fourteen-year-old Ministry successor leaning over him. It had taken nearly three decades to bring that moment full circle, decades that had changed him more than he would ever have imagined. Today, his life was complete.

XV
The Bitterfruit Tree

The Opal Hall in the Qox Palace gleamed like an iridescent pearl. Its luminous moonstone walls shifted with traces of aqua and marine. Jaibriol sat on a white couch across from Parizian Sakaar, the Highton Aristo who served as his Trade Minister. Jaibriol's aide, Robert, had taken one of the wing chairs at the opal table. So had Tarquine, who had at least showed up this time.

Jaibriol felt ill. They were going over reports from the guilds that bred and trained providers. Before he had claimed his throne, he had served in the Dawn Corps of the Allied Worlds, which had helped newly freed worlds recover after the war. He had seen the pavilions where Silicate Aristos "designed" providers, the labs and examination tables, the discipline, memorization, testing, erotica, and isolation rooms. He had met providers huddled in their cubicles, slaves his own age or younger, staggeringly beautiful. The collars and cuffs they wore extended picotech into their bodies until the threads became so interwoven with their neural systems, it was impossible to remove them without surgery.

None of those providers had a name. None knew their age. None could read or write. An inventory had listed them by serial number. That night, Jaibriol had walked out among the whispering trees and been violently sick in the beautiful forest the Silicates had grown to adorn their pavilion. He had leaned over with his arms around his stomach and retched again and again until he felt as if he were tearing out his insides.

The Trade Minister sitting here had no idea of Jaibriol's reaction. Sakaar didn't consider his job abhorrent. He went over the files on the trillion-dollar industry as if he were reporting on inanimate objects. Jaibriol could tell the meeting disturbed Robert, whose father had been "trained" in a Silicate facility. But his aide accepted it as part of Eubian life. He had never known anything different. The other aides didn't think about it at all; they were simply doing their jobs, recording files and organizing statistics.

As Finance Minister, Tarquine tracked Silicate corporations and ensured they followed accepted business practices, at least as defined by Aristos. She hid her response behind the icy façade she had perfected, but Jaibriol caught the truth from her mind. The meeting revolted her. It was why she had altered herself so she could no longer transcend; late in her life, she had developed a trait shared by no other Aristos he knew except Corbal and Calope Muze. Remorse. His empress might be one of the most prodigiously crooked human beings alive, but she wasn't brutal. She could no more bring herself to inflict pain on providers than could he.

Yet sometimes in the sultry hours of the night, when Tarquine held him in her arms, he felt the hunger within her, her memory of transcendence. Deep within, a part of her wanted to hurt him, and that darkness chilled Jaibriol.

At the moment, she was frowning as she studied a holofile Sakaar had handed to her, a copy of the one he gave Jaibriol with reports on various Silicate facilities.

"This entry on the Garnet sale during the third octet last year," Tarquine was saying. "It appears less eminent than the predictions of my Evolving Intelligence codes."

Jaibriol blinked. "Less eminent" sounded like her way of saying the profits were lower than expected. Outwardly, the Trade Minister seemed unaffected by her observation. When Jaibriol concentrated on his mind, though, he realized Sakaar was hiding an unease greater than such a minor comment deserved.

"It is difficult to estimate eminence with elevation," Sakaar said.

Jaibriol almost laughed at the bizarre phrasing. Sakaar had a point, though; such predictions often weren't accurate.

Tarquine scanned another holopage. "And here, under the Mica Class Three-Eight product line, the fifth octet subprofits margin is only one-third as eminent as one might foresee."

Jaibriol wasn't even certain what she had said. Whatever it was, though, Sakaar didn't like it. With his mental barriers at full force, he could tell only that Sakaar was uncomfortable. Too uncomfortable. Her comments didn't sound threatening to Jaibriol, but the Trade Minister thought otherwise.

Jaibriol had long ago learned the value of letting his people probe and strike while he listened. Among Hightons, whose discourse branched like verbal fractals, an emperor who spoke so little frightened people. It could be useful; they often attributed more intrigue to his silence than it warranted. In his first years as emperor, when he had been a desperate teenager totally out of his depth, the silences had protected him, hiding just how thoroughly he had no idea what he was doing. Now they had become a tool.

"Claims of inconsistency would be premature," Sakaar said.

That caught Jaibriol's attention. It sounded as if Sakaar had warned Tarquine to stop accusing him without proof. Among Aristos, where appearance and reputation were everything, an unsubstantiated accusation ranked as a crime worse than marrying outside one's caste. Which of course turned such accusations into valued currency, but only if the accuser could make them stick. If not, the accuser suffered censure, loss of reputation, even legal penalties if the accused went to the courts. Sakaar's reaction was way out of proportion to Tarquine's comments, which made Jaibriol suspect his Trade Minister far more than if Sakaar had said nothing.

"Perhaps they would be premature," Tarquine answered, her voice smooth. "But premature development is no longer a danger with so many advances in modern science."

"Unless the development is itself flawed," Sakaar said.

Watching Tarquine, Jaibriol suspected she had evidence

of some Machiavellian scheme Sakaar had concocted, and she wanted him to sweat. Either that, or she was bluffing the hell out of the Trade Minister.

Robert's wrist comm beeped. An instant later, Jaibriol's buzzed, Sakaar's pinged, and Tarquine's hummed.

"What the blazes?" Sakaar said.

Jaibriol lifted his comm. "Qox here," he said. As soon as he moved, the others responded to their pages.

Corbal's urgent voice came out of the mesh. "Jai, turn on the Third Hour broadcast. You'll want to see this."

Puzzled, Jaibriol nodded to Robert, who had somehow managed the feat of simultaneously being attentive to the emperor and answering his comm. Robert flicked his finger through a holicon above the mesh film in his lap, and a holoscreen activated on the wall across from Jaibriol. As the others turned around to look, images formed in front of the screen. It was a Skolian transmission. The Eubian translation scrolled beneath it in three-dimensional glyphs, but he didn't need them; he was fluent in Skolian Flag.

The broadcast showed the Cathedral of Memories, a building of sparkling white stone, windows of blue glass, and flying buttresses that were works of art. A tall man was striding with four guards along a concourse to a huge arena. His dark skin had a disquietingly familiar gold sheen.

". . . must be his son," a newscaster was saying, her voice taut with excitement. "It's the only way he could walk in the Promenade *after* the Ruby Dynasty, but before Imperator Skolia."

A chill started at the bottom of Jaibriol's spine and

crept upward. Did she mean Kelric Skolia's son? *What* son?

"Who the flipping hell is that?" Sakaar demanded.

Jaibriol had no doubt that normally some Aristo would have responded with a veiled barb at the Trade Minister's lapse of language. But the only other Aristos present were Tarquine and himself, and he was far too riveted by the broadcast to give a flaming jump about what Sakaar said.

If he understood the broadcaster, the next person to walk the concourse would be Kelric. It meant the promenade was almost done; only the Ruby Pharaoh and her family followed the Imperator. But when the cathedral doors opened, a girl with gold skin walked out onto the top of the steps, the wind blowing back her distinctive gold hair.

"This is incredible!" the newscaster said. "A *second* child has appeared."

A man spoke, apparently another commentator. "I don't think much doubt exists as to her parentage, with that coloring."

"Why aren't they announcing her name?" the woman said.

Jaibriol was wondering the same thing. Didn't Kelric know his own children? The girl stood waiting, her head held high. He could tell what she felt, though, even if . sensing her mood was impossible across interstellar distances. After a lifetime of associating emotions with people's behavior, and ten years among Hightons, whose language was as much gesture and posture as words, he read body language like a book. She was scared.

A new voice spoke, what sounded like the official

announcer at the Promenade itself. "Roca Miesa Varz Valdoria—" The man inhaled deeply. Then he said, "Skolia."

"It can't be!" Sakaar shouted.

"Gods forbid," Tarquine muttered. "*Another* one of them?"

Jaibriol stared at her, his hands clammy. "Did you know?"

"I had no idea," she said. "But they must be legitimate heirs. He was wearing marriage guards when I bought him. He told me his ex-wife gave them to him."

This was news to Jaibriol; none of ESComm's files on Kelric included anything on an *ex*-wife. "Why was he still wearing them?"

"He said he loved her."

Jaibriol tried to fathom her reaction. If what she had just said bothered her, it showed on neither her face nor the surface of her mind. With Sakaar in the room, though, he couldn't let down his barriers enough to be certain.

The broadcasters continued talking, excitement spilling into their words. Jaibriol tuned them out, his focus solely on the scene. The doors of the cathedral opened again— and the Imperator walked out. He towered, broad of shoulder, long in the legs, massive in physique, huge and gold. His square chin, chiseled features, and close-cropped hair enhanced the effect, as did the grey at his temples. When Jaibriol had met him ten years ago, Kelric had been dying. Even then his presence had overpowered. Now he stood like an indomitable war god surveying his realms.

Nor was he alone. A woman stood at his side, nearly as

tall as Lord Skolia. Fiery hair was upswept on her head, and her eyes blazed, fierce and flooded with intelligence. She was one of the few people Jaibriol had ever seen who could match the sheer force of personality that Kelric projected.

And this time Jaibriol *felt* Tarquine's reaction. It jumped within her, so intense it burst past his barriers. *Anger.* In her mind, she owned Kelric, though he had attained his freedom ten years ago. To see him with another woman violated her sense of balance at a level so deep, it burned within her. In that moment, Jaibriol didn't want peace with Kelric's empire, he wanted to obliterate the Imperialate.

The Promenade announcer said, "Kelric Skolia, Imperator of Skolia, and Ixpar Karn, Minister of Coba."

"Minister?" Tarquine raised an eyebrow. "It seems you and the Imperator have something in common."

Jaibriol felt as if she had socked him in the stomach. The Aristo edge to her sarcasm came from her anger at discovering Kelric had a wife again—this one astonishingly formidable—and Jaibriol couldn't bear to see how much it affected her. He had one thing in common with Kelric: Tarquine. He couldn't reply, he could only stare at the broadcast as Kelric and his long-legged wife strode down the concourse.

Then the Ruby Pharaoh and her consort walked out onto the cathedral steps. The first time Jaibriol had seen a Promenade, seven years ago, they had appeared alone. Today their son accompanied them, a boy of eight. They had named him Althor, in honor of his uncle, who had died in the Radiance War.

Normally their heir would go first, as Kelric's had done. But not this child. Jaibriol knew about him from the ESComm files. The pharaoh and her consort were too closely related; they carried the same deleterious mutations in their DNA. The boy had been born without substantial parts of his body, including his legs. Hightons would never have allowed such a birth, but Althor's parents had cherished him. Over the years, surgeons had worked on the boy, giving him biomech limbs and organs, and an internal web more extensive than even for a Jagernaut. He appeared normal now, tall for his age, though thin. He walked slowly with the stiff gait of someone unused to his limbs, and his parents stayed with him. But he walked.

An exhale came from the crowd at the sight of the pharaoh's heir. The Promenade had served its purpose, assuring the Skolian people that their leaders were strong and well, and that their ruling house would thrive for generations to come.

Jaibriol wished he could stop the broadcast. He felt as if he had eaten from the bitterfruit tree of Aristo mythology. He lived a nightmare day after day, with no reprieve and no hope of escaping the pain or fear. He had to sit here and watch his family, knowing they shared the Ruby bonds forever denied to him, that they would always have the joy of that love. He would never know those gifts they took for granted. He couldn't even risk siring an heir with his own wife.

Jaibriol stood up abruptly, knocking the holofile on his lap to the floor. He had to leave before his crumbling defenses fell apart. Everyone scrambled to their feet. He nodded curtly to Robert and his guards, indicating they should accompany him.

Without a word, Jaibriol strode from the room.

Kelric stood with Ixpar at a starburst window in a tower of the Sunrise Palace on the planet of Parthonia. Outside, the mountains stretched in every direction, rolling in swell after swell of green, with blue-violet sky above and lowering dark clouds misting their peaks. Late afternoon sunrays slanted across Ixpar's face, silvering her grey eyes.

"Shall we?" Ixpar murmured.

Kelric took a breath. "Yes." It had taken years for this moment to come, and he had thought it never would happen. He would wait no longer.

She touched his arm with a gesture he remembered, as if she were simultaneously offering support and assuring herself he was real. Then she flicked her finger across the panel of the wrist comm he had given her this afternoon. It was odd to see her with Skolian technology, which had been forbidden to Cobans for so long. Even after only a few hours, she used it with ease. It had always been that way with her; sometimes she seemed to pick up ideas faster than he could articulate them.

A deep voice came out of her comm mesh. "Najo here, sir."

Ixpar quirked her eyebrow at Kelric and mouthed, *Sir?*

"He thinks you're me, because it's my comm." Kelric motioned at the device. "Go ahead."

Ixpar lifted her arm and spoke in accented but fluent Skolian Flag. "Secondary Najo, this is Ixpar Karn. Have Imperator Skolia's children arrived yet?"

Silence followed her words. Although Kelric was separated from his bodyguards by a wall and enough distance to mute his reception of their moods, he knew them well enough to interpret Najo's response; hearing Ixpar jolted him. His guards had been laudably discreet, given the curiosity he felt consuming them. They had no idea what to make of Ixpar.

Then Najo said, "Their flyer is en route, Your Majesty."

Ixpar blinked as if the comm had sprouted two heads. She touched the mute panel so Najo couldn't hear her. "My what?"

Kelric smiled. "Majesty. It's your title, as my consort."

"Are you one of these, too?"

"Well, yes. I go by Lord Skolia, though."

She regarded him dubiously. "*Majesty* seems rather grandiose. More like a mountain than a person."

"You can use your Coban title if you prefer. Just tell him."

She touched the send panel. "Thank you, Secondary Najo. Also, you may call me Minister Karn."

"Understood, ma'am." He paused. "Are you with Imperator Skolia? I have a message for him."

Kelric had no doubt "a message" was a prodigious understatement. Gods only knew how many people wanted to reach him. He and Ixpar had escaped the coliseum by the roof, where they boarded a flyer. They had spoken with no one. His children had sat below his box in the coliseum, and he had had them escorted to the palace as soon as the Promenade ended. If he had asked them to wait while he came through the tunnel to their box, people would have had time to catch up with them. He had waited twenty-six years for this moment. Maybe his children would accept him, maybe not, but he wanted whatever happened to be private.

He activated his comm. "Najo, tell anyone who wishes to speak with me that I will talk to them this evening."

"Yes, sir. They are rather urgent, though."

Kelric could imagine. "They'll have to wait." Ixpar was watching him, her stately figure silhouetted against the arched window. "Let me know as soon as my children arrive."

Najo answered quietly. "They're here, sir."

Kelric froze. What if they rejected the father they had never met?

After a moment, Najo said, "Imperator Skolia?"

Kelric took a deep breath. "Please escort them in."

An eternity passed for Kelric in the moments before anyone entered. The world seemed caught in another bubble, but this time he wasn't certain if he was within it or on the outside. The door opened, leaving Najo in its archway, a towering Jagernaut in black with a huge gun on his hip. He had a strange look, as if he had gone through a tunnel packed with the unexpected and come out the other end, no less stunned than before but able to accept whatever he found. He stepped aside, into the room—

A girl appeared in the doorway.

In that moment, Kelric *knew*. He needed no DNA, Promenade announcers, or Coban historians to tell him. Like knew like. Her mind glowed like the sun, as it had even before her birth, when she was barely more than a dream. She stared at him with his own eyes. She wore suède trousers and a gold shirt, so much like her mother, Savina; but unlike Savina, his daughter was tall, nearly the height of her namesake, Roca Skolia.

It was several moments before he could speak. Finally the Teotecan words came to him. "My greetings, Rohka."

His daughter inhaled abruptly, as if his voice reminded her that she needed to breathe. She walked forward, and if she knew anyone else but Kelric was present, she gave no sign. She stopped a few paces away from him. "Father?"

Somehow he smiled. "It seems I have that good fortune."

"Cuaz and Khozaar me!" she said, invoking Coba's capricious wind gods.

Her flustered expression so reminded him of Savina, he didn't know whether to laugh or cry. "Your mother used to say that."

Rohka hesitated. "Will you tell me about her?"

His voice softened. "Gladly."

He hadn't spoken about Savina since her death. Perhaps talking to Rohka would help him close the chapter on that terrible loss, so he truly felt free to love Ixpar. His bond to Ixpar had begun to form that first day he saw her leaning over him like a fire-haired angel, but so much had intervened in the fourteen years between when he met her and married her. Including Savina. It took him a long time to grasp his emotions; he was like a glacier flowing down a mountain. Patience wasn't a common trait of Coban women when it came to love. Savina had burst into his life like a solar flare, melted his reticence, and loved him passionately for five years. Losing her had nearly killed him. Only Ixpar had understood, and given him the time he needed to come alive again.

It finally dawned on Rohka that Kelric was standing next to the leader of her civilization. She flushed, her cheeks rosy, and bowed to Ixpar. "My greetings, ma'am."

Ixpar inclined her head. "And mine to you, Rohka."

A rustle stirred in the doorway. Looking up, Kelric saw Strava enter the room. She gave him a questioning look.

Taking a breath, Kelric nodded. Strava didn't turn around, but lights flashed on her gauntlets, as happened when his guards used their biomech to communicate. Then she stepped to the side of the entrance.

A man walked through the doorway.

Kelric saw him, but his tension was so high, he couldn't focus on the man's face. It was a blur. Then everything snapped into place and his heart wrenched. Jimorla. His firstborn. His heir.

Jimorla's face was achingly familiar, though Kelric had never seen him before today. He had the same violet eyes as Kelric's father. His brown hair curled in disarray, tousled from the wind. A gold shimmer overlaid his skin, but he had inherited his darker coloring from his mother, Rashiva. He also had her exotic beauty and upward tilted eyes, but in him it had the dramatic masculine strength of his desert ancestors.

His son showed no hint of a smile. By custom, a man from a desert estate never smiled in the presence of a woman unless only his kin were present. His Oath forbade him to speak to anyone Outside the Varz Calanya. Even knowing that, Kelric hadn't been able to stop himself from hoping Jimorla would speak, for his son had already defied tradition by traveling to Parthonia and walking in the Promenade. But those were breaks with custom, not the Oath. As much as Kelric knew that intellectually, he couldn't help but wonder if Jimorla's impassive silence came from more than his Oath.

Kelric spoke in Teotecan. "I am pleased you are here." It sounded as stilted as it felt.

And his son said, "I am honored."

An ache swelled within Kelric, one hard to define, for he had never understood his own emotions as well as he read those from other people. This came from deep within him, full of warmth, as if it held his heart.

"How is your mother?" Kelric asked.

"She is well." Defiance flashed in Jimorla's eyes. "As is my father, Raaj."

It felt like a punch. *What did you expect?* Kelric thought. Raaj had raised Jimorla. It hadn't been until age thirteen that Jimorla learned the identity of his biological father. Kelric knew he would have to work to become a father to his children. They were part of him, yet they were strangers. Their lives had been so different than his, they had no intersection with him.

Except for Quis.

He couldn't suggest playing Quis to Jimorla; it would be a great offense, especially given that his son had come without the Manager of his Estate. It astonished him that Stahna Varz had let her Calani travel to another world. It went against every tradition, custom, and expectation of her people. It violated Jimorla's Calanya Oath. No Manager would allow such, yet the most rigid of all Coban queens had done exactly that.

"I'm grateful Manager Varz accepted this visit," Kelric said. That sounded so paltry for what he felt.

"It wasn't Stahna who made the decision," Ixpar said.

Kelric stiffened and stared at her. *What had she done?* Started another war?

Whatever Ixpar saw in his expression, it made her smile. "Don't worry," she said. "I haven't kidnapped anyone."

Jimorla looked from her to Kelric, his gaze intent. Then he shrugged off the robe he wore over his shirt and trousers and folded it over his arm. At first Kelric wasn't certain why, except for the room being warm. Then he saw the gold bands in his son's sleeves, partially covered by the loose cloth. Three Calanya rings gleamed on each of his upper arms. The top band showed the rising sun insignia of Haka Estate, where he had been born, and the middle one had the Varz clawcat.

The third ring bore the Karn althawk.

Gods almighty. His son was a Karn Calani. Ixpar had made him a Third Level, probably one of the few on the planet, and he had achieved it at an incredibly young age. Jimorla had lived in the Calanya at two of the most powerful Estates, Haka and Varz, both adversaries of Karn. That combined with his heritage would make his Calanya contract exorbitantly expensive. It must have put even Ixpar's Estate into debt.

Another realization hit him. His son could have refused the Third Level. That he had accepted it, though it meant leaving his home to live at an Estate he probably viewed as hostile, meant more to Kelric than he knew how to say.

Jimorla was watching him, and Kelric saw the uncertainty in his eyes. He had no more idea how his father would accept him than Kelric did about his son.

Kelric's voice caught. Looking at both his children, he said, "Welcome to my home."

And to my heart.

XVI
Pillar of Light

Jaibriol stood in the Silver Room of the Qox Palace and studied the life-size holo image before him. It showed two military men, but they weren't ESComm officers. No, these were the warlords of his enemies. They were standing on a stage, listening to a speech. The one with steel-grey hair was Chad Barzun, who headed up the Skolian Imperial Fleet. The other was Admiral Ragnar Bloodmark.

A door hummed behind Jaibriol. He didn't need to turn; he saw his visitor's face reflected in the screen behind the holos. Tarquine came to stand at his side, studying the image of the Skolian commanders. Her faint scent drifted to him, astringent and bracing.

"An interesting couple," she said. "Did you know Bloodmark is one-quarter Scandinavian?"

"I didn't realize you were that familiar with ISC." He knew about Bloodmark because he had read the ESComm dossiers on all the top Skolian officers, but he hadn't thought she was interested in military details.

"I make it my policy to know the major players." She indicated Bloodmark. "He may look like a nobleman, but his mother was space-slag poor. Bad economics in that bloodline."

"That may be," Jaibriol said. "But he operates now at the top level of Skolian hierarchies."

Tarquine waved her hand in dismissal. "That can't be too difficult. They are only Skolians, after all."

He raised an eyebrow. "As opposed to, say, Iquars?"

She gave him a half-lidded stare, like a feral cat. "Iquars are in a class by ourselves."

When she looked at him that way, it could make him forget why he didn't like being the emperor of Eube. "So I've noticed."

She tilted her head at the images. "Why are you interested in these two?"

He refocused his attention on less flammable matters than his wife. "Of all the Skolian commanders, Barzun seems the one most likely to support a peace treaty."

"That's hardly saying much," Tarquine said, "given the allergic reactions they all have to the concept."

"I suppose. Bloodmark was more intractable at the talks, though. He carries a great deal of weight with ISC." Jaibriol rubbed his chin. "In fact, he has more seniority than Barzun. But the Imperator promoted Barzun over him. I wonder why."

"I take it you have a hypothesis?"

"I'm not sure." As much as he disliked discussing Kelric with her, she knew the Imperator better than did any other Aristo. "I had the impression during our negotiations that the pharaoh was the only one willing to talk peace. But maybe Imperator Skolia isn't as intransigent as we thought."

"Don't let them fool you," Tarquine said. "The Allieds have a very old saying. 'Good cop, bad cop.'"

"What is a 'cop?'"

"Police officer. When you want something from adversaries, you set two people to work with them. One person is easy on the target. Softens them up. The other is tough. Of course it's never true; they play off each other." She flicked her finger through several holicons on her wrist comp, and the image in front of them changed to one of the Ruby Pharaoh.

Jaibriol almost jerked; the pharaoh looked like a delicate version of his mother. The pharaoh was ethereal rather than robust, and where his mother had been fierce, the pharaoh seemed gentle. But both women had the same large green eyes and heart-shaped face. It hurt to see. He longed just once to talk to his Ruby kin, not about politics or war, but about the family he would never know.

"See how fragile she looks," Tarquine mused. "But she isn't in the least. She is steel."

"I wouldn't know." He kept his gaze on the holo, unable to meet Tarquine's gaze.

His wife spoke in a low voice. "They say the Ruby Pharaoh and her niece—the previous Imperator—were more alike than anyone realized."

Jaibriol felt as if she had caught him with a rope and spun him around. What did Tarquine expect, to hear him admit Soz Valdoria, the late Imperator, was his mother?

"People say many things," he told her.

"So they do. For example, that gold is softer than steel."

Gold? He gave her an incredulous look. "You think the *Imperator* is more likely than the pharaoh to consider peace?"

Tarquine thought for a moment. "I'm not sure. He's every bit the military commander. But I suspect he is less adamant against it than he seems."

As uncomfortable as this discussion made Jaibriol, her interpretations intrigued him. "Pharaoh Dyhianna is the ruler, though. Imperator Skolia answers to her and the First Councilor."

Tarquine gave him a dour look. "What sort of brain-addled decision was that? She deposes that Assembly, a very sensible thing to do. And then what. She gives them back half of the power. Maybe she would give me half if I asked."

Tarquine on the Ruby Throne. What a terrifying concept. He said only, "The blended government works."

She waved her hand. "That's a non sequitur."

"What, that their government is sound?" As much as he found her canny mind fascinating, she could exasperate the blazes out of him. "How the hell is that a random comment?"

"Well, they are Skolians," she allowed. "I guess one should make allowances for their bizarre notions."

Given that he was half Skolian, Jaibriol decided his blood pressure would remain lower if he changed the subject. He touched his wrist comp and replaced the holo with an image of Barcala Tikal, the First Councilor, who shared the rule of Skolia with the Ruby Pharaoh. A lean man with regular features, he had brown hair streaked with grey.

"What do you think of him?" Jaibriol asked.

She considered Tikal. "Sounder finances in his Line. But he could do a lot better if he paid more attention to his finances and wasted less time on the Assembly."

Jaibriol threw up his hands. "Tarquine, he's the Assembly leader! That's his job, for flaming sake."

She regarded him through sleepy eyes. "We certainly are direct today."

Jaibriol crossed his arms, refusing to let her distract him. "We would also like to be enlightened today, sometime before the sun sets."

Her lips curved upward. "Indeed. About what?"

"Tell me more about Tikal."

She studied the holo of Tikal as if he were a puzzle. "The pharaoh took a possibly fatal risk when she let him live. I doubt he has ever stopped thinking how much safer he would be if the Ruby Dynasty no longer held power." She tilted her head. "Of course, he is Skolian. You never know how they will act."

"That's because they aren't as predictable as Aristos." He didn't say "as unimaginative," but she knew what he meant.

"*Predictable* isn't the word for us," Tarquine murmured. "We're efficient. When methods work, why change them?"

"That assumes everyone shares the same view of what works."

"Oh, they never do," she said. "Consider your Diamond Minister, Izar Gji. He wants to increase commerce. He's far more interested in wealth than in war. The export coalition he and the other Diamonds were putting together had the potential to be highly lucrative. But they needed the Janq Line to make it work. After the Skolians stole the Janq merchant ships and caused such a ruckus, the coalition fell apart."

"The Skolians didn't 'steal' anything," Jaibriol said, annoyed. "They confiscated pirate ships that committed criminal activities in Skolian space."

She waved her hand in dismissal. "It doesn't change the outcome. Now that the coalition has fallen apart, Minister Gji will be looking for other ventures to achieve his goals." She paced in front of the holo, thinking. "Gji wants to expand trade routes. Approached in the right way—" She stopped in front of Jaibriol, blocking the holo of the First Councilor. "The *predictable* way—he may even consider exotic options."

He knew "exotic" meant Skolian. "He didn't seem interested to me," Jaibriol said, remembering his lackluster dinner with the Minister. "Nor is it only Gji I have to convince. I need the support of my Trade Minister." Flatly he added, "And Sakaar sure as hell won't give it to me."

Tarquine's gaze darkened. "Trade Minister Sakaar has many concerns he needs to consider."

Jaibriol thought back to what she had said to Sakaar during their meeting about the Silicate pavilions, her implication that she had discovered a problem in his reports. He had been so rattled by the broadcast about Kelric's unexpected children that he hadn't yet followed up on the Sakaar matter.

"Concerns such as—?" Jaibriol let the question hang.

"Sakaar hides well," she said. "So well, in fact, that he

could vanish from almost anyone's sight. Unfortunately for him, he has to deal with me rather than 'almost anyone.'"

Jaibriol didn't envy the Trade Minister. But Sakaar was clever. "He deals well, Tarquine."

"Very well," she murmured. "Astonishingly, extensively, extravagantly well." She waited a heartbeat. "After all, fraud is a form of dealing."

Good Lord. Sakaar's crime would have to be massive indeed if even Eube's unrepentantly corrupt empress considered it astonishing, extensive, and extravagant. "Such dealing," he said sourly, "has been known to give emperors mammoth headaches."

"Heads should only ache if one gets caught," Tarquine said. "You don't need medicine at all." In her dusky voice, she added, "But I do believe Minister Sakaar has a raging pain in his head."

"And precisely what caused this dire health of his?"

"Let us just say he misplaced the revenue of a few trades. For a little while."

He squinted at her. "What little while?"

"Well, perhaps the last five years."

Five *years*? "What the hell?"

Her lips quirked up. "That was articulate."

"Yes, well, I would very much like you to articulate more on the subject of Sakaar."

She switched into that terrifyingly incisive mode of hers. "Our illustrious Sakaar routed ten percent of the profits from every transaction he oversaw as Trade Minister into a series of hidden Allied financial institutions. He disguised his actions through an exceedingly labyrinthine process. It was brilliant."

"*Every* transaction?" He stared at her. "Tarquine, there are *millions* of those a year, some for millions of credits."

"Indeed. He is a very wealthy man." She paused a beat. "Or he was, before someone froze his assets."

Hell and damnation. "He must be brilliant, to have hidden this from you for five years."

"Actually," she hedged, "the pertinent time span in that case would have a different numerical value."

"Tarquine."

"So to speak."

"What numerical value?"

"Perhaps three."

"He hid it from you for three years?"

She scratched her ear. "Perhaps one might use the word months."

"*Months?*" She had known within three months and said nothing until now? "Then why the holy blazes did it continue for five years?" If she had made some deal with Sakaar, he would have her hide. And a very, very bad headache. "Just when did he find out you knew he was stealing my empire blind?"

"You needn't look so alarmed." She was almost purring. "I let him know at that last meeting we had with him. I imagine he was quite relieved when that broadcast about the Ruby Dynasty distracted you." Satisfaction saturated her voice. "Think of this, husband. A crime committed constantly for more than five years is far more serious than one done for three months. And the more serious the crime, the greater leverage it gives to the discoverer of that peccadillo."

"Peccadillo?" He could only stare at her. She was

talking about fraud on a massive scale. He had never heard of anything like this before.

"Don't worry," she added. "I will deal with it."

"When you deal with things, I get hives," he muttered. "I want a report, Tarquine, and it damn well better include the evidence you've gathered. I want everything. *Everything.*"

"Of course," she said smoothly.

Jaibriol wanted to groan. Whenever she agreed that easily, he knew it was time to worry.

The sixth implosion destroyed a gas giant in an uninhabited star system of Sphinx Sector.

Jaibriol strode across the launch hexagon with Robert and his bodyguards. Glory's sun was just rising. Seven of the fourteen moons were in the sky, four of them tiny chips barely visible to the eye. The largest, a huge red disk, glittered on the horizon opposite to the sun. Eube Qox, the first emperor, had surfaced it with ruby and named it in honor of his empress, Mirella. Overhead, the third largest satellite sparkled as a half-moon. Jaibriol's grandfather had named it Viquara after his empress and surfaced it in diamond.

The fifth largest moon was called Tarquine. Jaibriol had altered it both within and without. He surfaced it with a steel-diamond composite, brilliant and hard, but inside it had a beautiful crystalline structure in violet, blue, and white. A geode. It was the most fitting tribute he could think of for his wife.

The fourth moon should have been named after his mother. His father supposedly never had the chance, so

Jaibriol inherited the decision. He couldn't call it Sauscony, after a Skolian Imperator, which was undoubtedly why his father had never named it, either. Jaibriol finally christened it Prism, in honor of the world where his family had lived in exile. He let people think it was his father's nickname for his mother. He didn't know how to resurface Prism, though the name cried out for a substance that would split light into its colors. The choice should have been his father's, and it felt wrong for him even to choose the name, let alone decide how to change the moon.

All this business with moons and wives seemed hollow this morning. After seeing Kelric with his family—and knowing his own empress desired the Imperator—Jaibriol felt broken inside. Tarquine would never admit any desire for Kelric; she refused even to acknowledge the huge price she had paid for him. But he had felt her anger at seeing Kelric's imposing wife. Kelric had everything Jaibriol could ever want, and if Eube and Skolia ever found their way back to the talks, Jaibriol would have to meet him at the peace table without letting his envy interfere. Somehow, someway he had to find accommodation with the knowledge that he could never again have what he craved, the love of a family of psions. It was good he had matters to take him away this morning, for he didn't think he could have borne another day of the icy Aristo world that imprisoned him.

As Glory's small sun edged above the horizon, Jaibriol boarded his yacht. Robert sat next to him, and his bodyguards took other seats, with Hidaka as the pilot. They blasted off into a dawn of splintering clarity. Their destination: Sphinx Sector Rim Base. Jaibriol's purported intention: to discuss with the commanders there the possibility that the implosions could be a weapon of Skolian design. It could be coincidence that the path of the events pointed roughly toward the SSRB, but neither Jaibriol nor ESComm intended to take chances.

Jaibriol kept to himself the real reason for his visit. He didn't believe the Skolians had anything to do with the implosions. He feared a more ancient intelligence was at work, one he neither understood nor had reason to believe intended good will.

The Lock.

The War Room on the Skolian Orbiter served as one among several centers of operations for the Imperialate military. It was a Skolian counterpart to the Eubian SSRB complex. In the War Room, Skolian commanders planned strategies against the Eubian military.

Today the amphitheater in the command center thrummed with energy: officers worked at consoles, telops focused on the meshes, pages ran errands, and cranes with console cups swung through the air. High above the amphitheater, a massive arm held a command chair under the dome of holostars. Conduits from all over the War Room fed into the blocky chair and sent data directly into the brain of whoever sat in that technological throne.

Kelric entered the War Room in the holodome, far above the busy amphitheater, striding along a catwalk that stretched to his chair. Yesterday he had walked the Promenade with his wife and children on the planet

Parthonia; today he brought them to the Orbiter to see where he lived. He tried to forget they had to return to Coba. As much as he wanted them here, they had lives elsewhere; Ixpar ruled on Coba, his daughter was her successor, and his son a high-ranked Calani. But they were here now, and perhaps, just perhaps, they would consider staying.

The rest of his family wanted to know where the blazes he had acquired a wife and children. He had so far said little, except that he spent eighteen years on Coba. He intended to tell them more, but neither words nor expressing emotions had ever come easy to him. He needed time to answer their questions.

Dehya left him alone, patient with his silences, though he had no doubt she was investigating Coba. Roca also understood he needed time. She would have gone to Coba if he hadn't forbidden it and had a military force to back up his wishes. But in other ways her response was gentle. He remembered her pleased surprise: *You named your daughter after me?* Well, of course he had. Roca had been the greatest female influence in his youth. Surely at least part of the reason he loved so deeply was because his parents had loved their children that way.

The rest of his kin took their lead from Roca and waited, trying to be patient, but their frustration felt like a cloud of smoke. It was another reason he had come to the Orbiter; he needed time alone with his family. He and his children needed time to adjust to one another before he could open up to everyone else.

As Imperator, he also had to work. So today he had come to oversee the roaring, star-flung military known as

Imperial Space Command, squeezing in a few hours while Roca spent time with the daughter-in- law and grandchildren who were so new to her,

Holographic starlight from the dome silvered his blocky throne. As he settled into the chair, it folded a mesh around him and clicked prongs into his ankles, wrists, spine, and neck, linking to his biomech web. The hood lowered, and a spider-web of threads extended into his scalp. Data poured into Bolt, and the node organized the input, leaving Kelric free to think.

He laid his arms on the rests and sat back. This chair was almost identical to the one in the SSRB Lock command center. He would never forget. He had met an emperor there. He was almost certain Jaibriol the Third was a telepath, yet that was impossible; Hightons had deliberately eliminated the DNA from their gene pool. Gods help humanity if that had changed, and the Eubians created their own Kyle web.

Three Locks had survived the fall of the Ruby Empire. The Orbiter was one; this space station had drifted in space for five millennia before Kelric's people found it. Although modern science couldn't replicate the Locks, they still operated. They had opened Kyle space to humanity. A person didn't physically enter the Kyle; they accessed it with their mind. The laws of physics didn't exist there, including limitations imposed by the speed of light. The content of someone's thoughts determined their "location." As a result, the Kyle mesh, or psiberweb as some called it, gave telops instant communication across interstellar distances. ESComm's military inventories and personnel dwarfed ISC, but ISC could outmaneuver, outcalculate, and outcommunicate ESComm. The Traders lumbered and Skolia sailed. It was the only reason Kelric's people survived against Eube.

A sense of stirring came from Kelric's gauntlets. A warning.

Bolt? Kelric asked. **Did you get that?**

You'll have to be more specific than "that," Bolt answered. I'm receiving a large amount of data.

My gauntlets. Kelric didn't know how to describe it. **They're warning me.**

About what?

I don't know. You didn't sense anything?

I can't get impressions the way a human does.

At times Kelric thought the node was more human than some humans. **Did the gauntlets send you any data?**

Nothing. They seem quiescent. Bolt paused. Not quiescent, exactly. More as if they are waiting.

That sounded like an impression to Kelric, regardless of what Bolt might think of his ability to form them. **Waiting for what?**

I'm not sure. You, maybe.

Kelric concentrated on the gauntlets. **What are you telling me?**

HOME. It came from his gauntlets as a feeling rather than a word.

Where is your home? Kelric asked.

No response.

Bolt suddenly thought, Kelric, have you been reading the broadcasts from the Selei Science Meshworks?

No. Should I be?

I don't know. One just came up in my memory. I believe your gauntlets inserted it.

Kelric stiffened. **They can affect your memory?**

It's never happened before. However, I detect a sense of urgency.

What's in the broadcast?

It regards some space-time anomalies. Bolt gave him a summary of the implosions. Apparently no cause has yet been found.

Kelric rubbed his chin, bewildered. **They started on Glory?**

Yes. But they've moved into space. And grown more disruptive.

Where are they going?

Bolt accessed his optic nerve and presented a map that appeared to hang in front of the chair. It showed a region of space with the implosions highlighted in red. The line is roughly toward the SSRB, where the Traders have the Lock. Which is where you found the gauntlets and could be the place they consider "home."

Kelric concentrated on the gauntlets. **Is this linked to the Lock?**

No response.

Bolt, did they put anything else in your memory?

Nothing.

Kelric studied the massive gauntlets on his wrists. **What are you trying to tell me?**

A sense of an alien intellect washed over him. **HOME.** Home. If they wanted the SSRB Lock, he didn't see how he could help. He stared down at the War Room, and Bolt let the map fade. The dais on the far side of the amphitheater was empty, and the corridor to the First Lock lay beyond it. Transparent columns bordered the corridor, and ancient mechanisms gleamed within them, moving gears and levers that flashed lights. The path extended away from the dais until it dwindled to a point of perspective, as if it went on forever.

Have you detected anything unusual from this Lock? he asked Bolt.

Nothing. But I don't normally communicate with a space-time singularity.

Kelric smiled at its phrasing. A Lock didn't communicate, it simply existed. Even that wasn't certain. If someone who wasn't a psion tried to enter the Lock, they found nothing in the chamber at the end of the corridor. He suspected they could find the singularity only if they entered the room when a Ruby psion was already there. He had never tried to bring in someone else; it seemed wrong. The Lock wanted only its Keys to visit that surreal place where two universes intersected.

A psion who wasn't a Ruby *could* sense the singularity. They knew it was there, unlike someone with no Kyle ability. But the farther they went down the corridor, the greater the pressure on their mind, until they had to turn back or black out. Only a Ruby psion could endure its power and reach the chamber.

The Lock had never bothered Kelric. It felt *right*. He was always aware of it at the edges of his mind, and Dehya described a similar effect. That was the closest they came to communication with it. Kelric rarely walked that corridor.

He had no reason to; he was already a Key. Whether formation of the Dyad was its purpose or simply a side effect, he had no idea. He and Dehya took care never to disturb it, except in emergencies. He had no idea of such a situation now, but the warning from the gauntlets disturbed him. They either couldn't or wouldn't tell him more, and he couldn't go to the Lock where he had found them.

But he could go to the one here.

The Sphinx Sector Rim Base formed one of several command centers for the Eubian military. The base consisted of many space stations executing intricate orbits around one another. From far away, they sparkled like jewels in deep space; closer in, they resolved into giant habitats bristling with weapons, antennae, and space debris. The Lock that ESComm had stolen from the Skolians orbited in the center of the system. Most of the habitats supported lush biospheres and populations in the millions, but the Lock was small and purely functional, only machinery and metal.

Colonel Vatrix Muze had been in charge of the Lock station the first time Jaibriol had visited, ten years ago, and he still held the prestigious post. In the convoluted kinship relations among Aristos, Muze had ties to both Jaibriol and Robert. The colonel was the grandson of High Judge Calope Muze, Jaibriol's cousin, and Calope's uncle had sired Robert's mother, which meant Jaibriol and Robert were also distantly related.

Colonel Muze and a retinue of officers met Jaibriol in the docking bay. Muze bowed to him. "We are deeply honored by your visit, Your Glorious Highness."

Jaibriol knew he was lying. The colonel's mind grated even through his protections. Muze was no happier to see him today than the first time they had met, ten years ago. It wasn't only the relentless pressure of Muze's mind that bothered Jaibriol; he also felt the man's covert hostility, the most dangerous kind, antagonism hidden behind a veneer of deference.

Muze escorted him along a corridor that curved upward in the distance, following the curve of the rotating station. They were essentially walking on the inside of a huge donut in space. Jaibriol's guards surrounded them, Robert stayed at his side, and Muze's aides followed. Jaibriol felt as if his mind were splitting open. It wasn't only Muze; the colonel's three aides all had enough Aristo lineage to manifest that searching hunger for transcendence. It pressed down on Jaibriol, wore at him, exhausted him, until it was all he could do to keep from lurching forward. Robert glanced at him with concern, but Jaibriol didn't dare acknowledge it or otherwise reveal any sign of weakness.

"We have optimism," Colonel Muze was saying. "A team of distortion physicists is attending our discourse on the fabric of space-time. It is auspicious that they bring their ideas into our sphere."

Jaibriol wished the colonel would just come out and flaming say that the scientists sent to study the implosions had arrived. Nor had he ever heard of distortion physics. For all he knew, Muze had made it up. It would be a typical Highton ploy to ridicule someone.

"One would hope they don't distort their own name," Jaibriol said.

Muze glanced at him with a bland expression. "Your wit dazzles, Your Highness."

Wit, indeed. Muze's veiled antagonism jabbed at Jaibriol's shields. He lowered his barriers so he could probe the colonel's mind, but the pressure immediately increased, and he stumbled as his vision darkened.

"Your Highness?" Muze spoke smoothly, watching Jaibriol like a hawk that had spotted prey.

Jaibriol caught his balance and gave no sign he acknowledged Muze's implied question about his health. He struggled to rebuild his barriers. Mercifully, the onslaught receded, and the haze faded from his vision. It didn't bode well that Muze had caught his lapse; Hightons were experts at reading body language. Muze would interpret his dizziness as weakness, and when Aristos saw weakness, they attacked, often subtly, but they found ways to exploit any failing they perceived in a foe. And Jaibriol had no doubt Muze saw him in those terms. He had made enemies in ESComm when he opened negotiations with the Skolians.

Jaibriol had read the files on all his top ESComm officers. Many of them abhorred the Skolians. He had once thought their hatred derived from their conviction Skolians were a lower form of life. And that was part of it. They considered it repellent that a dynasty of "providers" had established an empire to rival their own. But as much as they refused to admit it, the Aristos also felt beaten down by the constant hostilities. They wanted to conquer Skolia because they were tired of war. It didn't create a desire in them to negotiate; the only solution they considered acceptable was eradication of the Imperialate and the enslavement of all Skolian peoples.

❖ ❖ ❖

The Lock corridor in the Skolian Orbiter lay in front of Kelric. Its lights seemed faster today. As a Key to the web, he was more attuned to the Lock than anyone else alive except Dehya. It was agitated, if one could apply a human emotion to a physical place. The corridor stretched out in front of him to that seemingly infinite point. Even knowing it lay inside a space habitat only a few kilometers in diameter, it unsettled Kelric. Perhaps it *did* go on that incredible distance, twisting into another place that wasn't aligned with this space-time.

Behind him, the War Room registered as a subdued hum. The Orbiter's thirty-hour cycle was deep into night. Even this late, telops were at work, monitoring the far-flung forces of an empire. Kelric knew they were aware of him, probably wondering what he intended to do. It was a good question: he wasn't sure himself.

He began to walk the corridor.

His boots clanged on the diamond-steel floor. He continued on, inundated with brightness from the brilliant surfaces, the pillars, the glow suffusing the area. On he walked, toward a point that never came closer.

And walked.

And walked.

Time seemed bent, as if it had curved away, around a corner. Surely it hadn't taken this long to reach the SSRB Lock. He felt as if he were walking forever down an endless path. He experienced none of the pressure other psions described in the corridor. Maybe he *couldn't* feel it; he lacked mental finesse, having an immense but blunt power.

The point of perspective finally began to change, growing into an archway that glowed as if it were white light. He stopped in front of it and set his hand against the side, convincing himself of its solidity. Then he stepped into the Lock chamber. Radiance enveloped him; with so much light, he could barely see the room. It was only ten paces wide, but its walls rose high over his head, lost in a luminous fog.

The Lock pierced the center of the chamber in a radiant column of light. It rose out of the floor and disappeared into the haze overhead. This was the singularity, the point where another universe punctured space-time. Kelric steeled himself, unsure what he would find but certain he needed to find out.

Then he stepped into the pillar of light.

XVII
Pillar of Darkness

"Your meeting with Colonel Muze and his staff is tomorrow at First Hour," Robert said. He rolled his mesh film out on the desk next to the armchair where Jaibriol had slumped. Glancing over, he spoke carefully. "They are all Aristos."

Jaibriol barely heard. He sat sprawled in his chair, too worn out to move. Tonight's dinner with the colonel and his top officers had been interminable. It battered his mental defenses. Nor did it help that the twenty-hour day here threw off his sleep cycle, which had adjusted to the sixteen-hour day on Glory. Muze had given him the best quarters on the station, but they were cramped and utilitarian. Jaibriol didn't care; he just wanted a reprieve from the pain in his head. He suspected his dinner companions had been transcending at a low level, unaware their good moods came from their emperor's splintering headache. In one of the grimmer ironies of his life, the very trait that made them so dangerous to him also improved their temper in his presence and ameliorated his tendency to antagonize them.

"Luminos down," Jaibriol said. He should answer Robert, but he barely felt able to talk. He needed time for the health nanomeds in his body to help him recover.

The lights dimmed, and the walls softened into soothing views of space with spumes of interstellar gas. With an exhale, Jaibriol slumped lower in his chair.

Robert was watching him with that concerned look he had worn ever since they had arrived. "Can I get you anything?"

"Thank you. But I'm fine." Jaibriol wasn't and never would be, but nothing Robert could do would change that miserable fact.

It felt strange to be so close to a Lock and sense nothing. No life. When ESComm had stolen this Lock from the Skolians, they had also captured Eldrin Valdoria, Kelric's older brother. As a Ruby psion, Eldrin could have become a Key, and with both a Lock and Key, the Aristos could have created their own Kyle web. The day they had enslaved Eldrin, the dream of Jaibriol's parents had ended, for Eube had gained the final ingredient it needed to conquer Skolia.

At the time, Jaibriol had been traveling as a member of a humanitarian organization, the Dawn Corps of the Allied Worlds. Desperate to protect both his parents' dream and his uncle, he had offered Corbal a trade: himself for Eldrin. It was the only exchange Corbal would consider for his captive Ruby psion: a Qox emperor he believed had the energy to conquer Skolia and raise Eube to greater heights, in exchange for the Skolian prince who might make it possible to conquer Skolia despite having no Qox heir to assume the throne. The death of Jaibriol's father had left Eube tottering on collapse; a vibrant young emperor could mean the difference between survival and breakdown.

Corbal's decision to accept Jaibriol's offer had outraged many Aristos. They also questioned why Corbal gave up his claim to the throne. Jaibriol had no doubts on that— Corbal had expected to rule from the shadows, manipulating the boy emperor. It had taken him longer to realize that Corbal had recognized his secret; Jaibriol lacked the same neural structures Corbal had eliminated in himself so he would no longer transcend. Only someone who had done the unthinkable among the Aristos would have uncovered the truth:

Jaibriol's great-grandfather had been Aristo.

His grandfather had been half Aristo, half Ruby.

His father had been a Ruby psion.

Jaibriol was a Ruby psion.

The Qox Dynasty had created its own Key.

Corbal hadn't just wanted to rule from behind the throne; he wanted Jaibriol to join the powerlink, make the Dyad a Triad, build a Kyle web, and conquer the stars. Corbal had sought to rule the sum total of humanity, all of it, Skolia and the Allieds included, through a puppet emperor. Except Jaibriol had proved far less malleable than he expected. Jaibriol couldn't deny the lure of the power, but he could no more inflict Aristo rule on all humanity than he could transcend. He had also realized his cousin didn't transcend, for Corbal didn't have that immense cavity in his mind. So the two of them had reached an impasse; they each kept the other's secrets.

Jaibriol could never trust his cousin. And yet . . . over the years, something had happened. Corbal's attitude toward him had changed. If Jaibriol hadn't known better, he might have called it familial love. He did know better, of course; he wasn't that naïve.

A chime sounded. Disoriented, Jaibriol opened his eyes and blinked at Robert. "What is that?"

Robert frowned at his mesh film. "Colonel Muze wishes an audience with you."

Jaibriol swore under his breath. "Tell him I'm asleep."

"If that is what you wish,' Robert said formally, "I will take care of it."

Jaibriol wanted to groan. He hated it when Robert talked that way. "In other words, you think I should see him."

"You need his good will," Robert said. "Or at least the best relation you can establish with him. It isn't unreasonable for the station commander to pay his courtesies during a visit such as this. Refusing his request would be an insult."

Jaibriol didn't feel up to dealing with Muze, but what he avoided today could escalate tomorrow. "Very well," he said tiredly. "Bring him in."

As Robert set up the audience, Jaibriol sat up and rested one elbow on the arm of his chair, a posture he had learned by studying portraits of his ancestors, who were often shown seated this way in some imperially elegant place. He had noticed the posture had a subtle effect on people; they viewed him as more regal. It disquieted him that it felt so natural.

His bodyguards ushered Colonel Muze into the room.

Hidaka walked at Muze's side, looming over him, his boots clanking. All of Jaibriol's guards were present, six counting Hidaka, one at each wall of the hexagonal chamber. They had that preternatural stillness of Razers, like waiting machines.

Muze bowed to Jaibriol. "My honor at your revered company, Glorious Highness."

Jaibriol nodded stiffly, an acceptance of the greeting with no indication the honor was either returned or refused. He didn't want to alienate Muze any more than he did just by being himself, but neither did he want to encourage the colonel. He lifted his hand, indicating a brocaded armchair identical to his. Both had extensive mech-tech that read body language and adjusted for comfort. On this utilitarian habitat, though, the brocade was more of a rarity than the smart tech.

After Muze was seated, Jaibriol waited. The colonel had requested the audience and he was lower in status than the emperor, so protocol required he broach the discussion first.

"Your visit brings fortune to our station," Muze opened.

"It would appear the vagaries of space-time also bring theirs," Jaibriol said, referring to the implosions. His nanomeds had eased his headache, but it was growing worse again.

"It is great bravery to set oneself in a path of the inexplicable." Muze tilted his head slightly to the left, a hint of contradiction.

Jaibriol knew what he implied; only a fool traveled into the path of an unexplained violent phenomenon. He gritted his teeth, but he could live with the barb. As long as Muze viewed him as callow and ill-advised, he wouldn't suspect Jaibriol's real reason for coming here. Muze didn't seem surprised by his interest; the Lock was, after all, their most valuable acquisition from the Skolians. No one knew if it could revive, and securing a Ruby psion had proved inordinately difficult, but as long as they had the Lock, the chance of creating their own Kyle web remained.

Jaibriol said nothing and let Muze stew. Eventually the colonel would get around to his reason for inflicting this audience. Jaibriol just hoped his head hadn't split open by then.

"It is rare that we have the pleasure of such a magnificent visit," Muze said.

"Indeed," Jaibriol said, and hoped his agreement stuck in Muze's craw. It probably wouldn't; Aristos expected their emperor to think of himself in grandiose terms.

"Would that we could offer your Glorious Highness a better environment," Muze added, his expression cagey.

Jaibriol didn't mind about the small quarters; he would be just as miserable in a bigger room. He said only, "It would be auspicious." He was running out of inflated adjectives.

Muze's eyes glinted. "Perhaps we could provide Your Magnificence a small token of our esteem."

With his headache, it took Jaibriol a moment to absorb what Muze meant. Then he felt sick. The colonel had just offered him a provider so Jaibriol could torture some psion even more unfortunate than himself. He wished he could toss the colonel out, but he didn't dare stir suspicion, especially during this visit. Jaibriol usually avoided "gifts" of providers using his fidelity to his wife as the reason, which was considered bizarre but not abhorrent. But at times, he couldn't avoid it without crossing what Aristos considered an unacceptable line, which meant he had to be present when they transcended. Sometimes it made him so deeply ill, he thought he would lose his mind, and right now he felt close to the edge.

Somehow he managed to say, "Your magnanimous character is noted." He almost gagged on the words.

Muze should have been pleased with the response. But he only seemed warier. Wary . . . and something else. What?

Then it hit Jaibriol. The colonel was *transcending*. With growing horror, Jaibriol realized Muze suspected his good mood was linked to the emperor. Jaibriol shored up his barriers, but it didn't help; his defenses were too strained.

"I shall arrange matters to your taste," Muze was saying.

Alarm flared in Jaibriol. He had to stop Muze from bringing a provider. He would experience the psion's agony as if it was his own, and if that happened in his current weakened state, he would crack open. But he couldn't form the words to extricate himself for the situation. His thoughts fled the intricacies of the Highton language like a cornered animal in pain.

"Your Highness?" Muze asked, his gaze hard.

A chime sounded.

Jaibriol blinked. As he turned toward the sound, Robert looked up from the desk where he had been occupying himself. Until now, he had apparently been too inconsequential for Muze to bother noticing.

"Your Glorious H-highness." Robert sounded terrified. "Please excuse my deplorable interruption. I beg you to forgive me. It is an urgent message from his eminence, Lord Corbal Xir. He requests you attend it soon. Sire!" He slipped out of the chair and knelt with his head down. "I beg you, forgive me."

Jaibriol would have gaped in utter astonishment at his aide's peculiar behavior, except the agony in his head overcame every other reaction, even his falling over in shock. Whatever had afflicted Robert?

It took him a moment to realize Robert was giving him an out. Corbal ranked well above Vatrix Muze in Highton levels of power and influence, enough so the colonel would have to accept a dismissal. At the same time, Robert implied the emperor would see that his aide paid for such an unwelcome interruption from an evening of pleasure. With his mind so raw, Jaibriol knew Robert *was* terrified, not of him, but *for* him. Robert feared that if this audience continued, the emperor would reveal himself in ways better left unknown.

Jaibriol lifted his hand to Muze, palm upward, the gesture meant to indicate apology and displeasure with the source of the infraction, Robert in this case. "It appears my cousin is more eminent than usual," he said wryly.

Muze gave a startled laugh. Apparently Jaibriol's attempt at a Highton joke hadn't fallen flat. He didn't know whether to be relieved he could pull it off or dismayed he was becoming that much of an Aristo.

He initiated the process of dismissing Muze without insult. The entire time, Robert stayed on his knees, shaking. When Hidaka escorted the colonel from the room, Jaibriol had an odd sense, as if Hidaka stayed too close to Muze. It wasn't enough to be an overt threat, but he wondered if the Razer was subconsciously trying to intimidate the colonel. It couldn't be conscious; Razers were designed to consider Aristos supreme beings. It was imprinted in their biomech webs and neural nets. Unless Muze endangered or attacked the emperor, Hidaka could no more threaten him than he could turn inside out. Given that Muze had done nothing more than offer Jaibriol a pleasure girl, the Razer could hardly consider him a danger.

After Muze was gone, Jaibriol said, "Thank you, Hidaka. You all may go as well."

"If it pleases Your Highness that we leave," Hidaka said in his deep voice, "we will esteem and honor your wishes." Then he added, "But I beg you to ask us to commit suicide instead, for we would rather take our own lives than leave yours undefended."

Hell and damnation. The last thing he needed was his Razers arguing with him under the guise of spurious threats to commit suicide. "Hidaka," he said softly. "Go. My head hurts."

The captain stared at him. Hightons never admitted weakness. The shock of it had the desired effect; Hidaka offered no more objections, just motioned for the other guards to leave with him.

As soon as he and Robert were alone, Jaibriol slid down to the floor next to his aide and slumped against the desk. Robert had scanned the room earlier for monitoring devices, but Jaibriol didn't want to take chances. Audio bugs were harder to find than optical, so instead of speaking, he tapped a message on his wrist comm and held it so Robert could see it even with his head bowed.

=Why are you on the floor?= Jaibriol asked.

Robert raised his head. Then he tapped out a message on his comm. =You must not let them harm you.=

=I am the emperor. They cannot.= That wasn't true, but he had endured too much truth for the night. He just wanted to go to bed and give his meds a chance to treat his aching head.

=They can,= Robert wrote. =And they will.=

Robert never openly contradicted him. It scared Jaibriol. =I'll be all right.=

=We must leave this place,= Robert answered. =It is worse for you here.=

A chill went through Jaibriol. Just how much did Robert suspect? =I can't go yet.=

=Cancel the meeting tomorrow. A crisis has arisen. Lord Xir bids you to attend it.=

Jaibriol thought he must be even more dazed than he had realized, to have forgotten what elicited Robert's reaction in the first place. Reorienting, he wrote, =If Corbal sent a message by starship and it's already arrived, he must have sent it just after I left Glory.=

Robert met his gaze squarely. =Forgive me. I lied.=

Jaibriol gaped at him. Robert was supposed to be incapable of misleading a Highton. That he admitted it without a flinch also put the lie to his performance of terror in front of Muze. When Jaibriol didn't immediately respond, Robert paled. But he never averted his gaze.

Jaibriol took a deep breath. =Very well. I will leave for

this "emergency."= As relief suffused his aide's face, he added, =But first I must visit the Lock.=

Robert's brow furrowed. =You are already in the Lock.=

=Not the station. The singularity.=

=But it is dead, Sire.= Robert grimaced. =Unless evil spirits haunt its grave. This station is a grim place.=

=It has no spirits. Just technology.=

Robert didn't answer, and Jaibriol doubted his aide believed him. Jaibriol rubbed his head with his fingertips. Regardless of his condition, he couldn't leave before he did what he had come here to do. He feared that what had begun as a small anomaly could become an interstellar catastrophe by the time it reached the SSRB. The implosions had started where he lived. Maybe it was coincidence, but he didn't believe that. The Lock was seeking him. Maybe it wanted any Ruby psion, and he happened to be closest.

He had to find out what it needed before it was too late.

XVIII
The Ward of Lives

Radiance filled Kelric Skolia.

Light flowed, liquid and brilliant.

A thought formed in his mind, with the sense of an alien intelligence. **KEY.**

Yes, Kelric thought. **I am your Key**. His body no longer existed. He had become thought. Light. Radiance.

NOT KEY, the Lock answered.

I am your Key. He could never stop being one. His brain was so thoroughly intertwined with the Dyad, it would cause fatal brain damage if he tried to withdraw.

DEATH. The luminosity dimmed around Kelric.

Whose death? Kelric asked.

ALL.

Foreboding rose in Kelric. If the Lock ceased with him in it, he would stop existing as well. His gauntlets had thought of "home," which suggested the SSRB where he had found them. Could that Lock be dying because he had deactivated it?

How can I help? Kelric asked. **What do you need?**

STRENGTH.

That I can do. He gathered his power into a great wave and flooded the Kyle. The fading of the light slowed, but it didn't stop.

ENDING, the Lock thought.

Then I must go, Kelric answered. If he didn't return to his own universe, he could vanish here. The first time he had entered a Lock, he had no trouble leaving. He had thought of doing it and found himself stepping out of the singularity. But now, when he tried, it didn't work—and without a body, he had no other way to go back.

The universe darkened. **END.**

NO!

The Kyle vanished.

Jaibriol Qox, Emperor of Eube, stood at the threshold of the corridor that led to the SSRB Lock and stared down the dead, dark pathway. Columns rose on either side, shadowed and filled with motionless gears. Nothing glowed here except a small Eubian safety light on the dais behind him.

He had come alone into this graveyard. He had evaded his guards by leaving his quarters through a disguised exit Robert had discovered when he swept the room for monitors. Convincing Robert to let him go by himself had been more difficult. His aide feared the Lock and had no desire to enter it, but he had even less desire for the emperor to do so. When Jaibriol told him to remain behind, he had thought for one astonishing moment that Robert would refuse an Imperial order. Then his aide had knelt to him, his face flushed, and Jaibriol had felt smaller than an insect.

No sense of life awaited him. No intellect tugged at his mind. Before Kelric had killed this Lock, Jaibriol had felt its presence. It had filled the station. Apparently no one else sensed it, certainly no Aristo or taskmaker, possibly not even a provider. But Jaibriol had known. Now that presence was gone.

Are you dead? he thought. Maybe he was deluded, to imagine this place as anything more than a big room with defunct machines and a path that led . . .

Where?

He started down the Lock corridor.

Darkness surrounded him. The wan light from the dais dimmed to nothing. It should have trickled down the pathway, yet nothing penetrated the gloom. He walked in blackness.

Jaibriol stopped, uneasy. He looked back the way he had come, but he could see no more in that direction. Turning forward again, he took another step. The darkness drew closer. He knew, logically, that a lack of light wasn't "close." Yet he felt as if it wrapped around him, heavy and dense.

He continued on.

Jaibriol had no idea how long he walked. Unable to see even his hand in front of his face, he felt dissociated from reality. This place between space-time and some other universe had gone wrong. He considered returning to the dais room, but he feared if he walked the other way, he would never reach the end of the path in that direction either. He existed in a limbo of nothing.

His hand hit a surface. With a relieved grunt, he felt along the barrier and found an opening. When he stretched out his arm, his hand hit another side. An archway, perhaps. He leaned against the lintel, his heart beating hard. Although he had no idea where he had ended up or if he could escape this place, at least it *was* a place.

When his pulse settled, he took an exploratory step through the archway. He almost fell; the floor on the other side was a hand span lower than on his side. He felt his way along a cool, smooth wall and figured out that he had entered a small room with eight sides. An octagon chamber. It had an octagonal depression in its center about two paces wide.

Jaibriol rubbed his hand over his eyes. Worn out, he slid down one wall and sat on the floor. He was no closer to discovering if the Lock had a connection to the implosions.

"What should I do?" he asked the air.

Silence.

After he rested, he climbed to his feet and made his way along the wall again, headed toward the doorway. Maybe he should go back to his quarters and sleep, before his body gave out.

His knee hit a hard surface.

Jaibriol paused, startled. Then he explored the barrier. It felt like a console. Yes, here was the seat. He sat down and slid his palms over the panels until his fingers scraped a line of engraved hieroglyphics. He felt it carefully. He didn't recognize the language, but it had elements in common with both Iotic and Highton, which derived from the same roots. He pieced out the inscription:

To you, Karj, comes the ward of lives.

Karj? Could it mean Kurj, the man who had been Imperator before Jaibriol's mother? But he had died only twelve years ago, and this inscription was probably thousands of years old. The name Kurj dated from before the time when Skolia and Eube had split apart, back when they had all been one people.

He tried to activate the console, but nothing worked. Finally he gave up and went back to the center of the chamber. Kneeling in the depression, he felt around the floor, searching for clues to understand this place. The sleek surface offered no answers.

Frustrated, he sat with one leg bent and his elbow resting on his knee. His thoughts felt muted, but at least it eased the damage from his exposure to Aristos, especially Colonel Muze, whose mind had grated like sandpaper on a raw wound. The darkness settled over him like a blanket and muffled his brain.

In the darkness of a space that didn't exist, Kelric Skolia strained to keep his identity intact.

Begin.

He shored up Kyle space like the Atlas of Earth's mythology holding up the world.

Begin.

His power beat like a deep pulse.

Begin.

The darkness stabilized, an absence of light but no longer of existence. And Kelric began to understand.

When he had deactivated one of the Locks, he had eliminated one of three nodes that sustained Kyle space. The Locks balanced the Kyle web; with only two operating, it strained and snapped. Humanity had created million of gates that connected the Kyle to space-time, and each one added to the strain. Just as earthquakes relieved pressure in a planet's crust, so the implosions relieved stresses between the two universes. The instabilities had built for ten years, until something had to give. When the disruptions reached the SSRB, they were going to rip apart space-time between the three Locks like fault lines cracking. It would be an interstellar disaster of unprecedented proportions.

Kelric saw no choice. He had to reactivate the Lock. A universe where the Traders had access to Kyle technology wasn't one he wanted to contemplate, but destroying a substantial portion of space could be even worse. Gods only knew how many people would die and star systems perish.

He had no idea if he could restart the Lock from so far away, but as a Key, he had more resources than anyone else, probably more than he had plumbed. The SSRB Lock existed at the fringes of his awareness, quiescent, distant and vague, but alive.

Resume, he thought.

No response.

I am your Key. Come to me.

Like a leviathan awaking, the Lock stirred.

Jaibriol sat in the darkened SSRB Lock and tried to understand its emptiness.

Come to me, he thought, he wasn't certain why, except that the words felt right.

The Lock stirred.

Jaibriol froze. **Who?** he asked.

NOT KEY. It was as if a distant monolith turned toward him.

I'm not a Key, that's true, he admitted.

DEATH.

He swallowed, wondering if it thought he had killed it. **Do you mean this Lock?** Uneasily, he added, **Or me?**

ALL.

Both of us?

NO.

I don't understand.

END.

His frustration built. **What ends?** He felt foolish questioning a thought that was probably a figment of his imagination.

THE CORRIDOR OF AGES.

I don't understand. He didn't know if the thoughts came from the Lock, the machinery, or something else.

Nothing.

You have to help me. That felt wrong. He delved deeper into his mind—and words came as if Kyle space itself revealed them.

Come to me, Jaibriol thought. **I am your Key.**

Kelric's thought thundered throughout the Kyle.

RESUME.

With a gigantic, shattering surge of power, the Lock awoke.

Light flooded the chamber where Jaibriol sat, brilliant and painful. He cried out and covered his eyes. In that instant, the Kyle singularity shot up through the floor and pierced the chamber—

Right through Jaibriol.

XIX
A Chilling Blue

Crush the petals of a night-fragrant vine,
In bitter dreaming sweetness.
Hold its vulnerable, frail beauty,
Cherished beyond all reason.

The night offers surcease, heart-aching hope,
Or painful, streaming cruelty.
Pray withhold your chilling blue transcendence
In the deep, purpling dawn.

The singing of the ancient provider broke Jaibriol's heart, for the music was impossibly beautiful and impossibly sad. He grieved for the love of the family he had lost, for the family he would never know, and for the crushing, bitter weight of Aristo cruelty that would be his for the rest of his life.

Deep within the Kyle, the emperor wept.

XX
Traid Quis

Jaibriol dragged himself out of the singularity on his hands and knees. He sprawled on the floor while his head reeled with power. It was unbearable. He would drown in the streaming blue of the Kyle.

His fingers spasmed as he clawed the floor. For ten years he had hidden, repressed, constrained, and constricted his mind, and now the Lock had ripped it wide open. Power flooded him as his thoughts encompassed a universe. He wanted to scream, but he could barely breathe.

His muscles clenched as if he were convulsing. It could have been seconds, minutes, hours. Then they released, and he choked out a sob. He crawled another few feet, pulling his body along the floor. Light filled the chamber, mercilessly bright. With tears streaming down his face, he pushed up on his hands—

And stared into the maw of a laser carbine.

Too much in shock even to register fear, Jaibriol raised his head. In the brilliance of the Lock, he could barely see the man who held the gun. But he recognized the eyes. They were the only color in the chamber, red and hard. And when the man spoke, Jaibriol knew his voice.

"The fates of Eube are truly capricious," Colonel Muze said from behind the gun, "that they would give us a Ruby Key in the person of our own emperor."

The Lock had shredded Jaibriol's defenses, and the Aristo mind of the colonel surrounded him in a great icy void that froze his thoughts, his heart, his being. He felt Muze transcending, and he silently screamed with the torment. In one horrifying moment, he had given Eube everything it needed to conquer the Skolians and condemned himself to a life of agony so much worse than what he already lived that he knew he would go insane.

"**No.**" Jaibriol thought he whispered, but the word thundered in the chamber as if he were one of those fates Muze had evoked.

The colonel backed away from him. "Get up."

Jaibriol couldn't move.

"*Get up!*" Muze shouted, and his fear saturated the air.

Jaibriol dragged himself to the console, which glowed like alabaster. Clutching the chair, he pulled up to his knees. With his arms shaking, he struggled to his feet. Then he just stood, staring at Muze. The violation couldn't have been worse than for an Aristo to enter the Lock.

"For ten years, you've corrupted the throne." Loathing filled the colonel's voice. "I always knew you were flawed, but I had no idea just how great the filth you brought among us. We will cleanse Eube of your stain." His voice was harsh with revulsion. "And you will serve us, provider.

Have no doubt; you will pay for this crime beyond all crimes."

The light suddenly flared even brighter, blinding him. A backlash of violence hit Jaibriol, not physically, but crashing through his mind. He stumbled away from the console and tried to scream, but no sound came. He teetered at the edge of the pillar of light, the singularity that had thrown him into Kyle space, and he knew without doubt that if he fell into it again, the power would kill him.

The singularity died.

Darkness dropped around Jaibriol. The pillar was gone. He no longer felt the presence of the Lock. The astringent smell of a laser shot and the stench of melted composites filled the air—that, and another smell he couldn't identify but that raised bile in his throat. He couldn't handle the sensory onslaught; his mind was shutting down.

He staggered backward and hit a wall. The blackness wasn't complete; dim light filtered into the chamber from the corridor, enough to show him that whatever had killed that Lock had also slagged the console. Vatrix Muze no longer stood anywhere Jaibriol could see. He didn't understand why the colonel had fired. Did he sicken Muze so much that the Aristo would seek to destroy a Ruby Key who had joined the Triad? If that were true, Aristo thought processes were even more alien than he had ever comprehended.

He stumbled toward the entrance, a vague octagon of lighter shadows. A towering figure appeared there, silhouetted against the dim light. Jaibriol lurched to a stop, unable to push himself any farther.

A deep voice spoke. "Can you walk, Your Highness?"

Jaibriol wanted to weep. **"Hidaka?"** He barely whispered it, and yet his voice echoed.

"I have stopped the assassination attempt." Hidaka's usually impassive voice sounded shaken. "You must leave this place, Sire."

Jaibriol stared at his bodyguard. Hidaka had to know what he was seeing. He had to have heard what Muze had said. Why would a Razer call a false emperor *Sire*?

Something grotesque lay in a twisted, smoldering pile across the chamber. Then Jaibriol recognized the stench that filled the room. Cauterized human flesh.

Hidaka was holding a laser carbine. His bodyguard had murdered a high-ranking Aristo who had just made possibly the most valuable discovery in the history of the Eubian empire.

"Ah, no." Jaibriol swayed, and his vision dimmed.

"Sire!" Hidaka lunged into the chamber.

Jaibriol's legs buckled, and Hidaka caught him as he fell. The giant Razer lifted Jaibriol into his arms as easily as if the emperor were a broken doll, and blackness closed around him.

Kelric slowly lifted his head. He was sitting sideways at a console in the Lock chamber on the Skolian Orbiter. The singularity glowed next to him, but it seemed oddly dim. Although his head throbbed, he sensed no damage to himself. None of his internal warning systems had activated.

Bolt? he asked. **Are you there?**

Yes. I'm fine.

How did I get here? The last Kelric remembered, he had been deep within a fracturing Kyle space. He had reactivated the SSRB Lock many light-years distant at a Eubian military complex.

I don't know. Bolt, who was supposed to have no personality, sounded bemused. My memory has a gap. I have no other data until you became conscious of sitting here.

Kelric gazed at the pillar of light. He no longer had to squint against its brilliance. **Something damaged the Lock.**

I detect no damage here.

It's weakened.

Perhaps the problem isn't with this one.

Kelric rubbed his temple. **I feel strange.**

Are you injured?

I don't think so. After a moment, he added, **I've a shadow.**

All people have shadows, assuming proper light conditions.

Not that kind, Bolt. In my mind.

Is your link as a Key weakened?

No. It has a— He struggled to define his impression. **Not a shadow, exactly. When you have a solar eclipse, the moon shadows the sun. The moon is present, but you don't see it, only the shadow. It's as if a moon cast its shadow across Kyle space.**

"Kelric?"

He jumped to his feet and whirled around, his body toggling into combat mode as he raised his arm to strike.

Dehya had entered the chamber and stood bathed in radiance from the singularity. Small and frail, she was little more than a third his weight. She looked up at his giant fist raised above her head.

Kelric stared at her, dismayed. What if he hadn't stopped his reflexes in time? He could have killed her with one blow.

He lowered his arm. **"You surprised me,"** he said—and froze. He had spoken in low tones, but his words resonated with power.

"What did you do?" Her voice sounded as if it came from far away, blowing across the blue spaces of the Kyle.

I called the Lock at the SSRB, he thought. Usually mindspeech drained him, but in this interstice separating space-time and the Kyle, it felt right. **Something went wrong.**

It died, she answered. *Or ended somehow.*

I can't tell what happened. My mind is too blunt.

I can't tell, either. My mind hasn't the strength.

We must combine efforts.

Kyle space is damaged. If we go in together, we could strain it too far.

Kelric feared she was right. With the combined power of their minds focused in the Kyle, they might destabilize its weakened structure and accelerate the implosions. But if they didn't find out what was wrong, they could be inviting a catastrophe of interstellar proportions. Something had happened when he touched the SSRB Lock, something so intense it had pushed him out of the singularity and seared his memory.

Dehya was watching his face. *It called to me for help, too, I think.*

My gauntlets sent me a warning about the SSRB Lock. A memory leapt in Kelric's mind: he had met Jaibriol Qox there, ten years ago.

Dehya's thought drifted over him like mist. *Let me see.*

Here in the chamber, his mind flexed as it never could in normal space. And he and Dehya were Keys. Their minds linked in ways no other humans could manage. He lowered his barriers so she could see pieces of the memory he had stored in Bolt ten years ago . . .

The emperor stood at his full height, over six feet tall. He was a boy, no more than seventeen. He crossed the dais to Kelric. When he stopped, only a rail separated them.

"Go now," Jaibriol said. "While you can."

"You would let me go?" Kelric asked, incredulous.

Jaibriol regarded him steadily. "Yes."

Kelric didn't believe it. "Why?"

The emperor answered in cool, cultured tones. "Meet me at the peace table."

"You want me to believe you wish peace," Kelric said, "when you have a Lock and two Keys."

"What Lock?" The youth spread his hands. "It no longer works."

Kelric knew Jaibriol had seen him suspend the singularity. Yet the emperor hadn't asked if he could bring it back alive.

"We had one Key," Jaibriol added. "We gave him back."

"Gave who back?"

"Your brother. Eldrin Valdoria."

"Don't lie to me, Highton." Kelric knew the Eubians

would never free his brother. Now that they had a Lock and a Key, nothing would convince them to surrender either.

"Why would I lie?" Jaibriol asked.

"It's what you Hightons do," Kelric said. "Lie, manipulate, cheat."

It happened then. Jaibriol's aloof mask slipped. In that instant, his face revealed a terrified, lonely young man trapped in a role beyond his experience. And his gaze was wrenchingly familiar. Kelric *knew* him, but he didn't remember how.

Then Jaibriol recovered, and once again the icy emperor faced Kelric. "I've little interest in your list of imagined Highton ills," he said. His disdain was almost convincing.

Kelric tried to fathom him. "Eube would never give away its Key. Not when you had a Lock. Nothing is worth it."

"Not even me?"

That stopped Kelric cold. "You, for Eldrin?"

"Yes."

It was the one trade Kelric could imagine them making. A vibrant young emperor on the throne would revitalize Eube. But at the price of their Key? It must have ignited furious debate.

"You are right," Jaibriol said. "It wasn't a universally popular decision. But it is done. I am emperor and your brother is free."

Kelric wondered if his face betrayed that much of his thoughts. He didn't fool himself that they had let Eldrin go. This new emperor was toying with him while guards waited outside.

"I am alone," Jaibriol said.

Kelric froze. "Why did you say that?" If he hadn't known better, he would have thought Jaibriol was an empath. But no Aristo could be a psion.

"You didn't wonder if I had guards?" Jaibriol asked. "I find that hard to believe."

"And you just happened to come in alone when I was here."

"Perhaps you could say I felt it."

"Perhaps," Kelric said. "I don't believe it."

"I suppose not." Jaibriol rubbed his chin. "I detected your entrance in the station web."

Kelric knew the boy was lying. But why? And why did Jaibriol look so hauntingly familiar?

"Imperator Skolia." Jaibriol took a breath. "Meet me when we can discuss peace."

"Why should I believe you want this?"

Jaibriol motioned upward, a gesture that seemed to include all Eube. "It's a great thundering machine I hold by the barest thread. If I am to find a way road to peace, I need your help."

It hit Kelric then, what he had known at a subliminal level throughout this surreal conversation. He felt the youth's mind. Jaibriol had mental barriers. They had been dissolving as he and Kelric talked, probably without the young man realizing it. His luminous Kyle strength glowed.

Jaibriol the Third was a psion.

Kelric spoke in a stunned voice. "You're a telepath."

"No." Pain layered Jaibriol's denial. He became pure Highton. Polished. Cold. Unreal. "I am what you see. Qox."

"At what price?" Kelric asked. "What must you suffer to hide the truth?" He couldn't imagine the hells this young man lived, surrounded by Aristos, never knowing surcease.

Jaibriol met his gaze. "Was anyone here when I came into the Lock? I never saw him."

Kelric spoke softly. "Gods help you, son."

Strain creased Jaibriol's face. "Go. Now. While you can."

Kelric stepped into the Lock corridor. Then he turned and started the long walk down the corridor. His back itched as he waited for the shot, a neural blocker to disable him or rifle fire that would shred his body.

"Lord Skolia," Jaibriol said.

He froze. Would the game end now? He turned to face the emperor. "Yes?"

"If you make it to Earth—" Jaibriol lifted his hand, as if to reach toward him. "Go see Admiral William Seth Rockworth."

"I will go." He wanted to ask more, but he didn't dare stay longer. He set off again. As he strode down the corridor, he had a strange sense, as if Jaibriol whispered in his mind:

God's speed, my uncle . . .

The memory faded, and Kelric became aware of Dehya. He didn't recall moving, but they were both sitting on the floor. The light of the singularity rippled the air in the chamber.

He is a psion. She didn't make it a question.

It took Kelric a moment to reorient. **Yes, I think so.**

We need to know more about him.

Have you had contact with Seth Rockworth? Qox lived with him for two years. He regretted needing to ask the question; he knew she avoided the topic of her former husband. Neither the Imperialate nor his government had formally acknowledged their divorce for fear it would invalidate the treaty established by their marriage. For Eldrin's sake, she kept the subject out of their lives.

I haven't spoken to Seth in years, she thought. I doubt the Allied would let me near him. They've watched him continually since they learned he had Jaibriol Qox as his ward.

I'm not surprised.

I too have wondered about Qox, though.

Kelric tensed. **In what way?**

It's hard to explain.

He waited, but she said no more. It was her way; she often thought in patterns or equations that evolved in sub-shells of her mind before she spoke of them. It disconcerted most people, but it never bothered him. When she felt ready, she would explain.

In any case, he had another way to communicate with her. He took off his pouch and spilled his Quis dice onto the floor. The gems sparkled against the silvery-white composite, but the light that saturated the chamber washed out their glitter. He lowered his defenses carefully, so he wouldn't injure her mind with the force of his own. He wanted her to understand Quis at a level deeper than even she could glean from a few sessions.

Kelric offered his knowledge of Quis, and he felt her mind blending with his as she absorbed the concepts. He placed the first die, an onyx octahedron he used for the Qox dynasty. Dehya studied it and then set down a gold dodecahedron. They built patterns of the Traders, the Imperialate, and the Ruby and Qox dynasties. At first, she did little more than mimic his moves. Then she began to mold the structures on her own. He felt the change on a visceral level, as her Quis took on the luminous character of her extraordinary intellect.

Kelric wasn't certain when he realized what Dehya was trying to show him. She knew too little about the game to clarify her patterns, but she learned fast. Incredibly fast. Her theory became clear; the implosions began on the planet Glory because the Lock was seeking the nearest Ruby psion.

Jaibriol the Third.

No! He built structures to overpower hers, yet no matter how hard he tried, they evolved back to the same pattern: the Lock sought a Key. It hadn't reached out to the Orbiter or Parthonia or anywhere else the Ruby Dynasty called home. Instead, it had touched the Qox Palace.

As to why Dehya believed Jaibriol was a Key, either she didn't know Quis well enough to develop the pattern or else she was holding back. Kelric pushed harder, building structures centered on the Aristo compulsion with the so-called purity of their lines. They were fanatical about their genetics. They would consider it an abomination for a psion to sit on the throne.

Dehya's patterns echoed his, but a stronger one swamped them out. Aristos had an even greater obsession: subjugating the Ruby Dynasty. They found the power wielded by the House of Skolia more intolerable than diluting their DNA, enough even for the Qox Dynasty to breed a Ruby psion in their Line.

Kelric exhaled. He had to acknowledge the possibility. He already believed the emperor was an empath. If Qox had the sensitivity of a Ruby psion, the young man's life had to be a never-ending hell.

A grim thought hit him. **If I restarted the Lock, Qox can use it.**

Dehya looked up. *We must discover what happened and decide what to do.*

Affecting the SSRB Lock from so far away is difficult. I'm not sure what I'm doing.

I may be able to tell.

The Kyle might not support both of us at the same time.

We must try.

Kelric nodded, his motions slowed in the space of this interstice chamber. He put away his dice, and they stood up, regarding each other. Whether or not they would survive, neither of them knew, but the consequences of trying nothing were too serious to ignore.

Together, they stepped into the column of radiance.

XXI
The Broken Pillar

Jaibriol awoke into dimness. He lay on his side with blankets pulled over his shoulders. Opening his eyes, he stared across the room, which was lit by no more than a small night-panel next to an unfamiliar door. He felt queasy and dull . . .

His memories trickled back then: the Lock, Colonel Muze, Hidaka, the nauseating stench of scorched flesh. Jaibriol groaned, and his stomach lurched.

A rustle came from across the room. "Your Highness?"

Hidaka? Jaibriol thought he spoke the name, but nothing came out. His giant bodyguard was walking out of the shadows, a projectile pistol large on his belt, his boots thudding on the floor, his tread slowed in the lower gravity of the space station. The gunmetal collar around his neck glinted.

Jaibriol laboriously pulled himself up to sit in bed. The covers fell around his waist. He still wore the black trousers and shirt from before, but someone had taken off his shoes.

Hidaka stopped by the bed, looking down, his face shadowed. "Are you repaired?" he asked.

Jaibriol squinted at him, disoriented. When his Razers talked that way, they did sound like machines. "I don't know." His voice was thick. "How long have I been unconscious?"

"Six hours, thirty-two minutes, and twelve seconds."

That long? His fear grew. "You shot Colonel Muze."

"Yes, Your Highness. He threatened you. I am tasked with guarding your life. So I removed the threat."

"What did you see?"

"You went into the corridor. It was too dark, and I couldn't find you."

"You followed me into the Lock?" Jaibriol hadn't had any idea. He had thought he gave his bodyguards the slip.

"Yes, Sire. So did Colonel Muze. When the Lock activated, it lit up the dais room. I saw him at the start of the corridor. He did not see me. He went down the corridor, and I followed."

Good Lord. Hidaka must have heard everything. But maybe he didn't realize what it meant.

"Do you know who I am?" Jaibriol asked. He wished Hidaka didn't loom so ominously over him.

"You are the Emperor of Eube." Hidaka seemed puzzled by the question.

A cautious relief spread over Jaibriol. "Yes, that's right. I was checking the Lock to see if it had sustained damage related to the implosions."

"Yes, Sire."

"That is what you saw."

"Yes." Then Hidaka added, "I didn't see the emperor join the Triad."

Jaibriol felt the blood drain from his face. He stared at Hidaka, and the captain met his gaze steadily. In a voice more human than many Aristos, Hidaka said, "I would never see anything, Your Highness, that would bring harm to your reign." His gaze darkened. "Nor would I let anyone else."

Everything about Jaibriol's life as he had understood it these past ten years was tilting askew. "What have you told the station authorities?"

"That Colonel Muze tried to murder you."

Sweat broke out on Jaibriol's brow. "Has anyone tried to take you into custody?"

"No, Sire."

"An Aristo is dead, Hidaka." He strove to keep his voice even. "No one can kill a Highton with impunity."

"I was protecting you." The captain paused. "Security here does wish to question me. They also wish to ascertain you are alive."

"Why haven't they ascertained it yet?"

"We will let no one near you, Sire, until we are assured of your safety."

We? If more people than Hidaka were involved in this business, he could be in even more trouble than he thought. "Who is 'we'?"

"Myself and your other bodyguards."

"You have protected me well. I'm immensely grateful." He meant every word. At the moment, he was also terrified of the Razer, who had broken God only knew how many supposedly inviolable restraints on his actions. "I must speak now with the station authorities."

"I cannot risk your safety."

He wasn't certain if Hidaka was holding him prisoner or guarding him. The captain had been conditioned to protect Aristos. *Only* Aristos. Then he had seen the emperor revealed as a Ruby psion. He should have *helped* Muze make the capture. Jaibriol wouldn't wish anyone's death, but he was grateful Hidaka had intervened. Now, though, he had no idea what the captain intended for him.

"Is Robert here?" Jaibriol asked.

"He has been staying in his quarters."

"Is this his suite?"

Hidaka shook his head. "Mine, sir."

"Ah." Jaibriol spoke firmly. "I must speak with Robert."

Hidaka's gaze never wavered. "I cannot bring him, Sire."

Jaibriol thought he must be hearing wrong. Hidaka couldn't refuse, not if he acknowledged Jaibriol as emperor. Jaibriol lowered his barriers and probed Hidaka's mind, but he received only a metallic sense of thought.

"You must bring him," Jaibriol said.

"I cannot put you in danger."

Jaibriol rubbed his face, groggy and disoriented. "What are you going to do with me?"

"No harm will come to you." Incredibly, strain sounded in the captain's metallic voice. "I have sent a starship to the Qox Palace, summoning backup. When the rest of your Razers arrive, we will escort you to Glory."

"Because you trust the other Razers."

"Yes, Sire."

Jaibriol's hand clenched on the blanket. "Are you going to tell anyone what you saw in the Lock?"

Hidaka met his gaze. "I saw nothing except an attempt by Colonel Muze to murder you."

He didn't know whether to be relieved or afraid. Hidaka had the ultimate case for blackmail. "What do you expect in return?"

For a moment the Razer looked confused. Then comprehension washed over on his face. Jaibriol almost missed it; in the dimness, he could barely see the cybernaut's shadowed features.

Hidaka went down on one knee and bent his head. "I ask nothing in return, Your Highness, but that your reign be long and glorious. I serve you today, tomorrow, next year, and for as long as I live."

Jaibriol stared at him, astonished. When he had ascended to the throne, his Razers had disturbed him, for they had been more than half Aristo. He had gradually replaced them with these guards who couldn't transcend, but he never forgot that his secret police were conditioned to hold Aristos and their principles above all else, including the emperor's life, should it turn out he violated those principles by his very existence. Never in a thousand years would he have thought Hidaka would, or even could, choose loyalty over that conditioning.

When Jaibriol found his voice, he said, "Captain, I— Rise. Please, rise."

Hidaka rose to his feet, towering. Jaibriol looked up at him, aware of how vulnerable he would be if Hidaka ever decided to act against him. "I am grateful for your protection and your loyalty. I will never forget, Captain. But I must see Robert."

"He is called Robert Muzeson." Hidaka's voice was steel.

Then Jaibriol understood. Robert was related to the colonel. Distantly, but still, he had a kinship tie with Vatrix Muze.

Jaibriol spoke quietly. "I'll be safe with him. And you'll be here."

It was plain Hidaka wanted to object. Jaibriol would see now how far his bodyguard could go in holding him captive.

For a moment, Hidaka did nothing. He finally took a deep breath and bowed to Jaibriol, then crossed the room to the door. When he opened it, Jaibriol glimpsed his other guards outside. Hidaka spoke to them, four giants conferring, then closed and secured the door.

The Razor turned back to Jaibriol. "I have sent for Muzeson."

Jaibriol's grip on the blanket eased. If he was a prisoner, at least they didn't intend to completely isolate him.

Robert arrived within moments, and strode across the room. He looked as if he hadn't slept in ages. Dark rings showed under his eyes like smudges and his hair was a mess. Jaibriol could imagine him raking his hand through it as he argued with Hidaka.

When Robert reached the bed, he knelt and bowed his head. "My honor at your presence, Esteemed Highness." His voice shook.

"Robert, you don't need to do that." When his aide looked up, Jaibriol motioned to the chair by the nightstand. He congratulated himself that his arm only trembled a bit, for he felt as wobbly as a newborn pup. "Sit. Be comfortable. Tell me what's going on."

Robert sat in the chair, stiffly, on its edge, obviously

anything but comfortable. "Are you all right, Sire? I've been so worried. They refused to let me near you."

"I'm all right. Hidaka didn't want to do anything until I woke up." That wasn't exactly true, but it would do. "How much has he told you?"

Robert's posture tensed more, though Jaibriol wouldn't have thought that possible. "He said Muze tried to kill you and destroyed the Lock instead. Hidaka managed to shoot him before he shot you."

Jaibriol could pick up more from Robert than with Hidaka, enough to know his aide believed the tale. "I'm grateful for Hidaka's quick action." More than grateful. Indebted for life.

Robert glowered at him. "It is my fervent wish, Most Glorious and Esteemed Highness, that you will remain glorious and esteemed by resisting the impulse the next time you feel inspired to dodge your bodyguards."

Jaibriol almost smiled. He didn't, knowing that if he softened, Robert would continue the lecture. He thought of Muze, and his humor faded. "The colonel's staff must be upset."

Robert answered dryly. "You've a gift for understatement."

"Have they demanded we turn Hidaka over to them?"

Robert gave him an odd look. "You are the emperor. They can't make demands against the captain of your guards, especially after Muze tried to kill you. They are treading with care. And Hidaka sent for backup before anyone knew what he was doing."

Jaibriol was beginning to reassess his fear of the guard. Maybe Hidaka had been the only one thinking straight. "Is the situation here that bad, that we need backup?"

"I'm not sure," Robert said. That he made such an admission relieved Jaibriol; the aides who served most Hightons would never risk such a statement, lest they bring down punishment on themselves. Jaibriol thought it was a stupid way to manage staff. In his experience, people did better work when they weren't afraid they would be skewered for problems beyond their control.

"The colonel's aides are terrified," Robert continued. "I suspect they are waiting to see who you want executed." After a moment, he added, "If you do."

Jaibriol stared at him. "Executions for *what*? Were they in a conspiracy with Muze?" He doubted it, given that Muze hadn't actually tried to assassinate him. But he would have asked the question if Hidaka's cover story were true. Besides, one never knew with Aristos. Their plots and counterplots bubbled everywhere like overactive carbonation.

"I haven't seen evidence of one," Robert said. "That doesn't mean it doesn't exist, of course."

"So they expect me to kill a few of them just to make sure."

"Yes, Sire."

It sounded to Jaibriol like a good way to decimate the station. He didn't intend to execute anyone. However, he needed to appear as if he were acting from a position of power rather than waiting to see if the station authorities would demand an investigation.

"I want Muze's people questioned." He glanced at Hidaka, who was standing back, a dark figure in the dim light. "Captain, you're in charge of the interviews. I want to know how far this conspiracy went." They both knew it went nowhere, but he had no doubt Hidaka could make it look as if he believed otherwise.

Jaibriol started to say more, but his vision blurred and the room swirled around him. Although Robert was saying something, Jaibriol couldn't concentrate. As he sagged to one side, Robert jumped up and reached to catch him. Suddenly Hidaka was there, his large hand covering Robert's shoulder, holding him back with that huge grip.

Robert froze, staring up—and up—at Hidaka. Moving with great care, the aide straightened, keeping his arms at his sides and his hands in plain view.

Jaibriol rubbed his eyes, trying to regain his equilibrium. "What did you say?" he asked Robert.

Robert spoke carefully. "You need a doctor."

Jaibriol shook his head, then stopped as his nausea roiled. He didn't dare see a doctor. He had no idea what a physician could tell about his condition. Did becoming a Key alter him in a measurable way? He didn't feel any three-way Triad link, but he was too shaken to think straight. Power roared within him like an ocean, but it was all muddled and confused. He dreaded what it could mean. His uncle had killed his great-grandfather by joining the powerlink. Their minds had been too alike; it couldn't support them both. Jaibriol prayed he hadn't harmed his kin, the Ruby Pharaoh or the Imperator.

With a sigh, he collapsed onto the bed. He was aware of Hidaka pulling the covers over him. Then he passed out.

❖ ❖ ❖

DARKNESS.
INJURY.
DEATH.

Kelric?
The name reverberated in the darkness.
Dehya? he thought.
I am here.
They existed in blackness. The Lock Chamber on the Orbiter had vanished the moment they stepped into the singularity. But where light normally inundated Kyle space, now only the dark surrounded them.

Kelric poured out his power. Dehya added her nuance—

Kyle space burst into existence, a radiant blue ocean under a sky roiling with dark clouds. Kelric swelled in a giant wave, a tsunami that could drown a person by breaking on the shores of their mind. Dehya existed everywhere as texture, detail, color, the *essence* of this space. Had Kelric had a body here, his breath would have caught. He had never seen the Kyle in such vivid beauty. When he was by himself, he experienced it only as a sense of light.

It's incredible, he thought.
I've never seen it so strongly, Dehya thought.
Or vast. In the far distance he saw blackness.
That's not a landmass, Dehya thought. *It's just gone.*
He swept through the ocean toward the empty place. As he neared the dark shoals, he arose in a tidal wave. His power roared into the darkness—

Into nothing—
Nothing—
Destruction—
Death—

Come back! Dehya's shout reverberated.

With a wrench, he pulled out of the void. The sea and skyscape reformed, but now they wavered and rippled.

Home, he thought.

Kelric became aware of his body. He was sitting at the console in the chamber again. Dehya stood on the other side of the octagonal room, partially hidden by the singularity. The light washed out his vision; he could barely make her out.

For a while he sat, unfocused. Eventually he realized Dehya was walking toward him. Each of her steps lasted a long time. Her mouth moved, but it took endless time for her to form one word. It vibrated in his mind, distant, long, drawn out.

Goooooooo . . .

Her slowed-time walk mesmerized him. How many hours would she need to cross the chamber? How long to say one sentence?

Dooooown . . . she thought.

Go down . . . ? He was comfortable on his stool. He could sit here forever.

Avennnnuuuuuue . . .

She had taken three steps, and the singularity no longer hid her from view. Her body was ephemeral, translucent, caught in transition from the Kyle.

Of Aaaages . . .

Go down the Avenue of Ages. She wanted him to leave the chamber. Urgency touched her voice despite her languid approach.

He slowly stood, rising to his full height, the floor receding below him. Dehya was partway into her fourth step. He turned toward the entrance. The corridor should stretch from that opening back to the Orbiter, but he could see nothing beyond the arch. He stepped toward it, and the thud of his boot reverberated as if he were some massive giant out of Lyshrioli mythology. He stepped again, but the entrance came no closer. Again. The opening was only four paces away, yet it seemed unreachable.

Huuurrrryyy . . .

Step.

Step again.

The archway was out of reach.

Reach . . .

Reach out . . .

Reach out his arm . . .

His hand closed on the edge of the arch.

Pull . . .

Pull body . . .

Pull body forward . . .

Lift foot . . .

Lift foot to Lock corridor . . .

Kelric lurched into the corridor and stumbled along its glittering floor. His time sense snapped back to normal, and he heaved in a breath, his chest expanding as he gulped air. Then he swung around. Dehya was inside the chamber, barely visible in the radiance. She had one foot lifted and one arm outstretched, but viewed from out here, her motion was so slow, he couldn't even see a change in her position.

Dehya!

Kelric had a strange sense, as if she strained to answer his mental shout, but her thoughts existed in a slowed time and couldn't mesh with his own. He grabbed the archway and stretched his arm back into the chamber. He felt as if he were pushing through invisible molasses. With maddening slowness, his hand closed around her forearm. He braced himself against the archway, one foot against the wall and the other planted on the floor behind him— and he *heaved*.

Dehya came out of the chamber like a child birthed by ancient forceps. Her body solidified and suddenly she was moving at normal speed—straight into Kelric. The force of his pull had already unbalanced him, and as she crashed into his body, he stumbled back, losing his hold on her. She lurched away and slammed into a pillar, her cheek bouncing against its transparent surface. The lights inside the column flashed as if panicked.

Kelric regained his balance like a tree almost felled, but still standing. When he started toward Dehya, she shook her head, warning him away. Her face was pale and her eyes large. She spoke, or at least her mouth moved, but he heard none of her words. He stretched out his arm, pointing to the corridor that should—he hoped—take them to the Orbiter War Room.

Dehya slowly pushed a straggle of hair out of her eyes and started down the corridor. Far in the distance, a point of light glittered.

They walked together.

And walked.

And walked.

For hours.

The point of perspective never came closer. They were in a broken corridor, forever trapped between two universes.

XXII
The Path Home

Jaibriol awoke, slept, and awoke again. Robert hovered over him, his face strained, always with Hidaka nearby, like a bulwark.

The next time Jaibriol awoke, he was lying in a new bed. Someone had changed his clothes into silk pajamas with the imperial seal of a Eubian jaguar on the shirt. The small light on a nearby wall illuminated very little, but he could tell this room was smaller than his quarters on the station. Although the hum around him was familiar, he couldn't place it. He lay on his back and stared at a white ceiling curving above his head, so close he could touch it if he lifted his arm.

Eventually it came to him. The hum was an engine. He was on a star yacht. He didn't recognize this cabin, but his own yacht had a bulkhead that arched above the bed this way. As he turned on his side under the silver covers, a beep came from nearby. Undoubtedly a panel somewhere had just notified some person he was awake. He didn't know how the monitors could tell the difference between his turning over while he slept and while he was awake, but they seemed to know.

Sure enough, someone soon appeared: Corbal Xir, his elderly cousin. "Elderly" was relative; Corbal had the health of a man in his prime. Only his eyes showed his age. Jaibriol wasn't sure how to define what he saw in them. Wisdom, perhaps, but other Aristos possessed that trait. A human being could be wise and still be harsh. It wasn't the presence of something he saw, but its lack. No cruelty. His cousin might be avaricious and power hungry, but he wasn't brutal. Jaibriol had no doubt Corbal would manipulate him for gain if he could, but he felt closer to the Xir lord than to any other Aristo except Tarquine.

Corbal walked quietly through the cabin, his pace slow in the low gravity created by the yacht's rotation. When Jaibriol realized his cousin thought he was sleeping, he sat up and swung his legs over the edge of the bed. Corbal paused, his face unreadable in the dim light.

"Luminos, half power," Jaibriol said. The lights brightened, though not enough to bother his eyes.

"My greetings, cousin," Corbal said. He came over and sat in a chair near the bed.

Jaibriol rubbed his eyes. "Is this your yacht?"

"It is indeed." Corbal frowned at him. "I thought you had outgrown this penchant of yours for traipsing all over Eube without proper guard or backup."

"My guard is fine," Jaibriol said coolly. "Hidaka sent for more Razers."

"He did. I came, too. I thought you might prefer a yacht to a military transport."

He was right, but he was also evading the point. "How did you know Hidaka had sent for more guards?"

"Why wouldn't I know? Your safety is my concern. Your bodyguards know this."

Jaibriol wasn't fooled. His bodyguards didn't trust Corbal any more than he did. "They wouldn't tell you if they thought I was in danger. For all they know, you plotted with Colonel Muze, another of my dear relatives." He scowled at Corbal. "Your spies are nosing into my affairs again. I want you to cut it out."

His esteemed cousin looked as if he didn't know whether to feign offense or astonishment. "I cannot 'cut out' what I haven't done."

"You know what I mean. How did you get past Tarquine?"

Corbal crossed his muscular arms. "I fail to understand why I would need to pass the empress."

"Oh, I don't know. Maybe because her spies are watching your spies watch me to make sure they report nothing back to you that she doesn't want you to know about me."

Corbal snorted, and this time his annoyance sounded genuine. "Your wife has a high opinion of her intelligence. Someone should remind her that the point where self-confidence becomes folly is closer than most people realize."

Jaibriol had long ago learned never to underestimate the force of nature he had married. "I'm glad to hear you say that. It eases my mind to know you won't let it happen to you."

Corbal raised an eyebrow. "You might warn the

empress of the same. Otherwise someone might turn her merchant fleets over to the Skolians."

Well, hell. So he also suspected Tarquine of helping the Skolians catch Janq pirates. Corbal would never accuse her without proof; otherwise, the accusation would do him more harm than Tarquine. And they both knew that if Tarquine had leaked covert information to the Skolians, she would never leave a shred of evidence.

Jaibriol thought of his dinner with Diamond Minister Gji, the one where Tarquine had never shown up and Corbal had come instead. "I can well imagine what might happen if an Aristo Line lost its fleets and believed the wrong person had caused it."

Corbal's voice hardened. "I would like to believe that the throne supports its allies."

"Well, you should believe it," he said, irritated Corbal had misunderstood his warning. He wasn't the one Corbal needed to fear. "I can't promise, however, that those who sit next to that rock-hard chair of mine don't have their own agenda."

Corbal raised his eyebrows. "Your Glorious Highness would never accuse, without proof, those who sit next to him."

"Well, guess what. I wouldn't accuse her *with* proof. Maybe I'm just worn out with the two of you bickering all the time."

Corbal shook his head at the direct speech and didn't respond, but Jaibriol could tell he appreciated the warning even if the craggy Xir lord would never make that admission.

"It pleases me to see you well," Corbal said instead. "The Line of Muze has much to answer for, but at least murder isn't among their crimes. Not that a lack of success makes the attempt any less of a betrayal."

If you only knew, Jaibriol thought. He said only, "Indeed." He had to admit, that word could come in useful.

"Muze's sentence fit his crime," Corbal said. "But now we will never know what he could have told us. Others may have plotted with him."

Dryly Jaibriol said, "Along with how many other Aristos who don't consider me fit to rule?"

"Of course you are fit to rule. The Emperor of Eube is exalted beyond and above all humanity."

"Corbal, don't." He wasn't up to listening to the standard Aristo line. It didn't help that most of his trillion subjects believed it, and even many Aristos, those who weren't convinced he was going to bring about the fall of Eube through his youth and "eccentric" notions of peace.

"Don't what?" Corbal said. "You must never express doubt. It only invites more such incidents."

He knew what his cousin meant: *Don't slip up.* But today Jaibriol could barely maintain his façade; his mind was too thick to form coherent thoughts. If Corbal ever learned what had happened, he would do everything within his prodigious power to use Jaibriol as a member of the Triad. Jaibriol felt ill when he contemplated the potential interstellar ramifications. He didn't even know why the Lock had awoken. The words he had thought while sitting in it hadn't felt like his own. Nor did he know what it meant to join the Triad. Should he sense the other two people in the link? He prayed the destruction of the Lock hadn't also killed them.

"How long have I been out?" Jaibriol asked.

Corbal had an odd expression, as if Jaibriol were a riddle for him to solve. "About six days, planet time. Ninety hours."

Jaibriol leaned against a bulkhead. "What do the doctors say is wrong with me?"

"Well, that is a problem."

That wasn't what Jaibriol wanted to hear. "It is?"

"The captain of your Razers says you gave him an Imperial order. No doctors. He says he will kill anyone who violates your order."

"Oh." Jaibriol couldn't recall giving the order, but it was a good one. "I didn't trust anyone on the station."

"You are no longer on the station."

"Razers are very literal."

Corbal was studying him. "They are designed like machines. Yours, however, seem to have more personality."

Jaibriol had no intention of letting Corbal interrogate him about his bodyguards. Hidaka had saved his life in more ways than he could count, but it also put Jaibriol at risk. It wasn't like with Corbal and Tarquine; he knew secrets about them as damaging as what they knew about him. They kept their silence to protect themselves as well as him. He had nothing, however, to ensure Hidaka never revealed him, and the Razer held an even greater secret. Corbal and Tarquine knew he could join the Triad; Hidaka knew he had *done* it. That the Razer hadn't yet tried to blackmail him offered no guarantee it wouldn't happen.

An image tugged at Jaibriol's mind: the light in his room reflecting off the Razer's gunmetal collar. He realized then his mistake. He kept forgetting his bodyguards were taskmakers. He saw them as free men, deserving of the same respect as every human. But they always knew: he could turn them off, reprogram them, kill them with impunity. Even if he forgot that ugly truth, they never would. No Razer would blackmail the emperor. In Highton culture, it would be an immediate death warrant. If he had been thinking clearly, he would have realized that sooner.

Nor could a guard betray him to another Aristo in the hopes of furthering himself. The Aristo might go along with it until he learned the emperor's secrets, but then he would destroy the Razer. Hidaka should have let Colonel Muze take Jaibriol prisoner. He should have served as a witness. Instead, he defied a lifetime of conditioning to protect the emperor, choosing fidelity over the brainwashing that had defined him since birth. Why, Jaibriol didn't know, but it was finally soaking into his overwhelmed brain that Hidaka genuinely wanted to protect him.

Jaibriol exhaled as if he were a balloon losing air. It was good his guards looked out for him, because he felt too dazed to do it himself. He closed his eyes and slumped against the wall.

Corbal spoke quietly. "You should see a doctor."

"I'm only tired." Jaibriol lifted his eyelashes halfway, just enough to see Corbal. "I will speak with you later."

His cousin obviously wanted to object. But even he couldn't defy an Imperial dismissal. "As you wish, Your Highness." He rose and bowed, then took his leave. At the doorway, though, he paused to look back. Jaibriol met his gaze with no encouragement in his expression or body language, and after a moment, Corbal nodded with reserve and left the room.

Jaibriol slid back down into bed. He wondered if he would ever feel normal again. Did all Triad members live with this vertigo and sense of mental displacement? He hated it. And what good did it do him? He had no idea how to build a Kyle web or anything else. If he could have left the Triad, he would have done so in a second. But Hidaka had sacrificed the Lock to save him, and no one knew how to repair the ancient, arcane technology. If Jaibriol needed it to stop the implosions, he was out of luck, because that Lock would never again operate.

The dreamlike universe of the Lock corridor was neither space- time nor the Kyle, but somewhere in between. Kelric and Dehya walked in limbo. When Dehya mouthed words, he couldn't decipher them. Their thoughts interfered like waves and cancelled each other out. The too-bright corridor sparkled until it hurt Kelric's eyes.

Bolt, he thought. He had an odd sense, as if his node responded, but the firing of its bioelectrodes was out of phase with his brain. Its thoughts were waves whispering against the shores of his mind.

He and Dehya walked and walked and went nowhere.

Kelric became aware of a tug on his thoughts. **Dehya?** he thought. **Is that you?**

Nnnnnnnn.

He wasn't certain if that came from her, but he took it as *No.* An image flickered in his mind . . .

A Quis die?

That didn't come from Dehya. Kelric focused inward,

and the image of a topaz octahedron intensified. It was the piece he used to symbolize Haka Estate, where his son had grown up. A second image formed: a gold octahedron. His daughter. He wasn't forming the images; they came from outside of him.

Rohka? he thought.

Come hoooooome . . .

The thought originated from beyond this corridor. It coiled like a rope, and he grabbed it with his mind. He grasped Dehya's shoulder to ensure they didn't get separated in this endless place, his huge hand covering her from neck to upper arm. Dehya glanced up at him, but she didn't object.

Kelric followed the mental rope of Quis dice. Nothing changed in the corridor: it remained an infinite pathway that ended in a point. But the image of the dice stayed in his mind, drawing him home . . .

Like a shutter opening, the point ahead of them suddenly expanded into an archway a few meters away, its transparent columns filled by gold, silver, and bronze gears, with lights racing across them like sparkflies. Kelric lengthened his stride, afraid the arch would disappear before he and Dehya reached that portal back into their own universe.

As they staggered under the arch, his mind *rippled* as if it were a lake and the thoughts of people in his universe were stones dropping into the water, creating circles that expanded outward in ever widening waves. In that moment, he saw the Lock corridor as if he were watching it through hundreds of eyes, all the people in the War Room. He and Dehya were stepping out of a white mist, she staggering in slow motion, he with his limp exaggerated, his large hand gripped on her shoulder.

Kelric's thoughts snapped back into his mind as abruptly as they had jumped outward. He and Dehya stumbled onto the dais in the War Room, and people surged around them. With a groan, he sank to his knees, reeling with vertigo. Doctors knelt around him, monitoring him with scanners and asking questions he couldn't hear. Dehya collapsed a few paces away, and one of her huge Jagernaut bodyguards knelt protectively over her while people crowded around.

Kelric didn't realize his bodyguards were also on the dais until Najo brushed his shoulder. Looking around, Kelric saw Strava on his other side, her stoic face impassive, and Axer behind him, huge and bulky, a giant with a bald, tattooed head.

Chad Barzun, the commander of the Imperial Fleet, knelt next to Kelric. Even as short as he kept his iron-grey hair, it looked disheveled, as if he had raked his hand across it. Wrinkles creased his blue uniform, though it was designed from smart cloth that could smooth out normal crumples. Dark circles showed under his eyes.

Kelric's mind swam, thick and woozy, with a sense of mental dislocation. Chad was talking, but Kelric couldn't understand him. It wasn't that Chad spoke out of phase, but rather that Kelric had spent so long in a distorted space-time, his mind couldn't readjust to his natural universe.

He looked past all the people and commotion. At the edge of the dais, his mother Roca and his brother Eldrin stood waiting—with a tall woman whose regal face would have caught his eye in any crowd. Ixpar. His wife. He had never seen her so pale. He didn't know how long he had been gone, but during that time, she would have been stranded in a place she had little context to understand and where she knew almost no one. She had taken the irreversible step of breaking Coba's isolation, risking the well-being of her people, even their identity, all based on his vow that he could protect them. And what had he done to honor her tremendous act of faith? Vanished the day after she came to him. Gods only knew what she thought now of his promises.

An ISC doctor was wrapping a med-string around Kelric's arm to monitor his blood pressure. Another medic was studying holos of Kelric's body that rotated above a screen he had unrolled on the floor. Kelric couldn't follow the discussion of the doctors at all, and Chad had given up trying to talk to him. The admiral was just sitting on the floor, an elbow on his bent knee, watching the doctors and Kelric.

Bolt? Kelric thought.

I'm here, his node answered.

Relief washed over Kelric. **Can you communicate for me? I can't understand anyone.**

I will access your gauntlets.

Good. Also, how long was I in the Lock?

I don't know. The singularity disrupted the atomic clock in your biomech web.

See what you can find out.

A deep voice came out of the comm on his right gauntlet. "Admiral Barzun, can you understand me?"

Chad jerked, then peered at Kelric and at the gauntlet

with that alert, wary style of his that Kelric knew well. When the admiral answered, his words were garbled and indistinct.

Do you understand him? Kelric asked.

Yes, Bolt answered. It's muddled, but I believe he said, "To whom am I speaking?"

Explain it to him.

"I am the primary node in Imperator Skolia's biomech web," Bolt said to Chad. "He is having trouble hearing you. I will interpret. Also, he wishes to know how long he has been gone."

As Chad answered, Bolt thought, He says you went into the corridor four days ago and Pharaoh Dyhianna about three.

No wonder I'm so hungry. He should have been starving; he needed huge amounts of food to fuel his large body. Is Dehya all right?

Bolt relayed the question. He says the pharaoh is having less problem communicating. However, she won't tell anyone what happened.

Kelric glanced at Dehya over the heads of the people around them. She was sitting up and talking to another doctor. Her guards hulked over her, dwarfing her body.

Dehya, Kelric thought. **Can you hear me?**

She glanced at him. *Are you still out of resonance?*

Resonance with what? And why doesn't it affect you?

I think whatever damaged Kyle space threw the Lock here out of phase with our universe. My mind adjusts faster than yours, that's all. It's probably the price you pay for all that power. She paused as someone spoke to her. Then she thought,

Kelric, we need to talk. We have to get rid of all these worried people.

Worried indeed. The people around them were pretending they didn't notice the pharaoh and imperator having a silent conversation. Although he and Dehya were trying to be subtle, it was hard not to use gestures or facial expressions when they communicated; he did it reflexively. It was awkward, like whispering in front of others, but at the moment he had no other option.

We can't talk just yet, he thought, tilting his head toward Roca, Eldrin, and Ixpar. **We must see to our families.**

Yes. Her face gentled as she gazed at Eldrin. He looked calmer now than when she had come out of the corridor, but Kelric could imagine how frantic he must have been after she vanished. Guilt washed over him for the worry he had caused.

Dehya's thought rippled. *You didn't do it. Something happened, I don't know what, but it's not good.*

It's still affecting us.

Can you speak at all with the people here?

Kelric turned his attention to the admiral, who had sat back on the floor. "Chad, do you understand me?"

Everyone around him froze, and the people tending Dehya turned with startled jerks. Ixpar had been lifting her hand to her face, probably to brush away a fiery tendril of hair, but now she stopped with her arm in midair.

For flaming sake. **Bolt, why is everyone staring at me?**

Your voice sounds odd, Bolt thought. It is unusually

loud and it echoes. I believe it is the type of sound humans associate with an elevated being.

Elevated, my ass.

It wasn't until Dehya laughed that he realized he hadn't shielded his mind from her. When he glowered, she thought, *I doubt your gluteus maximus has anything to do with it.*

Funny, he growled. Her doctors were asking if she was all right, probably because she had laughed for no obvious reason.

He climbed stiffly to his feet, his joints crackling and his knees aching. He towered over everyone. Chad and his doctors stood up as well, and the doctors backed away. Although Chad stayed put, sweat sheened his forehead.

"I'll need to meet with you and the other joint chiefs," Kelric said to him. From the way the admiral blanched, Kelric thought his voice must still sound strange.

"I'll take care of it, sir." Chad's answer had an oddly distant quality, as if he were far away. But he spoke with the same efficient confidence Kelric had always appreciated. Chad Barzun might not have Admiral Ragnar Bloodmark's brilliance, but Kelric would far rather have Chad backing him than Ragnar.

Kelric rolled his shoulders to ease his sore muscles. "Chad, did anyone try going into the Lock to find us?"

"We've been trying," Chad said. "No one with a trace of psi ability has been able to enter the corridor. Normally they can walk a short way before they have to turn back, but this time they couldn't even go under the archway. The path, well—disappeared. We sent in people with a zero Kyle rating, and they found the path, but they couldn't reach the end. They just kept walking. They couldn't communicate with us, either, until they came back. We finally found someone with a negative rating. She reached the end, but the chamber was empty. No singularity. She waited a day, until she ran out of water, but she never found a trace of you or Pharaoh Dyhianna."

"Gods," Kelric muttered.

"It was bizarre," Chad said. "No sensor registered either you or the pharaoh as anywhere on the Orbiter."

"Doesn't that always happen when we go in the Lock?"

"I don't know," Chad admitted. "We have so few records of anyone using this one."

It was true, Kelric realized. He and Dehya called on the Lock as sparingly as possible, for they had no idea what, if anything, might stir a backlash. Exactly what that backlash might be, he neither knew nor desired to find out.

"Sir, what happened in there?" Chad asked.

A good question. "I'm not sure. I'll brief you at the meeting." Kelric wanted to speak to Dehya before he discussed it with anyone else. He could also see Ixpar watching him, which made it difficult to concentrate on Chad.

The admiral followed his gaze and smiled. "Shall I see you at the meeting then?"

"Yes, that would be good." Kelric started toward his wife, but as soon as he took a step, one of his doctors blocked his way.

The man's face paled as he looked up at Kelric, but he didn't move. "I'm sorry, Lord Skolia. But we don't know if your phase shift can affect your family."

That gave him pause. He wasn't sure what was wrong

with him, but he certainly didn't want to shift anyone out of normal space or cause some other bizarre effect. After a moment, he said, "Please tell my wife what you just told me. It's her decision as to whether or not she will come over."

Ixpar was watching him with that intense quality of hers, as if she were barely contained energy. Her red hair had escaped its braid and was curling about her face. It reminded him of her personality, civilized on the surface, but with the atavistic queen simmering just below. She had always fascinated him, a study in contrasts, an enlightened leader dedicated to the advancement of her people with the soul of an ancient warrior burning within her.

Although the doctor was obviously uneasy, he went over to where Ixpar stood with Kelric's mother, Roca. Eldrin wasn't there anymore. Glancing around, Kelric saw Eldrin embracing Dehya, his head bent over hers, tears on his face. Kelric was feeling worse by the moment for causing all this upset.

He turned back to see Ixpar walking toward him in her graceful, long-legged gait. She didn't look the least perturbed by the prospect that her husband might suddenly phase out of space-time. A smile curved her lips. She might be the newcomer here, submersed in a culture strange and sometimes inexplicable, but if she felt any apprehension, neither her posture nor her mood revealed it. But then, Ixpar had never been easily daunted.

Roca stayed back. Kelric doubted she was worried about Kyle space anomalies; more likely, she knew he wanted to see Ixpar alone. It was an aspect of her personality he had always appreciated, for all that she frustrated him at times.

However much she might want to talk to him, she stayed back, respecting his privacy. Although she had raised her mental shields, he could sense her response to Ixpar. She approved of his new wife. As well she might; they were both formidable women. He detected more than that, though. She had always feared he would overwhelm his loves with the sheer force of his personality and mind. With Ixpar, she had no worries.

Ixpar stopped in front of Kelric, almost eye to eye with him. He wanted to embrace her, but he felt restrained with so many people on the dais: doctors, bodyguards, telops, and mech-techs studying the entrance to the Lock Corridor. He had never had Eldrin's ease with expressing his emotions even one on one, let alone with other people present.

Ixpar brushed a curling tendril out of her face and spoke in formal tones. "It's good to see you."

His voice softened, as it so rarely did nowadays. "I'm glad you're here."

"Kelric—" Her self-assured exterior slipped, and in that instant her worry for him showed. Then she took a breath and once again became the composed queen.

The hell with restraint. Kelric pulled her into his arms, feeling the smooth sweep of her hair under his cheek. With a sigh of release, she put her arms around him, supple in his embrace. She felt like a tiger, slim and sleekly muscled.

"I thought I had found you only to lose you again," she murmured.

"Ai, Ixpar, I'm sorry. I had no idea that would happen."

"Where did you go?"

"I'm not sure." He drew back, his arms around her waist. The faint sprinkle of freckles across her nose was almost impossible to see, except this close up. "You sent that message. The Quis dice."

She touched the dice pouch hanging from her belt, though he didn't think she realized she had taken that reflexive action. "No one could send you messages," she said. "Your officers tried to contact you, but it didn't work."

"You didn't send me mental images of Quis dice?"

"I wouldn't know how."

He realized it was true. Although she empathized strongly with others, he didn't think she was a full psion, certainly not a telepath who could send mental pictures. If she hadn't done it, though, then who? Neither his mother nor his siblings knew anything about Quis.

"Were either Rohka or Jimorla here?" he asked. He had been silent about his children for so long, it felt odd to say their names, as if it made both him and them vulnerable.

"We've been taking turns." She shifted her arms, and her muscles flexed against his back, stirring pleasant memories of their evening together on Coba.

"Hmmm." Kelric drew her closer and nuzzled her cheek.

She laughed softly. "We have an audience, you know."

Well, hell. He lifted his head with reluctance and let her go. "Were either of them here just before Dehya and I came out?"

"Rohka was here until a short time ago," Ixpar said. "She was tired, though. In fact she almost passed out. Your mother sent her to the house so she could rest."

Perhaps his daughter had almost passed out because she had reached between universes to contact him. She had the Ruby power, but no training; such an effort would probably exhaust her. He didn't know who else besides Jimorla would send images of dice, and he didn't think Jimorla had the Kyle strength.

"Has she ever talked about mind pictures?" he asked.

Ixpar shook her head, her brow furrowed. "Nothing. If she has a talent like that, she lets no one know."

It didn't surprise Kelric. Cobans didn't believe psions existed. If Rohka talked about what she could do, they would think her daft. He doubted she had told anyone here, either. Being sixteen years old was difficult enough even without the culture shock she was facing. She had no context to understand her gift. The moment the speaker at the Promenade had given her name as Skolia, almost everyone across three interstellar civilizations had understood its import—except Rohka herself.

"I need to talk to her and Jimorla," he said.

Ixpar's face gentled. "It would be good. They need to see you're all right."

Kelric didn't know if he could assure them of that. He feared none of them were all right, that what he and Dehya had discovered in the Kyle threatened the stability of space itself.

XXIII
The Lost Covenant

Corbal's yacht landed at a private spaceport in the Jaizire Mountains on Eube's Glory, capital planet of the Eubian Concord. Jaibriol had no doubt Corbal told his crew to make sure no one notified the empress. Corbal's spies would triple-check their security to ensure she didn't know her husband had come home.

Tarquine was at the port, of course.

She had come with a flyer, ready to whisk Jaibriol away to his private retreat in the untamed forest of the high peaks.

Corbal scowled as he stood in Jaibriol's cabin, watching the emperor prepare to meet his wife. "You should return to the palace," Corbal growled. "Not gallivant around the mountains."

Jaibriol shrugged into a conservative black-diamond shirt and sealed it up the front. Corbal was trying to unsettle him with the direct speech, but his cousin should know by now it wouldn't work.

"I need a rest, remember?" Jaibriol said. In truth, he was heartily sick of resting. His vertigo had receded, and he felt almost human again.

Corbal crossed his arms and leaned against a table. The furniture was genuine wood, a rarity on any space-faring vessel. Jaibriol liked it, though not for the reason most Hightons approved of such extravagance, because it showed their wealth. During his first fourteen years of life, he had lived on a world where his family had only what they made themselves. He didn't know if the planet had been terraformed or developed flora on its own, but the mountains had been lush with trees. His family had built everything they needed from that wood. He would never tell his cousin the true reason he liked the tables on Corbal's yacht: they reminded him of home.

"Hiding in the hills will hardly present a courageous face to your subjects," Corbal said. "They want to see their emperor hale and hearty." Dryly he added, "And alive."

Jaibriol fastened his elegant sleeves with carnelian links at the cuffs. "Surely you don't suggest they know I might not have been alive." If someone had already leaked news of the murder attempt, he would have their hide. Not literally; he wasn't that much like his ancestors.

"No." Corbal straightened his posture, which in Highton meant he intended to convey a supposed truth. "But they will suspect problems exist if you don't attend your duties."

"Robert is going back with you." He cocked an eyebrow at Corbal. "If any dire duties come up that need attending, I'm sure he'll let me know."

His cousin frowned. "Sarcasm doesn't become an emperor."

"Oh, admit it, Corbal. You don't want me with Tarquine." Jaibriol finished fastening his cuffs. He could have had a valet dress him, but he had never liked other people doing what he was perfectly capable of doing himself. For public appearances, he let his protocol people work on him, mainly because they wouldn't leave him alone until he agreed, though somehow they always made it seem as if it were his idea.

"Your wife is most esteemed," Corbal said, holding his thumb and forefinger together. "So exalted, in fact, that she is up in the ozone. Such lofty heights can asphyxiate a person."

"Yes, well, she doesn't trust you, either."

His cousin made an exasperated noise. "Jai, your language will be your downfall just as surely as your empress."

Jaibriol scowled at him. "Stars forbid I should actually say what I mean."

"You want direct speech? Fine. Your manipulative wife is power mad."

Jaibriol went over to him. "If power is what she wants, why would she cause my downfall? If I go, so does she."

"A desire for a man's power isn't synonymous with a desire for a man's best interests."

The corners of Jaibriol's mouth quirked up. "I believe her desire is for the man."

"Then you have my sympathy," Corbal said sourly.

"Whereas you of course have no desire for my power."

Corbal met his gaze. "You were safer with Colonel Muze and his laser carbine than you are with Tarquine Iquar."

Jaibriol walked to the doorway, where he paused and looked back at his cousin. "I will see you when I get back."

Then he went to meet his wife.

Tarquine was waiting on the landing hexagon with her own Razers. Jaibriol could usually read her expressions even when she was a cipher to everyone else, but today her face was inscrutable, and he didn't dare lower his mental shields with his mind so sensitized by the Triad.

Her clothes bothered him, though he couldn't say why. She wore a violet jumpsuit, fur-lined jacket, and boots, all suitable for the cold mountain weather. Her hair hung in glittering perfection around her face and shoulders, and her sculpted features showed no hint of strain. But something was wrong. He was as certain of it as if someone had shouted the news.

Captain Hidaka stepped down from Corbal's yacht, his carbine gripped in both hands. Jaibriol followed, and then the rest of his guards. The conduits on Hidaka's arm were flashing, as were those of the captain for Tarquine's guards, as they communicated via implants in their bodies. The entire time, Tarquine stared at Jaibriol with no hint of emotion. He didn't know what to think. She didn't seem angry, nor did he know of any new crises beyond the usual state of Aristo life.

Hidaka turned to Jaibriol. "You and Her Highness are cleared to approach each other."

Jaibriol nodded, wondering if it sounded as bizarre to

Hidaka as it did to him, that they had to clear the empress and emperor to meet each other like ships cleared to land.

Tarquine approached Jaibriol, her walk stirring him in ways he tried to ignore. She wasn't trying to be seductive; she never showed or sought affection in public. But he knew the way her muscles were moving under that jacket and jumpsuit. He had been alone for days, and he wanted his wife. More than that, he wished she had come to meet him because she wanted him, not because she had to assert to Corbal that she wielded greater influence over the throne.

"My greetings," Jaibriol said.

She stopped in front of him. "Are you all right?"

Her directness jolted him. In Highton, it could be an invitation to intimacy. It would shock other Aristos, not because of the sexual overtones; given the bondage orgies some of them had with their providers, a subtle hint of sensuality would hardly outrage anyone. But in this case, it came from an Aristo to her spouse in public. Rather than inviting his warmth, she would normally follow the strictures of their caste, including a reserve so extreme, it felt like a straightjacket to Jaibriol. Today she seemed distracted.

"I'm fine," he lied. He wondered if she sensed a difference in him. Space-time had literally shifted under his feet, yet everyone treated him exactly as always, even Hidaka, the only person alive who knew the truth.

"I find myself pleased," Tarquine said, her voice duskier than usual.

Jaibriol realized what he sensed in her. Strain. He

could believe she would worry about an attempt on his life. It threatened her position as empress, especially given that he had no heir. If he died, the line of succession would go to Corbal. And he believed—or perhaps deluded himself—that she cared for him in her own Highton way. But he wasn't certain why her concern would translate into strain *with* him.

"It pleases me to see you looking so well," he said, which was more tasteful than *I want to throw you onto a bed.*

"It should," she murmured. "Much better than Corbal."

"It was generous of him to pick me up," Jaibriol said. Wryly he added, "Magnanimity is always a virtue."

"How very Highton," she said. "Using a five-syllable word where one or two would suffice."

He gave a startled laugh. "Now you sound like me."

"Far better to sound like you—" Her gaze shifted to a point beyond his shoulder. "—than certain others."

He turned to the yacht. Corbal was standing in the hatchway, leaning against one side, his arms crossed as he watched them. Although his shirt and trousers didn't look as if they had climate controls like the clothes Jaibriol was wearing, the Xir lord seemed unaffected by the cold.

Jaibriol walked back to the ship. He took care, when he was with both Tarquine and Corbal, never to appear as if he favored one over the other, at least not too much, lest their subtle war escalate to uglier proportions.

When Jaibriol stopped below the air lock, Corbal waited a moment before jumping down, just the barest pause—

but it could get him arrested, for no one, even the highest
of the Hightons, could deliberately stand above the
emperor. Corbal was pushing to see how much favor
Jaibriol would show in front of Tarquine. It irritated
Jaibriol, because it forced him either to do nothing about
Corbal's lapse in respect, and so appear weak by Highton
standards, or else to think of some stupid punishment he
had no wish to apply.

Jaibriol frowned at him. "I should invite you to dine
with Tarquine and myself."

His cousin cocked an eyebrow at him. "What offense
have I given, that you would threaten me with such?"

"Corbal, if you ever do that again, you won't be happy
with the result."

The Xir lord answered in a deceptively mild tone. "Be
assured, whatever point I might have intended is already
made—and obvious to the only people who need a
reminder of it."

Jaibriol knew he meant Tarquine. "Asserting favor with
the throne by depending on the good will of kin has risks.
Don't leave me no choice but to take actions I would far
rather avoid."

"Favor works in two directions."

Jaibriol understood his point: enmity also went two
ways. He didn't want Corbal as an enemy any more than
Corbal wanted his disfavor.

"My greetings, Lord Xir," Tarquine said as she came up
next to Jaibriol.

Corbal bowed to her. "My greetings, Your Highness."

"I do hope the cold doesn't bother you," she murmured.
"I've never put any credence in the maxim that blood

thins with age, but I wouldn't want you to inconvenience yourself for us."

Jaibriol almost groaned. It was a double barb, both against Corbal's age and her suggestion that his relationship with Jaibriol would weaken over time.

"How kind of you to express concern," Corbal said. "I've heard it said that advanced years bring with them a greater understanding of others."

"Oh, I'm sure," she replied. "Or even, say, advanced decades. All fourteen of them."

"Or eleven," Corbal said. "An unusual number that. Eleven. It's prime, you know."

"Of course," she said. "Always prime. At the top."

Enough, Jaibriol thought. They were giving him a headache. He had no desire to hear them taunt each other about the supposed decrepitude of their advanced age when they were so obviously hale and hearty. It only heightened how raw he felt around them.

"Prime," Jaibriol said. "As is the hour." Which meant absolutely nothing, but might distract them.

Corbal was focused on Tarquine. "A prime number has no divisor, you know. Except one and itself." Softly he added, "One. Not two."

Jaibriol blinked. What the blazes? Tarquine, however, apparently knew exactly what he meant. She said, "As in father and son, hmmm?"

"One's heir is his immortality." Corbal seemed puzzled by the reference to his son, but his voice had that too smooth quality Jaibriol dreaded, because it never boded well. "Assuming one has an heir."

For flaming sake. So that was the point of Corbal's

barbs about prime numbers. The empress had yet to give birth to the Highton Heir.

Jaibriol was about to tell them to cut it out when Tarquine said, "Immortality comes in many guises. Intelligent—or otherwise. Of course, what one would like immortalized varies. Some things are better left to their mortality."

Ah, hell. That sounded like she had discovered some misdeed of Corbal's son Azile, the Intelligence Minister, and was threatening to expose him if Corbal didn't quit insulting her.

"I find myself wishing to dine," Jaibriol said shortly. He held out his hand to Tarquine. "Attend me, wife." He had no doubt she would find his order inexcusably abrupt, but he didn't have the energy to deal with the two of them. If he didn't put a stop to this, he might end up with his Intelligence Minister discredited and Corbal as his enemy, which could be a disaster. He needed both Corbal and Tarquine, and just *once* he wished they would try to get along, if only for his sake.

Tarquine regarded him with her unreadable crystalline gaze, and for one nerve-wracking moment he thought she would refuse him in front of Corbal, forcing him to lose face or reject her. Then she laid her hand in his. Instead of releasing her, as protocol demanded, Jaibriol lowered his arm and stood holding hands with his wife.

"I thank you for bringing me home," he told Corbal. "May the gods of Eube smile upon you."

Corbal bowed, and Jaibriol caught the flicker of relief in his eyes. He hadn't wanted his son discredited, but

neither had he been willing to back down in front of
Tarquine.

Jaibriol took leave of his cousin and returned to the
flyer with Tarquine. They boarded with all eight of their
oversized bodyguards. Inside, she waited until the molecular
air lock solidified, hiding them from Corbal's yacht and
undoubtedly from his spy sensors as well. Then she jerked
her hand out of Jaibriol's hold as if he had developed a
plague.

She spoke icily. "Never speak to me that way again."

"Damn it, Tarquine, I need my Intelligence Minister."
He was painfully aware of their guards listening. Most
Aristos assumed that Razers thought only of military
matters, but he knew better. "And I need Corbal's good
will."

He expected her to tell him why he needed neither.
Instead she just shook her head. "Let's go home, Jai. I'm
tired."

Concern replaced his anger. "Are you all right?" She
never admitted anything she considered a weakness.

"Of course." She waved her hand. "We have better
matters to concern us than your inconsequential cousin."

He wasn't fooled. If she considered Corbal inconsequential, she wouldn't devote so much effort to monitoring
his activities or spying on his spies.

"I would have rather awoken on your yacht," he said.
His smile quirked. "In your cabin." And bed.

She gave him a quelling look, but it wasn't convincing,
given the spark of desire in her mood. "Then where would
I have slept?"

He pulled her toward him. "I can think of someplace."

She tensed in his hold, and at first he thought she would pull away. Then she exhaled and relaxed into his kiss.

After a moment, Jaibriol drew back, though he kept his arms around her waist. "I was surprised to see Corbal," he admitted. He would have expected Tarquine to reach the SSRB ahead of even his shrewd cousin.

She started to speak, then shook her head.

"What is it?" he asked

"I was—preoccupied."

His unease stirred. "By what?"

"It isn't important." She took his arms and pulled them away from her waist. "We should go."

It isn't important was as bad as *Don't worry.* And her rebuff stung. He turned away and went to a passenger seat at the front of the craft. Hidaka took a seat against the hull that faced inward. Two of Tarquine's guards took the pilot and copilot's seats, and the others settled into passenger chairs.

Tarquine sat next to Jaibriol. "Don't sulk," she murmured as if he were a boy. At least she said it too softly for anyone else to overhear. Then again, all their bodyguards had biomech-augmented ears.

"You tell me not to give you orders," he said. "You don't like it. Fine, Tarquine. Don't treat me like a child."

He expected her to respond with a convoluted Highton remark that meant, *Then don't act like one.* Instead she said, "You know, for all that Corbal offends the bloody hell out of me, he's right. Both he and I are old. Maybe too old." She glanced at him. "I can't help it if you seem young to me. But I don't mean to offend."

It was a fair comment, and more than he had expected. "You seem pensive today."

"No. I just—" She shook her head as if to discard the mood. An aloof smile came to her face, and she was Tarquine again, Empress of Eube, and Finance Minister of the wealthiest empire in human history.

"It is interesting the news one hears," she said.

He regarded her warily. "I'm afraid to ask."

"The Diamond Minister has suggested, rather obliquely, that we consider Skolians as a possible market for Eubian products."

Jaibriol stared at her. "You talked to Gji?"

"I talk to him often. We are both Ministers, after all."

He remembered now why her clothes tugged at him. She had been wearing that same outfit the night she hadn't shown up for his failed dinner with the Diamond Minister. "That time Gji and his wife dined at the palace and you didn't show up—was it because you were up here?"

She gave him an odd look. "Why would I have been here? I had a meeting in the city." She stretched her arms. "Minister Gji actually has the notion that opening trade negotiations with the Skolians is a good idea."

He couldn't help but smile. "How did you convince him it was his idea?"

"You know, Jaibriol, you waste many of the resources at your disposal." She wouldn't look at him, which was odd, because she could stare him in the eye even when she was committing financial fraud on an interstellar scale.

"What resources?" he asked, which was about as

direct as a person could get, and it wasn't an invitation to intimacy, but she had him worried enough to slip out of Highton.

Her eyes flashed at his unintended insult. "Oh, I don't know. Maybe all those providers you ignore."

Jaibriol suddenly felt ill. She couldn't mean what that sounded like. "We had an agreement."

"What agreement? I don't recall signing anything."

No. She *couldn't* had done what he thought. Neither of them touched their providers, and they never offered them to any other Aristo. They had kept that agreement for ten years. "You know what I meant."

"Sometimes," she said, "bargains must be rethought."

"You hosted Minister Gji and his wife at a dinner." He was having trouble breathing.

"A dinner, yes. I invited many of the Diamonds."

"Many?" Jaibriol knew what they would expect. "Tarquine, who served the meal?"

"You know, your providers lounge around all day, using your wealth and giving nothing in return."

He stared at her. According to the books, he had sixteen providers on Glory. They lived in a wing of the palace distant from where he spent most of his time, and he told Robert to give them whatever they wanted. He avoided them assiduously, not because he disliked them, but because they might recognize what no Aristo could sense, that he was a psion. Like them.

Somehow he spoke calmly, though he was raging inside. "You had them serve at the dinner."

She met his accusing gaze. "As they should. I entertained the Blue-Point Diamonds in the most esteemed style of the palace. You made many allies that night, Jaibriol." Then she added, "Despite yourself."

She might as well have punched him in the stomach and kicked him while he was down. He had protected the providers entrusted to his care for ten years, and in one night she had destroyed all that. The Blue-Point Diamonds numbered more than fifty. God only knew what horrors that many of them could inflict on sixteen helpless slaves. He felt sick. He had to hide his reaction, lest the guards grow suspicious; that for some merciful reason Hidaka had chosen to protect his secrets was no guarantee others would do the same. But the anger that surged within him was almost more than he could contain.

He sensed no satisfaction from Tarquine, only fatigue. She didn't like what she had done, either. Why do it, then? Knowing her mood didn't reveal the reason for it, and she was guarding her thoughts even more than usual. Maybe she truly did want to increase Eubian wealth, even if it meant doing business with their enemies. She had always valued finance over war. But it didn't fit. Plenty of other methods existed that didn't require dealing with Skolians or hurting his providers. The only reason she had suggested opening trade negotiations was because she thought it could restart the peace process.

Jaibriol couldn't bear to reach for his dream at the price of committing the very crimes that caused hatreds between his people and the Skolians. Tarquine knew he would never do what she believed necessary to win support for his ideals. So she had waited until he was gone, and then she had done it herself.

He had known her nature when he married her, and yes—he had known it worked to his advantage. That he chose at times to forget that knowledge didn't make it any less true or him any less responsible.

God forgive me for the day I married you, he thought. *For I don't think I can.*

XXIV
A Father's Debt

"It is like an enormous, glaring machine," Rohka said. "It flashes and rings, with too many parts to count, and it has so much light, it blinds you." Her voice had that same quality Kelric remembered in her mother, a sweetness and energy he had never forgotten.

They were sitting on the sofa in the sunken living room of his house on the Skolian Orbiter. The place had seemed empty in the year since Jeejon's death. Having Ixpar and the children here changed that, but it was hard to absorb. It always took him time to adjust to new circumstances. Yet for all that he struggled to adapt, it brought him great pleasure to know he would find them in the big stone rooms of his house when he returned at night.

"I've never heard Skolia described quite that way," he said, smiling, more for the joy of her presence than for her less than complimentary depiction of his civilization.

Rohka winced, with no attempt to hide her emotions. She was open and unjaded, like a fresh wind blowing through his life. "I don't mean to insult your home. It's all so much to understand." Her large eyes were like his mother's. "When you vanished down that corridor, we feared never to see you again. I thought your people knew so much, but no one could say what happened."

"I didn't mean to frighten you."

"I'm just so glad you came back."

He agreed heartily with the sentiment. "How did you know to send me the Quis images?"

"Jimorla suggested it. He said a Sixth Level Calani would have to respond to dice." She shifted her weight on the couch. "Ixpar told your military people, but I don't think they believed it. She tried sending the images, but she can't do it. Jimorla said he wasn't strong enough. Your family tried, but they don't know Quis. So I did it."

He spoke with gratitude. "I don't know if either I or the pharaoh would have made it back, otherwise."

"I don't understand." Her young face brimmed with emotions: uncertainty, curiosity, fear, relief. She didn't hesitate to let him know how she felt, and to Kelric, that was a gift. "I study physics with my tutors. But none of it sounds like anything your family tells me about space and time and these places where neither exist."

"You can learn." He was balanced over an emotional chasm. If he asked and she said no, it would be worse than if he never asked. But the words came out before he could stop them. "We have a school on the Orbiter. It's among the best in the Imperialate. If you would like— you could study here." Then he stopped, for fear of her refusal.

"Stay here?" Rohka seemed relaxed on the other end of the sofa, turned sideways to face him, one hand on a large cushion. But he saw the way her posture tensed. Nor did she know how to shield her thoughts. Her mind was a blaze of warmth, golden and untouched by the harsh universe beyond Coba. She was a miracle, and she had no idea.

"If you would like to stay," he said, self-conscious. "It's your choice."

"I don't know." Her smile flashed like sun breaking through the clouds. "It's so incredible! All my life, I've known my father was Skolian. But I never understood what it meant."

Kelric grinned at her. "Just think of what you could see."

Her mood doused as fast as it had flared. Her emotions changed so quickly, it was hard to keep up. It was like sunlight glancing off a sparkling lake, then suddenly banished by clouds.

"I have duties to my people," she said.

He spoke quietly. "You will someday rule Coba. You'll live through the era when your world becomes part of the Imperialate. What better way to prepare yourself for that responsibility than by getting an Imperialate education."

She regarded him with approval. "That's a good argument. I will try it on Ixpar."

That was so much like something Savina would have said, it made Kelric want to laugh and cry at the same time. "Does that mean you would like to stay?"

"Maybe. But I have to talk to Ixpar."

His heart swelled. Her response might not be a ringing agreement, but it was a start.

"Kelric?" A man spoke in a rich voice.

"Eldrin!" Kelric jumped to his feet and turned to look over the couch. "My greetings."

Eldrin stood in the wide entrance across the room. He was about six feet tall with broad shoulders but a leaner physique than Kelric. He wore an elegant grey and white shirt and blue trousers. He had violet eyes, and his lashes glinted with a hint of metal. Burgundy hair, glossy and straight, brushed his collar, longer than most Skolian men wore it, or at least those in the military, which defined Kelric's world. It was no coincidence Eldrin looked like an artist; he was known throughout settled space for his singing. His spectacular voice had a five-octave range that normal humans couldn't achieve, a gift he had inherited from his father, the Dalvador Bard.

Eldrin inclined his head. "It's good to see you."

Rohka stood up, watching Eldrin with wide eyes.

Kelric smiled at her. "This is my oldest brother. Eldrin. Your uncle."

Rohka bowed to Eldrin, charmingly awkward. She spoke Skolian Flag with a heavy accent. "I am honored, Your Majesty."

Although it pleased Kelric that she knew Eldrin's correct title, he didn't want her to think she had to address his family with such formality. He regarded Eldrin with an intent focus and tilted his head. His brother nodded almost imperceptibly and walked over to them.

Eldrin smiled at Rohka. "It is a pleasure to meet you. But please, call me Eldrin." He hesitated. "Or if you like, Uncle Eldrin."

Rohka's cheeks turned rosy. "I would like that."

Eldrin glanced at Kelric, but he sent no mental images

or thoughts. Rohka might "overhear." He could tell Eldrin wanted to talk to him alone, but Kelric didn't want Rohka to think he was pushing her away when they had just begun to know each other.

Rohka glanced from Eldrin to Kelric. Then she spoke with courtesy to Kelric. "Is it all right if I go talk to Ixpar now? I would like to tell her what we discussed."

"Yes, certainly," Kelric said, touched by her sensitivity. In that way, too, she was like her mother, rather than blunt like him. "Ixpar went to the pharaoh's home to get Jimorla."

"They're still there," Eldrin said. He gave Kelric a bemused look. "Mother and Dehya are asking your wife about that dice game. It seems Minister Karn plays it rather well."

Minister Karn. The title startled Kelric, for he would always think of her as Ixpar. But to the rest of humanity she was the enigmatic minister who had appeared out of nowhere. The broadcasters knew nothing about her, and Kelric didn't intend to tell them. He had promised Ixpar no one would bother her world, and he meant to keep his oath. With the defenses around Coba fortified even more than before, no one could even go near the solar system without having their ship confiscated.

"Ixpar knows Quis better than most anyone else alive," Kelric said.

"She trounces me all the time," Rohka grumbled.

Kelric couldn't help but smile at her irate expression. "Give it time. You'll see."

Rohka blushed and smiled. Then she took her leave, as charming in her departure as her presence.

After Rohka left, Kelric walked outside with Eldrin. They went higher on the hill, above the house. The weather was, as usual, perfect. They strolled under trees with shushing leaves.

"She's quite striking," Eldrin said.

"Do you mean Rohka?" Kelric asked, pleased. His daughter, it seemed, was brilliant, beautiful, and charming.

His brother glanced at him and grinned. "You should see the look on your face. Yes, she is impressive. Mother is delighted with her, as you've probably noticed." He stopped under a tree and leaned against its papery trunk. "I meant your wife, though."

Kelric rested his weight against another tree. "Ixpar is more than striking."

"Imposing might be a better word."

Kelric thought of the time he had seen Ixpar striding across the Calanya common room, her waist-length red hair in wild disarray, belts of ammunition criss-crossed on her chest, and a machine gun gripped in her hands. "Yes. Much better."

"Your son is—" Eldrin paused. "I want to say reserved, but that isn't right. He seems almost in shock."

It was what Kelric had feared. "He's lived in seclusion his entire life. I'm astonished he was willing to come here at all."

Eldrin was watching him closely. "Those bands he wears on his arms—they're like the ones you have in your office."

"Hmmm," Kelric said.

"Just hmmm?" When it became clear Kelric didn't intend to add anything more, Eldrin spoke curiously. "Does wearing those bands mean living in seclusion?"

"Possibly," Kelric said.

His brother waited. Then he thought, *Kelric?*

Kelric kept up his shields. He didn't feel ready to speak about this. It wasn't that he intended to cut out his family; he would tell them about Coba. But it didn't come easy. Although he had always admired Eldrin, they had never been close in his youth. Eldrin was fifteen years his senior and had left home a year after Kelric's birth. Their lives hadn't intersected much; Kelric had joined the J-Force as a Jagernaut, and Eldrin had already been a singer. Only in these last ten years, with both of them living on the Orbiter, he had begun to know his brother.

"I don't mean to intrude," Eldrin said.

"You're not." Kelric exhaled. "I just need more time."

Eldrin smile wryly. "Your son is a lot like you. He won't talk to me at all. To no one, in fact, except Minister Karn. He never smiles, either."

"He doesn't mean it as a rebuff." At least, Kelric hoped not. "A Calani never speaks to anyone Outside his Calanya. And men from the desert never smile in the presence of women, except their wives or kin."

Eldrin was watching him with fascination. "Good gods, did you live like that?"

"For a while." The topic was making him uncomfortable. "I wanted to ask you about the Lock. You were there when Dehya and I came out this afternoon, weren't you?"

Eldrin obviously wanted to stick with the subject of his "little" brother living in seclusion. But he relented and said, "It was eerie. The two of you appeared in the corridor, slowed down. You looked translucent. You solidified as you came through the arch and started to move normally.

It was about twenty minutes, though, before your voice sounded normal."

"Did you feel anything? Mentally, I mean."

Eldrin thought for a moment. "When I reached out to Dehya's mind, it felt strange. Disorienting."

"Is it still that way?"

"Not anymore. But something is bothering her." He regarded Kelric uneasily. "She says you and she must talk. That was why I came to get you."

Kelric rubbed his hand over his eyes. "Yes."

Eldrin waited. Finally he made a frustrated noise. "You're a regular fount of information today."

"I'm not trying to be obscure. I just don't know what to tell you."

"According to Chad Barzun, before you went into the Lock, you looked up those implosions. He thinks it could be important."

"Possibly." Kelric had thought it destabilized Kyle space to have two Locks carrying the load of three, but in trying to reactivate the SSRB Lock, he feared he had damaged it. Whether or not his efforts had eased the strain on the ancient centers, he had no idea, but if they hadn't, he dreaded the results.

"I've never seen Dehya like this," Eldrin said.

"Like what?"

"Scared, but she won't tell me about it."

Kelric understood the feeling. "I'll talk to her."

"Right now you have company." Eldrin indicated the hill below them. Four people were climbing it: Ixpar, Roca and her namesake Rohka, and a robed, cowled figure that could only be Kelric's son, Jimorla.

"First I need to talk to someone else," Kelric said. It was his son who had realized how to pull them out of the corridor.

Jimorla wandered with Kelric through the house, inscrutable in his robes. His cowl covered his head and the Talha hid his face except for his eyes. He had inherited the height of the Valdoria men, but with a slimmer build. Apparently in his youth, he had trouble eating some foods and had to boil his water, following the same diet Kelric had used on Coba. But whatever illness Jimorla had endured as a child, in the end Coba had agreed with him; as an adult, the young man was strong and fit.

When Kelric had caught up with Jimorla on the hill, Roca had taken one look at his face and ushered everyone else off, leaving him alone with his son. Kelric wasn't sure how she managed it so smoothly, but he was grateful. She seemed to realize that without privacy, he and his son couldn't converse.

Jimorla stopped in a doorway. "Is this your office?"

"That it is." Kelric lifted his hand to invite him inside.

Jimorla walked to the desk, which was stacked with jeweled Quis dice. He glanced up, only his eyes showing within his cowl.

Kelric understood his unspoken question. "Those are mine."

His son pushed back his cowl then and pulled down the Talha so the scarf hung around his neck. With a start, Kelric realized his son considered this office the closest equivalent of a Calanya, and therefore a place he might relax.

The light pouring through the window struck metallic glints in Jimorla's hair. His violet eyes were a color never seen in Coban natives. Prior to his son's birth, Kelric had assumed he didn't carry the gene for violet, because it was dominant on his home world and his eyes were gold. But the genetics of eye color had always been convoluted, and his people had altered their own DNA over the millennia, further complicating the patterns of their inherited traits.

"I feel as if I should ask for a Speaker," Jimorla said.

Kelric understood. In a crisis, if a Calani needed to talk to an Outsider, he could do it through the Calanya Speaker.

"You and I are in the same Calanya," Kelric said. "Now that you're at Karn. So we can talk."

"It's true, isn't it?" Jimorla seemed bemused. "I never expected to leave Varz."

"But you said yes." It meant the world to Kelric.

His gaze darkened. "How could I refuse? It would be tantamount to defying the Imperator."

Dismayed, Kelric said, "Is that how you saw this, as an order from me to come here?"

"Isn't it?"

"No. It's your choice. Always."

Jimorla gave no outward hint of his thoughts, but he didn't shield his mood any better than his sister. His mind evoked the aqua waters of a sun-drenched ocean. Thoughts swam below the surface like silvery fish, a flash of color, then shadows. Kelric couldn't follow most of the emotional currents, but he felt Jimorla's resentment. It wasn't only that his son hadn't wanted to come here; the anger went much deeper.

Jimorla? Kelric thought.

The youth tilted his head. "Did you say something?"

Kelric suspected his son rarely mind-spoke on Coba, if ever. Rohka was the only one strong enough there, and his children would rarely have the chance to interact.

"I thought it," Kelric said.

The color drained from Jimorla's face. "Don't."

"My apology." With regret, Kelric raised his barriers. He seem less able to connect with his son than his daughter.

"Why do you want us here?" Jimorla asked.

Kelric searched for the right words. "I hoped we could get to know one another." It sounded so bland for such a great longing within him. He hoped he hadn't acted precipitously by contacting them, that his wish to know them hadn't outweighed his common sense in protecting them.

Anger flashed on Jimorla's face. "Why would you want to meet me now, after ignoring me for twenty-seven years?"

"I had no choice on Coba. I wasn't allowed to see you."

"You didn't have to leave my mother."

That felt like a blow to the chin. "She said I left her?"

"No. She didn't say anything."

"She turned away from me."

His son looked incredulous. "Why would she do that?"

"She didn't want me."

"Yes, she did." Now Jimorla seemed bewildered. "Why else would she refuse to fight in the war?"

That was unexpected. In military terms, Jimorla's mother had been the strongest ally of Ixpar's greatest foe. "I didn't know she refused."

"She was in love with you." Defiance sparked in his voice. "But she loves my father more."

My father. The words cut like blades. With difficulty, Kelric said, "Raaj is a good man."

Jimorla hesitated. Then he spoke in a quieter voice. "Why did she turn away from you?"

Kelric wondered if the young man had any idea of the knives he was turning. But he owed his son the answers. "She didn't like my past."

"That you had been in prison for murder?"

"No. She could live with that."

"What else could it have been?"

"Tell me something. Have you ever kissed a woman?"

Deep red flushed Jimorla's face. "Of course not."

"Have you ever smiled at one? Besides your kin."

"No. You know I'm not married." His voice tightened. "Why do you ask these insulting questions?"

Kelric couldn't imagine living the constrained, controlled life of a Haka nobleman since birth. It had been hard enough for just one year. "I don't consider them insults."

"And that offended my mother?"

"In a sense. I had lovers before I married her."

Jimorla stared at him for a long moment. When he found his voice, he said, "Oh."

Kelric had no regrets for the women he had loved. But in the rigid culture of the desert Estates, it was illegal for a man even to smile at a woman. Even now it angered and bewildered him that Jimorla's mother had been able to look past the fact that he had killed someone, but not that he had taken lovers outside of marriage.

Jimorla could have reacted many ways, most of them

negative. Rather than offended, though, he looked puzzled, perhaps because he had lived away from the desert long enough to adapt to less restrictive customs. But he seemed unable to fathom his own father having such freedoms.

After a moment, Jimorla said, "When I was thirteen, my mother said you wanted to meet me."

Kelric nodded. "I always did. But it wasn't until then that the Managers agreed to let you visit me."

"What changed?"

It was almost more than Kelric could bear to talk about those days. But he forced out the words. "I was dying. By the time the doctors figured it out, I had only a few months to live."

The tense set of Jimorla's face softened. "I didn't know."

"The war started before you and I had the chance to meet."

"Everyone thought you died in the fires."

"It was better that way."

"Why?!" Jimorla's anger surged. "Why was it better for us to grieve for your death?"

Kelric spoke grimly. "I caused the first war your people had seen in a thousand years. It tore Coba apart, and as long as I was part of your culture, that would continue. I wouldn't—I *couldn't* be responsible for more death and misery." Quietly he added, "Especially not of my own children." Jimorla breathed out, his face strained, but he didn't dispute Kelric's words. As a Calani, he had to know the truth; it saturated the Quis of Coba.

"You waited ten years to come back," Jimorla said. It was an accusation more than a statement.

"It took that long to make certain I could protect you." Kelric wished he were better with words. "I haven't always been Imperator, Jimorla. And having a title is no guarantee of power. Had I revealed Coba when I had no power base, it could have done great harm to your world. I can stop that from happening now. I couldn't when I first escaped."

"You could have found a way."

"I did," Kelric said quietly. "That is why you're here." He lifted his hands, then dropped them. "I'm no good with explanations. I'm sorry."

He feared his son would find that answer a poor excuse. Instead, Jimorla said, "I've never been good with words, either." He glanced at Kelric's dice. "But with Quis . . ."

Kelric exhaled. Technically, they were in the same Calanya. So they could sit at dice. In reality, Kelric was as far Outside as a man could go, and Jimorla's Oath to Ixpar forbid him to play Quis with Outsiders. Yet here he stood, waiting, and Kelric could no more turn down his son than he could cut off his arm.

Forgive me, Ixpar, he thought. He gathered up his dice and indicated a table. He and Jimorla sat across from each other.

Then they rolled out their dice.

XXV
The Fountain

The Qox retreat for the Emperor of Eube had no name. No map listed its location. No mesh address existed for it. The retreat nestled within a valley hidden among the highest peaks of the Jaizire Mountains, and no one could visit that range without permission from the emperor. Forests surrounded the boar-wood lodge. The trees grew unusually tall, their trunks huge and gnarled, clustered close together as if they had joined ranks to repel invaders. Vines dripped from their spiked branches like tatted lace in dark shades of green. Tangle-wolves and blue-spindled pumas stalked the peaks.

Jaibriol loved the retreat. It didn't remind him of home; the land here was too stark and brooding. The wild beauty, untamed and untainted by Aristos, called to something within him. Usually he enjoyed the time he spent here with Tarquine, a respite from the grueling days of his reign. But today they walked into the lodge in cold silence.

The walls had no tech to distract him, only smooth wood with whorled knots. A boar-wood exterior surfaced the console against one wall. The floor had the best available controls to remove insects and dirt, and keep the temperature comfortable, but it looked like simple wood softened with rustic throw rugs.

Jaibriol went to a bar by one wall and poured a drink of the strongest liqueur he could find. The label on the fluted crystal bottle said, simply, "Anise I." The Anise burned a path down his throat and flared heat throughout his body. Ten years ago he would have gagged at its strength; now he hardly blinked.

Tarquine poured a tumbler of Taimarsian brandy. Unable to look away, Jaibriol watched her raise it to her red lips. The muscles of her alabaster throat barely moved as she swallowed. She was physical perfection by Aristo standards, and it suddenly made him ill.

"Did you join them?" he asked.

She glanced at him, the tumbler at her lips. She took another sip, then slowly lowered the glass. "Join who?"

"At your 'dinner' for the Blue-Point Diamonds." His voice was low and dark, like the anger within him. "Did you join their orgy and use my providers?"

"Your language seems to have lost its elevation." Her oh-so-perfect voice had a chill that symbolized everything he hated about Aristos, but today it also had an edge, as if she were struggling to keep her icy veneer.

"Don't play Highton games with me." Something was building in him, something hard and full of misery. "Answer me."

"Why should I?" Her voice was heating up. Tarquine—the

ultimate ice queen—was losing her cool. "You violate all standards of Highton decency and then accuse *us* of immorality."

"You did, didn't you?" He felt as if acid were burning inside of him. "Oh, I'm sure it was sublimely tasteful by Highton standards, right, Tarquine? You were all discreet when you tortured and raped the providers I expected no one ever to goddamned *touch.*" His fists clenched at his sides. "Did you enjoy it? I know it's still in you. I feel it at night, when you 'make love' to me. Or whatever you call it."

Her voice struck like a weapon. "At least other providers didn't talk while I enjoyed them."

He stared at her. *Other* providers. Had she forgotten their guards were here, that they could hear her imply the emperor was a slave? It was insane to argue; he and Tarquine were losing the hard-fought composure they needed to survive. But too much had happened, and his life was out of control. The thought of her spending time with some pleasure boy while he agonized in the crucible of the Lock was more than he could bear.

"Did you enjoy committing adultery?" he said, his voice honed like a knife. It was an insult even more grave than the accusation that she betrayed their vows, for an Aristo could only commit that crime with another Aristo. To suggest that for her, lying with a provider was adultery, put her on the same level as the slaves lowest in the hierarchy of the Eubian empire. "I don't even know how many male providers I have. Or maybe you didn't care—male, female, they're all good."

Jaibriol didn't know she was going to strike until her

palm hit his face, and his head snapped to the side. Her voice was deadly. "Never speak to me that way. *Never.*" She set her drink on the counter. Then she turned and walked away from him, her back stiff under her jumpsuit.

He stared at her, his fist clenched on the bar. Her betrayal affected him at a deeper, more primal level than he ever wanted to admit. It killed him, and he hated knowing he had come to need her so much. That her actions might motivate the Diamond Aristos to support his foolish dream of peace made it even worse. The contradictions of his life had become more than he knew how to endure, but he had no choice, he had to live with them no matter how they ravaged his soul.

Jaibriol downed his drink in one swallow. Then he swung around and hurled the glass with biomech-enhanced strength. It flew across the lodge and shattered inside the antique hearth. Hidaka had been bending over the console, but now he straightened up with a jerk, glancing from Jaibriol to the pulverized glass strewn across the stone. The guards posted around the walls came even more alert, if such was possible. They were all being discreet. None gave any hint they had just heard the emperor and empress have an argument that could tear apart Jaibriol's claim to the title. They probably assumed he and Tarquine had been so angry, they hurled unforgivable insults. Even that violated the icy code of Aristo behavior. Since his experience in the Lock, he was losing the restraint so vital to his life.

Jaibriol walked over to Hidaka, his adrenaline racing even as he tried to appear calm. Although the captain regarded him with a neutral look, Hidaka was expending so much effort to hold the expression, Jaibriol could practically see his strain.

"Do you need the console, Your Highness?" Hidaka asked.

Jaibriol nodded, not trusting himself to words. As Hidaka moved aside, Jaibriol settled into the cushioned seat and entered his mesh- globe, the "world" tailored to his needs, where he kept records, personal data, and correspondence, what people had called their "account" in the antique world of early mesh systems. He knew he should leave this business with Tarquine alone, but he couldn't stop himself. He accessed the list of his providers, the "inventory" he hated, for he lived in fear that someday he would become an entry in that seductive, brutal catalog.

He had inherited fourteen of them, not from his father, who according to the records had never even visited them, but from his grandfather. Despite their gorgeous and sensual appearance of youth, most were in their thirties or older. One was even fifty-two, though in her holo she looked fifteen.

The last two providers, both women, were gifts given to Jaibriol by other Aristos. Although six of his grandfather's were male, it said nothing about his grandfather's preferences; an Aristo could transcend with a psion of either sex. Pain was pain regardless of who experienced it. He didn't see how Aristos lived with themselves, let alone considered it their exalted right to hurt other human beings, especially those who were so helpless. He hated knowing the providers had suffered during his absence, and he loathed even more knowing that heritage was within his own DNA, that he was one- eighth Aristo.

Unexpectedly, the records for Corbal's providers came up as well, apparently because Tarquine had nosed into his private affairs. Sunrise was the only one Corbal lived with. She had a physical age of sixteen, but Jaibriol was startled to discover Corbal had first bought her decades ago, during his marriage. His Highton wife had sent her away, which suggested his interest in Sunrise had been considered more than acceptable even then. After his wife passed away, Corbal brought Sunrise back to his home. The sweet "girl" Jaibriol knew was actually a woman over twice his age.

He locked Corbal's files. It wouldn't keep Tarquine out if she put her mind to breaking in, but he didn't see why she cared. Even if she hadn't already copied the record, it wasn't anything that offered her economic or political advantage.

The holos of his providers remained. They stood on a screen in front of him, each about one hand span high, the beautiful pleasure slaves he owned. He couldn't stop wondering who Tarquine had slept with. Probably the men; his wife was definitely heterosexual. The thought made him want to smash the console. Gritting his teeth, he took a long look at the women. In the reflection of the console, he saw Hidaka behind him, gazing at one of the images with a strange look Jaibriol couldn't interpret. The girl's large bronze eyes glimmered in the holo, and her hair shone like polished bronze, falling to her waist in huge curls. She wore nothing but a glittery G-string and a chain halter with a few topazes hiding the parts of her he most wanted to see.

Jaibriol stared at the image. "Hidaka, contact Robert and let him know I am returning to the palace." He indicated the bronze girl. "Tell him to have her ready for me."

❖ ❖ ❖

Robert was waiting when Jaibriol stepped out of the flyer on the roof of the palace. He hadn't told Tarquine he was leaving. He hated himself for expecting her to act as anything but an Aristo, and he couldn't bear to look at her. His loneliness crashed in, the pain that he kept at bay only by the intricate delusion he had built for his life, that no matter what miseries he endured as emperor of this sadistic empire, he had the respite of an empress who, beneath her chilly exterior, actually loved him.

He was a fool a thousand times over, for believing in his dream, for believing in her, for believing anyone could ever change this hell known as the Eubian empire. They had the strongest, wealthiest, largest civilization humanity had ever known and someday they would probably take over the entire human race. Nothing he did, nothing he endured, no desperate hope he carried within him would ever change that.

Robert stood in the circle of the flyer's lamps. They didn't need the light; it was never truly dark on Glory with so many moons. Tonight, Jaibriol counted nine, some crescents, some fuller, some tiny, others dominating the sky. The tormented ocean crashed so loudly against the glittering black shore beyond the city, he could hear the waves even here, atop his palace.

"Welcome back, Your Highness," Robert said.

"Thank you, Robert." Jaibriol strode past him, toward the bulb tower with the lift that would take them into the palace.

Robert caught up with him. "Should I tell the staff to prepare for the empress's arrival?"

"No." Jaibriol kept going. "Did you have the girl brought to my rooms?"

"Yes, Your Highness." He sounded upset.

"Good." Jaibriol stopped at the onion dome. A molecular air lock shimmered in its side and vanished, leaving a horseshoe arch. He stalked through it, headed for the collapse of his personal life.

The bedroom suite was dark; only a red crystal lamp burned on the nightstand, and its dim light barely reached the voluminous bed. Even from so far away, Jaibriol saw the mound under the covers. He crossed the room silently, past the sitting area and breakfast niche. At the bed, he stared down at the girl sleeping under the velvet spread. Her hair veiled her face, leaving it only partly visible. Bronze lashes sparkled against her cheeks.

He pulled down the bedspread, uncovering her. She was wearing even less than in the holo, just the G-string. Her body was full and curved, and her face so pretty that his breath caught. She had a tiny waist and breasts surely too large to be natural, with huge nipples that looked permanently erect. From her file, he knew she had enhanced pheromones as well, designed to attract and intensify a man's sexual response.

Jaibriol didn't even take off his shoes. He slid onto the bed and sat against the headrest, still wearing his leather jacket, and under it, his black-diamond clothes with carnelian at his cuffs and belt. When he pulled the girl between his legs and slid his hand over her breast, she murmured in her sleep.

"Wake up." He rolled her nipple between his fingers, trying to recall her name from the file. "Wake up, Claret."

She sighed and opened her eyes, her lashes taking forever to lift. "My honor at your glorious presence, Most Esteemed Highness," she murmured drowsily.

Jaibriol bent his head and kissed her hard, too full of anger and hunger to be gentle. He gripped her between his knees, with her torso against his chest. The conduits on his coat scraped her skin, but if it bothered her, she gave no sign. She molded against him, pliant in his hold, far more lush than an Aristo, compliant in a way he would never find in his wife. Her scent surrounded him, intoxicating, and he should have savored every moment with her. He owned the most desirable sex slaves alive—and he couldn't enjoy them even after his wife had goddamned cheated on him.

Jaibriol stopped kissing her and sat with his head bent over the girl, his arms around her. He wanted to smash something inanimate, because he didn't want her, he wanted Tarquine. Even immersed in the aphrodisiac of this lovely girl's pheromones, he couldn't make love to her because he couldn't be unfaithful to his wife.

Claret pulled herself up so she could look into his face. "Why are you sad, Your Highness?"

"I'm not sad," he lied.

She slid her hand across his chest. "What would you like?" she murmured. "Whatever you want. Anything."

He folded his hand around hers. "I couldn't imagine a sweeter night. But it seems sweet isn't what I want."

Fear sparked in her gaze. A brutal image jumped into her mind, what she had endured at the hands of the Blue-Point Diamond Aristos, and Jaibriol felt as if he would die.

"Claret, I'm not going to hurt you." He brushed the tousled hair from her face. "How could I harm such a gift?" Her Kyle strength was a balm on his traumatized mind. He kissed her again, more gently. "You can sleep here tonight. Whatever you need, just let the house staff know."

Her puzzlement washed over even his guarded mind. She had no mental barriers. Of course Aristos never taught their providers how to shield their thoughts. The more open a psion, the more the Aristo received their pain. Jaibriol couldn't imagine how they could have tortured this tender girl and taken enjoyment from it, and for a moment he hated them so much, he felt capable of murder. The only person he hated more was himself, for not protecting the people in his care.

"I'm sorry," he whispered. It was an insane thing for the emperor to tell a provider, but he couldn't stop the words.

Claret touched his temple. "You hurt so much."

"No." He could never let her know. "I don't."

"It's in you." Her eyes were luminous. "Such terrible pain. It is yours rather than mine. And you have no void."

"No. It isn't true." Tears he could never shed burned in his eyes. He had known he couldn't hide from a psion, but he had thought for just one night he could keep his nature a secret.

She leaned her head against his shoulder. "That you are a gift of the gods," she whispered, "we have always known."

His voice rasped. "What does that mean?"

"You are kind."

He had no answer to that. He wasn't kind, he was a monster who had let them be misused on a terrible scale.

"If only I could give you kindness," Jaibriol said.

"You have given me all I need," she answered, but she was lying, for an image jumped into her mind of what she wanted and could never have.

Hidaka.

In her memory, that taciturn monolith he knew as one of his deadly cybernetic guards was instead a man full of affection and loving words, though the two of them had never dared act on their feelings, lest they be caught and punished, even executed. Jaibriol wanted to die then, as he realized what Hidaka's "odd" look had meant at the lodge. It was a man in pain and trying to hide it. Hidaka had saved Jaibriol's life in a thousand ways when he shot Muze, and in return Jaibriol had taken the woman he loved.

The foyer outside of Jaibriol's bedroom was dim. Hidaka was standing with his feet apart and his arms crossed, his face a study in impassive neutrality. He lowered his arms and bowed as Jaibriol walked into the foyer.

"Are my other Razers outside?" Jaibriol asked.

"Yes, Sire." Hidaka guarded his voice well. If Jaibriol hadn't realized what had happened, he wouldn't have noticed the captain's strain. But he couldn't miss it now. He remembered Hidaka leaning over the console in the lodge. He had assumed the guard was checking security, but now he wondered if Hidaka had been trying to discover whether or not Claret was all right. Jaibriol had noticed her because of the intensity of Hidaka's response to her holo, and he felt like a swine for not realizing *why* his guard had reacted that way.

"I'm not going to stay," Jaibriol told him.

The captain nodded, and if Jaibriol hadn't been looking for it, he might have missed the relief in Hidaka's gaze.

"But I want you to remain here," Jaibriol added. "Tonight."

"Sire?"

Jaibriol spoke gently. "She is yours, for as long as the two of you want to stay together. She can move into your rooms in the palace if you would like."

Emotions burst across the face of his guard—his stoic, mechanical Razer. Alarm, fear—and hope. "I would never presume—"

Jaibriol lifted his hand, stopping him. "Just promise me this. You will treat her well."

Hidaka took a deep breath. Then he said, simply, "I will."

"Go on." Jaibriol tilted his head toward the bedroom. "The suite is yours tonight."

For one instant a full smile lit the Razer's face, a flash of white teeth. It only lasted a second, but that single moment spoke volumes against his supposed mechanical nature.

Jaibriol felt even smaller than before. They acted as if he had given them a great gift simply by allowing them to love each other. He could never say the words they deserved, never free Claret or Hidaka or Robert or anyone else, and most of all, he could never reveal his aversion to the foundations of Aristo life, for if he did, he could end up in the same inventory where he had found Claret.

Glory's six-hour night was half over by the time Jaibriol returned to his mountain lodge with his three guards. He couldn't find Tarquine. The central room was empty except for one of her Razers monitoring the console. That the guard had stayed here had to mean she was in the lodge. He could have one of his Razers find her. But he couldn't bring himself to show even that hint of how much he needed the woman he had insulted beyond forgiveness.

She wasn't in any room, including the bedroom. They should have been asleep together, but apparently neither of them could rest. Guilt and insomnia seemed to be partners tonight.

Standing by the perfectly made bed, he noticed a line of light across the room, under the antique door to the bathing chamber. Puzzled, he went over and pushed it open. No one was visible in the room beyond, with its round pool and earthen colors. A lamp with a blueglass shade glowed on a table in one corner, and a fountain burbled in the center of the blue-tiled pool.

Jaibriol turned to the Razer with him. "Wait here."

His bodyguard bowed. "As you wish, Sire."

Jaibriol went into the chamber and closed the door. The fountain was a scalloped bowl shaped like a flower with arches of water that curved up into the air and sheeted down the bowl.

He found Tarquine on the other side.

The empress was sitting by a sculpted bowl at the edge of the pool, hidden from the door by the water spuming through the air. She had leaned over the bowl, her head bent, her hair hanging around her face.

"Tarquine?" He stopped, bewildered by the strange tableau. He had seen her look many ways, but never vulnerable like this.

She lifted her head. Dark circles rimmed her eyes, and her pallor frightened him. Jaibriol knelt beside her, dismayed that while he had been stealing away to the palace, his wife had been sick. Except she couldn't be ill. Like him, she had health nanomeds, molecular laboratories that patrolled her body.

"What happened?" Jaibriol asked.

"Nothing." Her voice was low. "Where have you been?"

"At the palace."

Her voice turned acid. "Did you enjoy yourself?"

"No." He whispered the word.

"Neither did I." She pulled a lock of hair out of her eyes. "I never touched your providers."

He stared at her, incredulous. "You sure as blazes made it sound like you did."

She rested her elbow on the edge of the bowl and rubbed her eyes. "Perhaps I wanted to hurt you."

"Why?" She had succeeded, more than she knew.

"Because you make me care too much." She lowered her arm and met his gaze. "You force me to care if you are happy, if you are well, if you are satisfied with your life. And you never are, Jaibriol. Your sorrow saturates everything."

"I thought you had betrayed our vows."

She didn't tell him an Aristo could never betray a spouse with a provider. Incredibly, she said, "So you had to as well?"

"I couldn't." He spoke bitterly. "I don't know what hells

our marriage exists in, Tarquine, but it seems I love you too much to act in a manner any other Aristo would consider normal."

Her voice softened. "You express your love in strange ways."

So do you, he thought, but he couldn't say it, for he was never certain of anything with her, especially whether or not she loved him, and it hurt too much to ask her, for she would never acknowledge anything she believed made her weak. So instead he touched the bowl where she was leaning. Its purifying systems had cleansed its water to a pristine perfection, but he had no doubt she had thrown up in it.

"How can you be sick?" he asked.

"I'm not." She said it with a straight face, though she looked too exhausted even to stand.

"You just happen to be hanging over this bowl?"

Her gaze never wavered. "I lied to you, Jaibriol."

He didn't know which amazed him more, that she admitted it or that she stated it so simply. "About what?" He could think of so many possibilities, he hardly knew where to start.

"About why I missed your dinner with Minister Gji."

"You were in a meeting that night."

"No. I was here, in the mountains."

Although he had suspected as much since he saw her clothes, her confession made no sense. "Why lie about that? The lodge is here for us to use."

"I didn't come to the lodge."

"Where did you go?"

"A clinic."

"What clinic?" He had no idea what she was about, and he couldn't bruise his mind further by lowering his barriers.

"The Jaizire Clinic. The late Empress Viquara, my niece, established it, accessible only to the Qox Line." Bitterly, she added, "Modern medicine can accomplish almost anything our glorious empire requires it to do."

Jaibriol was beginning to understand, but he shunned the knowledge, as if doing so would protect him from this new agony she was about to inflict. "Tarquine, don't."

"It is already done," she said. "That night, after I came back, when we made love."

"*No.*" His hand spasmed on the edge of the bowl.

"You need an heir," she said tiredly. "You will have one."

"You cannot!" He refused to believe it. "You're too old."

She gave him a dour look. "How complimentary."

"I don't mean an insult. But it can't happen."

"Yes, well, that which can't happen is making me very sick."

"You have to see a doctor!" Alarm flared through him. "I'll summon—"

"No!" She caught his hand before he touched his wrist comm.

"*Why?*" His mind reeled. This woman who sat slumped here, her face pale from illness, might carry the Highton Heir. "Haven't you gone to one?"

"Not once." She had that unrelenting quality he knew all too well. "Nor will I."

He took her hand. "You must take proper care of the baby. And yourself."

"That is why no doctor must see me." She squeezed his fingers, then released his hand so she could motion at the room around them. "And why I came here to rest."

"You aren't resting. You're sick."

"I'm fine. *Only* in here can you know otherwise."

"Why?" His heart was beating too hard.

"I've secured this room to the best of my ability."

Jaibriol knew that euphemism. *To the best of my ability* meant she had turned her prodigious and shady resources to the task. If any place existed where they could talk in private, she could create that refuge.

"Why would you hide the event the entire empire is waiting for?" he asked. The unending speculation as to if and when she could provide him an heir had been a bane on their lives.

"Because any child of yours," she said, "won't be what the doctors expect."

He wanted to rage then, for she was right, and he would have seen it right away if he hadn't been so shell-shocked. She carried the full Aristo genes, but he was only one eighth. It was why he avoided medical experts, and why he had doctored his own DNA to appear more Highton, both within and without. Could a physician discover the Highton Heir wasn't Highton? As his great-grandfather had protected his grandfather, and his grandfather protected his father, so Jaibriol would protect his heir. But how had they managed without endangering the mother or the baby? They had left no records that could help Tarquine.

He stared across the bowl at her. "You can do checks on yourself, can't you? To see if the child is well?"

"Yes, to both." With exquisite misery, she said, "It is a boy. The next emperor."

Jaibriol wanted to feel joy, but his emotions were ripping him apart. "My grandfather was only half Aristo."

"*Never* say it. Never *think* it. Even with my safeguards, you never know."

She didn't understand. "Whatever his genes, he was Highton." Like a train hurtling over a cliff, Jaibriol couldn't stop. "He thought like a Highton. Behaved like a Highton. Valued being Highton." He spoke in a low voice. "Aristo genes are dominant, Tarquine. The Kyle genes didn't manifest in the Qox Line until my father, who inherited them from both his father and his provider mother."

Her fist clenched the rim of the bowl. "Your grandmother was the empress Viquara. My niece. Your mother was the Highton empress Liza. *Never forget.*"

"Our child will transcend." She had to acknowledge the truth. "He will grow up to crave his father's agony. And he'll know what I am. I can hide from my Ministers, my advisors, my judges and military officers and aides. But I can't hide from my own child."

"No child of mine will betray his father."

He felt as if his heart were cracking open. "You don't know that. My grandfather was a monster."

"Your grandfather was the esteemed emperor of Eube."

"That doesn't change his brutality."

"He didn't have you as a father."

That caught him off guard. "What?"

She spoke quietly. "Bring your son up as your father brought you up, and the Highton Heir will be a far better man than any of those around him."

He didn't know where to put her admission, one no other Aristo would even think let alone speak, that raising their child without Highton influence would make him a better human being. "I can't live in exile with him. Secluding him won't change the fundamental nature of what he and I are. My grandfather stayed away from my father to protect him. But who will protect me from my son?"

She started to speak, stopped.

"What is it?" he asked.

"It can be done."

Something in her expression set off his alarms. "You know of another case?"

"It doesn't matter."

"Yes, it does!"

"Ah, Jai, no, I don't know. We will handle what comes."

"You had no right to do this without telling me."

"That may be," she said. "But I will not undo it."

"I wouldn't ask you to."

"Your grandfather survived."

"I would rather die," he said flatly, "than have my son follow the brutal footsteps of my grandfather."

Tarquine watched him as if her cast-iron heart were breaking. "Love our son. It's all you can do."

His life was disintegrating, and he didn't know how to stop it. "Even if he never betrays me, what if someone uncovers the truth? What will happen to our son then? If I am unmasked, so is he."

She pushed back the hair tangled around her face. That she had let it become so disarrayed told him far more about her distress than any claim she might make to feel otherwise.

"Go to the Skolians," she said.

"They would never accept the son of Jaibriol II, grand-son of Ur Qox, great-grandson of Jaibriol I. To them, I embody everything evil in the universe."

"You are their kin. They will accept you."

"And leave Eube in the hands of whom? You? Corbal? Calope Muze? My joint commanders? What sins against humanity would our empire commit because I was too great a coward to face my own reign?"

"Then endure, husband." Her gaze never wavered. "Endure and never grieve for what you cannot have."

"If I am ever discovered," he said, "you must take our son and yourself to safety, even if you have to go to the Ruby Dynasty. They won't like your Aristo heritage or his, but they won't turn away family." He could never know for certain if what she believed about his kin was true, but what he knew of them through his mother supported her conviction. And they had the means to shield his family.

"I will protect our child no matter what it takes." A fierce light glinted in her eyes. "But I will never throw myself on the mercy of the Ruby Dynasty."

He thought of the power roiling within him, tearing apart his carefully built defenses. "I can't promise we will survive."

"We are Qox and Iquar. We do more than survive." She was darkness and whiskey, mesmerizing. "We thrive. And we conquer."

Jaibriol had no wish to conquer humanity. But the moment he joined the Triad, that possibility had come within his grasp. Even knowing his child would be every-thing he feared, pride stirred within him, and another emotion as well, one so intense and painful, it might be love. He had within him the power to give his child an empire greater than any ever known.

The events whirling around him had gone beyond his control. He would do anything to protect his son, even if it meant he had to become the greatest tyrant in human history.

XXVI
Tides of Sorrows

Kelric had known the best Quis players on Coba. He had sat in the Calanya of the most powerful Estates. He recognized the hallmarks of brilliance even after years away from Coba.

His son had no parallel.

Jimorla's talent blazed. No wonder Ixpar had been willing to put her Estate into debt for him. Had Kelric not been the Imperator, he doubted the Varz Manager would ever have agreed to trade such a spectacularly gifted player to her greatest foe.

He didn't have the words to tell Jimorla how proud he was of his son. So he put it into his dice. Jimorla responded with a vibrancy totally unlike his enigmatic demeanor. They built structures of Coba. Kelric told his son about his life. He wasn't certain Jimorla truly understood; the culture that had molded his son was so different, Jimorla might never comprehend the life Kelric had known. But the young man's hostility faded.

Kelric's concerns for the Imperialate percolated into

his dice. He hadn't intended it to happen, but his worries were too big, and Jimorla was too talented to miss them. His son grasped his concerns exactly as would a Calani playing Quis with his Manager during a session dedicated to studying problems faced by the Estate. It was a gift of trust Kelric hadn't expected, and it meant as much to him as if Jimorla had spoken words of welcome.

Kelric described the Lock, the Keys, and the history of his people. He modeled what he knew of Jaibriol Qox, their meeting ten years ago, and his suspicion about Qox's mind. As the picture unfolded, Jimorla evolved it with his prodigious Quis. Untouched by anything Skolian, he offered Kelric a view unlike any other Kelric had considered. His son compared the Locks to three great dice, vital pieces in an interstellar game of Quis. He played them in structures that defined which empire gained advantage.

Yet despite Jimorla's luminous talent, his models of the Eubian emperor faltered. He described Qox as Kelric's son. It made no sense. It was impossible for Kelric to have fathered Qox; he had been on Coba fathering Jimorla. Yet his son remained convinced. Kelric soon realized Jimorla knew too little about the Ruby Dynasty to understand what he implied. He had no context. As Kelric told him more about his family, his son's structures changed. Yet still he persisted in making impossible patterns. He developed a convincing model to explain all of Qox's actions given one simple—and terrifying— assumption.

The Trader emperor was a member of the Ruby Dynasty.

❖ ❖ ❖

Kelric hiked with Dehya up behind his house, and they sat at the top of a long hill that dropped into a gorge. Far below, a river frothed and rushed through the valley.

The walk had tired him. He had never fully recovered from his years on Coba and his escape from the Traders, and he felt his age even more lately in the many aches of his body.

"A void as large as the one you found in Kyle space," Dehya said, "could mean a substantial part of *that* universe imploded."

"Maybe the strain there is as great as here." As far as he knew, no implosions had occurred in their space-time since he found the void. "I couldn't sense the Lock, just emptiness."

She regarded him uneasily. "If the implosions start again, we may have little recourse without that third Lock."

Frustration welled within him. "I was sure I did nothing more than wake it up. If I hadn't already been a member of the Dyad, I doubt I could have done even that much. But from so far away, it's impossible to tell what happened."

Dehya grimaced. "Gods only know what Jaibriol the Third might do with access to a working Lock."

In that splintering moment, watching her, Kelric knew she suspected what Jimorla had tried to tell him with Quis, that Qox was a member of the Ruby Dynasty. A chill ran through him.

"No," he said. *No.*

"Soz and the previous Trader emperor spent fifteen years stranded together on some planet," Dehya said.

"They weren't stranded together." Damn it, Dehya

knew that. "ISC had imprisoned him. He escaped and Soz went after him in another ship." Everyone knew the rest, that Soz had spent fifteen years searching for Qox.

"Convenient how it looked as if they had died," Dehya said. "Yet here they were on some unknown world."

"A planet is a large place to hide."

"So it is." Dehya looked at him, and he at her. Neither of them wanted to think it, what Soz and Qox might have done *together* in fifteen years. Soz couldn't have been anywhere near Qox when ESComm pulled him off the planet, for they would have blasted the entire region to make certain no one survived. By all accounts, she and Qox had never found each other. Kelric thought surely a person could go insane if they spent fifteen years alone, struggling to survive. As emperor, Qox had been reclusive; no one knew anything about him. From all accounts Soz had been single-minded in her pursuit of victory against the Traders in the Radiance War, driven, obsessed even. But insane? It didn't fit with what Kelric knew of his sister's indomitable strength of will.

He and Dehya could never reveal their suspicions to anyone else, for the more people who knew, the greater the chance it would leak and endanger Jaibriol, ending the reign of the only emperor who might actually negotiate with them.

"Jaibriol the Third can't be a psion," Kelric said, a protest as much to himself as to Dehya.

Dehya regarded him uneasily. "His parents *both* would have had to have had the genes. So his grandfather would have had them as well."

"I find it hard to believe even an adult psion could

survive among the Aristos. In my time with Tarquine, I could hardly bear to be around her colleagues." Kelric shook his head. "I can't imagine how a child would bear it. He would go crazy."

"Unless he was kept separate from the Aristos."

And there it was. Jaibriol the Third had been secluded throughout his childhood. No one knew he had existed until he was an adult, for all appearances the perfect, ultimate Aristo.

Kelric thought of Tarquine, the only Aristo he had met whose mind didn't exert that suffocating pressure. The empress. Was that why Jaibriol had married her? Kelric knew he and Dehya might be mistaken about their fears; they had no way to tell, not without meeting Jaibriol Qox. But they couldn't take any chances.

And so, in one of the greatest ironies of their lives, they would protect the Emperor of Eube.

"You cannot!" The words exploded out of Barcala Tikal, the First Councilor of the Skolian Assembly. He and Kelric were both on their feet, facing each other across the table on the dais of the Orbiter War Room. Dehya, Eldrin, Roca, Chad Barzun, and Ragnar Bloodmark were all seated, though Kelric thought they were ready to jump up, too, and argue with him. No matter. He didn't intend to change his mind.

"I can," Kelric said. "And if he agrees, I will."

Tikal hit the table with his fist. "No. It's insane."

Kelric planted his fists on the table and leaned forward. "But it's perfectly sane for our armies to hammer each other and slag planets instead?"

"We have no choice," Tikal said.

"We make our choices!" Kelric shot back at him.

"Gentlemen, stop," Roca said quietly. "Sit down. Please."

Kelric and Tikal continued their hostile stares. Then Tikal took a breath and settled in his chair. Kelric stood for a moment, his adrenaline racing, annoyed at Roca for being so blasted *moderate*. Then he grunted and sat down as well.

His brother Eldrin was watching him with a puzzled frown. "Interstellar leaders never meet in person even when they are allies," he pointed out to Kelric. "For you and Jaibriol Qox to meet, even through the Kyle mesh, would be unusual. What makes you think he would ever agree to a face-to-face meeting?"

"He might very well refuse," Kelric admitted. "But we'll never know unless we ask."

"Oh, I don't know," Ragnar said lazily, tapping a light-stylus against his other hand. "Our Imperator seems to have no trouble meeting with the wives of interstellar leaders."

Kelric gritted his teeth. Years had passed since his meeting with Tarquine, and still Ragnar wouldn't let it go. She had contacted him during the initial peace talks and requested the private conference, using the Kyle connection that Skolia had set up for Eube. When Kelric met with her, she claimed she wanted to know his intentions, whether or not his people honored the Eubian emperor's "desire for peace." It was absurd, and Kelric hadn't believed her, but he had spoken with her anyway. Why? They had each been taking the measure of the other. The Allieds had a phrase for it: Know thy enemy.

Although neither he nor Tarquine had committed a crime, it took no genius to see that a meeting between the Skolian Imperator and Eubian Empress—who had once been lovers—could be considered improper, to put it mildly. He had secured their communication, but it hadn't surprised him that Dehya found out. Unexpectedly, Ragnar had also broken his security and recorded the meeting. The admiral hadn't trusted him since.

Dehya spoke tiredly. "Ragnar, let it go."

"Why should he let it go?" Tikal demanded. "It has a direct bearing on this discussion."

"The problem," Roca said, "isn't some long ago meeting where nothing happened." She regarded Kelric. "What you want to do goes against every diplomatic protocol. Those protocols exist for a reason. They make it possible for our governments to deal together without destabilizing our already volatile relations. What you suggest endangers that balance. As Foreign Affairs Counselor, I strongly advise against this meeting."

"I also, as commander of the Imperial Fleet," Chad said. "Even if Qox did agree, where would you meet him? Certainly not in Eubian territory. It would be impossible for us to guarantee your safety. If the Eubians tried to capture or kill you, it would start the very war you say this meeting is meant to avoid. The only way ISC could assure your safety would be for Qox to meet you in our territory. And of course he won't, for the same reasons you can't go to him."

"Then we'll meet on Earth," Kelric said.

"That's even worse!" Tikal told him. "The last time you went to Earth, they wouldn't let you go."

"That was during a war," Kelric said. "They held onto the members of the Ruby Dynasty who sought refuge there because they didn't believe ISC had the resources to pull us out. They were wrong then, and they know they would be wrong now, even more so, given our current military strength. They aren't stupid, Tikal, and they want a war even less than the rest of us."

Chad leaned forward. "No one 'wants' the destruction and death of war, but it can be far preferable to the alternative—Aristo dominance over the human race. Jaibriol the Third is a Qox. A Highton. The descendant of a line of despots. Talking to him in person won't change that."

"You also have to consider your safety in another sense," Ragnar said. "It's only been a few months since someone tried to kill you, Imperator Skolia. We don't know yet whether or not a more extensive conspiracy exists."

Unfortunately, he had a good point. Kelric looked up at Najo, who was standing near his chair. "Has any evidence surfaced to indicate a larger conspiracy?"

"As of yet, no," Najo said. "However, security hasn't finished their investigation."

Kelric knew they would keep on looking unless he told them to stop. To Ragnar, he said, "I admit, it's a risk. But some risks are worth the danger."

"Not this one," Roca said. "Kelric, I fear it will *increase* hostilities. The Traders know what that vote in our Assembly meant, that it handed you more support for ISC. We need to convince them we're interested in treaties rather than battles. If you ask the emperor to meet with you under the conditions you describe, it is going to look more like a threat."

"I have to agree," Chad said. "If anything happened at that meeting to you or their emperor, it would inflame both sides. That's why we never have two rulers meet this way."

Tikal spoke tightly. "Lord Skolia does *not* rule the Imperialate."

"No, he doesn't." Dehya spoke for the first time. "Nor does he have any wish to undermine either of us, Barcala."

Tikal scowled at her. "I haven't heard you objecting to this madness."

"Perhaps because I don't consider it madness," she said.

Everyone went silent. Kelric had little doubt he was the only one who wasn't surprised by her response.

"You support this idea?" Roca asked with astonishment.

"I trust Kelric's judgment," Dehya said.

"I don't hear you volunteering to meet Qox," Tikal countered.

"Only one of us should go," Kelric said.

"Why?" Chad asked. "Because it is safer than having both of you in the same place, yes?"

"That's right," Kelric said.

"It's even safer with neither of you there," Chad told him.

"One of us should go," Dehya said.

"Why?" Roca seemed bewildered. "And why Kelric?"

He couldn't reveal the truth, that he could only reach Qox's mind in person. As to why it had to be him, that was harder to explain. His son, who knew almost nothing of Skolia's tortuous politics with Eube, had interpreted Kelric's relationship with Qox as father and son. Kelric didn't understand why; as far as he knew, he had given Jimorla no reason to suspect he could be even the uncle of the Trader emperor, let alone his father. But that Quis session had convinced Kelric that if anyone went, it should be him. He was also the only one of them who had met the emperor in person. He couldn't put into words why he thought he had a bond with Qox, but nevertheless, the thought remained.

He could say none of that. So he spoke another truth. "Any mesh communication, no matter how well secured, can be monitored. Only if we meet in person can we be assured of confidentiality."

"And why do you need this confidentiality?" Tikal demanded. "What are you planning to discuss with the emperor that you want no one else to overhear?"

"An end to the wars," Kelric said. "We can never speak freely in front of our top people. Neither of us can show any sign the other side would interpret as weakness. But with just the two of us, we might find an accommodation."

"Or you might try to kill each other," Chad said. "You do realize that will be ESComm's first thought."

"I don't see why you think he would have any interest in finding an accommodation anyway," Tikal said.

"Jaibriol Qox was the one who suggested the peace talks ten years ago," Roca pointed out.

"Yes, well, look how successful those were," Ragnar said sourly. "His own military wouldn't support him."

Kelric scowled at him. "Neither would mine. It takes two sides to negotiate. Maybe if he and I meet, just the two of us, we can find common ground on our own."

The First Councilor shook his head. "When the

Assembly voted to eliminate hereditary control over the Triad voting bloc, I knew it would increase your power base, even lead to military action against the Traders. It was my one hesitation in supporting the ballot. I did anyway, because I know someday we *will* face the Traders. We can't avoid it. Until one of our empires falls, we will remain set against each other. Our fundamental values and needs are too opposed. No common ground exists."

"We have to try," Kelric said, frustrated. "I need to do this, Barcala."

Tikal slapped the table. "The rest of humanity may view you as an Imperialate sovereign, but you don't rule here. You answer to me. And I say no."

"He answers to us both." Dehya said sharply. "I say yes."

"I won't give on this one," Tikal told her.

"My loyalty is always and firmly to ISC," Chad told Kelric. "But in this, I must agree with the First Councilor."

"I concur with Admiral Barzun," Ragnar said.

Damn. Kelric knew he could never sway them without the support of ISC. Technically, only Dehya and Tikal could make the decision. But with Tikal so adamant against the idea and no support anywhere else, he had little recourse.

Dehya met Tikal's gaze. "I won't give on this one, either."

"Then we're deadlocked," Tikal said. "We'll have to turn it over to the Assembly for a vote."

Kelric made an incredulous noise. "What the hell kind

of secrecy is that? The whole point is that Qox and I would meet in private, unaffected by outside influences."

Tikal sat back and crossed his arms. "It's the only way to resolve a deadlock between Pharaoh Dyhianna and myself."

Even if Kelric had been willing to send it to the Assembly, he knew it would never pass. If Roca, the voice of the Moderate Party, refused to support him, he would never convince the more bellicose factions of that voting body.

Kelric spoke with difficulty. "Very well. I withdraw the proposal."

Tikal didn't look triumphant, only weary. No one else spoke. Kelric felt defeated on a much larger scale than with this one question.

Then he looked at Dehya.

Her face showed only disappointment. Nor did her mood hint at any other response. But she was the most nuanced empath alive; if anyone could hide from even the psions at this table, it was Dehya. Kelric understood her as no one else, because he had worked with her in a Dyad for ten years—and the moment he looked at her, he knew. She wanted to do this without Tikal's consent.

She wanted him to commit treason.

The Emperor of Eube sought refuge in the night, out on the sparkling dark beach. The waves roared and crashed, rising to the size of houses and hurling their fury against twisted black outcroppings along the shore. Their spray leapt into the sky, coruscating against a night washed with moonlight in gold, white, and red. Driven by the satellites of Glory, the violent tides battered the coast.

Jaibriol knelt in the sand with no company except Hidaka and three other Razers. They were like a wall separating him from the rest of the universe, one monolith with four parts. Hidaka had discussed names with them and they all had them now, but they hadn't responded to his oblique inquiries about what to call them. They lived in their own universe, intersecting humanity yet never truly like humans. But they never wavered in their protection.

Jaibriol was fragmenting.

He couldn't control the Triad power coursing through his mind. He didn't understand it. He had no context, no preparation, no training, no advisors. *Nothing*. He had only the incontrovertible knowledge that he had to hide what had happened, push it into a recess so deep, no one could ever detect it, neither the Aristos who would prey on his pain nor the providers who would recognize him. He didn't know how to suppress the forces raging within him like the tides driven against this tortured shore. Nor could he escape. Colonel Muze had destroyed the Lock, and no one knew how to rebuild it. To survive, he had to stop being a member of the Triad. And he couldn't.

Jaibriol pressed the heels of his hands against his temples and squeezed his eyes shut. He couldn't do this. He couldn't keep the secret. His life and mind were unraveling. If he continued as emperor, he would fall apart in front of everyone, the Hightons, his advisors, his aides, and his enemies.

"Sire." The deep voice rumbled.

Jaibriol lifted his head and stared through the veil of his pain at Hidaka. "I cannot," he whispered. He wasn't even certain what he was telling his Razer.

The captain spoke with atypical softness. "Shouldn't we return to the palace? Your absence will soon be remarked."

Jaibriol struggled to his feet. "You can protect my person," he said dully. "But what about my thoughts?"

Hidaka regarded him uncertainly. "You will recover."

Not this time. Wearily Jaibriol pulled himself upright. "Let us return."

He headed to the path that wound up the cliffs to the palace. The Razers fell in around him, and lights flashed on their biomech arms. Hidaka acted as a conduit, interpreting Jaibriol's actions for them. Jaibriol had no idea how deep a network among them could go, for to his knowledge no other Aristos had let their bodyguards develop such extensive links. When given the freedom to act as their own beings, they became neither machine nor human, but something else. Yet still they served him with deadly versatility. The best defenses on the planet guarded his person and his palace.

But nothing could protect him against his own mind.

XXVII
The Hall of Providence

"I trusted you." Ixpar's low voice pulled Kelric awake. Startled, he sat bolt upright, his pulse surging as his mind caught up with his reflexes.

Ixpar was kneeling next to him, wearing the silky shift he loved to take off her. But no invitation showed in her posture tonight. Starlight flooded the Orbiter, reflected through panels that had opened after the Sun Lamp set, and it poured through the windows of his bedroom, silvering her body. She knelt by him with one clenched fist resting on her thigh.

"You should trust me," Kelric said, trying to wake up the rest of the way.

"You knew you would contaminate his Quis if you sat at dice with him," Ixpar said. "It was bad enough you agreed. But to pour so much Skolian and Eubian politics into your first game? It is unconscionable."

"I'm not sure how it happened," he admitted. Caught by the luminous genius of Jimorla's Quis, he had instinctively sought his son's input.

"It's obvious how," Ixpar said. "He asked you to play Quis. You said yes. You should have said no."

"He is my son." He met her gaze. "I will not refuse him."

"So you make all Coba pay the price?"

"It was one session."

"One devastating session." The calm of her voice belied the anger in her gaze, which reflected the starlight. "Everything he took from you, he will bring to Coba. And his influence has no small effect on our Quis. He is a Calani like no other. You must know that after your session. His patterns of Skolia and Eube will flood Coba."

He knew it was true. "I'm sorry."

"And you would take my successor as well."

"Rohka talked to you?"

"She wishes to study at the school here."

"Will you say no?" he asked. Her anger was a fog around him.

"I cannot. By Coban law, she is an adult." She sounded worn out. "I hate the idea. It will contaminate her Quis past repair. But you spoke truly. She should know your people. To rule Coba well, in this era when we become part of your empire, she must understand Skolia."

"So must Jimorla," Kelric said. "Otherwise, he'll create distorted pictures, as he did with myself and Emperor Qox."

"It isn't the same." The heat faded from her voice. "I'm sorry, Kelric. But Jimorla wants to return home."

He made himself nod, though it hurt. He couldn't fight this. He even agreed. Rohka would serve as the conduit from the Imperialate to the Calanya, filtering the input they gave the Calani. It would protect the Quis of Coba. But knowing that made it no easier to hear how his son felt.

"And you?" Kelric asked. "Will you also go back?"

"I cannot stay."

What could he say? She couldn't stop ruling Coba because he missed her. He thought of Jaibriol Qox, who symbolized everything he could never have. Qox ruled Eube. Period. No Assembly, no First Councilor, no one to interfere. Tarquine stood by his side, brilliant and unmatched, she who had never seen Kelric as anything more than a slave. She would give Jaibriol heirs, and his children would honor their father as everyone esteemed the emperor. Kelric's son barely even acknowledged him.

You are a fool to envy Qox, he thought. The man probably lived in hell, if what Kelric suspected were true.

"I'm sorry," Ixpar said, watching his face. "Would that I could tell you otherwise." She spoke softly. "I wish you could return with me, Kelric, live in my Calanya, be my husband." With pain, she added, "We both long for the impossible."

"We can visit each other." It was poor compensation, but it was better than nothing. He took her hand and ran his thumb over her knuckles. "Jimorla is truly a genius."

Her face gentled into a smile. "He is his father's son."

"Perhaps someday he will accept that."

"Ah, Kelric." She lifted his hand and pressed her lips against his knuckles. "I can only tell you what I tell myself; never grieve for what could have been. We do what we can."

Never grieve. He wondered if she realized she asked the impossible.

"If I defy a veto from the First Councilor," Kelric said, "I'm breaking the law." He and Dehya were walking on the hill behind his house, high above the gorge with the river.

"We could tell the Inner Council we think Jaibriol Qox is a psion," Dehya said. She even sounded serious.

Kelric slanted a look at her. "Either they would think we were crazy, or even worse, they would believe us. The more people we tell, the more likely it will hurt Qox."

"He's already in danger." She stopped and stared down at the foaming river that rushed against the rocks. "We need to talk to him."

"It's not that easy." Kelric had no way to contact Jaibriol outside of formal channels, which required extensive procedures through both governments. He didn't see what he would achieve by trying, except to get arrested. He might secure his part of the communication, but not the Eubian side. It wouldn't be private.

"I'll support any decision you make," Dehya said.

Kelric crossed his arms. "I don't want your support."

"Why the hell not?"

"Because the penalty for treason is execution."

She pulled him to a stop. "What, they're going to execute both the Ruby Pharaoh and Imperator?"

"When you overthrew the Assembly, you made enemies," Kelric said. "Blending the government may have been genius or madness, but either way, it's divisive." He rubbed the aching muscles in his neck. "You saw the ballot on

Roca's votes. It was almost even. Take a vote on whether or not the Ruby Dynasty should share the rule of Skolia with the Assembly, and it would be even less in our favor. They can't take that vote; we have the power to enforce your decree that neither side can disband the combined government. But that power comes from ISC. If I were to lose my title—say by committing treason—our power base among the military would crumble." He thought of the day she had announced the blended government. "If you had disbanded the Assembly and returned to the days of pure hereditary rule, you would have had to execute Tikal. I doubt he's ever forgotten how close he came to death. At your hands."

"I didn't execute him," Dehya said.

"That just makes him more dangerous."

"He's an inspired leader," she said. "If my taking the Ruby Throne meant his death, it was wrong. We need the Assembly. The time for an empire ruled solely by a dynasty is gone."

"Yes, well, too many people agree with you, Dehya. In fact, a lot of them think the time for *any* dynastic rule is gone."

"The Traders don't," she said dryly.

"Unfortunately." He gazed at the river as it frothed and churned over the rocks. "We don't have a Prime line to Qox the way we do to the Allied President on Earth. We've had nothing but hostilities and war with the Traders for half a millennium. I can't imagine that changing."

"Yet here is Jaibriol Qox," she murmured, "acting oddly."

"Which is the greater treason," he asked. "To defy First

Councilor Tikal and meet a tyrant in secret, or to obey and go to war when Qox may wish otherwise?"

Dehya met his gaze. "I wish I knew."

Jaibriol strode with Tarquine down a wide hall of the palace, under soaring horseshoe arches that shone with gold and emeralds. They were headed to the Amphitheater of Providence. The boots of his Razers rang on the jade-tiled floor, four mammoth human-biomech hybrids. But today they couldn't help him. It would be agony when he entered the amphitheater, for over two thousand Aristos had arrived to attend the economic summit. Tarquine would preside as Finance Minister, but Jaibriol couldn't avoid the sessions or attend via the mesh, not if he wanted to maintain the political edge that kept him sharp, even kept him alive. To give the appearance of neglecting such a confluence of powers could be ruinous.

As they neared the enormous doors of the amphitheater, a retinue of Hightons approached them from a hall that came in at an oblique angle to theirs. Jaibriol knew it had to be one of his top people, because no one else could get this close to him. With a sinking sensation, he recognized the tall man in the center of the retinue; General Barthol Iquar, Tarquine's nephew and one of ESComm's ruthless joint commanders.

He had no wish to see Barthol; the general's abhorrence of the peace process was matched only by his personal dislike of Jaibriol. But Tarquine was slowing down. As their two groups reached each other, everyone stopped. All of the aides and even Barthol's Razers went down on one knee to Jaibriol.

The general bowed to him with military precision. "You honor the Line of Iquar with your presence, Esteemed Highness." His harsh voice grated, and his Highton presence ground against Jaibriol's mind until he wanted to groan.

Jaibriol barely managed a nod. It was a marginal courtesy, one that suggested displeasure, but at this point it was all he could do without revealing his agony. He was about to resume his walk when he heard his wife speak through the haze of his pain.

"It pleases me to see you, Barthol," Tarquine said.

Barthol bowed to her. "It is my great honor to be in your presence." This time, he even sounded as if he meant the words.

"Indeed it is," Tarquine murmured.

Jaibriol thought of going on by himself, but he couldn't insult Tarquine by leaving her behind, and he had no intention of inviting his own incineration by ordering her to come with him.

"You look well today," Barthol told her.

"As do you," Tarquine said.

Barthol tilted his head slightly, a gesture that hinted at appreciation. "It esteems the Line of Iquar that its leaders are in good health."

"It does indeed," Tarquine said with a cool smile. "They plan to continue that way."

Jaibriol couldn't figure out what Tarquine was about. The contrast between his curt greeting and her welcome to Barthol hadn't been intentional on his part, but if it bothered her, she gave no sign. More to the point, he picked up nothing in her mood. He had a good idea what she meant by "continue," though. She headed the Iquar Line. No one knew yet she carried the heir to the Iquar title, and she hadn't chosen a successor to follow her if she died without an heir. Barthol was a logical choice, given his seniority within their Line and his power in ESComm.

"The throne wishes honor for your Line," Tarquine added to her brother.

Jaibriol blinked at her. *Your* Line? She and Barthol shared the same bloodline. Of course she wished them honors, but it was an odd way to say it, especially bringing in the throne. He had no desire to offer Barthol anything. The general had blocked him at every damn junction in the talks, adamant that Skolia pass a law requiring the return of any slaves who escaped into Skolian territory. Jaibriol had thought the Ruby Pharaoh had been willing to search for a compromise, but after Barthol took a hard line, her military became intransigent as well. It was a major reason the negotiations had stalled. As far as Jaibriol was concerned, Barthol could rot in perdition. He said nothing to the general, just met his gaze, an omission that glared all the more harshly given Tarquine's friendlier greeting.

"Your generosity benefits the Line of Iquar," Barthol told Tarquine, which meant zero given that she *was* the Line of Iquar.

"Indeed it does." Her words flowed over them, smooth and potent. "As it does for those who stand behind the head of any Line."

Jaibriol stiffened. If she was referring to heirs as those "who stand behind," she better not be planning to reveal she was pregnant. He couldn't let her do it with no warning or preparation, and without his agreement. Of course if he cut her off, she would turn him into metaphorical ashes, but he would have to live with it. He was already so beleaguered from his Triad entry, he doubted even Tarquine could make it worse.

Jaibriol couldn't read her intent; her face was inscrutable, and she had raised mental barriers, which no other Aristo would use, because they had no reason to learn. Barthol had his focus completely on her. His posture indicated caution, but he had turned his hand by his side so his palm faced away from his body, a subtle gesture that indicated curiosity. He wanted to know what she meant, too.

Barthol spoke smoothly. "It is the honor of those who stand behind them."

Well, hell. Was she leaving open the possibility she would name *Barthol* as her heir? That was bizarre. Whatever she hoped to achieve with such a temptation, it could only last a few months, until it became public knowledge she carried a child who was both the Highton and the Iquar Heir. If Barthol knew she had done it when she fully realized it meant nothing, he would only be angry.

Jaibriol didn't think he could take any more intrigues. He spoke curtly to Barthol. "It has been our pleasure to see you, General." He nodded to Tarquine, trying to make it appear as an invitation rather than an order.

To his relief, she inclined her head to her nephew. "May you fare well."

"And you always." Barthol bowed to Jaibriol. "I thank you for the honor of your presence."

Right, Jaibriol thought. He left with Tarquine, his retinue sweeping away. He expected Tarquine to frown at him for disrupting her machinations. Instead she put her hand on his forearm, as one would expect for the empress. Given that she never did the expected unless it served her purposes, it didn't set his mind at rest.

"An auspicious day," she said.

He spoke in a low voice. "Your esteem gives me hives, dear wife."

Her smile curved. "As often as you imply such to me, I have never seen a single hive on your beautiful body."

He flushed, and decided to keep his mouth shut on that one.

The doors to the Amphitheater of Providence rose to the height of ten men. They swung open as Jaibriol approached, apparently on their own volition, though he knew aides monitored his every step. As his retinue entered the hall, a thousand voices poured over him. He was coming in far above the floor, at a balcony that overlooked the gigantic hall with its many benches and the dais in the center.

Aristos filled the amphitheater.

Jaibriol's mind reeled from the thousands of them: Hightons, Diamonds, Silicates. He was dimly aware of Tarquine's hand on his elbow. To everyone else, it looked as if the emperor strode firmly into the amphitheater, attended by his empress and Razers. But he knew the truth; without the pressure of her hand, he would have stopped, frozen in place.

He and Tarquine took their seats in a balcony above the entrance, with his Razers around them like a human shield. This area was well removed from the rest of the amphitheater. He had selected it that way to protect his mind, but to the rest of Eube it was yet another example of his remote character. He had discovered it didn't matter. No one expected him to act normal. Broadcasters extolled his imperial demeanor. His behavior fit all too well with the Eubian belief that their emperor was a deity. Their attitude disturbed Jaibriol at a deep level; it felt like a trespass against the Christian religion he had converted to on Earth, which acknowledged only one God. But it also meant his people accepted his behavior, which at times was all that allowed him to keep from drowning in the cruelty of his life.

His distance from the other Aristos muted the effects of their minds, usually enough for him to tolerate these summits. Today even that wasn't enough. His head throbbed as the hum of voices swelled. Everyone knew the emperor had entered. They were an ocean of alabaster faces, glittering black hair, and hard carnelian eyes.

Tarquine turned to Jaibriol. "I must open the session."

He nodded stiffly, able to do little else. "Of course."

She didn't leave yet, though. Instead she spoke in a voice so low, even Robert wouldn't hear, though he sat only a seat away on Jaibriol's other side, reading holofiles. This was the best secured location in the amphitheater, with audio buffers for privacy, even visual buffers that hazed the air around them so no one could read their lips.

"Do you know why Corbal fears for his son, Azile?" she asked, intent on him.

Jaibriol narrowed his gaze. "Corbal fears no one. Not even you, Tarquine."

"He loves Azile, you know."

"I'm sure he does." Jaibriol even believed it.

"It is Admiral Erix Muze," she murmured.

"Why would Erix threaten Azile? They like each other."

"Suppose they were related."

"What do you say, 'suppose?'" Jaibriol couldn't see her point. "Azile is the grandson of one of Eube Qox's sisters and Erix is the great- grandson of the other. They're related to each other and to me." He pressed his fingertips into his temples, a sign of vulnerability no emperor should show in public, but he couldn't help himself.

"Erix married Azile's daughter."

"I'm aware of that." He was being too blunt, even for his wife, but he had no resources left for anything more. The impatience of the Aristos in the amphitheater grated against his mind like grit. "You have to start the session."

She leaned toward him. "Remember this, Jaibriol. Not all implications refer to your exalted self."

For flaming sake. She knew he didn't assume that. Unlike his predecessors. "Nor do all implications make sense."

"Erix loves his wife," she said.

Dryly Jaibriol said, "Truly astonishing."

"Just as Corbal loves the dawn. Except Erix doesn't know."

The dawn? That sounded like she meant Sunrise. He didn't see what this had to do with Erix's wife, who was Corbal's granddaughter and Azile's daughter—

A thought came to him, too impossible to consider, but he considered it anyway. Could *Sunrise* be Azile's mother? Azile looked and acted the perfect Highton, and he transcended. He had an Aristo wife and daughter. Of course his daughter was a Highton. Erix Muze would never have married her otherwise. If Erix felt an unusual affection for his wife, it might be seen as eccentric, but nothing more. He had no reason to think he might like her better because she had inherited traits not normally associated with an Aristo, such as kindness. Of course he would never suspect she was other than the ideal Aristo woman. Such an idea was preposterous. Outrageous.

Jaibriol stared at his wife and a chill swept over him. If Azile wasn't a Highton, Corbal had hidden a lie almost as huge as what he knew about Jaibriol. No one would discover it, not even Erix Muze. Corbal was too savvy. No one could outwit him.

Except Tarquine.

"What have you done?" Jaibriol said in a low voice.

"Prepared for the summit, of course." She rose gracefully, and he was aware of everyone below turning to look. The empress bowed to the emperor with perfect form and spoke in a voice that carried. "If Your Highness does so wish, we will began."

Jaibriol's pulse was racing, and his temples ached. He inclined his head, determined to keep his cool in front of the massed powers of his empire.

Tarquine walked with two Razers to the edge of the balcony. A robot arm had docked there, and she stepped into the Luminex cup at its end. As it ferried her across the hall, the dais in the center rose to meet them. A comm officer was seated at a console on that great disk, monitoring communications in the hall.

Within moments, Tarquine and her guards were stepping

from the cup onto the dais. The robot arm withdrew, leaving her in full view. The shimmer of a security field surrounded her. It all had a surreal quality to Jaibriol, as he were watching a play through the veil of a mental haze.

Tarquine stood at the podium while the dais rotated, giving her a view of the entire hall. When she spoke, opaline spheres rotating in the air throughout the ampitheater sent her throaty voice everywhere.

"Welcome," she said. "The two-hundredth and twenty-second Economic Summit of Eube is now in session."

A rumble of voices greeted her announcement. Thousands of Aristos activated their consoles and settled in for the triennial meeting where the powers of the empire gathered to plot, argue, and conspire about increasing their already obscene wealth.

Jaibriol struggled to concentrate as the session proceeded. He neither spoke nor participated in either of the two votes, a ballot to increase Gold Sector tariffs and one to decrease the tax on merchant fleets. Technically, the vote didn't matter; the final decision rested with him. But he ignored the summit at his own risk. If he went against a vote, he weakened his power base with whatever group he opposed. It was an unending game of intrigue, and right now he couldn't handle it. Mercifully, he didn't have to. His aides were recording the session, and he would look at it in detail later.

When Iraz Gji, the Diamond Minister, stood up behind his console, Jaibriol thought he meant to speak in support of the tariffs. Gji had actively lobbied for their passage. Given Gji's stature as a Minister, the comm officer jumped him ahead in the queue, and the *active* light glowed on his console. The rumble of voices quieted; it was unusual for a Minister to address the proceedings, and delegates stopped their maneuvering to listen.

Gji's voice rumbled as spheres carried it throughout the hall. "I wish to enter a new form in these proceedings."

Jaibriol scowled. "Enter a new form" meant Gji wanted to call for a vote on a ballot that had neither been on the agenda nor discussed on the floor. No one had informed Jaibriol, and he never liked surprises, especially from his Ministers.

Tarquine inclined her head to Gji. "Proceed."

"The exaltation of Eube rises each summit," Gji began.

Jaibriol silently groaned. He might be dying in pain, but he swore, half of it came from the interminable ability of Aristos to speak for hours without saying anything. Given that this was an economic summit, Gji's "exaltation" undoubtedly referred to the wealth of the empire.

"It is our desire to see the rise continue," Gji said.

Jaibriol watched Tarquine, noting her perfect composure, and he suddenly knew she expected this. A tickle started in his throat. She claimed Gji had softened to the idea of trade with the Skolians, but that was only a first step. Surely Gji wouldn't put the matter to a vote now; without extensive preparation, probably over a period of years, such a vote would never pass.

"At its highest," Gji continued, "our exaltation will spread throughout settled space."

A ripple of chimes came from the amphitheater as Aristos tapped their finger cymbals in approval of his implicit suggestion that Eube should conquer the rest of humanity, as if owning two trillion people wasn't enough.

"Many avenues of commerce exist," Gji said. "Some venture into exotic realms. Fertile realms rich with resources."

More cymbals chimed, and Aristos discreetly opened their hands on their consoles with palms facing upward, expressing their curiosity. Jaibriol just wanted him to get to the flaming point. So far it sounded as if he were suggesting the usual, that they conquer those exotic realms, which was no more obtainable today than at the last two hundred summits.

"New avenues can mean new means of travel," Gji added.

No cymbals chimed. *New* was not a favored word among Aristos. They sought to operate, think, and act as one mind. Variation was anathema.

On the dais, Tarquine gave the appearance of listening with a posture that suggested wary attention. She no doubt fooled everyone else, but Jaibriol knew better. Gji had said exactly what she wanted to hear.

"New is always a risk," Gji said, acknowledging the unease in the amphitheater. "Unless, of course, it adds to the exaltation of Eube. It might then inspire a call for concord."

Ah, hell. Jaibriol clenched the edge of his console. A "call for concord" meant Gji wanted to vote *now.* Surely he didn't mean the trade expansion. They had no preparation. It would fail miserably.

Jaibriol stood behind his console, and the rumbles died in the amphitheater. Tarquine looked up at him with a calm face, but he sensed her alarm. He wasn't certain himself what he intended, he only knew he couldn't sit here while events spiraled out of his control.

Jaibriol spoke, and his comm sent his voice out to the spinning orbs. "You orate well, Minister Gji." In truth, Highton discourse annoyed Jaibriol no end, but what the hell. It was true Gji had mastered the style. "We are, after all, the Eubian Concord."

Gji bowed to him. Every screen in the amphitheater showed him as an inset, with Jaibriol as the main figure. Jaibriol hardly recognized himself. He stood tall and somber, broad-shouldered, dressed in black with his black hair glittering, his eyes like rubies, his face with the bone structure that supposedly made him one of the most handsome men alive. He hated what he saw, the Highton emperor.

"You honor our proceedings with your voice," Gji said.

Tarquine said nothing, but she lowered her mental barriers and let a warning fill her thoughts. She had no reason to hide her efforts; no one but Jaibriol could sense what she was doing.

"It pleases us," Jaibriol said, "that you wish for more concord in our exaltation."

"I am honored, Your Highness," Gji said.

That was certainly different from Gji's chill disinterest when Jaibriol had met with him over dinner. Jaibriol didn't want to remember what had changed the Minister's attitude.

"It would please us even more," Jaibriol said, "to hear how we might achieve this greater exaltation."

Gji raised his head. "The exotic realms of humanity

control much wealth. To bring that wealth into concord with our own goals might be achieved by means other than Annihilators."

A shocked, discordant clamor of cymbals broke out. Often the cymbals expressed approval, but the syncopated beat the Aristos were using now told a different story. They were angry. It had taken Gji forever to get to the point, but when he finally reached it, no one missed his meaning. He had just called for a vote on opening trade relations with the Skolians.

Tarquine's voice rang out over the clamor. "Minister Gji, the Clerk in Session will attend your call."

Jaibriol stared at her. Her response was required; as the Minister who presided, she had to attend such details as whose clerk did what. But he knew her too well; she had set up this vote. Why? It was certain to fail. Perhaps that was the intent. She might have never wanted him to succeed.

Jaibriol had to make a decision. Only he could stop the call. No one would object if he made that choice, but it would do great damage to his hopes that it might pass another time. If he let the call go forward, it would also fail. Either way he lost. He watched Tarquine, wondering why she had done this.

He made his decision. As a clerk approached Gji, Jaibriol resumed his seat. That he hadn't objected didn't mean he agreed with the call, but it allowed the vote to proceed. For a ballot this outrageous, even if delegates suspected it had his support, that wouldn't stop them from voting against it. If anything, it would increase their determination to make their positions clear. Trade with the Skolians? Anathema. With carefully laid plans over time, he might have brought around enough Diamonds to garner the support he needed. This doomed the vote to failure, but at least he wouldn't go on record as opposed to the idea.

The clerk who took Minister Gji's call was a taskmaker and as such could present the ballot in direct language. It read simply: *Proposal: the Eubian Concord offer to open trade with the Skolian Imperialate for foods and curios.* Maybe Gji thought limiting the potential products for sale would make the idea more palatable. He might have been right if they had approached this in a rational manner. Nothing would help now.

As soon as the Clerk in Session read the ballot, Parizian Sakaar jumped to his feet. The Trade Minister's voice rang out above the turmoil. "Consorting with humanity's amoral dregs is no exaltation!"

Jaibriol had no doubt Sakaar meant the insult implicit in his blunt response. A widespread clash of cymbals indicated support for his outburst from the gathered Aristos. It sickened Jaibriol. He well remembered his meeting with the Trade Minister, when Sakaar had spoken about providers as if they were inanimate products. He called Skolians the "amoral dregs" of humanity because their psions were free rather than controlled by the brutal pavilions where his Silicate Aristos tormented providers.

Minister Gji stood again, another dramatic break with protocol, and regarded his Trade counterpart. "Indeed, Minister Sakaar, we would wish no loss of eminence due to consorting with dregs." He paused a beat. "Or due to other octet errors that create less exaltation."

Octet errors? What the hell? It sounded as if Gji was referring to the evidence of fraud Tarquine had found against Sakaar. None of the gathered Aristos showed any sign they caught the reference; as far as Jaibriol knew, Tarquine had told no one else. Members of the summit were talking agitatedly among themselves or notifying the comm officer they wanted to speak. The Trade and Diamond Ministers could get away with breaking protocol because of their high position, but Jaibriol suspected Sakaar wished now he had waited. Although his face maintained the Highton cool, Jaibriol recognized his strain.

Jaibriol rubbed his temples. His vision was blurring, and he had to wait until it cleared before he could search the hall. Both of his joint commanders had attended. Barthol Iquar was in the section reserved for the highest members of the Iquar Line. He wasn't speaking to anyone, just staring at Tarquine. It gave Jaibriol pause; he would have expected Barthol to assert the lack of military support for the vote.

Admiral Erix Muze was talking with his aides, and Jaibriol could see one of them preparing a statement. His protest would come soon. Tarquine was speaking into the comm on her podium, probably responding to a demand or question. The comm officer worked frantically, queuing requests to speak. Given the stature of the delegates who probably wanted to make their views known, Jaibriol didn't envy the officer her job, having to rank them.

The officer finally decided, and the *active* light glowed on the console of the Janq matriarch of the Diamond Aristos. Although the Janq Line had lost stature because of their economic troubles, few Aristos cared that the Janq had pirate ships. If anything, they admired Janq for the size of their fleet and their daring in pushing so far into Skolian space. The outrage, in their minds, was that the Skolians had "stolen" them.

Janq waited until the amphitheater quieted. Then she said, "The dregs of humanity have made clear their lack of eminence. It lowers us to consider them as a source of exaltation."

General Barthol Iquar rose to his feet.

Alarm flashed across the face of the besieged comm officer; she could hardly tell a joint commander to sit the hell down. Only Jaibriol could do that. She glanced up at him, almost imploring, but he didn't move. Barthol should have signaled the officer, but now that he was standing, Jaibriol had no intention of ordering him to sit. If he denied his joint commander the chance to speak against a ballot, especially one of direct concern to ESComm, it could backfire spectacularly.

The comm officer worked fast, and an *active* light glowed on Barthol's console. Even though he had violated protocol by interrupting the Janq matriarch, she offered no objection. He was a powerful ally. His protest added to hers would strengthen her position.

"Exaltation comes in many forms," Barthol said. "Dregs may be elevated through their association with superior life-forms."

Jaibriol gaped at him. *What the blazes?* Either he had lost his ability to understand Highton, or his bellicose General of the Army had just supported the Diamond Minister's call for trade with the Skolians.

For one moment, silence reigned. Then a roar of voices and cymbals erupted throughout the amphitheater. Tarquine would normally have called for order, but it looked as if she was swamped with messages blazing across her podium screen, the hologlyphs flaring like electronic fire.

Admiral Erix Muze, ESComm's other joint commander, stood up abruptly, the fourth time in moments that one of Eube's most powerful Hightons had broken the rules, this in an empire that prided itself on its lack of variation. The comm officer shot a panicked look at Tarquine, but she was too busy organizing the flood of messages she was receiving to respond.

The officer jabbed her console, and the *active* light blazed red on Erix Muze's console. The admiral's voice rang out. "It has been suggested here today that Eube may gain advantage by bringing rabble into concord with our goals. This, using means other than Annihilators and their kin." He fixed his gaze on Barthol. "However, it should be stated that fleets outfitted with such kin sail exotic seas far more profitably."

Jaibriol's shoulders relaxed. Although Admiral Muze had just declared his opposition to the ballot, he phrased it without offering challenge to his counterpart in ESComm. He seemed puzzled more than anything else, no doubt wondering what could possibly motivate Barthol to support the measure. Jaibriol had exactly the same question.

Barthol met Erix's gaze. With icily perfect intonations, he said, "And such profitable ships shall ride in the new dawn."

Jaibriol felt as if he were reeling. To anyone else, it must have sounded as if one joint commander had told the other that whatever their differences in this ballot, he expected to continue working profitably with him. But Jaibriol knew now what Tarquine had warned him about. Barthol had just hit Erix with a threat so huge, it could tear apart the Xir and Muze Lines. He could reveal Azile's daughter—Erix's wife—as the granddaughter of a provider.

Erix probably had no idea what it meant, but Jaibriol had absolutely no doubt Corbal knew. When Corbal rose to his feet, Jaibriol wondered if he should just kill himself now, because he didn't see how he would escape this madness unscathed. It was going to blow up in their faces rather than pass any vote. He glanced at Tarquine, but she was leaning over the comm officer's console, for all appearances doing her best to help sort the deluge of messages. The desperate officer turned on the *active* light of Corbal's console, her face flushed. Jaibriol sympathized. He had never seen even two speakers active at once, let alone five. It wasn't done. Period. Aristos were a great machine that operated in synch. They never deviated. If someone tossed a bolt into the proceedings, they scrambled in chaos.

Corbal's voice rang out. "Let us remember that those who ride in profit do so for the glory of the emperor."

Jaibriol felt like putting his head in his hands. Corbal had just invoked his royal heritage, that he was the son of Eube Qox's sister. On the surface, his statement was a suitably phrased Highton pledge of the loyalty they all gave to the Carnelian Throne, a reminder they were of concord and should behave accordingly. It sounded impeccably appropriate, but Jaibriol knew exactly what he meant. Corbal had just told Barthol Iquar to back the bloody hell off or Corbal would use his imperial connections to destroy him.

The head of the Janq Aristo Line was still standing. Her voice carried. "Such wisdom is of inestimable value, Lord Xir." Her words suggested she honored Corbal, but her stiff posture implied hostility. "As does all such wisdom—especially those truths about our sailing ships."

Jaibriol pressed his palms against the console as if that could stop him from falling when all these threats avalanched onto his throne. Janq believed Corbal had helped the Skolians capture her merchant fleets. She had to have evidence she believed good enough to withstand any claim of false accusation. She was telling Corbal that if he didn't either support her side or shut the hell up, she would reveal his treason to the summit.

"This is out of control," Jaibriol muttered.

"It is—unusual," Robert said. He sounded stunned.

Jaibriol had to stop this before it took him down with everyone else. Before he stood, he focused on Tarquine. She seemed unconnected to the monumental confrontation; her attention was on her work with the comm officer. She was simply doing her job, keeping order amid the blaze of emotions. No one suspected *she* told the Skolians about the Janq ships, she set up Corbal, she discovered Corbal's secret, and she had the evidence that would implicate either Corbal or else the Janq Line for a false accusation. No one—except Jaibriol.

Her bizarre exchange with Barthol before the summit

made all too much sense now. Somewhere, someplace, she had promised to declare him as her heir instead of her own child. His branch of the Iquar Line would become ascendant after this generation and hers would lose the title. All he had to do was support this ballot. For Barthol, it would be a great coup. What did it matter to Tarquine? Her child would inherit the Carnelian Throne. Except Jaibriol knew she would never give up that power, especially not the rule of such a powerful Aristo Line.

Jaibriol rose to his feet, and the hall quieted as everyone turned to him. The comm officer seemed frozen, unable to deal with yet another break in protocol, this time from the emperor himself. It was Tarquine who leaned over and turned off the lights on the consoles of Janq, Barthol, Erix, and Corbal. They all sat down; to presume they had the floor after Jaibriol had taken it was a crime against the throne, as decreed by one of Jaibriol's particularly narcissistic predecessors.

His words rolled over the amphitheater. The first time he had heard his voice amplified, he had thought the techs did something to give it that deep resonance. But he had checked. They did nothing. He actually sounded this way.

He directed his first comment to Janq. "Your Line has always done great honor to our empire." Jaibriol let neither his posture nor the position of his hands refute his statement. She nodded with a hint of relief, accepting the support.

"It is our hope," Jaibriol said, "that such continues. And certainly it is within our power to see that it does."

Her eyes widened the slightest bit, enough to tell Jaibriol she had taken his true meaning, despite his apparent support. If she pursued an accusation against Corbal, the emperor himself would discredit her evidence. He hoped to high heaven that Tarquine could nullify whatever proof Janq thought she had, because he had no idea how to refute her evidence.

Corbal lifted his chin with triumph. So Jaibriol spoke to him next. "We are pleased with the words of Xir, that those who ride in profit do so for the glory of the emperor."

Corbal inclined his head in acceptance.

Jaibriol waited a heartbeat. The frightened boy who had no idea how to speak among Hightons had vanished years ago and in his place stood a stranger Jaibriol barely recognized as himself. To Corbal, he said, "May the dawn always shine on those who sail for you, from here to realms exotic and new."

His cousin froze. No sound came from the amphitheater. Everyone knew what Jaibriol meant by realms exotic and new; incredibly, the emperor looked with favor on the ballot. That was shock enough. Only Corbal would hear the hidden warning; if he went against the ballot, he endangered Sunrise, his son, and his granddaughter. Jaibriol didn't want any of them hurt, but he couldn't protect them if someone without Corbal's best interest in mind—such as Barthol Iquar—chose to expose him.

Seeing Corbal go pale, Jaibriol felt like scum. But he had to continue. He turned next to Erix. The admiral sat behind his console, his attention focused on Jaibriol as he undoubtedly tried to unwind the conflicting tangles of alliance and confrontation.

Jaibriol said, "Admiral Muze."

Erix inclined his head, his posture wary.

Amplifiers carried Jaibriol's words to every inch of the amphitheater. "It is interesting that to become an admiral one must first be—" He paused. "A colonel."

The blood drained from Erix's face. Although the palace had released no formal announcement about the "attempt" against Jaibriol's life, word had leaked. The Aristos knew: Colonel Vatrix Muze had tried to assassinate the emperor. Vatrix and Erix were first cousins. Jaibriol had no reason to act against Erix; according to the investigation, the admiral hadn't seen Vatrix in years, and they had been estranged for longer. But in the elegantly vicious universe of Hightons, none of that mattered.

In ancient Highton tradition, Jaibriol could execute Erix or any other Muze for the sins of his kin. It would create a crisis for ESComm; the precipitous loss of a joint commander was no small matter. But Jaibriol wouldn't be the first emperor to retaliate against a highly placed member of a Line that had trespassed against him.

For a long moment no one moved. Then a rustle came from the dais. The comm officer was looking up at Jaibriol with a questioning gaze. When he inclined his head, she spoke in a subdued voice, and her voice went out over the spheres.

"Your Highness," she said, "do you wish to respond to this call for concord?"

Jaibriol met her gaze. "I call for concord as well."

It felt as if a mental quake shuddered through the hall. Jaibriol no longer cared. He just wanted this to end. "It would please us," he told the officer, "for you to continue the call."

She nodded, her face pale, and called the roll, starting

with the highest delegate present. "Minister of Intelligence, Azile Xir."

Azile rose to his feet. He stared at Jaibriol, his gaze hooded, and Jaibriol knew he had made an enemy. Azile spoke slowly. "I call for concord."

Voices rolled through the hall like a collective groan.

As Azile took his seat, the comm officer said, "Minister of Finance, Tarquine Iquar."

Tarquine straightened up from her attempts to organize the messages. She looked startled, as if she had been so busy, she had forgotten she was involved in the vote. Jaibriol didn't believe it for a moment, but she did a hell of a convincing job.

"I abstain," she said.

No surprise there. The Finance Minister often abstained, given her position as moderator of the summit. With her husband making his preferences known atypically early in the vote, she also chose the tactful response, neither going against him nor appearing to use her position to influence the call. With a sense of shell-shocked awe, he realized she would escape this entire business with no one ever suspecting her involvement.

"Minister of Diamonds, Iraz Gji," the officer said.

Gji stood up behind his console. "I renew my call for concord." He sat down again, his expression satisfied.

"Minister of Trade, Parizian Sakaar," the officer asked.

The Trade Minister rose heavily to his feet. For a long moment he stared at the Diamond Minister. Then he spoke as if he were gritting his teeth. "I call for concord."

"Saints almighty," Robert muttered.

My sentiments exactly, Jaibriol thought. Tarquine had

stored up her evidence of his mammoth crimes for exactly such a time as this.

"General of the Army, Barthol Iquar," the officer said.

Barthol rose to his great height. "I call for concord."

The comm officer stared at him with her mouth open, and the rumbles in the hall swelled. Even having already heard Barthol sound as if he supported the measure, apparently few Aristos believed he would actually vote in its favor. They had probably thought his earlier comments were so elegantly abstruse that they hadn't yet figured out his true meaning.

The officer finally recovered enough to say, "Admiral of the Navy, Erix Muze."

Erix stood up as if he were going to his own funeral. He knew what he had to say if he wanted to avoid exactly that event. He answered in a tight voice. "I call for concord."

The officer inhaled sharply. "High Judge Calope Muze."

Jaibriol felt like crawling under his seat. He hadn't even realized Calope had attended the summit. She was the only other Highton he liked. She had always treated him with respect, as if she actually believed he made a good emperor. Now she had witnessed him threatening to kill her grandson without a shred of evidence. Every screen in the amphitheater showed her standing up at a bench far across the hall, her face strained. She stared in his direction for a long moment. Then she looked at Erix, her grandson. In a heavy voice, she said, "I call for concord."

I'm sorry, Jaibriol thought, though he knew she could never hear his thought. None of them ever would.

The comm officer looked as if she were having heart failure. Nor was she the only one. But she spoke evenly. "Lord Xir?"

Corbal rose to his feet, his face clenched. "I call for concord."

Jaibriol doubted Corbal would ever forgive him. Or Calope. Or any of them. He lived on an island of his own slow dying.

The roll call continued, but the rest made no difference. The major players had spoken—and with the exception of one abstain, they had agreed to support what would rank as one of the most stunning upsets in Eubian history.

Tarquine glanced up at him and inclined her head as was appropriate for a Minister to her emperor. No hint of triumph showed on her face.

But it blazed in her mind.

XXVIII
Mists of Discourse

Jaibriol left his bodyguards outside his office despite Hidaka's protests. The room was unlit when he entered, except for the light coming in the window across from the door. The sun of Glory had set, leaving the sky a vivid red. A tall figure stood at the window, gazing out at the burning sky.

"I don't know why anyone bothers to say I sit on the throne," Jaibriol said.

Tarquine turned to him. "You are the emperor, my husband. You handled yourself brilliantly in the summit today."

"You set them up." He didn't know whether to be horrified or grateful. "All of them."

"Ah, Jai." She walked over, more relaxed than he had seen her in days. "You have your chance to talk to the Skolians. This strong expression of support from your top people offers the opening you need to contact the Ruby Dynasty." She stopped in front of him. "What you do with that opening—sell curios or negotiate peace—is your choice."

This felt surreal. "It isn't that simple."

"No, it isn't. It never is. But you have the opportunity."

Knowing she was right didn't cool his anger. "Why bother to send me? I couldn't come close to your expertise."

"In what?" She set her palm against his chest. "Yes, if you put me on the Carnelian Throne, I could be the ultimate Highton sovereign. No other Aristo would match my reign."

"Or your modesty," he said dryly.

"Eube doesn't need the ultimate Highton sovereign."

"No? What does Eube need?"

Her voice had a sense of quiet. "Someone with the decency and strength of character to make the best *leader*. It isn't the same as the best Highton sovereign." She lowered her hand. "Go to the Skolians. Do what no one else among us can. Make the universe a better place for everyone, not just Aristos."

He stared at her. "If any Aristo overheard what you just said, they would consider it grounds for assassination."

"Do you?"

"Never." He couldn't believe she would give up the Iquar title for his hopeless dream. "You offer me the impossible, but the dreamer who sought that shiny hope has become tarnished past recovery."

"I will always be Highton." Her voice had a still quality. "I could no more change than I could alter the laws of physics. I am what I am." The dim light shadowed her face. "And you will always be decent."

Decent. He felt anything but. She had given him a second chance, but the boy who had approached the Skolians ten years ago was gone, and he feared the man who had taken his place had become too much of an Aristo to claim that dream.

The communication from the Eubians came into the Office of the Ruby Pharaoh on the planet Parthonia, capital of the Skolian Imperialate. They forwarded it to the equivalent office on the Orbiter space station. It went through twelve layers of security before it reached the Advisory Aide to the Pharaoh. At the time, Dehya was deep within the Kyle, working on the vast network of meshes. So the Advisory Office of the Pharaoh forwarded the message to the Advisory Office of the Imperator.

Seated in the command chair above the War Room, Kelric barely noticed when the light on the armrest turned blue. It was a moment before he touched the *receive* panel.

"Skolia, here," he said.

His aide's voice floated out of the mesh. "Sir, we have a communication from the Emperor's Office on Glory."

What the blazes? "Play it."

"Forwarding."

A new voice spoke, this one in elegant Iotic with a Highton accent. "My honor at your Esteemed Presence, Pharaoh Dyhianna. I am Robert Muzeson, Personal Aide to Emperor Qox." The light on the comm indicated the message was prerecorded; without access to the Kyle web, Eubians couldn't send in real time. They weren't without recourse to Kyle technology; they could always petition

Skolia for the loan of a node. Of course they liked that idea about as much as they liked moldy food. Maybe less. Moldy food didn't taunt them by challenging their ascendancy.

The message continued. "His Glorious Highness, Jaibriol the Third, desires a mutual audience of himself and Pharaoh Dyhianna."

"Good gods," Kelric muttered. He had never heard of anything like this. It gave him one hell of an opening, though. He could have the techs bring Dehya out of her Kyle session, but that would take time— and involve her in ways he wanted to avoid.

Kelric tapped a panel. "Major Wills?"

A man answered. "Here, sir."

"Prepare the omega protocol." Kelric had designed omega himself, in case he ever wanted to hide his communications from ISC and the government. "Use it to send the following to Emperor Qox's people."

"Recording, sir." Wills sounded stunned. He couldn't miss the implication, that Skolia's Imperator wanted to conceal his contact with Eube's emperor.

"And Wills," Kelric said. "You are bound by the protocol confidentiality." It was the weak link in the process, that Wills knew he had sent the message.

"Understood, Lord Skolia."

"Message begin," Kelric said. "The Imperator desires a mutual audience of himself and Emperor Qox, real-time, virtual."

"Sending." Wills spoke with efficiency, but Kelric didn't miss the shock in his voice.

And you don't know the half of it, Kelric thought.

The Luminex console curved around Kelric. Normally a crew tended his VR sessions: today he came alone. He fastened himself into the chair. The mesh folded around his body and plugged into sockets in his wrists, ankles, and spine, linking to his internal biomech. He had told no one what he was doing, and he used security he had designed himself. If this worked as expected, no one else would ever know about this session. He didn't fool himself that it would be impossible to trace, but if someone did unravel what he had done, he hoped it would be too late.

He touched a panel in the arm of his chair. "Bolt?"

"Here," his node said. It had accessed the console through Kelric's biomech link to the chair.

"Do you have a Kyle node prepared for Emperor Qox?"

"Everything is ready," Bolt said.

A chill went through Kelric. No communication between Eube and Skolia at this high of a level had taken place for years, since the breakdown of the negotiations. In the beginning, their staffs had continued to speak, trying to restart matters, but when one attempt after another failed, those communications had fizzled as well.

"Let's go." Kelric lowered the visor over his head, and the world turned black.

"Wait," Bolt said, a disembodied voice in the dark.

"Is something wrong?" Kelric asked.

"Are you sure you want to do this?"

"He requested the communication."

"You know what I mean."

Kelric closed his eyes, not because it mattered in the dark, but out of reflex, as if that would let him evade the concern in the voice of his supposedly emotionless node. "Yes, I'm sure."

"Activating VR," Bolt said.

The surroundings lightened into a mist and took form: a glossy white room with no furniture or exits. As real as it seemed, he had to remind himself he was in a chair on the Orbiter. He had changed nothing in his appearance except his clothes; instead of the casual slacks and shirt he actually wore, here he had a dark gold uniform with the insignia of an exploding star on his shoulder.

Kelric walked toward one seamless wall, and a door appeared. He exited into a hall of blue marble columns and airy spaces. Normally the computer would create an honor guard and whatever other retinue his protocol people felt necessary for a meeting with the emperor. Kelric had activated none of those simulations. The less resources he used, the less likely he was to draw attention to his proscribed use of the Kyle web.

Jaibriol stood by the Luminex console that curved around his chair. Robert waited a few paces back, checking a holofile. Hidaka was monitoring the area with his cybernetic arm, and Jaibriol's other guards stood posted around the chamber. Several Hightons waited with him: the Protocol Minister, the Diamond Minister, and Tarquine. Corbal hadn't approached him since the vote, and Jaibriol didn't blame him, given what had happened.

His head ached continually. No nanomeds could cure it. He wondered dully if he would have to endure this pain for the rest of his life.

A tech approached and knelt to him, her gaze downcast.

"Please rise," Jaibriol said.

She stood, favoring her knee. "We're ready, Your Highness."

He nodded formally and took his seat in the console. As she fastened him into the chair, its mesh folded around him, clicking prongs into his wrist, ankle, and spine sockets.

"Are you comfortable?" the tech asked.

"Yes, good," Jaibriol said. The taskmaker minds of the techs working around him offered a mental wall that eased the pressure of the Aristo minds in the room.

She tapped the console. "This will link to the Kyle web."

"You're sure they have a node we can use?" he asked. The Skolians had promised to create one, but unlike with the peace talks, this time no crew had contacted his people. They had dealt only with an EI that called itself Bolt. Jaibriol had no idea what it meant, and he didn't like it. But he wasn't meeting Kelric in person, only as a simulation. What happened at the other end couldn't physically affect him.

"The node is set," the tech said. "Ready, Your Highness?"

Jaibriol's pulse jumped. "Yes. Go ahead."

She lowered his visor, enclosing him in darkness. A voice said, "Initiate," and another said, "Activating VR."

The world brightened, and Jaibriol found himself standing in a white room. A *square* room. The right angles disoriented him. He expected a door to appear and an avatar to enter, to serve as his host. When nothing happened, he went to the wall, uncertain what to do.

A message in English lit up the surface: Privacy requested.

Jaibriol tensed. Kelric wanted to talk to him alone, with no one else in the connection? To call it a strange request was akin to saying it was odd that the vote on opening trade relations with the Skolians had passed.

Jaibriol had asked to meet the Ruby Pharaoh. The Imperator had answered. Technically, it was an insult; in theory, Kelric didn't rule Skolia. In practice, no one doubted his power, especially since the recent Assembly vote. But communications between potentates weren't done in private, not without inviting suspicion of collaboration with the enemy. In this situation, though, that verged on ludicrous. Jaibriol suspected that if he refused the private conference, he would never learn what Kelric had come to say. He also knew that if he cut his advisors out of the link, they would have collective heart failure.

He laid his palm against the wall. "I accept."

The surface shimmered and vanished, revealing a fog beyond.

"Emperor Qox!" The alarmed voice of his Protocol Minister cut the air. "You just activated a security field!"

Hidaka's deep voice rumbled. "Sire, please go no further."

"I've accepted the field," Jaibriol said.

"Jai, don't." That was Tarquine. "You don't know what it means."

"It's just a simulation," Jaibriol said.

Hidaka spoke. "Your Highness, simulations can be used to cause injury, even at a distance. You could risk brain damage."

Jaibriol hesitated. Then he said, "I'll be fine."

"Jai, no!" Tarquine's voice rang out.

I have to find out what your former lover wants. Then he walked into the mist.

Kelric didn't have to wait; Jaibriol soon materialized out of the fog. The emperor looked as if he were cloaked in the night. He wore black-diamond trousers and shirt, and a black belt studded with carnelians. Red gems glinted in his cuff links. His black hair splintered light, and his red eyes had a jeweled quality. Kelric was no judge of appearance, but even he could tell Qox was uncommonly good-looking even among Hightons, who raised the pursuit of narcissistic "self-improvement" to an art. The emperor exuded vitality, a man at his peak, broad-shouldered and tall, long-legged and narrow- hipped, the embodiment of every standard of perfection in Eube and across the stars.

Kelric hoped Qox had enhanced his avatar in the simulation, because if the emperor really looked like this, it had to violate some law of the cosmos. No one deserved so many advantages: the greatest wealth of any human alive, the highest title in what many considered the most powerful empire in human history, the worship of trillions who considered him a deity, and an empress whose sultry, devastating beauty was outdone only by her deadly efficiency as a political weapon. Kelric was acutely conscious of his advanced years, the grey in his hair, and the limitations on his power, his life, and his family. He had been nothing more than a high-priced slave to the woman this man called wife.

They stood taking each other's measure, neither willing

to speak first, for it was an implicit admission that the other occupied the dominant position. They had held their titles for roughly the same time, but Jaibriol was hardly more than a third Kelric's age. He had also initiated contact, which meant he should go first. But Kelric's status wasn't formally equivalent to Jaibriol's title as emperor.

Then Jaibriol spoke in Highton. "Imperator Skolia."

Kelric responded in the Aristo language. "Emperor Qox."

"It intrigues us that you requested a secured conference," Jaibriol said.

Kelric's first reaction was that Qox had learned Highton discourse too well. Instead of simply asking why, he approached the question obliquely. Fast on the heels of that reaction came the shock; the emperor had spoken to him—a former slave—as he would to a Highton. As an equal.

Kelric could read nothing from Jaibriol except what Qox wanted him to see, the perfect, aloof, alabaster Aristo. If Jaibriol had ever been a naïve high school boy on Earth, those days were gone.

"Emperor Qox." Kelric spoke formally. "You honor me with your language. I haven't the proficiency in Highton to return the honor. If you will forgive my direct language."

Jaibriol inclined his head. "There is nothing to forgive."

"I come to you with a request."

Jaibriol watched him with his carnelian gaze. No, not carnelian. His eyes looked like rubies.

"Go on," the emperor said.

"Meet me on Earth. In person. Just the two of us."

Jaibriol's face showed no hint of his reaction to that

outlandish suggestion. He spoke coolly. "Why would I do such a thing?"

"Because I can help you. I may be one of the only people who can. But only in person." If he and Dehya were right, if Qox were a psion, the emperor would know what he meant.

"I have many people who can help me," Jaibriol. "Billions, in fact. Why would I need the aid of a provider?"

Kelric gritted his teeth and was glad the simulation edited it out. "You once asked me to meet you at the peace table. We met. It failed. Are you willing to try again? We will get nowhere surrounded by aides, officers, and advisors who limit our discourse. Meet with me. Just me. If you truly meant what you said that day in the Lock."

Even in the simulation, Jaibriol's gaze darkened. "I spoke the truth."

"Then come to Earth."

For a long moment Jaibriol just regarded him, with no hint he would consider the suggestion, and Kelric's hope died.

Then Qox said, "Very well. Let us meet."

XXIX
Refuge and Fire

Jaibriol left Eube's Glory without telling Robert. He rose in the predawn stillness and went with Hidaka and three other Razers to the starport. Hidaka never balked. If he thought it bizarre that the emperor would steal away from his palace without telling even his most trusted aide, he said nothing.

Jaibriol couldn't fathom what Kelric wanted. At least he knew now that he hadn't killed his uncle by joining the Triad. He couldn't tell whether or not the pharaoh survived; if it was possible to detect the Triad across space, he didn't know how. But if she had died, surely he would have picked up some hint from Kelric of such a massive grief. And if anyone could help him deal with becoming a Key, it was Kelric. What would possess the Imperator to do such a thing, he had no idea. More likely Kelric would try to kill him.

By agreeing to see the Imperator in secret, Jaibriol knew he risked much. Despite the torment of his life, he

had no desire to die, for he would soon be a father. He
would love his child no matter what, even if his son might
become everything he abhorred. But he could end up as a
slave if he couldn't learn to control his mind better than
he had done since he joined the Triad. And no Aristo
could teach him that control.

So he went to meet his enemy.

Kelric's ship landed in a private berth at a starport in
West Virginia. He came with Najo, Strava, Axer, and no
one else. He had no wish to involve his bodyguards in
actions that could end in an accusation of treason, and he
had tried to leave them on the Orbiter. But ever since he
had snuck off to Coba without them, they had been even
more alert. They understood the stakes; if he was caught
doing this, they all risked execution. They still refused to
stay on the Orbiter.

As far as the port authorities knew, he was a rich
Skolian who wanted no fanfare during his vacation on
Earth. If his security worked as well as he intended, neither
they nor anyone else would ever know otherwise.

Jaibriol would come in a similar manner. He hoped.
That the emperor had agreed to the meeting supported
Kelric's suspicion he was dealing with a psion, but he
couldn't be certain until they met. Even then, he didn't
know what he would find. If Jaibriol had lived among
Aristos for ten years, gods only knew how badly it had
damaged the Kyle centers of his mind.

Or maybe he was wrong about everything, and Jaibriol
agreed to come because it offered a chance to kill the
crazy Imperator.

Jaibriol's only stipulation had been that they meet in the Appalachian Mountains. It made sense; if the Aristos discovered what he had done, he would have an excuse, weak as it might be. He had gone on retreat in a place he had once called home. Kelric had no such cover for visiting Earth. The only time he had spent on this world had been against his will, as a political prisoner.

He went to an isolated mountain region, to a cabin owned by an elite establishment that catered to the wealthy. He spoke with no one and needed no check-in. Among the Allieds, one could buy anything if he paid enough, including anonymity. In some ways, it had been easier to arrange security here than for a military operation. Bolt had simply told his contact that his "patron" didn't wish to be disturbed and then arranged a large transfer of funds. Very large.

Kelric's guards were also securing the area. With all these precautions, he doubted a bug could get past them. On a solo mission like this, though, he still had significantly less protection than if ISC had been involved.

While Najo and Strava checked the rustically opulent cabin, Kelric sat at a desk built from knotted wood and unrolled his mesh screen. Axer stood behind him, solid and silent, but Kelric felt his agitation. His guards hated this trip.

He scanned Earth's public meshes in their military, government, academic, and entertainment spheres. It was interesting from a cultural standpoint, but he couldn't concentrate on the entertainment sites and the rest offered nothing his security people hadn't told him in greater detail.

Kelric put away the screen and took the dice pouch off his belt. He played Quis solitaire for a while, but he couldn't focus on that, either. His structures kept evolving in patterns of tension, which was hardly eye-opening, or else predictions of his execution. Too much could go wrong, and his dice kept portraying every possible way. He finally stuffed them back in the pouch and sat back in his chair, rubbing his eyes.

Strava walked into the room. "Sir?"

Kelric looked up with a start. "Yes?"

"You have visitors." Her face was pale.

Kelric stood slowly, aware of Earth's uncomfortably heavy gravity. "Where?"

She tilted her head toward the front of the cabin. "They're on the forest road that leads up here."

"Do you have an ID?"

"Nothing," she said grimly. "We can't crack their system."

He met her gaze. They both knew what that meant. His guards had the best sensors available to a Skolian Imperator. None could match them—except those for a Eubian emperor.

"Keep me posted," Kelric said.

"I will, sir." Strava went to a window and edged aside the curtains so she could look out into the night. It wasn't necessary; she could have monitored the approach from within the security room she and Najo had set up within the cabin. But Kelric appreciated her presence and Axer's. He was more nervous than he wanted to admit. What if instead of Qox, a murder squad showed up? He had defenses, but so would they. Qox knew Kelric had come here alone, in secret, without ISC backup.

Kelric joined Strava and pulled back the curtains. Outside, pine trees rustled. The night otherwise had that deep silence of a land that knew no cities. Knowing his silhouette would be visible from outside, he let the curtain fall back, in case killers arrived instead of Qox. Strava stood at his side with the poised look of a fighter ready to shoot someone, preferably a Trader, he had no doubt.

Kelric paced restlessly across the room. He was a fool to trust Qox. He had to be wrong. No psion could survive among the Aristos, not and retain his sanity.

One thought haunted him. When Jaibriol Qox had lived on Earth, the school authorities there had incorrectly recorded his birthday, listing him as a few months *younger* than his true age. The Qox Palace had fixed the mistake. The date on Earth had to be wrong; otherwise, Qox would have been conceived *after* his father "died." The previous emperor hadn't died, he had been lost on an unknown world, but he could hardly have impregnated his empress from there. Many people assumed she had used sperm stored by her husband to become pregnant after he disappeared. It went against Highton mores, however, which would explain why the palace found the "error," so Jaibriol didn't suffer the supposed shame of such a birth. Kelric had come to fear it hid a far greater bombshell, that Jaibriol's father had sired him while stranded on that planet.

Stranded with Kelric's sister, Soz.

He didn't want to believe it. Qox couldn't have forced her; she had been a Jagernaut Primary, one of the most versatile killing machines alive. But she would never have willingly birthed the Highton Heir. Unless . . . Qox had been a Ruby psion.

He pressed his fingers into his temples. The idea so disturbed him, his head throbbed. Usually the nanomeds in his body could fix a headache, but tonight even they didn't help. He felt disoriented, off balance.

"Sir?"

Kelric jerked. Turning, he saw Najo standing nearby. He focused his blurred vision on the guard. "Are they here?"

"About half a mile away." He watched Kelric with concern. "Are you all right?"

"My head hurts."

Najo tensed. "Sir! It's a trick!" His hand dropped to the Jumbler on his hip.

Kelric smiled slightly, aware of Strava and Axer watching. "The Traders often give me a headache, but I don't think we can accuse them of a nefarious plot because of it."

They regarded him dubiously.

Kelric's smile faded, for he knew if anything went wrong, he may have condemned these three to stand trial, even to die. For ten years, they had guarded him. They were more than officers; they had become an integral part of his life. They were willing to put their lives on the line for his hopeless dream of peace, and that meant more than he knew how to say. But he had to try.

"I want you all to know," he told them. "Whatever happens, I—" He stumbled with the words. "I thank you. For everything." It sounded so inadequate.

Najo said, "We wouldn't have it any other way, sir." Strava and Axer both nodded. They seemed to understand, feeling it from his mind if not his awkward speech.

Suddenly lights flashed on their gauntlets, which linked their biomech to the cabin security. Najo went to the door, standing to one side with his Jumbler up and ready. Strava returned to the window and nudged aside the cloth with her mammoth gun. Axer took up position by Kelric with his weapon drawn. Their tension filled the cabin, and Kelric feared they would jumble the first person that walked through that door.

"Put down your weapons," he said.

Strava turned to him, incredulity on her face. "Sir!"

"All of you," Kelric said. "Lower the guns."

"We can't do our job if you restrict us," Najo told him.

"If it were me coming here," Kelric said, "and we walked into a room full of Razers who had their laser carbines aimed at us and Jaibriol Qox standing behind them, what would you do?"

Najo regarded him steadily. "Defend you. Shoot, if necessary."

"That's my point," Kelric said. "Lower the guns."

Strava blew out a gust of air. She was clenching her Jumbler so tightly, her knuckles had turned white. Najo exhaled as well. Then he said, "Weapons down."

As the Jagernauts lowered their guns, an engine rumbled outside. Kelric's head felt as if it were splitting apart, but he knew now that nothing within his body caused the pain. It came from someone on the other side of that door.

Heavy footsteps sounded on the porch. The metallic sense of a mind came to him, one so augmented, it didn't feel human. The hair on Kelric's neck prickled. He hoped he hadn't made a mistake having his guards lower their weapons. A great deal could happen in the fraction of a second it took to raise a Jumbler.

Someone pushed the door. Perhaps they had expected it to be locked; Kelric didn't know. It opened slowly, swinging past Najo, who gripped his Jumbler, but with his arm straight down by his side, the tendons standing out along his tensed limb.

A giant stood framed in the doorway. A Razer.

Kelric had seen them on broadcasts. They served as the emperor's secret police and bodyguards. This one towered, his harsh features clenched. He did indeed hold a laser carbine—

Down by his side.

Kelric let out a breath, more relieved than he would ever admit. The Razer entered the room, his boots clanking on the wooden floor. Strava flanked his steps, matching him in height if not mass, her gauntlets flashing with so many warning lights, it cast an eerie red glow over her and the Razer.

Another man appeared in the doorway.

The moment Kelric saw him, he knew just how much the VR simulation had edited Qox's appearance. This man wasn't the perfect, untouched emperor. Jaibriol the Third stared at him with haunted eyes, his face haggard. But what Kelric felt most of all, undeniable and inescapable, was the raging Kyle pain in Jaibriol's mind. It was so huge, he wondered the cabin didn't catch fire and burn with its heat. No psion could miss it; he saw his own horror mirrored in the faces of his Jagernauts.

Incredibly, the Razer still didn't raise his weapon. He looked from Kelric to Jaibriol, his gaze far too perceptive.

Kelric found his voice. "Come in. Please."

Jaibriol entered the cabin, his gaze fixed Kelric. He

spoke in that deep, spectacular voice that people all across the stars heard every time he appeared in broadcasts. It hadn't been doctored; he truly possessed that resonant voice—just as had Kelric's father, the Bard of Dalvador.

"You look the same as in the simulation," Jaibriol said.

Kelric blinked, startled. Of all the openings he had expected—an abstruse Highton greeting, stilted diplomacy, or questions—none included that statement. Jaibriol hadn't changed his appearance, either; physically he was the same. But no EI was here to edit out the agony in his gaze.

"I don't usually alter my appearance," Kelric said.

Jaibriol nodded stiffly, as if he didn't know what else to say and had been as caught off guard by his comment as Kelric.

Three more Razers entered, until the room was bursting with guards. Kelric felt how much it strained his own to keep their weapons down; the slightest hint of a threat, and they would fire. He didn't like the odds, either, four Razers and three Jagernauts. Despite the augmentation of the Razers, however, he suspected the Jagernauts were more formidable. But he doubted they cared a whit about their specs compared to Qox's bodyguards. They just wanted to shoot.

Jaibriol's splintered pain tore at Kelric. The emperor was struggling to hold the monstrous barriers he must have lived with every day of his life for the past ten years. But nothing could cut him off from Kelric, not when they were face to face. The mental defenses Jaibriol had built crumbled without Kelric doing anything. How could they help but come down to him?

The Triad knew its own.

Kelric knew then that matters were far worse even than he and Dehya had feared. Their nightmare had been given reality. Jaibriol Qox had become the third Key.

Qox stared at him with eyes that had seen more than anyone his age should have endured. "Father in heaven," he whispered.

In Iotic.

"Sire!" The Razer captain stepped toward the emperor as if to protect Jaibriol from himself. Strava jerked as if she had been struck. Najo gaped at Jaibriol, and Axer's confusion jolted over Kelric. Jaibriol had spoken the language of Skolian nobility, what Kelric would have taught his children had he raised them. Yes, certainly, the emperor knew Iotic, just as Kelric knew Highton. But what Eubian emperor would revert to perfect, unaccented Iotic under stress?

Jaibriol looked around as if he were trapped. Watching him, Kelric felt certain that if he bolted back to Eube without aid for his traumatized mind, he wouldn't survive. He needed help far more desperately than Kelric had ever guessed.

Strava cleared her throat. "Shall I close the door?"

Kelric started, as did everyone else. Then he glanced Jaibriol. The emperor took a deep breath and nodded.

"Yes, go ahead," Kelric told her.

They all waited while she swung the door shut on rustic but well-oiled hinges. Qox shifted like a thoroughbred racehorse ready to spook at the wrong word, the wrong gesture—or the wrong thought. Kelric could have mind-spoken to him; the emperor's Kyle strength filled the room. But it had a fractured quality, and Kelric feared to do more damage. How any psion could survive with such injuries, he had no idea. Jaibriol had to have a phenomenal strength of will. Kelric had known only one other person with that tenacious, enduring strength. Soz.

After another strained moment, Qox spoke in Highton, aloof and cool. "Well, we are here. Perhaps now you will tell me the reason for this."

"I needed to meet you in person," Kelric said.

A muscle twitched in Jaibriol's cheek. "Why?"

Kelric looked at the captain looming next to Jaibriol, his arms flickering with lights, except the Razer had no flesh and blood arm under all that tech.

Jaibriol glanced up at the Razer, then at Kelric. "What you have to say to me, you say to Hidaka. My guards remain."

Najo regarded Kelric, his gaze dark and tense.

"Stay," Kelric told the captain.

Relief flashed across Najo's face. He would have refused an order to leave, and Kelric had no intention of putting either himself or his guards in that position. But having so many people present hobbled him. He couldn't reveal Jaibriol in front of their guards.

Jaibriol ran his finger around the collar of his black tunic. "It always was hot and humid here in the summer."

Kelric almost smiled. Talking about the weather he could handle. "Is this where you lived while you were on Earth?"

"Not anywhere near here, actually. But the mountains around Seth's home are in the same range as these."

Kelric nodded. By "Seth," he had to mean Admiral Rockworth, the man who cared for Jaibriol and three other children during the two years of the Radiance War. Kelric wanted to ask him so much, especially if he was related to the other children, but he feared to push, or even nudge the emperor, lest it drive him away.

"Would you rather walk outside?" Kelric asked. From the alarmed expressions of their guards, he might have suggested he and Jaibriol throw themselves in front of a speeding magtrain.

Qox made a visible effort to relax his shoulders. "That would be good."

Strava scowled at Kelric, but when he gestured at the door, she stalked over and opened it. As he stepped forward, every guard in the room lifted their gun. Sweat gathered on his palms but he didn't wipe them on his slacks. When he came up next to Jaibriol, the emperor tensed, and the Razer he had called Hidaka clenched his half-raised carbine.

With care, Kelric lifted his hand, inviting Jaibriol to the door. The emperor inclined his head, and a line of sweat showed at his hairline. Together, they left cabin, accompanied by seven guards, all wound as tight as coils. Najo also had his Jumbler up and ready, but neither he nor Hidaka had aimed at anyone.

Although the humidity was worse outside, a cooling breeze ruffled the pines. Strava left the lamps on in the cabin so they had enough light to see. They stepped into a clearing ringed with trees, and Jaibriol exhaled, then breathed in the pine-scented air. The shattered sense of his mind eased.

"It's never this dark on Glory," he said. "The sky is full of moons."

"The Orbiter always has starlight," Kelric said.

Jaibriol hesitated, started to speak, then stopped. Finally he said, "Have you talked with Seth Rockworth?"

Kelric knew why he asked; ten years ago, when they met in the Lock, Jaibriol had suggested he go to the admiral. Rockworth had told the Allied authorities he had never known Jaibriol's identity, but Kelric had always wondered.

"I'm afraid not," Kelric said. "Earth's military won't let us near him."

"I'm not surprised." Jaibriol gave a tired laugh. "I doubt they were happy when one of his wards turned out to be a little more than a harmless schoolboy."

Jaibriol, Kelric thought.

The emperor froze, stock-still. Kelric waited.

Jaibriol's voice rasped. "The nights here are so strange. So long. Yet so short."

Kelric held back his impulse to try the link again. If Jaibriol had barricaded his mind at an extreme level for ten years, he might find any telepathic contact painful.

Kelric said only, "Long and short both?"

"Nights on Glory are only a few hours." Jaibriol began to walk. "But if you live on a world that is part of a binary system, with the planet orbiting one star, which orbits another star, the nights and days can last for hundreds of hours."

Kelric's breath caught. No one except the ESComm ship that had found Jaibriol's father knew the location of the world where he had been stranded. Rumor claimed the records had been lost and that the crew of the ship had died in the war.

"Did you grow up in a place like that?" Kelric asked.

"I lived with my mother," Jaibriol said. "Empress Liza."

Kelric could only nod. Everyone believed that story. But unless the last Highton empress had been a Ruby psion, it was complete fiction.

"Sir!"

The shout came from Strava in the same instant Najo shoved Kelric at the ground. Before Kelric had a chance to respond, his enhanced vision toggled on and the world slowed down.

The Razers leveled their guns at Kelric's bodyguards, but Strava and Axer weren't facing the Eubians, they were aiming at the trees. As Kelric's augmented speed kicked in, everyone seemed to move in slowed time. He hit the ground, catching himself on his palms, and his breath went out in a grunt. Najo shoved him down, protecting Kelric's body with his own. Strava stood above them, her feet planted wide while she fired into the forest. The beam from her Jumbler created sparks in the air and exploded the trees in a harsh orange flashes.

He was aware of Jaibriol falling next to him and the Razers firing their carbines. For one gruesome second Kelric thought they were shooting his guards; then he realized they were blasting the trees. Kelric twisted around to see Axer sweeping the area with his Jumbler. The trees disintegrated in orange explosions, lighting up Axer's body as if he were on fire. With his bald, tattooed head and muscled physique, he looked like an avenging demon.

And in that instant, as Kelric stared at the guard who had protected him for years, a projectile burst out from the trees—

And hit Axer.

The Jagernaut's body flew apart in gruesome slow motion.

"*No!*" The shout burst out of Kelric. He tried to jump up, but Najo shoved him down even as he fired. The trees around them truly were in flames now, from the Razer's carbine shots.

"It's you they're after," Jaibriol shouted at him. "They're trying to kill *you*. Are they insane? They could rid the universe of a Qox and they go for the good man instead?"

Kelric wondered what sort of nightmare Jaibriol lived, that he expected murder attempts to target him as the greatest evil. An explosion flared in the night, and a ball of fire ballooned above the trees barely fifty meters away. Another blast shattered the cabin, billowing debris, smoke, and flame.

Najo dragged Kelric to his feet. "Run," he yelled.

Hidaka heaved Jaibriol up so fast and so hard, he lifted the emperor off the ground. A third explosion rent the air, this one barely ten meters away.

"Go!" Hidaka shouted at Jaibriol, shoving him away from the blasts. "*GO!*"

Kelric grabbed Jaibriol's arm and took off with enhanced speed, literally dragging the Eubian emperor—

The ground exploded under them.

XXX
A Brace of Kinsmen

Jaibriol floated in a sea of flames. He had no sense of time or place, just dislocation.

Then he hit the ground and gasped as rocks stabbed his body. Debris rained around him. He tumbled down a slope, rolling, rolling, hitting rocks and underbrush, out of control. He smashed into a cluster of boulders and pain shot through him. With a groan, he scrambled to his feet, driven by adrenaline. Far up the slope, flames roared in the cabin. He couldn't see anyone; if Kelric or any guards still lived, they were no longer standing.

Jaibriol started up the slope—and tripped over a body. Lurching and dazed, he fell to his knees. A huge man lay sprawled in front of him, his lower leg twisted at a bizarre angle.

"Kelric?" His voice cracked. "God, no." Terrified to find the Imperator dead, he grabbed Kelric's wrist—and gasped with relief when he found a pulse. But Kelric wasn't breathing. Jaibriol pumped on his chest, using emergency techniques his parents had taught him on the planet Prism, where they had no medical care but what they could do for themselves.

Kelric suddenly jerked and choked in a breath. He coughed harshly, gulping for air.

"It's all right," Jaibriol said. "You'll be all right." He hoped it was true.

"Najo—" Kelric's voice rasped.

"Your guards are up there." Jaibriol stretched out his arm, pointing to where the fire blazed. "So are mine."

Orange light limned Kelric's face. "We must help them."

"Can you walk?"

Kelric paused, then said, "Bolt says my leg is broken."

Jaibriol scooted down to check Kelric's right leg. It had twisted back on itself in a way impossible even for a biomech joint. "This looks bad." He lifted his head. "Who is Bolt?"

Kelric pushed up on his elbows. "My spinal node."

"Can your meds administer pain medicine?"

"The hell with that. I don't want my focus dulled."

"We have to get out of here," Jaibriol said. "I don't think you can walk on this."

Kelric grimaced as he sat up. "I'll manage."

Jaibriol looked up the hill. With foreboding, he said, "No one has come down."

"They can't be dead." Kelric spoke as if his words could ensure their lives. "They *can't.*"

"Hidaka—he—" Jaibriol couldn't go on. He couldn't lose the captain. Angry at himself, he grabbed the outer seam on Kelric's slacks and ripped it hard, two-thirds of the way up Kelric's leg.

"What the hell are you doing?" Kelric shoved him away.

"Finishing the job your people started?"

"They didn't start anything," Jaibriol said. "No one knows I'm here."

"You knew someone was trying to kill me."

Even realizing Kelric had sensed the truth about him, Jaibriol couldn't admit he had picked it up from the minds of their attackers. He had hidden too long. He couldn't reveal himself even to someone who already knew.

Jaibriol cast about on the ground. "They shot at you first."

"They could have been going after both of us. Maybe they just missed you. How could you know otherwise?"

Jaibriol found a long, straight branch and broke off its smaller twigs. "They didn't even know who I was." He gave a ragged laugh. "They could have killed the tyrant of Glory, and instead they went after you. What idiots."

Kelric's voice quieted. "You got it from their minds."

"Don't be absurd." He picked up several more branches and leaned over Kelric's leg. "I'm going to set this. So we can get out of here."

"Where did you learn how to splint a broken leg?"

Intent on examining the injury, Jaibriol spoke absently. "My mother taught me." He looked up at Kelric. "It's going to hurt. I'm sorry."

The Imperator had a strange look. The firelight from above glinted on his metallic skin. "It's all right."

Jaibriol carefully pulled away the shreds of cloth from Kelric's leg. He remembered when his mother had splinted his arm, after ESComm had pulled out his father and "cleansed" Prism. It was one reason everyone believed

Soz Valdoria had been nowhere near the emperor. No one could have survived the mountain-slagging sterilization ESComm had inflicted on Prism.

Except.

As a Jagernaut Primary, his mother had had access to technology available to almost no one else. She had brought a quasis generator into exile. Just seconds before ESComm attacked, she enclosed her children in a bubble of the generator's field. Quasis froze the quantum state of anything within its field. Particles couldn't change state, which meant the bubble couldn't collapse, not even when a battle cruiser in orbit destroyed the mountain range. Jaibriol's arm had broken as the sterilization slammed around their bubble of safety, and his mother had splinted it while their family hunkered in the dark, bruised and terrified.

"Gods almighty," Kelric whispered. "What happened to you?"

Jaibriol jerked up his head. "I don't know what you're talking about." He struggled to fortify his mental barriers and hide his memory.

Kelric spoke in an unexpectedly gentle voice. "My mind is powerful, but blunt. I didn't pick up anything from the minds of our attackers up there. But other of my siblings have more mental finesse. They might catch what I missed." Quietly he added, "As might their children."

Sweat trickled down Jaibriol's neck. He could never answer Kelric's unspoken question about his parentage. He had hidden the truth for too long; he couldn't let go and speak of it. The secrecy was too ingrained within him.

"I'm going to set this now," Jaibriol said. "Are you ready?"

Kelric nodded, his face strained. "Go ahead."

Jaibriol went to work, gritting his teeth. He hated how it agonized Kelric; pain blazed in his uncle's mind. But the Imperator never cried out once. Jaibriol pulled off his black-diamond tunic, leaving only his undershirt, and ripped the tunic into cords so he could tie Kelric's leg to the splint. When he finished, he sat back, sweat streaming down his face. Kelric had one fist clenched on his thigh and he had dug the fingers of his other hand into the ground. He looked as if he had aged ten years.

"Yes, I'm an old man," Kelric said, his voice uneven.

"Don't say that." Jaibriol climbed to his feet and offered his hand. "You're going to live decades more. Centuries."

With help, Kelric struggled to his feet and stood with one hand on Jaibriol's shoulder, staring up the slope. The flames had died down rather than starting the forest fire Jaibriol had feared. He saw no one, neither his nor Kelric's guards.

"Do you sense anyone?" Kelric asked.

Jaibriol wanted to deny he could sense anything. But he wanted even more to survive. "No," he said dully. "No one. Not assassins and not bodyguards."

"I don't, either," Kelric said. "But it's hard to focus." Although he spoke calmly, he couldn't disguise the pain flaring in his mind.

"Can you walk?" Jaibriol asked.

"I doubt I can make it up that slope."

"I'll go look—no, I can't leave you here." Jaibriol stopped, torn with indecision.

"Go look," Kelric said.

Jaibriol took off, running up the hill. He slipped and

slid on the steep slope, but compared to the peaks where he jogged in the Jaizires, this was nothing. He slowed as he neared the top and bent down to crawl the last few meters.

A blast crater spread out before him, and beyond it lay the scorched remains of what had been a beautiful tangled forest. The devastation bore no resemblance to the woods where he and Kelric had so recently walked. It looked like a battlefield.

Jaibriol sensed no one's mind except Kelric. Whoever had attacked them was either gone or dead. He searched the crater first, and then the smoldering remains of the forest beyond. He forced himself to account for everyone, identifying them by what little remained of their blasted, charred bodies: his Razers, Kelric's Jagernauts, and six commandos, which matched the number of minds he had felt in the attack. None had survived.

When Jaibriol found Hidaka's remains, he fell to his knees in the ashes next to the body. Working doggedly, he scraped a scorched, dead chip out of the dirt, all that remained of Hidaka's node. He had some grief-stricken idea he would bring it back to Claret.

Clammy from shock, Jaibriol went back to the hill and half slid, half ran down the slope. Kelric was sitting on one of the boulders that had stopped Jaibriol's roll earlier. The starlight of the bizarrely moonless night glinted on his gold eyes. He seemed more metal than human, but Jaibriol could tell a man of compassion inhabited that metallic body.

"All of them are gone?" Kelric asked, his voice low.

"Yes. Our guards. The attackers." His voice cracked.

"All dead." He sat on the ground, braced his elbow on his bent leg, and put his forehead in his hand, too drained to move anymore.

"We can't stay here," Kelric said unevenly. He stood up and tried to take a step, but he immediately lurched and came down hard on his good knee.

"Ah!" The Imperator's sharp inhale ended in a groan.

Jaibriol raised his head. "Are you all right?"

"Fine," Kelric muttered. He grasped his splinted leg and maneuvered it around so it stretched in front of him. Then he just sat, silent. He obviously wasn't fine.

"I don't think you can go anywhere on that leg," Jaibriol said. "Not until you rest and your meds can start healing it."

Kelric started to speak, and Jaibriol thought he was going to object. Then his uncle just shook his head and fell silent.

Jaibriol felt something on his face. He touched his skin and his fingers came away wet with tears. Why did Hidaka have to die, one of the best men he had ever known? He was grateful beyond words that he hadn't told Robert or Tarquine he was coming. They would have insisted on coming with him. And they would be dead now; the first priority for his guards had been to save him, not his aides or even his spouse.

After a while, Kelric said, "Are their bodies destroyed?"

"That's a horrible question." Jaibriol's voice broke on the last word, and he decided to say no more.

"No, listen," Kelric said. "If their internal systems are even partially intact, it may be possible to revive them in new bodies."

Jaibriol stared at him dully until the words sank in. Then he said, "Not enough survived. It was bad."

"Oh." Kelric sounded subdued.

Jaibriol wondered if somewhere, some demon was laughing at them. He had so little, and now even that was gone.

"Hidaka saw." Jaibriol knew he should stop, but the words wrenched out of him. "He saw the whole thing. Yet still he supported me. He never wavered, never once."

"What did he see?" Kelric asked. The fires had died down, and his face was lost in shadows.

"Colonel Vatrix Muze caught me crawling out of the Lock," Jaibriol said. "So Hidaka shot him."

Kelric's voice went very quiet. "Why were you in the Lock?"

"The implosions." He took a ragged breath. "They were headed for the SSRB. I thought it might connect to the Lock. So I went to check."

"Did you find anything?"

"Nothing. It didn't work." He couldn't believe how calm he sounded. Inside he felt as if he were screaming.

"It was dead for ten years," Kelric said. "When I turned it back on, it was active for *one minute*. How could you know to be there for that one minute?"

"I don't know." Jaibriol wasn't even certain what Kelric meant. "I just sat there and the singularity appeared."

Kelric stared at him. "When the Lock reactivated, you were *sitting in it?*"

"Yes." He didn't know what else to say. "I will regret that moment for the rest of my godforsaken life."

"And you survived."

"If you call this survival."

"You had no preparation? No training? Nothing?"

"How would I?"

"Saints above," Kelric said softly. "What happened to you would have killed almost anyone else."

Jaibriol just shook his head. Although he was shielding his mind, Kelric's power was too great. It soaked into him, a great golden glow of warmth. These few minutes with his uncle had done more to ease the agony in his mind than anything else since he had become a Key.

"You need a medical facility with neurological experts," Kelric told him.

Jaibriol knew he would never get such treatment. Dully he said, "We both need help."

"Tell me that you betrayed our agreement," Kelric said. "Tell me that you let someone know you were coming here."

Jaibriol would have laughed if their situation hadn't been so bad. "No. I kept my word. Perhaps you told someone?"

"Not a soul. I secured the entire area."

"Enough to hide four explosions and a fire?"

Kelric exhaled. "I'm afraid so."

"The commandos were thorough. The cabin is gone. So are our vehicles."

"I picked this place because it was so remote."

"This is absurd," Jaibriol said, incredulous. "We're two of the most powerful people alive. We can't be without recourse."

Kelric didn't answer. His pain swamped out everything. After a while, though, Jaibriol felt it ease, and he suspected Kelric had let his meds dispense painkillers after all.

Eventually Kelric said, "We both have biomech enhancements."

Jaibriol nodded. "Even with your broken leg, we could probably walk out of here in a day or two."

"And then what?"

Jaibriol considered the question. "The moment we find help, we lose our secrecy. It will look strange for us to be together."

Kelric's laugh had a frayed edge. "You've a gift for understatement. Can the Emperor of Eube be executed for treason?"

Jaibriol jerked, startled. "I haven't committed treason."

Kelric spoke tiredly. "I have."

Good Lord. No wonder he seemed so subdued. "They can't execute the Imperator. ISC will stand behind you." The loyalty of his military to their commander was legendary.

"How do they know you and I aren't plotting here in secret? Why would they support me for committing the worst violation of ISC security in the history of the Imperialate?"

Jaibriol sat for a time absorbing the ramifications. He had come with such hopes, for a dream that never died no matter how much he lost. He took a breath and plunged ahead. "Then bring them a peace treaty."

"We don't have a treaty." Even in the dark, the lines on Kelric's face showed his strain. "Our generals and admirals and ministers and assemblies couldn't agree on one."

"Then let us agree, you and I." He tapped his temple. "I have the one we worked out years ago stored in my node. If you're willing to take a download into yours, we'll both have a copy. We can sign it with our neural and DNA imprints."

"Have you forgotten?" Kelric asked. "We never finished it. We couldn't come to terms on the most basic aspect of all."

It seemed to Jaibriol as if his whole life had narrowed to this moment. He knew the magnitude of what he suggested. But if they never tried, they would surely fail. He had nothing to lose by asking for the impossible.

He took a breath. "My joint commanders refused to sign because yours wanted to grant every escaped slave freedom. Yours refused to sign because mine demanded the slaves be returned."

"That hasn't changed," Kelric said. "My people will never agree to slavery. Not today. Not in a thousand years. My last wife was a taskmaker. I was a provider. I'll never subject another human being to what we lived through." Softly he added, "To what you must suffer every day of your life."

"No." Jaibriol doggedly evaded the words. "Give me three months. Any Eubian slave found within your territory must be sent back if they have been free less than that. After three months, they are free." He willed Kelric to consider the compromise. "The Ruby Pharaoh almost agreed to that during our talks, before ESComm balked."

Kelric made an incredulous noise. "ESComm will never agree to that. Nor will your Trade Minister."

"They've already agreed to trade negotiations. That was why my office contacted the pharaoh's office. To start this dance we always do when we want to communicate with each other."

"Trade?" Kelric's voice sharpened. "Of what? *People?*"

"No! Gourmet delicacies. Curios. That sort of thing."

Kelric squinted at him. "Your people want to export food and souvenirs to mine?"

"Well, it's a start."

"Selling us those tentacled monstrosities you call gourmet food hardly seems a step to better relations."

Jaibriol smiled. "Ah, well." He agreed about the Taimarsian squid. "It isn't the goods, but the motivation."

"Whose motivation?"

"General Barthol Iquar for one. He wants the Iquar title."

"Tarquine already has it," Kelric said flatly.

Just hearing him speak her personal name cut Jaibriol. He steeled himself and went on as if he didn't care, though it felt like broken glass were inside of him. "She'll give it to him."

"Give up control of the strongest Aristo Line after Qox?" Kelric didn't look convinced. "She would never do it."

"She's the empress," Jaibriol said. "Her child will sit on the throne. She can afford to give up her Iquar title."

"It doesn't matter how much power Tarquine has. She always wants more."

"Nevertheless, it seems she is going to do it."

"For you." Kelric sounded tired, as if Jaibriol's words made him feel old.

"I don't know for what."

"You think the title would assure Barthol's agreement?"

"It's possible."

"That's only one of the signatures you need."

Jaibriol made himself speak, though he hated to go on. "Admiral Erix Muze will sign because he wants to live."

Kelric snorted. "You can't execute your joint commander for refusing to sign. ESComm would revolt against you."

Jaibriol spoke quietly. "No one except Colonel Vatrix Muze and Hidaka saw me crawl out of the Lock. Hidaka shot Vatrix."

"I'm not sure how this connects to Erix Muze."

"Hidaka told everyone Vatrix tried to kill me," Jaibriol said. "A Razer cannot lie about such a thing."

"Did he know what he was seeing in the Lock? About you."

"Yes. He knew."

"And he didn't reveal you?"

"No."

Kelric's voice gentled. "No wonder you mourn him so."

It hurt even to think on. "As far as anyone knows, Vatrix Muze tried to murder me. By Aristo custom, it is my right to have his kin executed in retaliation."

Kelric was watching him closely. "Did Erix Muze have anything to do with what happened?"

"Nothing."

"So you're telling me that with no trial or evidence, you can have one of your joint commanders executed for a murder attempt he knew nothing about. And no one would condemn you for it."

Jaibriol forced out the answer. "Yes."

"A murder attempt that didn't actually exist because your Razer killed the colonel and lied about it."

"Razers can't lie."

"Like hell."

"Assassination is a serious matter."

"Gods," Kelric muttered.

"No, the world of the Aristos isn't pretty," Jaibriol said. "But it is mine. I deal with it as I can."

"Would you actually put Erix Muze to death?" Kelric asked.

Jaibriol didn't know the answer to that himself. "What matters is that he believes I will do it."

"What about the Trade Minister, Parizian Sakaar? You need his support as well."

"He won't object."

"Why not?" Kelric demanded. "The trade of people is the life's blood of your economy. He'll set himself against any treaty that dilutes his control of that godforsaken industry."

"Let's just say he has other interests to protect."

"In other words, you have something on him."

"It would seem so." It was Tarquine who had something, but Jaibriol had no intention of discussing her further with Kelric.

"Is it enough to make him sign?"

"I think so."

"Corbal Xir is next in line for your throne," Kelric said. "He won't support a treaty that weakens his power."

"Corbal won't fight it." Jaibriol also doubted Corbal would ever forgive him.

"Why not?"

"Because I know many truths about him." Corbal also had truths about Jaibriol, but if he revealed those secrets, Jaibriol could drag down not only him, but also his son Azile, his granddaughter, and the entire Xir Line. And

Sunrise. It killed him to threaten Corbal after his cousin had protected him, but his personal life meant nothing compared to what their peoples could gain. No matter how much the Aristos reviled him for seeking peace, he needed only four signatures on that treaty: himself, Corbal, Barthol, and Erix.

"If you and I sign this document," Jaibriol said, "I'll get the other signatures." He couldn't guarantee it, but he had a chance.

Kelric considered him. "For my people, the Ruby Pharaoh, First Councilor, and I must sign. And the Assembly has to ratify it."

"Will they?"

"The pharaoh, I think so. The First Councilor, I don't know." With a grimace, he added, "If I'm convicted of treason, my signature won't matter. In that case, our joint commanders must sign." Wryly he said, "You only have to deal with two of them. I have four." He thought for a moment. "Chad Barzun would probably sign. Maybe Dayamar Stone of the Advance Services Corps. Brant Tapperhaven of the J- Force? He's a wild card. But Naaj Majda, the General of the Pharaoh's Army, will never sign. She wants Eube broken. Period."

"They won't convict you." Jaibriol didn't know if he said it to convince himself or Kelric.

"Don't be so sure." Kelric sounded as if he felt heavy. "Many people abhor the split of hereditary and democratic rule in our government. If I'm accused of conspiring with you, it will weaken ISC support for the sovereignty of the Ruby Dynasty. The Assembly might well jump at the chance to remove me from my seat." He rubbed his eyes, his fatigue obvious. "As you may have noticed tonight, I am not universally liked."

"Nor I," Jaibriol said. To put it mildly. "But if we can complete this document tonight, would you sign it?"

For a long moment Kelric looked at him. Then he said, simply, "Yes."

Jaibriol couldn't believe he had heard the word. Fast on the heels of exultation came the sobering knowledge that even if he and Kelric signed, they had no guarantee their governments would support their agreement.

But they could try.

That night, beneath the stars of the planet that had birthed their race, two leaders sat together, a young man who was forever scarred and an aging man who had lost more in his life than he could measure. They had no lofty hall, no pomp, no protocols. They didn't go to work in a great amphitheater. No broadcasts covered their efforts. They sat on a rocky hill in the dark and went over the document step by step, sentence by sentence, word by word, until they agreed.

Then they signed together the first peace treaty ever established between their empires.

XXXI
The Meld

Kelric awoke as the sky began to lighten but before the sun lifted its orb above the mountains. The air smelled of smoke, ashes, and pines. Birds called in the distance. For a while he lay on his back, staring at the sky. Blue. On his home world, the sky had a violet tinge. As strange as Earth's looked to him, the color felt right in a way he couldn't define.

The events of last night soaked into his waking thoughts. Najo, Strava, and Axer were gone. He felt hollow without them.

Even with his nanomeds distributing painkillers, his leg ached. At least the hydraulics in his limb had kept it from snapping off. It would heal, he supposed, though his limp was going to be even worse. Of course, that wouldn't matter if he were dead. As much as he wanted to believe ISC wouldn't execute him, the realist in him knew otherwise. Too many people had too much to gain from his dishonor and death. Given who else had nearly died in this attack, he doubted the commandos had a link to ESComm. It wasn't that he didn't believe they might be involved in a murder attempt against their emperor; he wasn't that naïve. But Jaibriol claimed they hadn't known about him. With his mind so sensitized, he would have picked up an intent to kill him, and Kelric would have known if he lied about it.

The team investigating the last attack against Kelric had thought the would-be assassins operated alone. Either they were wrong or else other groups also wanted Skolia's Imperator dead. It was a grim thought. That the killers had known he was here suggested someone high in the government or ISC was involved.

Kelric slowly sat up. His muscles protested with stabs of pain, and he grunted, wishing he wasn't so stiff.

"My greetings," a voice said.

He looked around. Jaibriol was sitting on the rocks behind him, his booted feet braced on the ground, his elbows on his thighs, his hands clasped between his knees.

Kelric maneuvered around, dragging his leg until he was facing the emperor. "How long have you been awake?"

"About an hour." Jaibriol rubbed the back of his neck. "I looked for food, but I didn't find anything that seemed edible."

Although Kelric knew he was hungry, his biomech web muted the pangs by releasing chemicals that fooled his body into thinking he had eaten. It wouldn't stop him from starving, but it eased his discomfort.

"We should search the cabin," Kelric said.

"I did." Jaibriol lifted his hands, then dropped them.

"Nothing is left but debris. Not even water. The blast and fire destroyed everything, even the plumbing."

"Water must be here somewhere." Kelric motioned at the forest. "Otherwise this wouldn't grow."

Jaibriol grinned, an unexpected flash of teeth that made him look years younger. "We can make history with our treaty, but we can't find a drink of water. Strange, that."

Kelric smiled. "I guess so." He picked up a staff of wood that was lying next to him. "This wasn't here last night."

"I made it while you were sleeping." Jaibriol rose to his feet with a supple ease that Kelric envied. "If you can walk this morning, I think we should leave as soon as possible."

Using the staff, Kelric struggled to his feet. By putting his weight on his good leg and leaning on the staff, he was able to stand. Jaibriol was right. They shouldn't wait for rescue. That no one else had been with their attackers didn't mean no one would show up. They could just as easily be picked off elsewhere, but at least they would be getting closer to help.

Kelric looked up the hill. "I'd like to go up." He wanted to pay his respects.

Jaibriol seemed to understand. He offered his arm.

"I'll be fine," Kelric said. He took a step—and his leg buckled. Jaibriol caught him before he fell, but Kelric's weight nearly knocked them both over.

Kelric swore under his breath. Then he pulled away and tried another step. He managed by using the staff as a crutch and keeping the weight off his broken leg. On flat ground it worked reasonably well, if slowly, but when he tried to climb the slope, his leg gave out. He couldn't manage even with Jaibriol's help.

The emperor spoke quietly. "I'm sorry."

Kelric couldn't answer; it hurt too much. *Good-bye,* he thought to his guards. *You will be missed.*

Jaibriol motioned to a notch across the small valley. "I think we can get out that way, and the land stays flat."

Kelric nodded, already tired. Then he began the painful process of walking. Jaibriol stayed at his side, moderating his stride to match Kelric's speed. It was humbling. It was hard to believe he had ever been young and full of energy. That was the man Tarquine had desired, the prince she had seen in broadcasts. Why she had paid that amorally ludicrous price for a dying man, he would never know.

They made their way through a narrow gap between two hills. Needles and twigs crackled under their feet, and branches rustled overhead, inundating them with the deep scent of pines. It was surreal, walking here with Jaibriol the Third as if the two of them were on a vacation.

Jaibriol's hair shimmered in the early morning light and his red eyes were visible from a good distance away. Anyone who knew anything about Eube would recognize him as an Aristo. Nor could Kelric hide his own offworld heritage. People on Earth didn't have metallic coloring.

After a while, Jaibriol said, "I think those implosions are connected to the Locks."

It took a moment for Kelric to reorient his thoughts. The space-time implosions. He felt too tired to talk. Given what he had done, though, activating the Lock while the emperor was in it, he owed Jaibriol more than silence.

"When my people built the Kyle web," Kelric said, "we

knew almost nothing about the Locks. Everything was guesswork. But I'm starting to understand. I think the web strains the interface between Kyle space and our universe. Every time we add another gate, it adds to the strain. The Locks are a balance. When I turned one off, it destabilized the system. If we don't reactivate it, the implosions will get worse." Uneasily he said, "I think it could destroy large regions of space, entire solar systems. Maybe more."

He expected Jaibriol to be incredulous, ask a question, something. When the emperor had been quiet for too long, Kelric glanced at him. Jaibriol's face had gone pale. His fear hit Kelric like a bright light.

"What is it?" Kelric asked.

"The SSRB has no Lock." Jaibriol drew him to a stop. "When Hidaka fired at the colonel, we were inside that octagonal room that houses the singularity."

Kelric felt as if his pulse stuttered. "Are you telling me your guard fired a laser carbine inside the Lock chamber?"

Jaibriol nodded. "It missed me. But not much else."

"Ah, gods." Kelric suddenly felt bone weary.

"We've had no implosions I know of since then."

"Maybe it eased the pressure when I activated the Lock," Kelric said. "But I had the impression it only operated for about a minute."

"Yes." Jaibriol rubbed his neck again, a mannerism Kelric suspected came from the constant tension he lived with. "Three Locks. For a Triad."

Kelric resumed his painful limp. "As far as I know, the Triad doesn't require three Locks to exist."

"Then maybe neither does the Kyle. It had two Locks and two Keys. Now it has two Locks but thr—" He stopped abruptly, then spoke carefully. "If the Kyle once again had three Keys, maybe the two Locks would be enough."

"Maybe." It was plausible with what Kelric knew. He hoped it were true. In every way, the survival of his people depended on this young man. The emperor had gone to great lengths to attain the treaty, and Kelric had no doubt he wanted it. But if he changed his mind, he had within his grasp the ability to create a Kyle web for ESComm, negating the advantage Skolia had over Eube, the technology that kept them a step ahead of the Traders. Jaibriol didn't need a Lock to build such a web. The Triad Chair wasn't in the chamber, it was on a dais at the start of the corridor, well removed from the singularity. Jaibriol had been sitting in it the first time Kelric had seen him, ten years ago.

Back then, Kelric hadn't thought Jaibriol knew anything about the chair. Maybe that was still true. He strengthened his mental shields, blurring them, too, so Jaibriol wouldn't realize he had cut off his thoughts. Then he said, "You need the Lock to build a Kyle web."

"I don't have a Lock," Jaibriol said.

Kelric probed his mind as discreetly as he could manage. Jaibriol had no idea what to do with a Triad Chair. He just thought it was an uncomfortable throne. Nor did he comprehend what it meant to be part of the Triad. He only wanted free of its presence. He didn't know he could never leave the powerlink. Neurological changes had begun in his brain the moment he became a Key. To withdraw now would cause fatal brain damage.

Kelric didn't know how Jaibriol would survive among Aristos. His mind was a furnace, burning with power. Unless he learned to hide it better than this, the Aristos would soon realize the truth. Then what? They would have a Key. Jaibriol might have no interest in learning how to create a web, but if the Hightons turned their combined intellects to the problem, they would learn. And they would force him to build it for them.

"Kelric?" Jaibriol was watching him.

It startled Kelric to hear his personal name spoken by the Emperor of Eube. "Yes?" he asked.

"Your sister—" He stumbled over his words. "She was Imperator before you, wasn't she?"

Softly Kelric said, "Yes."

"Was she happy?"

"The last I saw her was almost thirty years ago." Kelric spoke with care. "Jaibriol, how could your mother teach you to splint a broken leg with tree branches?"

"She was good at—" He suddenly stopped, and panic flared in his eyes.

"That's an unusual skill for a sheltered Eubian empress," Kelric said.

Jaibriol turned his head away, and Kelric knew then that the young man could never speak the truth. It was locked within him by emotional scar tissue.

Kelric continued with the utmost gentleness. "When Soz was young, she loved to swim in a lake near our house. She would go up there when she wasn't supposed to be out and get into trouble when she came home."

Jaibriol gave an uneven laugh. "I can imagine."

Kelric remembered how Soz had laughed and teased,

how she could grin one moment and glare the next. Seven brothers and one Soz, and they had never been a match for her. He smiled with his memories, though they hurt. "When I was eight and she was seventeen, we went hiking in the Backbone Mountains. We got caught in a storm. It frightened me, the lightning, the rain, the hail. It so rarely happened in the lowlands where we lived."

Jaibriol spoke softly. "You could have taken shelter in a cave."

A pain jumped within Kelric, a stab of loss and mourning and something else that felt like bittersweet joy. That hadn't been a guess about the cave. Jaibriol knew.

"Yes," he said. "A cave. We huddled in it while lightning cut the sky and thunder shouted. We were afraid. It comforted us to merge our minds. A full Rhon merge." Only Ruby psions could join minds that way, but they rarely did, for it was too powerful a link for most people to endure and too intense to sustain. But in those few moments, he and Soz had blended their thoughts down to a deep level. From that day on, he had shared a bond with her stronger than with his other siblings.

"Anyone fortunate to share such a bond," Jaibriol said unevenly, "would value it forever. She might—might even share the treasured memory with her children."

Kelric put his hand on Jaibriol's shoulder. "I can't help you leave the Triad." When alarm flared in the emperor's gaze, Kelric said, "Just listen. You don't have to admit anything." Softly he added, "You cannot return to Eube in your condition. I've been protecting your mind, but when we part, it will all come back, the agony, the loss of control, the pain. You'll be wide open to the Hightons."

"Don't," Jaibriol said.

"You must learn to control it."

"I can't," he whispered.

An idea was coming to Kelric, forming with the clarity of jeweled Quis dice in the sunlight. He looked around for support. A nearby deciduous tree had a thick branch, almost a second trunk, that grew horizontally a few feet above the ground. He limped over and leaned against it, half sitting, half standing. Then he untied the pouch from his belt. For a moment he stayed that way, looking at the worn bag bulging with dice. He had carried it for almost thirty years. The dice were as much a part of him as his limbs, his thoughts, his heart. They shaped his life. To part with them would leave a hole he could never fill even if he had a new set fashioned with identical pieces.

Kelric extended his arm with the pouch. "Use these."

Jaibriol's forehead creased. He came over and took the bag. Turning it over in his hand, he said, "What is it?"

"Dice."

The emperor opened the sack and shook a few gems into his palm. They flashed in the sunlight slanting through the trees and sparkled as if they were bits of colored radiance caught in Jaibriol's hand.

"They're beautiful." He looked up at Kelric. "What do you do with them?"

"Play Quis," Kelric said. "When pressure from the Hightons becomes too much, when you can't take anymore, when you fight for control and can't find it, play Quis. It will calm your mind, help your control, perhaps even ease the pain."

Jaibriol looked bewildered. "I don't know how."

In the short time he had with Jaibriol, Kelric knew it would be impossible to teach him Quis at a high enough level to help. But he did have a way.

Kelric took a breath. "If you meld with my mind, I can give you the knowledge. Store it in your spinal node to study at your leisure." He felt as if a part of him were dying. If he joined his mind with Jaibriol, the emperor would probably pick up more than Quis from him no matter how hard Kelric tried to limit their meld—including how to use the Triad Chair to create a Kyle web.

"You would offer me this trust?" Jaibriol asked.

Kelric nodded.

"What if it injures my mind even worse?"

"You have to trust me. Just as I must trust you."

Jaibriol clenched the pouch until his knuckles turned white. "I cannot."

"You have to trust someone."

"I don't trust my own wife. Why would I trust you?"

"You came here to see me," Kelric said. "I can think of no greater show of faith."

Jaibriol's voice cracked. "I can. Asking me to let you into my mind."

Kelric waited. The decision had to be Jaibriol's; if the young man felt pressured, they couldn't create the blend. They stood in the early morning with sunshine filtering through the trees, a fresh green light that softened the day. Butterflies flashed orange and black among the foliage.

Finally Jaibriol said, "Yes."

Kelric released his breath. "Good."

"What do I do?"

Kelric spoke gently. "Nothing." Then he closed his eyes.

Bit by bit, Kelric lowered the barriers he had developed over his lifetime. He didn't have the crushing mental defenses Jaibriol used; his were more layered shields that had become so integral to his personality, he wasn't certain he could lower them enough. He concentrated on his memories of Quis. He also accessed files in Bolt where he had stored Quis concepts, rules, ideas, strategies. When he had been a Trader prisoner, he had even tagged his interpretations of their customs with Quis structures. He readied it all for Jaibriol.

Then he reached out a luminous tendril of thought.

Their minds touched, and Kelric scraped Jaibriol's mental scar tissue. He had never wished for Dehya's finesse more than now, for he feared his raw power would injure the emperor even more. But the scars gradually melted, like gnarled ice under the warmth of a sun. Slowly, he and Jaibriol blended, first the outer layers of their minds and then those that went deeper. Kelric offered his knowledge to the young emperor, the files from Bolt, then his own memories, both the vibrant images and those time had dimmed and bleached.

And he absorbed memories from the emperor.

Kelric saw Jaibriol's father, the previous emperor, and knew that those who had called the man a monster had erred on a mammoth scale. The father in Jaibriol's memories was kind, gentle, vulnerable. That same decency defined Jaibriol beneath the hard exterior he had developed to survive. The son had inherited his father's purity of soul. Kelric also saw what Jaibriol didn't realize, that his father hadn't been strong enough to survive the Aristos. The tenderness that had made him such a beloved father would have destroyed him as emperor.

And it was true: Soz was his mother.

Jaibriol had her incredible strength. Kelric saw his sister through her son, and it broke his heart. Soz laughed more with her husband and children. She could be tender with her babies and fierce when protecting them. Jaibriol's sole model for an adult woman during the first fourteen years of his life had been one of the most complicated, strong-willed warriors of modern times, but what he remembered most about her was the depth of her love.

When Kelric opened his eyes, Jaibriol was kneeling on the ground, his head bowed, his shoulders shaking as tears flowed down his face. Kelric lowered himself next to the emperor, then put his hand on Jaibriol's shoulder and bent his head. He didn't know what Jaibriol had taken from his mind, but if the memories were as intense, as treasured, and as painful as those he had gained from the emperor, it was no wonder Jaibriol cried.

They knelt together in the forgiving beauty of a summer day and wept for the people they had lost.

XXXII
Stained Glass

On a summer day in the Appalachian Mountains, Kelric and Jaibriol reached the outskirts of a small town. Jaibriol sought help in a church, and they entered during Sunday services. Kelric could no longer walk on his own, even with the staff; Jaibriol supported him with Kelric's arm draped over his shoulders. Both of them were half-starved and dehydrated, and neither had slept much for two days. Jaibriol staggered inside the door, just enough to see they had found people. Then he sagged to his knees, no longer able to support Kelric's massive weight.

Kelric collapsed to the ground and rolled onto his back, his eyes closing. Jaibriol stayed with him, kneeling, while people rose from the pews, staring in bewildered shock. They approached with care, the reverend from the pulpit and parishioners from the pews. As they gathered around Jaibriol and Kelric, they spoke in English. Jaibriol peered at them, exhausted, unable to interpret the language he hadn't heard for ten years, and that he had never spoken as well as the Eubian or Skolian tongues he learned from his parents.

Jaibriol chose a church because he hoped they were less likely to turn away two people in need. After he had converted to Seth's religion, he had been baptized and received First Communion. He didn't think this was a Catholic church, but it had the same serenity he remembered from St. John's. He stared over the heads of the people to a high, stained glass window aglow with sunrise colors and light.

Like Quis dice.

Patterns filled his mind, swirls of color and shapes.

The reverend knelt in front of Jaibriol and spoke in Eubian. "Can you understand me?"

Jaibriol tried to concentrate. "My friend is ill," he said. "He needs a doctor."

"We've sent for one." The man hesitated. "Can you tell me who you are?"

"You don't know?"

"No. I'm sorry."

It relieved Jaibriol that no one seemed to realize who had stumbled into their morning services. The idea that the Emperor of Eube and Imperator of Skolia would come into their church was probably too absurd for them to recognize either him or Kelric even if anyone had seen them on a news broadcast.

The other adults clustered around them. They were calm, but Jaibriol felt their confusion. Someone had taken the children away, or at least kept them back.

"Can you translate for him?" one of the women asked the reverend. She wore a blue dress with no shape.

"I speak English," Jaibriol said slowly.

Relief washed over their faces. "Can you tell us what happened?" the reverend asked.

"Someone tried to kill us." Jaibriol didn't know how much to say. "We need to contact your authorities."

"We've sent for the sheriff," the reverend said.

"What is sheriff?" Jaibriol asked.

"A law officer," the woman told him.

Kelric stirred and opened his eyes. He stared at the ceiling of the church and spoke in Iotic. "What is this place?"

"A church," Jaibriol said, his voice ragged. "They've sent for help." His head swam with dice patterns. He didn't know what they meant, but they soothed him.

Kelric laboriously sat up, huge muscles bulging under his sleeves. With difficulty, he grasped a pew and climbed to his feet. At nearly seven feet tall, with a massive physique, he had a build heavier than occurred in the gravity of Earth. He loomed over everyone like a titan. The parishioners backed away.

Jaibriol stood up next to Kelric. "Maybe you should sit," he said in a low voice. His Iotic sounded odd in this place.

Kelric nodded, his face clenched from pain, and eased into a pew. He crossed his arms on the pew in front of him, laid his forehead on his arms, and closed his eyes.

The reverend was one of the only people who had stayed with Jaibriol. He was watching Kelric with concern. "The doctor should be here soon. Will he be all right until then?"

"I don't know." Jaibriol had no doubt Kelric could

recover from a broken leg. What would happen when he returned home was another story.

A boy of about ten years old had inched over to them. He looked up at Jaibriol. "Are you a Trader?"

"Sean!" A woman pulled him back. "Leave the man alone."

"He looks like those pictures on the holovid," the boy protested as she hurried him away.

Glancing around, Jaibriol realized no other children remained in the church. The adults stayed back, watching him. They seemed bewildered. He didn't know what to tell them. The past two days had drained him: the attack, signing the treaty, the miraculous and terrifying mental blend, and two days of stumbling through the forest. He had hoped the destruction of the cabin would activate some monitor, but if it had, no one had responded. He and Kelric had hidden their visit too well.

The door of the church creaked open and sunlight slanted across the worn pine floor. A burly doctor with a balding head strode inside carrying a med box. He headed toward Jaibriol, did a double take, and then stopped and gaped.

"Good God," he said. "You're an Aristo."

"Yes," Jaibriol said. "I am."

The doctor looked around at everyone. "You want me to treat a damn slave lord?"

"Grant, don't," the reverend said. "They need our help."

"Well, hell's hinges," the doctor muttered. Either he didn't know his words would result in his arrest on a Eubian world or else he didn't care. He came over to the pew and peered at Kelric, who had lifted his head.

"You the patient?" Grant asked in English.

Kelric glanced at Jaibriol, a question in his gaze.

"He asked if you're hurt," Jaibriol said. He turned to the doctor. "He has a broken leg."

Kelric slid along the pew, making room for the doctor, though he watched Grant warily. The doctor sat with no fanfare and bent over Kelric's leg. He poked and prodded, and checked it with a med tape. Glimmering holos rotated in the air above the tape like jeweled Quis dice.

Watching the doctor, Jaibriol realized it could help Kelric that everyone knew he had come in with an Aristo. It increased his chances of avoiding recognition, because no one in their right mind would expect the Imperator to be running around Earth with a Eubian nobleman. Kelric was wearing marriage guards, but if someone didn't know much about Eube, they could mistake them for the ID restraints of a taskmaker.

Whether or not Kelric could return home without anyone realizing he had been here was a different matter. If any news service picked up the story that an Aristo had walked into a church, that was it. One picture of him or Kelric on the meshes and their secrecy would evaporate. Even if they avoided that exposure, they had to get off-world without raising questions. They had also left thirteen dead people in the mountains along with a blasted cabin and burned out swath of land. Someone wanted to kill Kelric, and Jaibriol didn't believe for a moment that whoever masterminded the attempt had died with those commandos.

One powerful thought stayed with him; his wife and future heir were safe. He hadn't wanted an Aristo child, but it no longer mattered, for he already loved his unborn son.

"How'd you get this break?" Grant asked Kelric as he removed the splint. "You look as if you've been sorting wildcats." He squinted at the Imperator. "Guess that would be tough for them, eh?" He chuckled and went back to work.

Kelric blinked at him, then looked up at Jaibriol. "Do you know what he is saying?"

Jaibriol smiled. "He thinks you look tougher than a wild animal."

The doctor glanced from Kelric to Jaibriol, then went back to work. He spoke tightly to Jaibriol. "He your slave?"

"No," Jaibriol said. For people to make that assumption was one thing, but it could backfire spectacularly on him and their attempts to establish a treaty if Kelric's people learned he had made such an offensive claim.

"What language were you talking?" Grant asked.

"It's Iotic," Jaibriol said. In the same moment Kelric shot him a warning glance, someone inhaled sharply. Glancing around, Jaibriol saw the reverend staring at him in disbelief.

Jaibriol pushed his hand through his dusty hair. He had to be more careful. Only Skolian nobles and royalty spoke Iotic as a first language. That didn't mean Kelric was either, but it was a good explanation of why an Aristo would speak to him in that tongue. The chances of someone here knowing that were small but apparently not zero.

"Iotic, idiotic." the doctor muttered. "Never heard of it."

He considered Kelric. "Who set your leg? He did a good job."

"I did it," Jaibriol said. He swayed, then caught himself. It occurred to him that he wouldn't stay on his feet much longer.

The doctor paused to study him. "When did you last have water or a meal?"

"We've found a lot of streams," Jaibriol said. "A few berries." He had to think about the food. "About two and a half days since an actual meal."

Grant scowled at the reverend, and then at the woman in the blue dress, who had come to stand with him. Seeing the reverend and the woman together, Jaibriol thought perhaps they were father and daughter.

"If we're going to help them," Grant told them gruffly, "I reckon we should get them some food. And a place to rest."

"Don't chew them out while I'm gone," the woman said. Then she bustled off.

"We can take them to the hospital," the reverend said.

"It couldn't hurt." The doctor stood up next to Jaibriol. "Does your friend speak English?"

"I don't think so." Jaibriol glanced at Kelric. "Can you understand any of what they're saying?"

Kelric shook his head. "My node can interpret Spanish, but not this language."

Jaibriol nodded and spoke to the doctor. "He doesn't, but I can translate for him."

"I need a release form to treat him," Grant said. "He has to sign it. We'll need your passports as well."

"Our what?" Jaibriol asked.

"Your documents. Your permission to be in our country, on our world, in our *free* space." Anger snapped in his voice. "No matter who you are, you need some authorization."

"No passport." Jaibriol decided he had better keep his answers short.

"How did you land?" Grant demanded. "They just let you traipse in here?"

"I don't know this word, *traipse*," Jaibriol said. "But if you mean, did I have permission to land, the answer is yes."

"Without a passport."

"Yes." He had no intention of describing the discreet and disguised manner he had used to enter Allied space.

The doctor jerked his thumb at Kelric. "He got documents?"

Jaibriol spoke to Kelric. "He wants to know if you have any papers allowing you entry into Allied space." Dice patterns swirled in his mind. He felt light-headed, as if he could float.

Kelric leaned back in the pew. "They were in the cabin." He lifted his gauntleted arm. "This comm has my military ID."

Jaibriol suspected Kelric wanted to give his identification as the Imperator about as much as he wanted another broken leg. He turned back to the doctor. "He doesn't have anything he can show you, either."

Grant shook his head. "This has to be the strangest case I've ever had."

The woman who had left earlier returned, walking into the sunshine that streamed past the open door of the church. She came to Jaibriol and spoke shyly. "We have rooms where you and your friend can stay. We've also a lunch for the two of you."

Jaibriol inclined his head. "I thank you." He barely stopped himself from using the royal "we." He felt her mood. She thought he was attractive, so much so, it intimidated her as much as his being a Highton. It was an odd reaction, but it took him a moment to figure out why. Hightons coveted beauty. They never had a simple appreciation for it; their possessive cruelty swamped out any softness. If a taskmaker noticed him that way, her reaction was lost in awe or fear. Providers were supposed to love him; they were bred, conditioned, and drugged for it. This woman's simple response so rattled him that it made him question whether, after ten years among the Hightons, he could ever again react like a normal human being.

Jaibriol stood in the dimly lit parlor with the curtains drawn against the afternoon sun. Kelric had fallen asleep on the couch in the "bed and breakfast" where the people from the church had brought them. Kelric had refused to go to a hospital, so the doctor reset his leg in the church, covering it with a med-sheath from thigh to foot. In sleep, his legendary face was at repose for the first time since Jaibriol had met him.

The married couple that lived here had fed them, fussing as if they were any tourists who had stopped in town. Jaibriol had discreetly looked into finding his siblings, but no trace of them came up in his searches and he feared to draw attention to their existence if he pushed any harder.

He had also spoken his request to his hosts, the other reason he had wanted to come to these mountains. It didn't have to be the Appalachians; he could have satisfied this request almost anywhere on this continent or several others. But he had once called this part of the world home, and it was here he turned for refuge.

His request had stunned his hosts. But they had been willing to help.

A soft knock came at the door. Jaibriol jerked up his head. He almost said, "Come," but stopped himself, not wishing to wake Kelric. Instead, he went to the door and opened it by the antique glass knob.

A priest stood outside. He wore a black collar with white underneath, and black slacks. Grey streaked his brown hair, and his calm face had a gentle quality. He started to speak, then noticed Kelric and stopped.

"Perhaps we should go somewhere else," Jaibriol said. "He needs to sleep."

The man nodded. His face was difficult to read, but he hadn't guarded his mind. Although he recognized neither Jaibriol nor Kelric, he had some idea what he was dealing with. What he thought about it, Jaibriol couldn't tell; except for his apprehension, the man's reactions were deep in his mind.

They went to a parlor with the curtains pulled. Jaibriol didn't turn on the lights; he preferred the dimness. Perhaps it made it easier to hide from himself.

"My name is Father Restia," the man said.

"Thank you for coming." Jaibriol knew he should introduce himself, but what could he say? His personal name was one of the most common among Aristos, but it was common because three emperors had borne it, including himself and his father.

"Missus Clayton didn't give me details," the priest said. "Normally I would ask that you come to the church. But when she described you, I understood why you preferred to remain in private." Quietly he added, "I've never spoken to a nobleman of any kind, let alone a Eubian. If I act in a manner that offers offense, please accept my apology."

It relieved Jaibriol that his hosts had found someone who didn't hate Aristos. "No need to apologize. I lived on Earth for two years, in another part of these mountains, in fact. I understand the customs."

Restia stared at him, and his face paled. So he knew. Only one Aristo had lived in the Appalachians for two years. Three empires knew that name. Jaibriol Qox.

The priest exhaled. "Is that when you became a Catholic?"

"My first year here. It gave me an anchor." Jaibriol had desperately needed something to give him hope while his parents waged war against—and for—each other.

"Then you know," Restia said. "Anything said between us remains in confidence."

Jaibriol inclined his head in acknowledgement. It made no difference. He had too much he couldn't say, and nothing this priest could tell him would change that. But perhaps Restia could offer a respite for Jaibriol's soul. He had little doubt that if hell existed, he would end up there, if he hadn't already, but he wasn't ready to give up yet.

He knelt at a small table and the priest sat on the sofa next to him. That in itself would have horrified Jaibriol's people, that their emperor knelt to any man, let alone one they considered a taskmaker. He put his elbows on the table and folded his hands so he could rest his forehead on them. It wasn't really a position of prayer; in truth, he couldn't look at the priest. After ten years, he had forgotten the proper phrases, so he went by what little he remembered.

"Bless me Father," he said. "For I have sinned. It has been ten years since my last confession. These are my sins." Then he stopped. What could he say? It would take a thousand years to confess.

After a moment, the priest said, "Go ahead, son."

Jaibriol sat back on the floor, leaning against a chair at right angles to Restia. Staring across the room, he said, "A man is responsible for the sins committed in his name as well as his own. The roster is too long, Father. No one can absolve me for the crimes against humanity inflicted in 'honor' of my name."

"You are not the keeper of an entire race."

"No?" Jaibriol finally looked at him. "The Hightons think I am. They glorify my name while they torture, enslave, and kill, with impunity. I own billions of people. Hundreds of worlds. I descend from a line of monsters who considered genocide an appropriate response to defiance. The populations I control live with that specter, and if I've never slaughtered, neither have I acknowledged I consider it abhorrent. I could free my people. I could turn against the Hightons. I haven't." He felt the darkness within himself, and he feared Restia could do nothing for him.

The priest spoke in a quiet manner that fit like a cover over another emotion. If Jaibriol hadn't known better, he would have thought it was grief. But this man had no reason to mourn the tyrant of Glory.

"And if you did these things," Restia asked. "If you turned against the ways of the Hightons, what would happen to you?"

Jaibriol gave a harsh laugh. "What do you think? They would kill me." Bitterly he said, "Not that they don't try anyway."

"Then answer me this," Restia said. "If you can do more good by living with the evil, is that a greater sin than turning your back on what you can accomplish?"

"It's killing me," Jaibriol said.

"I wish I could offer you better counsel." Restia spoke softly. "Perhaps God has given you a greater trial because you have a greater purpose."

"Do you truly believe in this God?" Jaibriol asked. "So many cultures have a pantheon. Ask the man sleeping in the other room. His people believe in many gods and goddesses. Yet here on Earth, it is only one. A merciful god, you say. Yet what deity of mercy would create the Aristos?" He felt too heavy to continue, but the words he had pent up for so long poured out. "What mercy will be left when the Hightons hold sway over the entire human race, across all the stars, when no one is free but a race of monsters who would murder me in an instant if they saw me sitting here, speaking with you?"

"If I told you," Restia said, "that the greater humanity believes it has become, the greater the trials we must face, I would sound sanctimonious even to myself. I can't imagine what you face. Or what you endure. I know nothing of you but what we see on broadcasts." Quietly he said, "If you have come to me for the absolution of confession, that I can offer. But the forgiveness you need isn't from me. It is your own."

"Then I will never have it," Jaibriol said. "I can reach for peace, Father, but I can't change the character of man, even within myself. In the coldest hours of my nights, when the specter of power lures with its siren call, will I turn away?" It haunted him, for he knew now what he had within his grasp. The knowledge had all been within Kelric's mind—the Triad Chair, the Kyle web. Kelric hadn't wanted to open that portion of himself, but Jaibriol had seen. In giving Jaibriol an inestimable gift that could allow Eube's emperor to survive, Kelric had also given him the knowledge to conquer humanity.

"Knowing I have within my grasp the power to rule it all," Jaibriol asked, "will I seek peace?"

Restia's face paled. "I pray you do seek it."

"So do I," Jaibriol whispered.

The rumble of an engine tugged Kelric out of his doze, back into a waking reality. He was sprawled on the couch in a pleasant room of the house. The people here seemed puzzled by his refusal to go to the hospital, but no one insisted. They couldn't know he wanted these last few moments of freedom before his world collapsed. Better a house than a hospital with doctors monitoring him on machines.

Kelric wondered what these people would do if they knew their two guests contained within their internal nodes a peace treaty of incredible proportions. Whether or not it would be ratified was a question he feared to look at too closely, for in giving Jaibriol the knowledge to protect himself, Kelric had also given him knowledge that would negate the need for any treaty, if the Highton emperor chose conquest instead of peace.

Jaibriol was standing across the room, gazing at holocube pictures on the mantel. Antique paper with flowers and leaves covered the walls, and the moldings that bordered the ceiling were painted a pale shade of rose. Kelric listened to the engines overhead and wondered if this soothing room would be his last sight of freedom.

He had watched with bemused fascination while Doctor Grant heckled Jaibriol all morning. He didn't have to understand English to figure out the doctor had thrown barb after barb at his Aristo guest. Jaibriol took it with equanimity, but still, it had to be strange for a man whose people considered him a god.

He sensed the haze of Quis patterns in Jaibriol's thoughts. It softened the scarred edges of the young man's mind. Given time and treatment Jaibriol might someday heal. He would never get that help, not as long as he ruled Eube, but perhaps Quis could give him relief. It had done so for Kelric, making his life bearable in times when he thought he could no longer go on. Seeing his dice pouch hanging from Jaibriol's belt wrenched him, all the more so because he knew what else he had given Jaibriol. If he was wrong about the emperor, he truly had committed treason at its highest level, and he deserved the execution looming before him. Jaibriol could return to Eube, erase the document he and Kelric had signed, and seek to enslave all humanity.

That Jaibriol was a decent man, Kelric had no doubt.

But no one could live with the lure of that power and deny its hold. In the moment Kelric had offered him Quis, he had faced the most difficult decision in his life. He had based it not on concrete principles or logic, but on the unquantifiable patterns evolving in his mind. Whether he had done a great good or committed unforgivable harm against humanity, he didn't know.

The grumble of the engines intensified, until it sounded as if they were in the street outside. Jaibriol turned around and met Kelric's gaze. He looked as if he had aged years in the past few days, but he seemed much calmer now than earlier.

Someone had left Kelric's staff by the sofa. He grasped it with both hands and pushed himself to his feet. The doctor had done his job well; only a twinge of pain shot up his sheathed limb. He hoped Grant didn't have heart failure when he realized whom he had given so much grief today. Then again, someone willing to talk that way to an Aristo would probably survive knowing he had spoken to an emperor. It might be bravery, but more likely the doctor simply had no idea his words could have him put to death among Eubians. The people of the Allied Worlds lived a sheltered existence in the shadow of their violent neighbors.

The roar of the engine outside muted. A moment later, someone pounded on some part of the house. Kelric tensed, his hand tightening around the staff.

"They do that here," Jaibriol said. He came up next to Kelric. "It's called knocking on the door. It's how they announce their presence."

Kelric relaxed his grip on the staff. "We probably won't have another chance to talk."

Jaibriol bit his lip, and for one moment, he wasn't an emperor, he was a young man of twenty-seven caught in events too great to bear. It was hard to believe he was the same age as Kelric's son or Jeremiah Coltman, the youth Kelric had rescued from Coba. Jaibriol seemed years older, decades, centuries. No one should have to see in a lifetime what he endured every day.

"Be well," Kelric said. "No matter what happens, know that you can survive."

Jaibriol looked up at him. **God's speed, Kelric.**

The thought was an unexpected gift. Before Kelric could respond, steps sounded outside. They stopped—and the door creaked open. A man in the uniform of an Allied Air Force colonel stood framed in the rectangular doorway, and more uniformed men and women waited behind him in the hall, as well as the couple who owned the house. Dust motes swirled in a shaft of sunlight that slanted past them.

The colonel's face paled when he saw Jaibriol and Kelric. He walked into the room, his pace measured, and bowed deeply from the waist, a gesture part Skolian and part Eubian but one rarely seen on Earth in this modern age. With foreboding, Kelric inclined his head, aware of Jaibriol doing the same.

The colonel spoke in English. Bolt had been analyzing the language, developing a translation program. He interpreted the words as *My honor at your presence, Your Majesties.*

Kelric glanced at Jaibriol, wondering if he were offended. Eubians used Highness rather than Majesty. But the emperor didn't even seem to notice.

So they began the complex process of sorting out what Earth would do with the two potentates who had appeared out of nowhere in a church in West Virginia, beneath the wide blue sky of Appalachia.

XXXIII
Mists of Jaizire

ISC imprisoned Kelric on Parthonia.

His "cell" was a suite of rooms in a mansion that the army owned in the Blue Mountains far from any city. The officers who had picked him up on Earth had said very little. They had worn that same stunned look as the Allied Air Force officers. When Chad Barzun met them at the starport on Parthonia, his questions had broken over Kelric in shards. Kelric couldn't answer. He didn't know what would implicate him. Nothing like this had ever before taken place.

He had no idea what had happened to Jaibriol after the Eubian ambassador from the embassy in Washington, D.C., had showed up in Virginia with an octet of Razers. Someone in the church had contacted Washington as soon as they realized an Aristo had walked into their service. It had taken longer for the authorities to realize they should be doing the same with Kelric, but his own people had soon arrived.

And arrested him.

An ISC legal team questioned him. He said nothing. He allowed no one to access his gauntlets or Bolt. No one seemed to know what to do. Should they demand the Imperator submit to a biomech search? Normally they could order a Jagernaut accused in an investigation to release his internal systems. But it didn't take a telepath to see they were afraid of him. Sooner or later, they had to decide what to do. He didn't deceive himself. He had done what they claimed. The only question was his sentence: prison or death?

Kelric was standing by a table, pouring a much-needed brandy when the door chimed. Apparently his momentary reprieve from questioning was over. As he turned around with the tumbler of gold liquid in his hand, the molecular air lock across the room shimmered away, leaving behind a horseshoe arch. The Ruby Pharaoh stood in the archway.

"Dehya." It relieved Kelric to see her far more than he wanted to show, given how many monitors were undoubtedly keeping track of his every motion, word, and breath. With Jagernauts on the job, they might even be trying to monitor his thoughts.

Jagernauts. As in Najo, Strava, and Axer. The memory broke over him with pain.

Dehya walked into the room, and Kelric could see guards outside, both his and hers. Except in his case they were no longer bodyguards. They were holding him prisoner.

Dressed in a blue jumpsuit, with her slight build and small height, her long hair drifting around her body, Dehya looked vulnerable. Fragile. Kelric knew better, but it reminded him how close she could have come to facing the same charges ISC had leveled against him. Fortunately, she hadn't known about the message from Qox.

As the door solidified, Dehya wandered around the room, looking at the glass statues on the glass shelves and peering at the luminous sculptures in the corners of the room. The diffuse light reflected off her glossy hair.

"Nice room." Her voice was quiet. Calm. Conversational. Kelric knew exactly what it meant. She was furious.

"I'm surprised they let you in," he said. "The prosecutors aren't allowing any other family members to see me."

Dehya turned to him, her slender form reflected in the mirrored wall behind the art objects. "I'm the Ruby Pharaoh. They can't refuse me." Her eyes blazed at him. "Unless of course they've neglected to tell me something. Like, oh I don't know, maybe that the Emperor of Eube contacted me while I was in the Kyle web. Just a little thing like that."

She certainly didn't waste time. "I didn't want you involved," he said.

Kelric, she thought.

He shook his head. Jagernauts were psions. He had trained many of them himself. Here, in the heart of an ISC facility, the chance was too great that someone might eavesdrop even on their minds if they dropped their shields and let their thoughts too close to the surface. *Someone* had figured out he went to Earth even though his security had been so effective that he and Jaibriol had staggered through the Virginia wilderness for over two days without anyone knowing. It had to be someone in ISC; no one else had access to that much of his security.

Kelric limped to the sofa in the center of the room, across the white carpet. His leg was healing, but not as fast as it would have when he was younger. Dehya watched him, her brow furrowed. When he eased down on the couch, she came over and sat on the one facing him across a crystal table.

"Are you all right?" she asked.

"I'll be fine." It was a lie, and they both knew it, but he didn't see the point in saying anything else. Instead he asked her what had haunted him the past three days. "Have the remains of my bodyguards been recovered?"

Dehya nodded, the anger fading from her eyes. She spoke with that infinite gentleness she could show. "I'm sorry, Kelric. Nothing is left."

He somehow managed to nod. He looked away, at the vases, the shelves, anywhere that would let him blink back the moisture in his eyes.

Dehya spoke softly. "Roca asked me to tell you that she will support you no matter what."

Kelric looked back at her. "Is she angry?"

"Furious," Dehya said. "Scared for her son. Worried. Relieved and grateful you're still alive."

For now, Kelric thought. "They won't let me see even her."

"Especially her."

He frowned at Dehya. "Why especially her?"

She spoke quietly. "Roca is your heir. If you die, she becomes Imperator."

It hadn't occurred to Kelric that anyone would think he and Roca would plot together. But if he really had intended to betray his people to the Eubians, of course

ISC would keep him away from his successor. He didn't want to talk to Roca, either, if it would bring down suspicion on her.

"The Allied authorities recovered the remains of both your and Qox's guards," Dehya said. "They found traces of the apparatus that set the explosions, and debris from weapons that don't correspond to those of our people or the Razers."

"But no commandos."

Her gaze darkened. "Someone else got there first."

He felt as if the ground were dropping underneath him. He couldn't reveal what he suspected. The three people who had tried to kill him in the plaza had seemed to act alone, but he had little doubt that someone else had arranged it. The commandos on Earth may not have known Jaibriol would be there, but whoever had masterminded the attempt would take advantage of the results. Kelric couldn't hide his meeting with Qox; news services all over had picked up the story. Whoever tried to assassinate him might have succeeded even though they failed. The attack hadn't killed him, but a conviction of treason probably would.

Dehya was watching him. "Jaibriol Qox."

"I don't think he planned it."

"It would be rather stupid to plan his own murder."

Kelric just looked at her. She looked back at him. They both knew what she wanted to ask: was Qox a psion?

Kelric said, simply, "Yes."

Her forehead furrowed. "He did plan the attack?"

"No."

Her eyes widened, just slightly, and he knew she

understood. She pushed her hand through her hair, pulling the locks back from her face. She spoke in a murmur, reciting a line from a famous Eubian poem. "'So the gods turned in the void of stars, their frozen grave unbound.'"

Kelric clenched his hand around the brandy tumbler. "I need to address the Assembly."

"You can't address the Assembly if you're under arrest."

"You're the pharaoh. Order it."

"I can get you before the Assembly," Dehya said. "But they aren't going to let someone they consider a possible traitor speak as if nothing had happened. You would first have to let them vote on whether or not they judge your actions treason."

"All right." If he didn't face the Assembly soon, he might end up dead before he could bring them the treaty. He didn't know how much longer he could stop ISC from forcing him to download the records in his gauntlets and Bolt, but he doubted it would be long. Given the murder attempts, he had no idea what would happen to that download; right now he trusted his own people less than he had trusted Jaibriol Qox.

She clenched her fist and hit the arm of the sofa. "Kelric, listen! If the Assembly votes to convict you, that's it. You don't get a trial. You saw the ballot against Roca. It was almost even, including your votes, and you don't get a say in this. You have the most powerful hereditary seat. Gods, you wield a larger bloc than *anyone* except the First Councilor and me. And this isn't as simple as whether or not one of us can cast ballots for a dead spouse. A vote against you is a vote against hereditary rule. The only reason we keep that rule is because ISC backs us. ISC—which has arrested you for treason." Her voice cracked. "If you do this, and the vote fails . . ."

Kelric knew she was right. But it changed nothing. He had one shot. Nor was betrayal within ISC his only fear. The longer he went without bringing the treaty to the Assembly, the more time Jaibriol Qox had to change his mind.

"The Assembly is in session," he said. "Get me a hearing. Today."

Her face paled. "Are you absolutely sure?"

He forced out the answer. "Yes."

Dehya looked as if she were breaking inside. But she said, "Very well. You will have your vote."

Jaibriol found Robert waiting as he stepped down from his flyer onto the roof of the palace. How Robert had managed to keep everyone else away, Jaibriol had no idea, but he was immensely grateful.

"It's all over the mesh," Robert told him as they strode to an onion bulb on the roof with a lift down into the palace. "The Skolian and Eubian services picked it up almost as soon as the Allieds started broadcasting the story."

"Any speculation?" Jaibriol asked.

"They've arrested Imperator Skolia." Robert practically had to run to keep up with Jaibriol's long-legged stride. "That's fact. Speculation? Everyone believes you arranged to meet with him under false pretenses and almost succeeded in having him killed. The Hightons think you're brilliant."

"For flaming sake. That's ridiculous." Jaibriol stopped

at the tower and smacked his hand on the entrance panel. "And assassinate myself in the process?" He wanted to hit something a lot harder than a panel.

Only one holo of him and Kelric had reached the meshes, a clip caught by a security camera across the street from the church. But the image had flooded settled space: him half carrying, half dragging Kelric into that church, the two of them covered in dirt and dust, exhausted, staggering. Broadcasters were calling it one of the most powerful images ever taken. Of course everyone had the same question: What did it mean? Jaibriol wished he knew.

The door shimmered open and he stepped into the lift with Robert and his quartet of Razers. These guards had no names. None showed any sign of humanity. They were part of an elite unit he had selected, but none of them had challenged decades of programming to save his life and his sanity in the Lock. He clenched his fist and bit the inside of his mouth until the pain stopped his tears.

"Where is my wife?" he asked Robert as the lift descended. "I'm surprised she isn't here demanding what the hell was I doing."

Sweat sheened Robert's forehead. "She isn't in the palace, Sire."

"Where is she?"

"I don't know. I'm sorry."

Hell and damnation. Didn't he have enough problems without Tarquine going off to do who only knew what? "What about my joint commanders, Barthol Iquar and Erix Muze?"

"General Iquar is downstairs. Admiral Muze has sent inquiries to the palace."

The last person Jaibriol wanted to see was Barthol. Ever since he had left Kelric, his mind had felt raw and unprotected. Barthol would be like sandpaper scraping over a bleeding wound. It didn't surprise him Muze kept away, given that Jaibriol had threatened to execute him.

"And Corbal?" Jaibriol asked.

"He is in your office." With impressive calm, Robert added, "He appears somewhat upset."

Jaibriol shot him a wry look. "And people tell me I'm the master of understatement. They haven't met you."

"Ah, well." Robert exhaled. "It is quite some business."

"Think they're going to arrest me for treason?"

Robert looked bewildered. "You are the emperor. No one can put you on trial. Who would you commit treason against? Yourself?"

"It was a joke, Robert."

"Ah." He gave Jaibriol a rueful look. "It has been lively here, Your Highness. But not with humor."

The door shimmered open and they stepped into a gold and black foyer that reflected their images in the polished marble. Jaibriol knew he had to talk to Tarquine. Her brother's agreement to sign the treaty would be contingent on what Tarquine did with the Iquar title.

If Jaibriol asked him to sign.

"It's insanity." Corbal slammed his hand on Jaibriol's desk. "Are you mad, meeting him on Earth so you can attempt to kill him and instead almost get yourself killed?"

"Why does everyone believe that happened?" Jaibriol asked. They were alone in his secured office, with his Razers outside.

"Didn't it?" Corbal paced back and forth. "Now his own people are going to kill him. Was that your intent, a false murder attempt followed by execution?" He turned to Jaibriol. "It's brilliant, worthy of the greatest Highton strategists." He came back over to the desk. "And it isn't your style."

"I never claimed to have plotted against the Imperator."

"No. You just met with him in secret." Corbal knocked a vase off the desk and it shattered on the floor. "Is that what you're trying to do to yourself?"

The archway across the room rippled open, revealing the captain of Jaibriol's bodyguards. Since Jaibriol had a security blanket in place, his Razers wouldn't know Corbal had knocked over the vase, only that something had crashed. He motioned with his hand, dismissing the captain, and the Razer bowed, then withdrew. The archway shimmered back into solidity.

Corbal was watching him, his jaw rigid. "Do you have any idea what could have happened if ESComm or your Ministers believed you orchestrated that meeting *with* Imperator Skolia instead of to kill him?"

Jaibriol came around the desk, his boots crushing the shards of glass. "You set this story in motion. To protect me."

"Why would I protect you?" Corbal asked bitterly. "After you threatened me, my son, my granddaughter, and my entire Line."

Corbal's words had gone so far beyond the accepted modes of Highton discourse even with one's kin that Jaibriol had no doubt he intended the insult. Jaibriol walked away, then swung around to face him. "I met with Kelric to talk about the treaty."

Corbal came over to him. "He will never sign. Not Kelric Skolia, not the Ruby Pharaoh, and not their aggravating First Councilor."

"You don't know that."

"It is the oddest thing," Corbal said coldly. "Who would have thought both your joint commanders *and* Trade Minister would all support opening trade relations with the Skolians. It is truly unprecedented."

"You voted for it."

"Funny, that." His voice grated. "And if you bring me a peace treaty, do you think I will sign that, too?"

Jaibriol met his accusing gaze. "Would you?"

Neither of them moved, both standing in the debris of a shattered vase, a work of art considered beyond price. Then Corbal said, "Some principles are more important than peace. And some are more important even than blood."

"Principles of Highton ascendance."

"That's right."

And if it means an end of your life as you know it? Jaibriol wanted to ask. If it became known Corbal had willfully passed off his son by a provider as a Highton, helped Azile rise to a position of great power, and let his granddaughter marry one of ESComm's joint commanders, Corbal would lose everything. Jaibriol had only to invoke that specter to force his agreement. But he couldn't do it. Corbal had protected him for years. He couldn't threaten him with exposure.

Jaibriol walked away from his cousin. When he reached

the opposite wall, he turned around. "You have to do what you believe right," he said, knowing he was giving up his only leverage against Corbal. "And so do I. Know this, my cousin. For me, the rise of the sun is as precious today as it has always been, and as I hope it always will be."

Corbal's shoulders slowly relaxed as he breathed out. He came over to Jaibriol, but this time he stopped farther away, keeping the appropriate Highton distance. "That sounds like the man I have come to admire."

It was the first time Corbal had ever expressed the sentiment to him. "But not the brilliant Highton strategist."

"Look to your wife for that," Corbal said quietly.

"Robert says she isn't here."

"She went to your retreat."

Jaibriol stiffened. "What for?"

"I don't know. She wouldn't take her bodyguards."

"*What?*" Jaibriol strode toward the exit archway. It started to shimmer, but he burst through the air lock before it finished changing permeability. The membrane dragged along his skin.

"Robert!" he shouted.

His aide looked up from his desk. "I haven't found—"

"She's at the lodge," Jaibriol said. "Get my flyer. Now!"

Jaibriol jumped down from the flyer to the landing hexagon, his black jacket flying open. As he ran to the lodge with his guards, the harsh mountain wind whipped his hair back from his head. He burst through the front door into the main room.

The empty room.

"Tarquine!" he called. She could hear or see him on any

screen; if she were here, she was either ignoring him—or she couldn't answer.

Jaibriol strode across the room. The lodge was too quiet, too still. He yanked aside the bead curtain in the morning alcove, but she wasn't there. He was running by the time he reached their bedroom. He turned in a circle in the middle of the room, looking around, his leather jacket crackling with the force of his motion, his hair disheveled on his forehead.

Then he saw it, across the room. Rumpled blankets lay bunched up on the mattress as if someone had lain in the bed. He strode over and jerked the covers off the mattress.

Blood covered the sheets.

"No!" He threw the blankets on the floor. The blood had spread in a terrifying stain. He looked frantically around for any sign of her, but there was nothing, *nothing*.

Jaibriol suddenly realized someone had closed the door to the bathing chamber. He ran to the wooden portal and threw it open. Mist filled the chamber beyond, rising from the pool, white and opaque. Heated water arched from the fountain into the air and sprayed across the pool, blue and clear. He went over and stared into the water, his heart dying as he looked for her body, a dark shape lying against the tiles.

The pool was empty.

Jaibriol gulped in a breath. He turned back and forth, looking, looking, but he saw no one. Steam and water dampened his hair and sheened his jacket. He was a dark shadow in a room of cloud. He strode around the pool and came into view of the back wall—

A woman was slumped there, a white shift dampened against her body, her black hair tangled over her face.

"*NO!*" Jaibriol ran to her, his boots hammering the tile floor, his Razers only steps behind him. Dropping to his knees, he heaved in air. "Tarquine." His voice broke as he cupped his hands around her deathly pale face.

She opened her eyes.

"Oh, God, my God." Jaibriol choked out the words. He pulled her into his arms, her slender weight limp against him. As he held her, his heart pounded in his chest and his arms shook.

"Your Highness," a voice said. "A doctor is on the way."

Jaibriol jerked up his head to see a Razer looming over them. "No," he said, knowing Tarquine would never want anyone to see her this way. "Leave us." He jerked his hand toward the door. "Go! No one is to disturb us."

"Yes, Your Highness." The startled guard bowed and quickly withdrew with the other Razers, closing the door behind them.

Jaibriol turned back to Tarquine and pulled the hair out of her eyes. "Are you all right?" He looked down, touching her, trying to find the injury. "Where are you hurt?"

She spoke in a dusky voice, as if her words were twilight. "Where is Hidaka?"

"Hidaka? What?" She was too pale; he was certain she had lost too much blood. "Who attacked you?"

She grasped his hand so hard, it hurt. "I have no injury. I am not the one they tried to murder on Earth."

"Ah, God. Hidaka is gone." He couldn't separate his shock over that loss with his fear for her. "You didn't know?"

"How could I not know?" Drops of water glistened on her hair. "Everyone across a thousand worlds knows. Your bodyguards died so that you could live."

"Tarquine, there's blood all over the bed."

"The blood of gods," she said. "Or is it slaves?"

"What are you talking about? Who hurt you?" He set his hand on his abdomen. "Is the baby all right?"

"No one hurt me," she said dully. "Your son, however, is dead."

He couldn't breathe. "It can't be."

Mist curled around them and blurred her face. "I can control the wealth of an empire and wield power our ancestors only dreamed of." Her voice cracked. "But it seems I cannot stop my body from losing a child."

He smoothed the tangles out of her eyes. "We'll call a doctor. The best. We'll—"

"Jai, stop." She laid her palm against his chest. "No doctor could have helped."

"I should have been here."

"It would have changed nothing."

"But why?" He couldn't see how his wife, a woman he had never seen ill, had lost her baby. "How?"

"Do you really believe I would birth a child who would grow up to crave his father's pain?" The murmur of the fountain muted her voice. "A child who might someday dethrone and enslave the man who most loved him?"

"What did you do?" he whispered.

"He was your son. Yours—and some long dead provider." She took a breath. "Your great-grandfather, Jaibriol the First, wanted a Ruby son. It took me years to unravel what he had done. The stored eggs still existed.

Your great-grandmother wasn't the only candidate who carried Ruby DNA." In a low voice, she said, "I would have given you a Ruby son."

"Tarquine, no." He was breaking inside. "You can't. Only a psion can carry a Ruby child."

"I believed I could do anything," she said numbly. "If I were just strong enough."

It hit him then, why she had been willing to relinquish her title to Barthol: it would keep it within the Iquar bloodline—for the child she had carried had no Iquar blood. For him, she had made a sacrifice considered the ultimate crime for an Aristo.

Jaibriol pulled her into his arms and laid his head against hers, his face wet with the mist. It had to be the mist. He couldn't cry. Hightons never wept.

"Did you get what you sought on Earth?" she asked.

"Kelric and I signed the treaty."

"So we can sell his people Taimarsian squid?" Her voice shook with an incredulous laugh that held more pain than humor. "He risked execution for that?"

"No." Jaibriol drew back to look at her. "For peace."

She went very still. "You signed the peace treaty?"

"Yes." His pulse lurched while he waited for her response.

"It isn't valid unless Barthol, Erix, and Corbal sign," she said.

"Barthol will."

"You are astonishingly optimistic."

"Not if he expects the Iquar title."

In a deadened voice, she said, "And why would I do that?"

"For the son we will never have." His voice caught on

what would have been a sob if he had let it free. "For the child who died because you loved your husband enough to offer him an heir who wasn't your own."

Incredibly, a tear formed in her eye and slid down her face. He had never before seen her cry, never once. "Erix and Corbal will never sign."

"They have motivation. As during the summit."

"Motivation is not enough," she said. "You must be willing to carry through the threats, my husband. Because if you can't, you are only bluffing, and they are far better at it than you."

Jaibriol no longer knew what he was capable of. To attain his goals, he would have to stoop to methods he despised, either with his people or the Skolians. He didn't know how much more of himself he would lose as he struggled to reach his dreams. He could think only that he would never know his son. He had thought Kelric sired a Ruby psion with his wife, the woman with the red hair, who wasn't a psion at all. He was wrong. He had seen Kelric's memories. The mother of Kelric's Ruby daughter had died in childbirth, in Kelric's arms while he wept. She couldn't survive the birth trauma of a child whose mind was so powerful, it tore hers apart.

"I can't lose you," Jaibriol said.

"If I cannot give you an heir to love you as you loved your father," she said in her throaty voice, "then someday I will give you an heir of unparalleled strength and brilliance. An Iquar heir." Darkness saturated her words. "But if you cannot raise a son, my husband, then raise an empire as none has ever been known, until all humanity everywhere, from here to the ends of space, kneels to you."

XXXIV
A Choice of the Ages

The Amphitheater of Memories overflowed with the session of the Skolian Assembly. No one knew Kelric was to appear. He entered the hall with Dehya and his guards through one of thousands of arches. A robot arm waited for them, with a console cup at the end large enough for six people.

All over the hall, the screens that usually showed speakers were instead replaying a broadcast that billions, even trillions of people had seen. Kelric stared at the images as they played throughout the amphitheater, larger than life. Less than two minutes of coverage had hit the meshes before the governments of three civilizations stopped it, but that was enough. Again he saw himself and Jaibriol stagger into the church. A few steps into the building, Jaibriol collapsed, half lowering, half dropping Kelric to the floor. Sunlight streamed over them, and Jaibriol's hair glittered. Exhaustion showed on his face, even desperation, but his haunted red eyes seemed to burn.

"Subtle," Dehya muttered. She sounded angry.

"His people think he set it up to kill me," Kelric said.

She looked up at him, and he knew her thought; if Jaibriol had set him up, Kelric was playing into his hands. By bypassing his right to a trial and throwing the decision for his fate to the Assembly, he left himself excruciatingly vulnerable. He saw no other choice; if whoever sought his death found the treaty, wiped it out of Bolt's memory, and denied knowledge of the document, no one would believe it existed. Without evidence, he could never justify his meeting with Jaibriol. Although the emperor had a copy, Kelric had no idea what he intended. He didn't believe Jaibriol had planned the attack, but Qox was perfectly capable of using it to his advantage. Jaibriol had a choice to make, and the fate of three empires hung on his decision.

Thousands of voices clamored in the hall. The tiers of seats started far below the level where he had entered and rose far above. Kelric felt as if he were entering a giant arena with himself as the gladiator set to fight for his life.

The dais was halfway up the height of the hall. Protocol sat at a console there, and First Councilor Tikal stood next to her, peering at one of her screens. Tikal suddenly jerked his head up and stared straight at Kelric. The robot arm was only one of many ferrying people through the hall, but Kelric had no doubt Tikal knew he was there. Protocol, who controlled the dais, apparently realized it as well, for the platform was rising to meet them.

Within moments the media wizards who controlled the screens had picked up his arrival. The images of Jaibriol blinked out, replaced by real-time views of Kelric and

Dehya standing in the console cup. A surge of emotions flooded him like storm waves; no psion, no matter how strong, could shut out that many minds in one place, all concentrated on him. Their shock poured over him, their disbelief, curiosity, hostility, and confusion.

Kelric knew he frightened people with his power, his size, his taciturn nature, and his unpopular decisions to use ISC forces on Skolian worlds. In the past, the good he had done ameliorated the effect, and yes, so did the protocol officers who endeavored to portray him as the handsome, golden prince rather than the hardened, metallic dictator. But now screens all over the hall showed him dressed in black, towering over Dehya, his huge bulk dwarfing her delicate form, and he knew they should never have entered together. Next to her, he looked like a monster.

Across the hall, Roca was staring at him, her face pale as she leaned forward. Her aides were working furiously at the console, undoubtedly trying to figure out what the blazes was going on. At the pharaoh's bench, Eldrin was on his feet behind his console, his gaze fixed on Kelric and Dehya. Kelric was grateful Ixpar and his children were on the Orbiter. He wished he could have spoken to them before all this happened, but perhaps it was better this way. If ISC convicted him of treason, he didn't want it to backfire on his wife and children.

As the robot arm docked with the dais, Tikal came forward, his expression thunderous. He spoke flatly to Kelric. "You cannot address the Assembly."

"He has the right," Dehya said.

Tikal swung around to her. "He betrayed his people, his

title, his oaths, and *your* family. By any law, this man has no right to stand before this governing body."

She met his gaze. "It is the Assembly's right to decide if he may address them. Not yours."

Tikal made an incredulous noise. "Imperator Skolia, you do realize, don't you, that you are asking the Assembly to decide your guilt or innocence? With no preparation?"

"That's right," Kelric said.

Tikal looked from him to Dehya. "Have you both gone mad?"

"He has the right to ask," Dehya repeated, her voice hollow. She looked up at Kelric. "If this is what you truly want."

He nodded, wishing he could tell her more. But he didn't dare. Too much was at stake.

Tikal shook his head. Then he motioned to the dais as if he were inviting Kelric to a guillotine.

As Kelric stepped out of the cup, the guards took positions on the dais that blocked him from Protocol's console. So he stood by the glass podium on the edge. When the robot arm swung away from the platform, only a force net that surrounded the great disk separated him from the chasm of air below.

Dehya was arguing with Tikal in low, heated tones. Kelric knew she was trying to convince him to let Kelric speak before they took the vote. Tikal would never agree. Before her coup, she and Tikal had been allies, even friends. As much as Kelric understood why she hadn't wanted to execute the First Councilor, her decision had left her open to any retaliation he sought against her or the rest of the Ruby Dynasty. Whoever had planned the attempts against Kelric's life didn't have to be in the military. Tikal had the necessary resources.

Bolt, Kelric thought. **Are you ready?**

I have prepared, Bolt answered. I don't think you can reach the console, however. If you go for it, the guards will shoot before you can do anything.

I know. But I'm right next to the podium.

It doesn't have what you need.

It can launch the emergency protocol.

Do you mean for evacuation?

That's right.

You don't want to evacuate the amphitheater.

No. I don't. But the protocol can link this dais to everyone's console.

The amphitheater techs have probably shut you out of the system.

It's been less than a day since the story broke, Kelric thought. **And no one had any idea I would come here. It's also a minor system, not one most people would think of first when closing me out.**

Perhaps.

Kelric watched Dehya and Tikal. **It doesn't look as if she's making headway.**

No. It doesn't.

Let's do it.

He leaned his arm on the podium as if he were resting, except he laid his wrist over a prong in the glass. The prong clicked into his socket through a hole in his gauntlet.

Downloading, Bolt thought.

Throughout the hall, red lights flashed on consoles, indicating the emergency protocol had activated. Kelric could have done without that glaring announcement that he had accessed the system, but at least it meant no one had closed him out.

"Councilor Tikal!" Protocol called. "He's sending out a file!"

"Block it!" Tikal shouted, whirling to face Kelric, his face contorted with anger.

Protocol's hands flew over the console. "Blocked, sir. I caught it in time."

I'm sorry, Bolt thought. I went as fast as I could.

Kelric felt as if his last supporting strut had broken. **You did your best.**

Tikal stared at Kelric with his fist clenched. "*Why?* Are you plotting the overthrow of your own Assembly? Gods, Kelric, what did they promise you?"

"I wasn't conspiring with Qox," Kelric said. "Let the file out."

"And give you access to every person in this hall?" Tikal asked. "Do you think I'm insane?"

"Kelric, what is it?" Dehya asked.

"It doesn't matter," Tikal said. "You asked for a vote from the Assembly on your guilt, Skolia. You're about to get it."

Kelric spoke angrily. "Was it you who tried to kill me, Barcala?"

"What?" Anger flooded the councilor's face. "You violate a ruling from your own government forbidding you to meet with Qox, you go in secret, you nearly get killed by his secret police, and then you have the gall to accuse *me?*"

"Councilor Tikal," Protocol said. "I have a copy of what he tried to send."

Tikal stared at Kelric, his face hard. "Erase it."

"Sir." Protocol spoke in a strained voice. "I think you better look first."

Tikal was still watching Kelric, but Dehya went to the console and stood by Protocol, reading the screen. Kelric saw the widening of her eyes.

"Gods almighty." Dehya lifted her head. "Barcala, *look* at this."

Tikal didn't move; he continued to stare at Kelric. Then the First Councilor took a deep breath and turned around. He stalked over to Dehya and clenched one fist by his side while he read Protocol's screen.

Comprehension dawned on Tikal's face—and something more, shock or anger, or both. Kelric wasn't certain and he couldn't risk lowering his defenses with so many minds pressing on him. The shock he understood. But he had an ugly sense Tikal would be angry only if he *wanted* Kelric to die, for he was staring at the only evidence that could clear Kelric's name.

Dehya looked up at Tikal. "Let him speak."

"This *has* to be false," Tikal said.

"Check the signatures," Kelric told him. "They're verified by DNA and neural fingerprints. We have records of Qox's from the negotiations ten years ago."

"You could have forged them," Tikal said.

"How?" Kelric demanded. "They're guarded by the best security available to ESComm."

"That's right," Tikal said. "Almost no one alive would have the knowledge, intelligence, and access to break that security. Except the head of ISC." He turned to Dehya. "Or the genius people call the Shadow Pharaoh." He shook his head when anger flashed across her face. "I've known you for decades, Dehya. We may have no proof you collaborated with him, but I don't believe for one second you didn't know about his plans."

"She had nothing to do with it," Kelric said. He had gone to great lengths to make sure nothing linked her to his actions. Tikal might have indisputable cause to remove him from power, but not Dehya.

No hint of the "frail" scholar showed in her face. "You have no proof, Barcala, because none exists. But know this—Imperator Skolia has my full support. Will you deny our people the only chance we've been offered for peace in *five hundred* years just to further your own power?"

Tikal looked more astonished than angry. "I'm not the one who overthrew the government. You damn near put me to death."

"But I didn't."

As they argued, thousands watched. No one could hear them, and during Assembly sessions images of the dais were blurred enough so no one could read the lips of the people there unless they were giving a speech. But anyone could see Dehya and Tikal were in a heated debate.

Tikal took a shuddering breath. Then he swung around with his fists clenched and spoke to Protocol. "Release the file."

Kelric sagged against the podium, and Dehya closed her eyes. As he straightened up, she looked at him, and he saw her shock over the treaty. It was probably one of the few times he had caught her by surprise. That he had brought them a peace agreement didn't mean they would absolve him of guilt. No guarantee existed Tikal would sign the document or that the Assembly would ratify it. But at least they had a chance.

Jaibriol Qox could still change his mind; instead of announcing a treaty, he could claim that one of his providers completed the Triad. If that happened, Kelric had no doubt ISC would kill him. The treaty would look like a lie. Even if he convinced them that Qox had betrayed him, he had still committed treason. And even if Jaibriol never revealed that Kelric had shown him how to use the Triad, ISC would suspect. The worst of it was they would be right—he would have betrayed everyone, his family, ISC, and the Imperialate. Eube would have its Kyle web and Skolia would fall. Only something as monumental as a genuine treaty would ameliorate his defiance of the First Councilor and his secret meeting with the emperor.

The ocean of voices in the amphitheater swelled as delegates received the treaty. Dehya stood with Tikal, both of them reading on Protocol's console while she paged through the file. Glyphs flowed across the screen, gold and black. Kelric waited, his pulse hammering. At first the delegates were quiet, with only a murmur rolling through the hall. As people finished the document, their voices rose, questioning, stunned, astonished.

Kelric steeled himself, for he had always dreaded speaking in front of crowds. Then he touched *send* on the podium. No one stopped him this time. His words went to every console and amplifiers in the hall.

"The treaty you are reading," Kelric said, "was signed

by myself and Emperor Qox. For it to go into effect, five more people must sign: the Ruby Pharaoh, First Councilor Tikal, General Barthol Iquar of the Eubian Army, Admiral Erix Muze of the Eubian Fleet, and Corbal Xir, heir to the Carnelian Throne. It must also be ratified by this body." He took a breath. "I have done what I can. What happens now is in your hands."

The noise surged until it felt as if he stood in a maelstrom. Lights flashed all over Protocol's console as delegates demanded a chance to speak. In the midst of the furor, Dehya came to stand with him. Absurdly, the podium was too high. When she touched a panel on its edge, a column rose from the ground. She stepped up on it and spoke into the private comm, so only those on the dais heard. "Transfer the file on Protocol's console to here."

A record of the treaty appeared on the podium.

"End of holofile," Dehya said.

The display changed to the last paragraph, and below it, the signatures of Kelric and Jaibriol. The emergency protocol was still in effect, which meant the display on the podium showed on every console in the amphitheater. Dehya picked up the light-stylus that lay in a groove of the glass.

And she signed the treaty.

The session seemed suddenly distant to Kelric, as if he and Dehya were on a mountain with a jagged range below them. They stood on a precipice. They might plummet down that long drop, but in this one exhilarating moment they had scaled heights no one had believed they could ever surmount.

Dehya smiled at him, her eyes luminous. "So we have." She turned and extended the stylus to Tikal. "First Councilor?"

He stood looking at her. Kelric waited for him to denounce the treaty, to say what it would mean if Jaibriol refused to acknowledge it. Instead, he took the stylus from Dehya. Then he stepped over to the podium and wrote his name under hers.

Kelric's pulse surged. Would it happen? Would Skolia and Eube finally, after more than half a millennium, find peace?

Tikal touched the speaker's panel, and his words rumbled throughout the amphitheater. "We are offered a treaty. It has been signed; the wording is not up for dispute. We must choose a time to vote on ratification."

"We have to do it now," Kelric said in a low voice, just to Tikal and Dehya. "If we're going to ratify it, we need to before Qox's people have a chance to weaken his position."

Tikal considered him. Then he turned to Dehya. "Would you accept a vote now, rather than waiting for the Assembly to discuss the treaty?"

She regarded him steadily. "Yes."

The harsh light of the amphitheater threw Tikal's features into sharp relief. He took a breath, his face creased by strain. Then he touched the panel. As he spoke, his voice rang out through the amphitheater. "The vote will commence immediately. A *yea* accepts the treaty; a *nay* refuses the treaty."

Clamor erupted again, and Protocol's console blazed. Kelric could well imagine the objections; they needed time to digest this extraordinary news. Unfortunately, they had no time, and he hoped anyone who knew the dynamics of Skolia and Eube would understand rather than voting against the treaty.

Protocol spoke into her comm. "Calling the vote." Her words glowed on the podium and came over the audio. She started with the lowest-ranked delegates and went through the roster. Ballot by ballot, the tally appeared on every screen. Vazar Majda stabbed her console when she gave her *aye*. Naaj showed more reserve, but she abstained rather than going against the treaty.

When Protocol called Ragnar Bloodmark, Kelric watched the admiral—and saw the flash of hatred. Ragnar covered it immediately, even as his *abstain* registered on the tally. But a chill spread through Kelric. He knew he would never find proof linking the admiral to the assassination attempts. But he no longer had a doubt who had masterminded them.

When the call came to Roca, she lifted her chin, staring straight at Kelric. Then she smiled, a radiant expression. Her huge bloc registered *aye* on every screen.

No one followed Roca; as signers, Kelric, Dehya, and Tikal couldn't vote. The tally glowed over the hall in bold red letters: 78 percent yea and 22 percent abstain.

"It is done," Tikal said, his voice resonant. "The Skolian Assembly accepts the treaty."

Kelric exhaled, flooded with relief. It was done. But they had only gone half way.

The rest depended on Jaibriol Qox.

XXXV
The Gift of Quis

Jaibriol kept his bedroom darkened as he stared out a window wall at the city below, Qoxire, capital of his empire. Its lights glistened, high above the thundering waves on the beach.

A door hummed across the room. Footsteps sounded on the deep-piled rug and someone stopped behind him. Jaibriol knew from his guards who had come, and he tensed as he turned around. Corbal stood about ten paces back, watching him, cold and hard. Behind him, on a table, the Quis dice Kelric had given Jaibriol lay in piles, sparkling in the gilded moonlight.

"Have you come to condemn me?" Jaibriol said. "Or bemoan your lost admiration for your emperor?"

"Ten years ago, you walked into my life," Corbal said. "Raw, unsophisticated, idealistic. Lethally innocent." He came over to Jaibriol. "That boy is dead. The man I saw in the meeting tonight—the man who blackmailed his joint commanders and his heir into signing that repellent treaty— is a Highton."

"Perhaps you wish to congratulate me, then." Jaibriol felt no triumph. They had signed—and he had become more an Aristo tonight than ever before.

"I find myself astonished at Barthol's cooperative nature," Corbal said. "He esteems you greatly, to offer such a success."

Jaibriol met his gaze. "You think much about succession."

"Of my Line, yes." His expression hardened. "Of my emperor's promises—or lack thereof, yes."

He doubted Corbal would ever forgive him for threatening to reveal his secret after Jaibriol had led him to believe he wouldn't do it. Yes, Jaibriol had been subtle with his threat. But Corbal had known.

"Many Lines have succession," Jaibriol said. "Say, Iquar."

"The Iquar Line may be one of great tribulation," Corbal said dryly, "but no one would deny its strength."

"Indeed. Barthol is a fortunate man."

"Barthol?" Corbal's forehead creased.

"Yes. Barthol." Tarquine had signed the documents making Barthol her heir directly after tonight's meeting.

Comprehension flooded Corbal's face, followed by disbelief. "*No one* is that fortunate. Not with the empress."

Jaibriol turned back to the window. "She is complicated."

Corbal joined him and stood staring out at Qoxire. "You know my thoughts on that."

"So I do." He also knew what Corbal really wanted to ask. Now that he had the signed treaty, what would he do? Even a few days ago, Jaibriol could have answered without doubt; he would seek peace. But everything had

changed. In meeting Kelric, in coming to know his Ruby
kin through his uncle's mind, Jaibriol had seen just how
great was the paucity of his life, even more than he had
already realized. It had forced him to confront what he
had given up the day he claimed his throne. He would
never share what Kelric and his family took for granted,
the kinship, the love, the Ruby ties. Jaibriol was the
wealthiest man alive, and he was dying from starvation.

But if he conquered Skolia, he could have his family.
He could protect the Ruby Dynasty. No Aristo would
touch his kin. He had learned an invaluable lesson
tonight; he had within him the capacity to do whatever
necessary to bend powerful Aristos to his will. In tonight's
meeting, he had been more a Highton than ever before in
his life.

A sovereign didn't have to be a tyrant. He, Jaibriol the
Third, could give the human race peace by following a different path. He could do such great good for his empire if
he wasn't locked in a constant struggle with the
Imperialate. Perhaps someday he could even free all his
people.

He would never have a Ruby son; all that survived of
his child was his memory of Tarquine's ravaged voice as
she told him their son had died. He bit the inside of his
mouth, using the pain to stop the tears that welled in his
eyes. Unless he conquered Skolia, he would never again
know a Ruby bond.

Images of Aristos cut through his thoughts. If he
brought them this treaty, they would revile him, condemn
him, even seek to end his life. That avenue to peace would
be an unending route to misery. But if he brought all

humanity together under his rule, he could offer protection instead of tyranny.

Jaibriol stared past the city at the violent waves battering the shoreline and leaping into the sky. "It is amazing," he said, "how difficult answers can be to the simplest questions."

"So I've heard," Corbal said. "It is amazing, too, how one can think he knows a man and yet be wrong on so many facets."

Each time Corbal brought up his betrayal, Jaibriol died a little more inside. "Gems have facets," he said. "People are more complex."

"Except for rubies, wouldn't you say? One should never underestimate their effect."

Jaibriol wasn't certain what he meant. Better to imply Corbal misjudged the situation than to admit anything. "I've heard it said misjudgment can be as dangerous as underestimation."

"Misjudgment and underestimation are two facets." Corbal paused. "A dyad, so to speak. You need a third facet. A triad."

His pulse jumped. Corbal couldn't know he had joined the Triad. *He couldn't.* He kept his voice cool. "To get a third facet, you must cut it. That can't be done if the tools are ruined." He doubted the Lock would ever again work.

"This is true," Corbal said. "One has to guess at so much in life. We can never be sure if speculation is no more than air bubbles that vanish when we look too closely. But let us suppose, purely for conjecture, that the destruction comes *after* the gem is faceted. A gem such as, say, a ruby."

"I prefer carnelians." It was a lie, but Jaibriol could say nothing else.

"Think of announcements." Corbal's words flowed like rich, forbidden oil. "One can proclaim many things. A signed document, perhaps. Or other things. Perhaps a trio of things."

"You seem fascinated with the number three tonight."

Corbal's voice hardened. "And think about this. What some call peace, others might call robbery of what belongs to them."

Jaibriol couldn't answer. He knew what lay within his grasp. He had thought of nothing else for the past two days. He could conquer the entire human race.

A man can be a benevolent ruler. He could make the existence of humanity better by changing the Aristos.

You haven't changed them in ten years, he thought. *You've learned only how to survive.* Was he becoming like them, the Aristos who believed they were so much higher than the rest of the human race while they inflicted such atrocities?

"*Think* of it," Corbal said. "Humanity has reached across the heavens, multiplied to incredible proportions, created wonders beyond any imagining. Our numbers are greater than any ever before known, more than our ancestors could even dream. We have achieved empires greater than anything we've found among the stars. We stand at the pinnacle of human achievement." His voice was like the call of a siren. "One person could rule it all."

Jaibriol's heart was beating too hard. "The Skolians have a saying," he answered. "'Across the stars the dynasty may trod, but yet the gods of Skolia are flawed.'"

"I wasn't talking about Skolians."

"Neither was I."

"Unlimited power," Corbal murmured. "Unlimited wealth. Unlimited realms."

"An empire fit for a man's heir," Jaibriol answered coldly. Until he and Tarquine had a child, Corbal was his successor.

Corbal's gaze darkened. "Or his wife?"

He thought of how Tarquine had walked at his side into his meeting with Barthol, Corbal, and Erix only hours after she had miscarried. In the lodge, he had seen her vulnerable in a way she would never show another human being, yet when she went to face the powers of an empire, she showed no sign of weakness. Corbal had no place criticizing her.

Jaibriol answered with ice in his voice. "A man's wife is his concern. Not his kin's."

"Nor should she be the concern of any facet in a triad."

Jaibriol felt as if Corbal had slammed him against the wall. He knew what "facet" Corbal meant. Kelric. Jaibriol would never be free of his uncle's specter. He had seen Kelric's mind. The Imperator thought of himself as aging and tired. He didn't see the commander who stood like a war god, the survivor who had defied two empires to claim his throne, the legend over which an entire world had gone to war.

The man Tarquine had wanted.

Jaibriol knew he could never match Kelric, neither in ten years nor ten millennia. The Imperator's shadow would forever leave him in its chill.

The moonlight cast Corbal's face into planes of light and shadow, making him look even more like their ancestors, especially Eube Qox, who had founded the empire. "I've heard the Skolians ratified a treaty," Corbal said. "I've also heard an Imperator's life depends on who else signs." His words were dark gems, hard and brilliant. "Announce a triad instead and he will die."

Jaibriol didn't want to hear Corbal—and he couldn't stop listening. On Earth, Kelric had offered him a means to survive. Quis. What it would come to, Jaibriol didn't know, but Kelric believed it could help. It had been an act of compassion. He didn't want to envy his uncle. He didn't want to fear Kelric's effect on Tarquine. He wanted to put aside these insidious thoughts. But he couldn't forget.

Jaibriol also remembered the boy who had needed to believe the lives of his parents had mattered, the boy who thought he could make the difference they had dared envision. Yes, he remembered. He knew what had happened to that young fool.

The boy had died, replaced by a Highton emperor.

Kelric found Ixpar on the balcony of his bedroom in the ISC mansion. Starlight silvered her face. He stopped at the entrance, needing a moment to absorb that she was here and not on the Orbiter.

"When did you come?" he asked.

She turned with a start. "Kelric." Then she said, "I've been trying ever since you returned. They wouldn't let me until tonight."

He joined her at the retaining wall of the balcony, which came up to their waists. Below them, the tangled foliage of a dense forest carpeted the mountain slopes. "I'm surprised they let you at all. I'm still under arrest."

"Why would they convict you?" she asked. "You brought them the treaty."

"Emperor Qox hasn't acknowledged it."

She had a strange expression, as if an avalanche were poised above them, ready to fall. "And if he doesn't?"

He indicated at the forest. "Look at that."

She glanced at the trees, then back to him. "It's beautiful. But I'm not sure how it connects to the treaty."

Kelric answered softly. "When you know it may be the last time you see a view, it becomes that much lovelier." He was gazing at her rather than the forest. She had let her hair down, and tendrils curled around her face, glossy in the starlight. "So very lovely."

Her face gentled. "They won't kill you."

"Perhaps I deserve it."

"How can you say that?" She had that look he remembered, the one he could never avoid, as if she could see past his silences and into the heart of his fears. "You offered your people a miracle."

"At what price?" He turned to the forest and leaned his elbows on the wall, staring at the rich green life. "I took a chance. I may have been wrong."

She stood with him. "You don't have your dice pouch."

"I lost it on Earth."

Her voice quieted. "On Coba, in our Old Age, the men in the Calanya had a custom. It was rare even then, and it fell out of practice many centuries ago."

"Coba has gone through many changes," Kelric said. Most of the recent ones, unfortunately, were because of him. He had sworn to protect them, and he had genuinely believed he could. He regretted it more now than he could say, for all he had offered them was upheaval and possibly his death.

"In the Old Age, men couldn't inherit property," Ixpar said. "But Calani found a way around that."

He looked over at her. "How?"

"A father would give his son his Calanya dice. They called it the Gift of Quis. It symbolized the father teaching the son how he played. And the Quis of a Calani is his essence. Almost his soul." Softly she said, "It was a great act of trust."

Kelric had thought his son meant it literally when he portrayed him as Jaibriol's father, but now he wondered. "Does my son know about this custom?"

"I don't think so." She rested her palms on the wall as she looked over the mountains. "But sometimes, with the most gifted Calani, the line between their Quis and precognition blurs." She glanced at him. "I used to see that in yours."

"Jaibriol Qox sees me as a rival. Not a father figure."

"Perhaps. Or it may be that neither of you sees himself as well as he sees the other."

"I don't know." Tiredly, he said, "I just wish my own son would see me as a father."

"Kelric, he does, maybe too much. He fears to lose you. For ten years we believed you were dead. Then you appear like a miracle, offering dreams." Her smile seemed to hold more sorrow than anything else. "We had you for so brief a time. Then you vanished into this place you call a Lock. Then you disappeared again, and it turns out you are on Earth with your enemy. They say you are going to die. Execution. Then you offer humankind its first peace in how many centuries? Five? Six? Now you say you may yet die." She gave an uneven laugh. "And how many days have we been with you? Ten? You live an eventful life."

"I'm sorry." That sounded so woefully inadequate.

"Don't apologize." Her eyes were luminous. "I am grateful to know you lived. I understand better now, both why you wanted to hide us and why you wanted to ensure we were prepared if you could no longer do it."

"I should have left you alone." The words came hard. "Yes, I protected you, and my children. No one can take your heritage now." Then he said, "And if Qox chooses war instead of peace? He knows about my family, including a Ruby psion heir."

"He won't betray your trust."

"He faces temptation greater than you know, Ixpar."

"You think it is true he set all this up to destroy you?"

"No. But he can use it for those purposes. He may not even fully acknowledge the lure of that power. He might convince himself, if he tries hard enough, that he can do more good if we all unite under one sovereign. Him." He forced out what had to be said. "More than anything, I wish for you to stay with me. I know you cannot. Nor can Jimorla or Rohka." He thought of the hatred on Ragnar's face. "I have no evidence one of my own people tried to kill me. But I know. It may yet happen. Anyone close to me is close to that danger." With pain, he said, "Take them home, Ixpar. I can't promise you will be safe there, but it is far better than here."

"I will," she murmured. "I'm sorry."

"Don't be." His voice caught. "They are miracles."

She touched his hand. "Your son told me that playing

Quis with you was a miracle, like riding on clouds or looking at the face of the sun and rising from its fire in rebirth."

Kelric swallowed. "Thank you."

"It is true."

"He will someday be better than me."

"He's like you. But he has played Quis almost from birth. It is a part of him in a way it never became with you." Her voice caught. "What he brings back with him, after his time here, will find its way into the Quis of Coba. Filtered through him. What Coba will do with that, I don't know, but I give you my oath, Kelric, we will seek answers for you. When you visit us—if ever you can come home—we will be waiting for you."

He drew her into his arms, bending his head over hers. His tears ran down his face, from the joy of knowing his family and the sorrow of losing them.

XXXVI
Duet

Dehya came to see Kelric after he sent away his protocol officers, when he could no longer take their fiddling with his clothes and hair. He was in a chamber near the Amphitheater of Memories where the Assembly met. Dehya stood by the door, and he could see her in the mirror. He pulled at his sleeves, trying to straighten them. He had dressed simply, despite the protests of his protocol team, choosing his unadorned black uniform.

"We've had a communication from the Qox Palace," Dehya said.

Kelric turned to her, and the room suddenly seemed too quiet. "What did they say?"

"The emperor will make an announcement today. They will time it to coincide with ours."

"Did they say what he was announcing?" It was a desperate question and they both knew it, but he asked anyway, in the groundless hope that he could know before he went before three civilizations and put his name, life, and empire on the line.

"They told us as much as we told them," Dehya said. She looked as if she had bitten into a sour fruit.

"Nothing, in other words."

She came over to him, small and slight in her sky-blue jumpsuit. "Whatever happens, know that I stand at your side."

"I don't want you at my side," he growled. "I want you to *live*."

Her voice gentled. "You hold so much within your heart, I think sometimes it may burst."

"Dehya, listen." He drew her to a table and sat across from her. "I can't go out there without warning you."

"I know you've secured this room." She sounded more as if she were warning him. "So did I. But nothing is certain."

"Even so." He had to do this. "Jaibriol Qox went to the SSRB to investigate the implosions." Kelric took a breath. "When I activated the singularity, he was sitting in the Lock."

Dehya stared at him for a full five seconds as her face paled. Then she said, "No."

"Do you remember what I told you about Soz and me?" Kelric asked. "What happened when we were children, during that storm?"

"I remember." Her voice had a deathly still quality.

"So does Jaibriol Qox, now. I showed him how to play Quis."

"Kelric—" Her hand clenched on the table.

"He needed something to give him control," Kelric said. He wanted to say more, to tell her that he believed Jaibriol's presence in the Triad had stabilized Kyle space and stopped the implosions. He didn't dare, even with mind-speech, given all the Jagernauts outside this chamber. He might have already revealed too much. But he didn't need to go on. He saw it in her eyes. She knew what Qox might do today.

"I'm sorry," he said.

"Don't be. I trust your instincts."

"I don't."

A chime came from the door. As Kelric and Dehya stood up, Dehya said, "I will see you in the amphitheater." Gently she said, "Be well, Kelric."

"You also."

Dehya left by a discreet exit that would put her in a hall with private access to the amphitheater. When he was alone, Kelric went to the main door. But he couldn't open it. Not yet. He stood with his palm against the portal, his head bowed as he centered himself. He felt as if a drum beat within him, steady, timeless. Perhaps it was his heart. Maybe it was a future his people had always faced and might now live. Or die for.

He touched a panel and the door shimmered. Eight Jagernauts waited outside. He saw it in their faces, what everyone wondered. Would Jaibriol give them a treaty today or destroy the military leader of his enemies?

Kelric set off down the hall, flanked by guards. His leg throbbed and his limp slowed him, but he kept going, headed for the Amphitheater of Memories.

Corbal came in when Jaibriol was alone, after the emperor had sent away his protocol officers. They were waiting in a chamber near the Amphitheater of

Providence, where the Aristos had assembled. Corbal stood by the door, and Jaibriol could see him in the mirror. Jaibriol pulled restlessly at his sleeves, trying to straighten them. He shimmered from his hair to his black diamond clothes to his polished shoes. Carnelians glittered in his cuffs and belt.

"We've had a communication from the Skolians," Corbal said.

Jaibriol turned, and the room suddenly seemed too quiet. "What did they say?"

"They have set up a Kyle node for us, since we can't create one ourselves." His eyes glinted. "Yet."

Jaibriol nodded formally. "Of course."

"With the connection, we will see it live when Imperator Skolia makes his announcement. And send yours live to them."

"Very well." Jaibriol went over to him. But he couldn't open the door. He wasn't ready. Not yet. He felt as if a drum beat within him, steady, timeless. Perhaps it was the beat of his heart. Or maybe his empire.

He touched a panel and the door shimmered. Barthol Iquar and Erix Muze waited outside, both in black dress uniforms with red piping on their sleeves. Four Razers waited with them.

And Tarquine.

Her red gaze was so intense, it looked as if it could burn through him. He thought he caught triumph from her, but she masked her emotions too well for him to be sure.

The minds of his joint commanders pressed on him, but he could endure it better today. When he had rolled out the Quis dice this morning, he had only intended to distract himself. But as soon as he drew on the memories Kelric had given him, his fascination with the game had swamped everything else.

The Imperator had been right.

Quis settled Jaibriol. With Kelric's memories to learn from, he could center the raging turmoil of his mind. It didn't take away the pain or give him control yet of that surging power, but it was a start. He had years to learn Quis. He didn't know yet what he would do with it, but it offered a lifeline in the ocean of his misery. It would help him rule Eube—

And beyond.

Jaibriol strode out of the room. Tarquine fell in at his right and Corbal to his left, with Barthol and Erix on either side of them. So they headed down the long corridor, the warlords of a conquering empire.

Kelric stood in the console cup at the end of a robot arm. Guards had accompanied him to the amphitheater and more waited on the dais, but he rode alone, and they hadn't insisted otherwise. He had seen it in their eyes, just as with Dehya. It wasn't condemnation; it was, incredibly, respect. He had tried to offer humanity the impossible. Peace. They knew he hadn't betrayed them. If this moment crashed, ISC would have to go through with the execution; to let him live would be to allow treason of unprecedented proportions with nothing to answer for it. How could they trust him in the Triad? But he would die knowing they understood why he had gone to Earth.

The Amphitheater of Memories hummed with the people of a thousand cultures. Giant screens showed him riding to the dais. He hadn't looked at the numbers, but he could tell from the crowds, even in aisles and between consoles, that more people had come today than to any other session he had ever attended. He felt the life, the vibrancy, the sheer *energy* of that gathering.

Don't let it end, he thought to Jaibriol, though he knew his nephew couldn't pick up that thought across the stars.

The robot arm docked at the dais, and Kelric stepped out, aware of the guards watching him. No one moved. Protocol was at her console, and Barcala Tikal stood by her chair. Dehya was standing by the console. She nodded to Kelric, and he nodded in return, though he felt as stiff as ice. He went to the podium, and screens throughout the hall showed him taller than life.

Kelric touched the speaker's panel. His voice went out to the amphitheater, and from there to Skolia, to his family, to Ixpar and his children, to the Allied Worlds, to Earth, to Jeremiah Coltman and Seth Rockworth and the people of a small Appalachian town. And to the Eubians. Three empires listened.

"Four days ago," Kelric began, "I met on Earth with Jaibriol Qox, the Emperor of the Eubian Concord."

The Razers swung open the great double doors, and Jaibriol walked with his retinue onto a balcony that over-looked the Amphitheater of Providence. Spread out before him, the hall hummed with Aristos, aides, officers, and guards, thousands in tier after tier. Giant screens showed images of Jaibriol, his hands braced on the waist-high balcony wall, Tarquine at his side, Corbal, Erix, and Barthol flanking them, Razers towering behind. He hadn't looked at the numbers, but it was obvious more people had come today than any other session he had ever attended.

He touched the speaker's panel on the wall and his words went out to three empires.

"My people of Eube." His voice resonated. "I come before you today to speak of triumph!"

"The treaty has also been signed," Kelric said, "by the Ruby Pharaoh and First Councilor, and ratified by the Assembly. All that remains is for the last three signers— the Highton Heir and joint commanders of ESComm—to add their names."

All across the amphitheater, people waited. Kelric looked at the private screen on the podium where a message would come only for him. It remained blank, and his heart thundered.

Jaibriol paused in the many honorifics expected from an emperor lauding his empire. He had said enough. He was tired of the overblown phrases. He glanced at Tarquine, and the intensity in her eyes terrified and exhilarated him.

"Four days ago," Jaibriol began, "I met on Earth with Kelricson Skolia, the Imperator of Skolia." He took a deep breath and lifted his chin.

Then he said, "Together, we signed a treaty for peace between Eube and Skolia."

❖ ❖ ❖

A message flashed on Kelric's private screen. He read the words, and a roaring started in his ears. He didn't think he could speak, that his voice would shake.

Taking a breath, he raised his head. And somehow he addressed the Assembly. "I have just received word from the Eubians." Despite his intention to remain calm, his voice crackled with hope. "They have signed!"

His words rang out. "We have a peace treaty!"

Jaibriol stood above the hall while it roared with voices and cymbals. Their shock and fury pounded his mind until he thought he would disintegrate. He stared at Tarquine, and she met his gaze. He could feel her mind now, as the onslaught wore down his defenses. It hadn't been triumph he had caught from her before, but an emotion even more powerful, grief and joy mixed together, her sorrow for the crushing path he had laid out for himself, but also, incredibly, her fierce exultation that he had dared the impossible and won.

His declaration of the treaty had gone to thousands of disbelieving Aristos, millions of news services, billions of settlements, trillions of people. The Aristos would revile him, hate him as they had hated no other emperor. But it was done. He had gone beyond and reached for something greater. For the first time in the history of Skolia and Eube, they had peace.

Jaibriol grasped Tarquine's hand so hard, he felt the bones in her fingers. She never flinched. They stood together, looking over the amphitheater, and he knew he could survive. With her at his side, he had done what he set out to achieve, and though the price might be greater than he could imagine bearing, he wouldn't let it defeat him.

His parents had not died in vain.

Characters and Family History

Boldface names refer to Ruby psions, also known as the "Rhon." All Rhon psions who are members of the Ruby Dynasty use **Skolia** as their last name (the Skolian Imperialate was named after their family). The **Selei** name indicates the direct line of the Ruby Pharaoh. Children of **Roca** and **Eldrinson** take **Valdoria** as a third name. The *del* prefix means "in honor of," and is capitalized if the person honored was a Triad member. Most names are based on world-building systems drawn from Mayan, North African, and Indian cultures.

= marriage

Lahaylia Selei (Ruby Pharaoh: deceased) = **Jarac** (Imperator: deceased)

Lahaylia and **Jarac** founded the modern-day Ruby Dynasty. **Lahaylia** was created in the Rhon genetic project.

Her lineage traced back to the ancient Ruby Dynasty that founded the Ruby Empire. **Lahaylia** and **Jarac** had two daughters, **Dyhianna Selei** and **Roca.**

Dyhianna (Dehya) Selei   = (1) William Seth
                              Rockworth III (separated)
                           = (2) **Eldrin Jarac Valdoria**

Dehya is the Ruby Pharaoh. She married William Seth Rockworth III as part of the Iceland Treaty between the Skolian Imperialate and Allied Worlds of Earth. They had no children and later separated. The dissolution of their marriage would negate the treaty, so neither the Allieds nor Imperialate recognize the divorce. *Spherical Harmonic* tells the story of what happened to **Dehya** after the Radiance War.

Dehya and **Eldrin** have two children, **Taquinil Selei** and **Althor Vyan Selei.**

Althor Vyan Selei = 'Akushtina (Tina) Santis Pulivok

The story of **Althor** and **Tina** appears in *Catch the Lightning.* **Althor Vyan Selei** was named after his uncle, **Althor Izam-Na Valdoria.** The short story "Avo de Paso" in the anthologies *Redshift,* edited by Al Sarrantino, and *Fantasy: The Year's Best, 2001,* edited by Robert Silverberg and Karen Haber, tells the story of how Tina and her cousin Manuel deal with Mayan spirits in the New Mexico desert.

❖ ❖ ❖

Roca = (1) Tokaba Ryestar (deceased)
(2) Darr Hammerjackson (divorced)
(3) **Eldrinson Althor Valdoria**

Roca and Tokaba had one child, **Kurj** (Imperator and Jagernaut), who married Ami when he was a century old. **Kurj** and Ami had a son named Kurjson.

Although no records exist of **Eldrinson's** lineage, it is believed he descends from the ancient Ruby Dynasty. *Skyfall* tells the story of how **Eldrinson** and **Roca** meet. They have ten children:

Eldrin (Dryni) Jarac (bard, consort to Ruby Pharaoh, warrior)
Althor Izam-Na (engineer, Jagernaut, Imperial Heir)
Del-Kurj (Del) (singer, warrior, twin to **Chaniece**)
Chaniece Roca (runs Valdoria family household, twin to **Del-Kurj**)
Havyrl (Vyrl) Torcellei (farmer, doctorate in agriculture)
Sauscony (Soz) Lahaylia (military scientist, Jagernaut, Imperator)
Denric Windward (teacher, doctorate in literature)
Shannon Eirlei (Blue Dale archer)
Aniece Dyhianna (accountant, Rillian queen)
Kelricson (Kelric) Garlin (mathematician, Jagernaut, Imperator)

Eldrin appears in *The Final Key*, *Triad*, *Spherical Harmonic*, and *The Radiant Seas*. See also **Dehya**.

❖ ❖ ❖

Althor Izam-Na = (1) Coop and Vaz
= (2) Cirrus (former provider
to Ur Qox)

Althor has a daughter, Eristia Leirol Valdoria, with Syreen Leirol, an actress turned linguist. Coop and Vaz have a son, Ryder Jalam Majda Valdoria, with **Althor** as cofather. **Althor** and Coop appear in *The Radiant Seas*. Vaz and Coop appear in *Spherical Harmonic*. **Althor** and Cirrus also have a son.

Havyrl (Vyrl) Torcellei = (1) Liliara (Lily) (deceased)
= (2) Kamoj Quanta Argali

The story of Havyrl and Lily appears in "Stained Glass Heart," in the anthology *Irresistible Forces*, edited by Catherine Asaro, 2004. The story of **Havyrl** and Kamoj appears in *The Quantum Rose*, which won the 2001 Nebula Award. An early version of the first half was serialized in *Analog*, May–July/August 1999.

Sauscony (Soz) Lahaylia = (1) Jato Stormson (divorced)
= (2) Hypron Luminar
(deceased)
= (3) **Jaibriol Qox**
(aka **Jaibriol II**)

The story of **Soz** at seventeen, when she enters the Dieshan Military Academy, appears in *Schism*, which is Part I of the two-book work *Triad*. The second part, *The Final Key*, tells of the first war between the Skolians and the Traders. The story of how **Soz** and Jato met appears in the novella, "Aurora in Four Voices" (Analog, December 1998). **Soz** and **Jaibriol**'s stories appear in *Primary Inversion* and *The Radiant Seas*. They have four children: **Jaibriol III, Rocalisa, Vitar,** and **del-Kelric.** The story of how **Jaibriol III** became the Emperor of Eube appears in *The Moon's Shadow*. **Jaibriol III** married Tarquine Iquar, the Finance Minister of Eube. The story of how Jaibriol and Kelric deal with each other appears in *The Ruby Dice*.

Denric takes a position as a teacher on the world Sandstorm. His harrowing introduction to his new home appears in the short story, "The Edges of Never-Haven" (*Flights of Fantasy*, edited by Al Sarrantino).

Aniece = Lord Rillia

Lord Rillia rules Rillia on the world Lyshriol (aka Skyfall). His realms consist of the Rillian Vales, Dalvador Plains, Backbone Mountains, and Stained Glass Forest.

Kelricson (Kelric) Garlin = (1) Corey Majda (deceased)
= (2) Deha Dahl (deceased)
= (3) Rashiva Haka (Calani trade)
= (4) Savina Miesa (deceased)
= (5) Avtac Varz (Calani trade)
= (6) Ixpar Karn (closure)
= (7) Jeejon

❖ ❖ ❖

Kelric's stories are told in *The Ruby Dice*, "The Ruby Dice" (novella, *Baen's Universe 2006*), *The Last Hawk*, *Ascendant Sun*, *The Moon's Shadow*, the novella "A Roll of the Dice" (*Analog*, July/August 2000), and the novelette "Light and Shadow" (*Analog*, April 1994). **Kelric** and Rashiva have one son, Jimorla Haka, who becomes a renowned Calani. **Kelric** and Savina have one daughter, **Rohka Miesa Varz,** who becomes the Ministry Successor in line to rule the Estates of Coba.

The novella "Walk in Silence" (*Analog*, April 2003) tells the story of Jess Fernandez, an Allied Starship Captain from Earth, who deals with the genetically engineered humans on the Skolian colony of Icelos.

The novella "The City of Cries" (*Down These Dark Spaceways*, edited by Mike Resnick) tells the story of Major Bhaaj, a private investigator hired by the House of Majda to find Prince Dayj Majda after he disappears.

The novella "The Shadowed Heart" (*Year's Best Paranormal*, edited by Paula Guran, and *The Journey Home*, edited by Mary Kirk) is the story of Jason Harrick, a Jagernaut who just barely survives the Radiance War.

Time Line

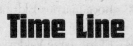

Circa 4000 BC   Group of humans moved from Earth
to Raylicon
Circa 3600 BC   Ruby Dynasty begins
Circa 3100 BC   Raylicans launch first interstellar
                flights; rise of Ruby Empire
Circa 2900 BC   Ruby Empire begins decline
Circa 2800 BC   Last interstellar flights; Ruby Empire
                collapses

Circa AD 1300   Raylicans begin to regain lost
                knowledge
         1843   Raylicans regain interstellar flight
         1866   Rhon genetic project begins
         1871   Aristos found Eubian Concord (aka
                Trader Empire)
         1881   Lahaylia Selei born
         1904   Lahaylia Selei founds Skolian
                Imperialate
         2005   Jarac born

2111	Lahaylia Selei marries Jarac
2119	Dyhianna Selei born
2122	Earth achieves interstellar flight
2132	Allied Worlds of Earth formed
2144	Roca born
2169	Kurj born
2203	Roca marries Eldrinson Althor Valdoria (*Skyfall*)
2204	Eldrin Jarac Valdoria born; Jarac dies; Kurj becomes Imperator; Lahaylia dies
2205	Major Bhaaj hired by Majdas to find Prince Dayj ("The City of Cries")
2206	Althor Izam-Na Valdoria born
2209	Havyrl (Vyrl) Torcellei Valdoria born
2210	Sauscony (Soz) Lahaylia Valdoria born
2219	Kelricson (Kelric) Garlin Valdoria born
2227	Soz enters Dieshan Military Academy (*Schism*)
2228	First war between Skolia and Traders (*The Final Key*)
2237	Jaibriol II born
2240	Soz meets Jato Stormson ("Aurora in Four Voices")
2241	Kelric marries Admiral Corey Majda
2243	Corey assassinated ("Light and Shadow")
2258	Kelric crashes on Coba (*The Last Hawk*)
early 2259	Soz meets Jaibriol (*Primary Inversion*)
late 2259	Soz and Jaibriol go into exile (*The Radiant Seas*)

2260 Jaibriol III born (aka Jaibriol Qox Skolia)

2263 Rocalisa Qox Skolia born; Althor Izam-Na Valdoria meets Coop ("Soul of Light")

2268 Vitar Qox Skolia born

2273 del-Kelric Qox Skolia born

2274 Radiance War begins (also called Domino War)

2276 Traders capture Eldrin. Radiance War ends; Jason Harrick crashes on the planet Thrice Named ("The Shadowed Heart")

2277–8 Kelric returns home (*Ascendant Sun*); Dehya coalesces (*Spherical Harmonic*); Kamoj and Vyrl meet (*The Quantum Rose*); Jaibriol III becomes emperor of Eube (*The Moon's Shadow*)

2279 Althor Vyan Selei born

2287 Jeremiah Coltman trapped on Coba ("A Roll of the Dice"); Jeejon dies (*The Ruby Dice*)

2288 Kelric and Jaibriol Qox deal with one another (*The Ruby Dice* novel)

2298 Jess Fernandez goes to Icelos ("Walk in Silence")

2326 Tina and Manuel in New Mexico ("Ave de Paso")

2328 Althor Vyan Selei meets Tina Santis Pulivok (*Catch the Lightning*)

The Following is an excerpt from:

Diamond ★Star

BY
CATHERINE ASARO

Available from Baen Books
May 2009
hardcover

★I★
Vault of Steel Tears

Del was sick of being interrogated. Supposedly he was a guest of Earth's government. Right. That's why they wouldn't let him leave their military base in this place called *Annapolis*. He was thoroughly fed up with their questions.

Today it was an Army officer. Barnard? Bubba? No, Baxton. That was it. Major Baxton. He had a green uniform and hair so bristly, it looked like a scrub brush. He sat across the table from Del in an upholstered chair that was obviously more comfortable than Del's metal seat. Holographic lights, or *holos*, glowed around the major, floating above the table as if he were a demon presiding over a laser-tech hell.

"All right, let's get started," Baxton said in English.

Del gritted his teeth. They all knew he didn't speak English very well. He could ask to use a language he knew better, but damned if he would show vulnerability to these people.

"Tell me your name," Baxton said crisply.

"My name?" Del thought he must have misunderstood.

"Your name," the major repeated. "Is that a problem?"

"You know my name." What was Baxton up to? Del felt off balance, unsure what these people wanted with him.

Baxton folded his arms on the table, and little green spheres floated near his elbows. "For the record."

"This is ridiculous." Del was so uneasy, his accent came out even more than normal. "You know name of mine. Your CO, he know it. *Everyone* here know it."

"For the record," Baxton repeated.

"Fine. You want my name? Have it all." Del leaned back and crossed his arms. "Prince Del-Kurj Arden Valdoria kya Skolia, Dalvador Bard, Fifth Heir to the Ruby Throne, once removed from the line of Pharaoh, born of the Rhon, Heir to the Web Key, Heir to the Assembly Key, Heir to the Imperator."

Baxton cleared his throat. "Uh, yes. Thank you. Age?"

"Why not look at this mesh file you all keep about me?" Del wondered when they would stop with all this business. "I am sure it say my name, age, home, what I eat, when I use bathroom, and how many wet dreams I have last night."

Baxton cleared his throat. "Your age, please."

Oh, what the hell. "Seventy-one."

"In Earth years."

Del wished he knew how to get out of this conversation. "That *is* Earth years."

Baxton spoke coolly. "Prince Del-Kurj, you are clearly not seventy-one years of age."

Del glowered at him. "Then maybe you tell me how old I clearly am."

"Seventeen?" Baxton's look suggested he thought Del was some defiant punk.

"Fine," Del said. "Have it your way. I'm seventeen."

Baxton glanced at the holos floating around him. Most were green, but one had turned red. "You're lying, Your Highness."

Del bit back the urge to tell Baxton what he could do with his lie detectors. Being rude wouldn't get him out of here. He wasn't sure of his age, anyway. Twenty-six maybe, but the year on Earth didn't match the world where he lived. Baxton could go look it up if he really wanted to know.

Del just said, "I am older than I look." The holo above the table turned green.

The major regarded him curiously. "Have you had age-delaying treatments?"

"Not really." Del laughed to cover his unease. "They say youth is curable. I guess in my case it isn't."

Baxton gave him a sour look. He tapped the table, and a new holo formed in the air, the image of a serpent curled around a staff, what Del had learned was a symbol of medicine here. When Baxton flicked his finger through the staff, words appeared below it on the table. He read for a moment, then said, "According to this, you have good genes, good health care, *and* good cell-repair nanomeds that delay your aging." He looked up at Del. "But don't your nanomeds get outdated?"

Del shrugged. "My doctor, every few years, he update them. I am scheduled for update a month ago." Dryly he added, "But I not get the update. It seems here I am, on Earth, instead of home."

"We could do it," Baxton offered, looking helpful, which was about as convincing as a wolf trying to look cuddly.

Right. Del saw their game now. This business about needing his name and age was a ploy in their endless search for excuses to analyze him. During his four weeks here, they had constantly tried to convince him that he should submit to their medical exams. His refusal stymied them, for they walked a fine edge between holding him captive and honoring him as a royal guest. They didn't want to look as if they were forcing him to do anything against his will.

Del didn't want their doctors to touch him. So far, no one had hurt him, but he had no idea what they intended or if they would ever let him go, really go, not just the few brief trips off the base they had so far allowed him with a guard.

He said only, "I update them when I go home."

"Hmmm." Baxton skimmed his hand through a holo hovering above the table.

Across the room, the wall shimmered and vanished, leaving a doorway. It bothered Del to see exits appear and disappear that way and left him feeling even more unbalanced. He had spent his life in a culture where doors swung open.

Mac Tyler walked inside and nodded to them. "Good afternoon, Your Highness. Major Baxton." A bit more than average height, with a lean build, Mac had regular features, hazel eyes, and brown hair. Although he came across as unassuming, it didn't fool Del. Mac's low-key exterior masked the intellect of a sharp negotiator.

Baxton nodded to the older man. "Good to see you, Mac." He didn't look the least surprised, and Del suspected he had signaled Mac when he brushed the table. Del always felt on guard here, and it exhausted him, especially because these people were older, more experienced, and savvier than him in just about every damn thing on their world.

Mac pulled out a chair and settled his lanky frame at the table. "I'm going to pick up some pizza," he told Del. "Would you like to come?"

Del had no absolutely desire to eat the Earth "delicacy" known as pizza. Mac and Baxton were probably doing what people here called "good cop, bad cop." Mac would rescue him, after which a relieved Del would relax with him and let slip useful information about his family. It exasperated him, but anything was better than this scintillating conversation with Major Baxton.

"I like, yes," Del said to Mac. He glanced at the major. "If we are done?"

"We can continue later," Baxton told him.

Del sincerely hoped not.

"It's stupid," Del said. He and Mac were walking down a hallway of the Annapolis Military Complex, which served Allied Space Command.

"They ask the same questions over and over," Del said. Instead of English, he was speaking Skolian Flag, his own tongue, a language his people had developed to bridge their many cultures. His ire welled up. "They want their doctors to examine me to see what they can learn about me and, well, I don't know what."

"They're frustrated," Mac said. "You won't do what they want."

Del slanted a look at him. "You're not doing your job."

Mac smiled. "My job?"

"You're supposed to trick me into a false sense of security and get me talking."

Mac didn't even deny it, "I guess my heart's not in this." Although he spoke as if he were joking, he sounded as if he meant it.

They continued on, Mac lost in his thoughts, leaving Del to his. It was one reason Del liked him despite their awkward situation; they didn't have to converse unless they really felt like it.

Del had met Mac when Earth's military had taken control of Del's home world last year. It still angered Del to think about it. His home was part of the Skolian Imperialate, an interstellar civilization that shared the stars with the Allied Worlds of Earth, supposedly as friends. Hoping to ease the strain, Earth's leaders had sent Mac as a "consultant" to establish good relations with Del's family. The tie-in was music; Del, his father, and one of his brothers were singers. Mac worked in the music business now, but he had been an Air Force major before he retired, which meant he also understood the military.

Although Del didn't usually get along well with military types, he liked Mac. The former major treated him fairly, and he didn't criticize or judge. Del could even forget his Air Force background because Mac didn't look the part. Today Mac had on dark slacks and a dress shirt, more formal than his usual pullover and mesh-jeans.

"Are you going somewhere?" Del asked.

Mac glanced at him. "Later. I have an appointment in D.C."

"More consulting?"

"No, not that." Mac smiled. "You're my only military job."

"What," Del said sourly. "Babysitting a captive prince?"

"You're not a captive."

"Fine. Then I want a berth on the next ship off this planet."

He expected Mac to come up with an excuse, the way the brass here at the base always did when Del pushed them to let him go. Instead, Mac said, "It may be sooner than you think. Your government is stepping up the pressure on us." Wryly he added, "You can always tell it's tensing up around here when people start ordering a lot of pizza."

"You know, I don't mean to offend," Del said, feeling awkward. "But I really don't like pizza." He slowed down as they reached a cross hall. "Would you mind if I went back to my rooms instead?"

"No problem." Mac seemed a little relieved, making Del wonder if he didn't like his babysitting job any more than Del liked being babysat.

"I'm working on a song," Del added.

Mac's interest perked up. "Mind if I listen?"

Even after knowing Mac for weeks, Del still felt that moment of shock, that this former Air Force major enjoyed his music. He knew the military had hired Mac to "like" it, but he would sense it if Mac were feigning his interest. Del was an empath.

It always amazed Del the strange ideas people had about empaths. He wasn't like a sponge that soaked up every emotion from the people around him. In fact, he shielded his mind to keep out their moods. When he did pick up something, he was never certain if he interpreted it right. Knowing someone's mood didn't explain *why* they felt that way. But as he had become more comfortable with Mac, he had relaxed his mental shields and discovered Mac genuinely enjoyed his singing. Del still didn't trust him, but he didn't resent his company, either. No one else wanted to hear Del sing. Or screech, as one of his brothers so kindly put it.

"Sure," Del said. "You can listen. I call the song 'No Answers.'"

Mac had always liked Del's rooms. No stark quarters here; Del had changed his apartment to evoke his home on the world Lyshriol. His wall panels showed views of the Backbone Mountains against a blue-violet sky. A Lyshrioli carpet covered the floor in swirls of green and gold, and red-glass vases graced the tables. It was a slice of Shangri-la hidden within the bleak walls of the Annapolis Military Complex.

Del leaned over an icer panel in the wall. "Want a beer?"

Mac settled in an armchair. "Sure." He had to remind himself that the "boy" offering him alcohol was legally old enough to drink.

Del might be young, but he sang like no one else. After spending so many years in the music business, Mac knew what the entertainment conglomerates looked for—and Del had it in bucketfuls. The holocam would love his face. Usually he looked like a scowling angel, but when he smiled, it was as if a light went on. Mac had seen women stutter to a halt at the sight. The violet color of his eyes and metallic quality of his eyelashes enthralled people, especially because they didn't occur naturally on Earth; they came from changes his forefathers had made to their genome. So did the wine-red color of his hair, which tousled in curls down his neck and on his forehead, sun-streaked with gold. His leanly muscled build had a lithe grace that would translate well into holographic media.

Of course, Mac could never send Del to an audition. The idea of a Ruby prince loose in the decadent ethos of the holo-rock industry broke him out in a sweat. It would be a security nightmare. Which was a shame, because Del was probably the most gifted rock singer Mac had ever met.

"Here they come." Del grabbed two bottles as they slid into the icer tray. He spun around and tossed one at Mac. "Catch!"

"Hey!" Mac grabbed at the missile, fumbled the catch, and cursed as it slipped through his fingers. The bottle looked like glass, but when it hit the floor, it bounced. He jumped out of his chair and managed to grab it on the fourth bounce.

Del grinned at him. "Sorry."

Sorry, hell. Mac grumpily scraped the bottle's tab as he dropped back into his chair. His infernal drink didn't open, it just hissed as it released gas from the frothed-up contents.

Del sprawled in a chair across from Mac with his legs stretched across the carpet. His beer, which hadn't been cavorting on the floor, opened right away. He took a long swallow, then lowered the bottle and regarded Mac smugly.

"You know," Mac said, "you can be extremely annoying." He tugged on the tab of his bottle, and it finally deigned to snap open. He took a long pull of his drink.

Del laughed. "I keep you awake."

Mac just grunted. "So what's this new song?"

Del's smile faded, replaced by a pensive look. "I'm still working on the lyrics. Tabor did the music for me."

"Tabor? Who is that?"

"Mac! You introduced us. Jud Taborian."

"Oh. Jud." Mac vaguely recalled running into Jud at some over-priced cocktail bar in Washington, D.C. That had been the first time Mac wrangled permission to take Del off base, so he had shown the prince around town. Mac barely knew Jud, though. The young fellow was a composer in the undercity music scene, which hadn't even dented the more lucrative planetary venues or bigger offworld markets. Many of its artists were mediocre or actively rotten, but a few were brilliant, and they all challenged accepted norms. Some tried to evoke the rock of earlier, less civilized eras. Although privately Mac agreed that present day music had become so "civilized," it was suffocating in its own conservatism, he couldn't sell musical anarchists to the conglomerates.

"I've been talking with Jud over the mesh." Del put his beer on the table and rummaged in a blue box he had left there. "He sent me this tech-tick." He pulled out a silver oval the size of his hand and squinted at it. More to himself than Mac, he added, "If I can just figure out how to use it."

"You've never used a ticker?" Mac knew Del had the device because Jud had sent it to Mac. The security people at the base didn't want Del giving out his address, so Mac let the prince use his for correspondence. Security had to clear any packages Del received, anyway. In fact, when Mac took Del off base, he acted as his guard and carried monitors that continually analyzed everything around them.

"I'd never even heard of a ticker," Del said. "Not before Jud gave me this one."

That surprised Mac. "Then how do you compose music?"

"At home, I'd hum the melody I wanted for a drummel player," Del said. "He'd figure out how to accompany me. Or I'd tell him the lyrics and he'd come up with something."

Drummel? Mac thought back to the instruments he had seen in Del's village. "You mean you've only played with those harp-guitar things?" Although Del had grown up in a rural community, he had mesh access to the resources of an interstellar empire. "No other media? No morphers?"

"Why bother?" Del shrugged. "I didn't really listen to offworld music. It's too much to sort through, and I haven't liked what I heard." His smile flashed. "Though if I'd picked up the undercity, *that* I would have listened to."

"I can imagine." No wonder Del sang so well. With no media enhancement, he's had no choice but to learn real technique.

Del studied the ticker. "Jud says I can edit the music he put on here. But I have no idea how." He tapped a button, and music played, slow and haunting, in a minor key, lyrical but with a raw edge, as if it were strumming under a violet moon.

"I like that," Mac said.

"The melody is right . . ." Del sat listening, his head cocked to one side. "The drums are too heavy, though."

Mac liked the driven quality of the drums, but he was

curious to hear what Del would do. "I can show you how to edit the song."

Del let the music fade away. "You know how to do that?"

"It's my job."

Del blinked at him. "I thought you were an agent."

"I'm called a front-liner," Mac said. "I get auditions and contracts for my clients. To sell their music, I need to understand what they do. I can't sing or compose, but I'm pretty good with the technical side."

"Then, yeah." Del grinned. "Show me."

They sat together at the table while Mac taught him how to use the ticker. When Del achieved the result he wanted, the instrumentals for the song had a beautifully eerie quality.

"It's good," Mac said. "Better than the usual undercity work."

Del shot him an annoyed look. "Just because you don't like undercity music, that doesn't make the musicians hacks."

"Oh come on. It's the quality I'm talking about."

"Why?" Del demanded. "Because they don't follow the boring mainstream?"

"No," Mac said. "Because a lot of them can't sing, play, or compose worth shit."

Del waved his hand as if to brush away the comment. But he didn't deny it. He was too accomplished a musician not to realize that for some, going undercity was little more than an attempt to define a lack of talent as progressive. The scene had produced some remarkable music, but they had also put out some of the worst dreck Mac had ever heard.

"You can sing circles around them," Mac said.

Del made a disgusted sound. "I doubt it."

It wasn't the first time Mac had heard Del make derogatory references to his own singing. He didn't understand why the youth felt that way. Del had no sense of his own talent. He was probably Mac's greatest find—and Mac couldn't do a damn thing with that discovery.

Well, almost nothing. He could listen. "So how does the song itself go?"

Del drummed his fingers on the ticker, set the oval on the table, then picked it up again. "I can't sing without something to hold."

Del wasn't the first vocalist Mac had seen who didn't know what to do with his hands while he sang. Mac almost laughed, thinking that some *did* have ideas, but they couldn't get away with it. The censors would come down on them like the proverbial ton of plutonium.

"Sing into the ticker," Mac said. "It'll record you. Then you can listen to your voice."

"Oh. All right." Del flicked on the ticker, looking self-conscious. "This is only a rough cut of the vocals."

The music began with an exquisite and simple melody played by only a harp, from what sounded like a Latin requiem. When it finished, the guitar riff played that started the music Mac had helped Del edit.

And Del sang.

His lyrics weren't the formulaic doggerel expected in the modern day universe of popular music. He varied the syllables more per line, sometimes drawing out words, other times rushing them. He used repetition to deepen the song rather than following a formula, and he gave the verses a freer form than current mainstream work:

> No answers live in here,
> No answers in this vault,
> This sterling vault of fear,
> This vault of steel tears,
>
> Tell me now before I fall
> Release from this velvet pall
> Tell me now before I fall
> Take me now, break through my wall
>
> No answers will rescue time
> No answers in this grave
> This wavering crypt sublime
> This crypt whispering in vines

He stopped, staring at the ticker, his lashes shading his eyes. "It's still rough," he said, as if apologizing.

"I like it." Mac wondered at the dark edge to the lyrics. Del wrote in a range of styles, from danceable tunes to ballads to hard-driving blasts. Sometimes he came out with these eerily fascinating pieces. Although the major labels probably wouldn't consider them commercial, Mac thought they had a lot more to them than the pabulum produced for popular markets.

"I've no idea what it means, though," Mac added.

"I suppose it's about never knowing answers even after you die. Or maybe that's what kills you." Del tapped his fingers on the ticker. "I don't like the third part. The first line is too long. 'Rescue' clunks. And 'Wavering crypt sublime' is idiotic."

"Why?" Mac asked, intrigued. "The sounds fit."

"The sounds, yeah. But the words are dumb. Crypts don't waver." He tilted his head. "Winnowing. Winnowing crypt sublime."

Mac smiled. "Crypts don't winnow, either."

"Sure they do. They winnow you out of life." Del pointed the ticker at Mac. "You can live for decades and never find answers." He lowered his arm. "Until death winnows you out of humanity and makes room for someone more useful."

Mac spoke quietly. "I hope you don't see yourself that way."

Del just shook his head. He had that far-off look that came when he wanted to practice. "I need to work."

"Would you like me to go?"

"I don't mind if you listen," Del said. "But it can get pretty boring when I'm working on a song. I just go over and over the same parts."

"It's not boring for me," Mac said. "I'd like to stay."

"Well sure, then." Del got up and walked around, holding the ticker. And he sang. He kept changing words, pacing like a caged lion. He sang a verse fluidly, then snarled the chorus. Yet somehow it all fit.

Although Mac liked to watch him sing, he knew it made Del self-conscious. So he closed his eyes and leaned his head back, enjoying the music. It was easy to submerge into Del's rich voice. The youth had trained his entire life, using techniques passed through generations in his family. Although Del could sing opera exquisitely, he preferred a far different style. He could croon one line, scream the next, wail and moan, then stroke the notes as if they were velvet, all without harming his voice. No one did anything that commercially risky in the mainstream, but undercity artists threw in all sorts of noise. Mac knew why Del had fascinated them that night in the bar; he easily achieved what they struggled to attain because he had the technique they lacked. To break the rules, they had to master them first.

Del wanted nothing more than to sing. He didn't care about the politics surrounding him. Although no one had physically hurt Del, Mac knew he had suffered emotionally. His people were torn by hostilities that had begun long ago, when humanity splintered into three civilizations: the Allied Worlds of Earth; Del's people of the Skolian Imperialate; and the Trader Empire. The Skolians and Traders had just fought a brutal war that had nearly destroyed them both and ravaged Del's family.

The Allied government had remained neutral, safe in their isolationism, but they agreed to shelter Del's family on Earth. When the war ended with no victor, Earth had feared the Skolians and Traders would send their world-slagging armies back out, again and again, until they wiped out humanity. So they refused to release Del's family. It did no good; the Skolians just sent in a commando team and pulled them out, all except Del, who happened to be apart from the others. So here Del remained, while Earth's government argued over what the blazes to do with him. Some thought having Del gave them a bargaining point with the Skolians. Others wanted to let him go and be done with the whole mess. Personally Mac didn't see the point in keeping him. What would they tell his family, the Ruby Dynasty—that if they started another war, they would never see their youngest son again? The bellicose Skolians were more likely to attack than bargain . . .

"Hey!" Del said. "You awake?"

Mac opened his eyes drowsily. "Just drifting."

"Admit it," Del said, laughing. "I bored you to sleep."

"Never." Mac stood up, stretching his arms. "I do have to go, though. I have a client who is auditioning today."

Del regarded him curiously. "What sort of audition?"

"It's with Prime-Nova Media, for a holo-vid cube."

"Oh. Well." Del squinted at him. "Good."

He smiled at Del's attempt to look as if he knew what the hell Mac had just said. "You've watched holo-vids, haven't you?"

"Not really. I see people playing them, but I don't stop to listen." Awkwardly Del said, "I don't want to intrude."

"You should see one. You'd enjoy it." Mac thought for a moment. "Would you like to watch the audition?" He had wrangled permission to take Del off the base by arguing that it reinforced their claim Del was a guest rather than a prisoner. He wanted to give Del at least those limited excursions; he felt like a cretin treating this youth as a prisoner when Del had never done anything to anyone.

He motioned at Del's ticker. "If we can get some mesh-box space, we could tech up a few holos for your cuts."

Del laughed, his eyes lit with interest. "I have no idea what you just said, but yeah, I'd like to go with you."

Mac grinned. "Come on. Let's go show you what I just said."

They headed out, into the freedom of a late morning turning red and gold with autumn.